Praise for THE CERTAINTY OF DOING EVIL

'Potent'

Scotsman

Praise for ROUGH JUSTICE

'A thoughtful analysis of the conflict between legality and justice, along with a relentlessly noir description of North London'

Hampstead & Highgate Express

'Excellent'

Birmingham Post

D1313502

Also by Colin Falconer

Venom
Deathwatch
Harem
Fury
Opium
Triad
Dangerous
Disappeared
Rough Justice

About the author

Colin Falconer was born in North London. He is a
journalist and author of nine previous acclaimed thrillers.
The Certainty of Doing Evil is his second contemporary crime
novel featuring the memorable Detective Inspector
Madeleine Fox. He now lives in West Australia.

The Certainty of Doing Evil

Colin Falconer

NEW ENGLISH LIBRARY
Hodder & Stoughton

First published in Great Britain in 2000
by Hodder and Stoughton
First published in paperback in 2000
by Hodder and Stoughton
A division of Hodder Headline

A New English Library Paperback

10 9 8 7 6 5 4 3

British Library Cataloguing in Publication Data

Falconer, Colin, 1953–
The certainty of doing evil
I. Suspense fiction
I. Title
823.9'14 [F]

ISBN 0 340 75033 2

Printed and bound in Great Britain by
Clays Ltd, St Ives plc

Hodder and Stoughton
A division of Hodder Headline
338 Euston Road
London NW1 3BH

The Certainty of Doing Evil

PART ONE

By normal sex life, we mean the forms of sex that commonly occur in healthy, natural people, and we group in abnormal sex all forms of sex that occur only rarely, and in their form deviate from ordinary forms in essential points. The borderline between normal and abnormal is, however, by no means sharp, and there are all kinds of intermediate stages.

J. Fabricius-Møller

Chapter One

Highgate, North London

She had been very beautiful once. She still was, if you could look beyond the waxy blue pallor of the skin, the half-lidded eyes, the nipple clamps, the protruding tongue. And yet the men in the basement, apparently dehumanised by their white overalls and their rapt concentration on micro-worlds, ignored her. Her dead body had become almost irrelevant to them. Only the pretty SO3 photographer, her long ebony hair brushed back in a tight businesslike pony tail, seemed at all interested in her, hounding her from every angle like an insatiable paparazza. The only sound in the room was the whirring of the electric motor in the camera.

DS Terry James winked at her. She ignored him, and took a close up shot of the woman's bound wrist.

Fox stood beside her colleague at the torture table. She was mostly indifferent to death now, but sexual crimes still made her feel uncomfortable, still gave her that tight, sick feeling in her belly. The other men, even though like her they were professionals, would not catch her eye. Something chilling, primordial about such acts, perhaps because the hatred that motivated these crimes was focused not against one person, but against a whole gender. It set anxious little shadows moving in the back of her mind; made it easy to misinterpret the hard stares of the men, forget that they were on her side.

'What have we got, TJ?' she said.

James – known to everyone on the squad as TJ – shrugged his shoulders. 'Just your basic S and M slaying,' he said. 'Spread and dead.'

'For Christ's sake,' Fox murmured. There was a lump in her throat. Backing up.

TJ grinned.

At that moment, the telephone rang.

All movement in the room stopped. The forensic team, the pathologist, Pakula, even the photographer, stared at the slender white telephone on the table beside the padded bench where the dead girl lay, a twentieth century instrument that jarred with the contrived medieval backdrop of the basement.

Fox waited for the answerphone to kick in, but apparently it had been turned off. That immediately struck her as curious. In the circumstances.

'Tell them she can't come to the phone,' TJ said. 'She's all tied up at the moment.' If TJ was disappointed that no one laughed at his joke, he didn't show it.

'If you were going to engage in a complicated sex session with bondage, surely you'd put the answerphone on,' Fox said, thinking aloud.

'I always do,' TJ said.

Fox, who was wearing latex gloves as well as white overalls, picked up the telephone. 'Yes?'

It was a male voice. 'Do you do enemas?'

4

Fox looked around the subterranean cell. There were no windows, and various torture implements hung on the walls: a plaited black leather whip, a switch, a riding crop. *And here I am, a good Catholic girl, talking to a stranger about enemas.*

She caught a glimpse of herself, framed for a moment in the wall-mounted mirror at the end of the room, a thirty something blonde with an austere, if not forbidding expression, no make-up, perhaps a little too tall. Not the sex goddess that TJ's fevered imagination had typecast her as, but still not bad for this time of the morning. Even though she looked like a bit player in an alien movie in the white overalls and overshoes.

'Who's speaking, please?' she said.

'Do you, or not?'

'Who gave you my number?'

'This is French Kitty?'

No, this is Detective Inspector Madeleine Fox; French Kitty is lying about a foot away from me, spread and dead, as TJ has so elegantly characterised it. But let's not bother ourselves with details right now.

'I need to know who referred you to me, before I can discuss my arrangements with you,' she said, and tried to avoid TJ's eyes.

'It was Bunny.'

'Bunny?'

'This *is* French Kitty?' the man said.

'Perhaps you could come around this afternoon at about three,' Fox said, but the caller had already hung up the phone. She replaced the receiver.

'Got yourself a hot date?' TJ said.

'He hung up,' she said.

'What did he want?'

'An enema.'

TJ bit his lip. Even Pakula struggled with that.

'I hope you told him to stick it up his arse.' Rely on TJ to flatten any piquant moment with a sledgehammer.

'He wanted French Kitty.'

'Give a name, ma'am?'

'His friend's name is Bunny.'

'Christ. It's like pets' corner.'

The forensic team went back to their business, dabbing at various surfaces with brushes, looking for latent prints. One of them found a fibre strand on the cement floor and placed it almost reverently in a small evidence bag, as if it were a sacred relic; the laborious but invaluable minutiae of a murder investigation. French Kitty, naked, spreadeagled on a wooden table, was once again ignored, her dignity forfeited with her vitality.

Fox watched Peter Gold, the new wonderboy in the forensic unit, go about his job, directing the other scientists in their work. The hackneyed image of Sherlock Holmes poring over a murder scene in a deerstalker, a magnifying glass pressed against his eye, was not completely false. Modern murder investigation followed a precise formula based on a singular premise: every contact leaves a trace.

It was not altogether impossible to commit an act of violence against another person and leave nothing of yourself behind, but it was becoming increasingly difficult. It was said that crime was becoming more sophisticated; so, too, was criminal investigation. Murder was no business for amateurs.

Fingerprints could be lifted from almost any surface, even human skin, their presence on a bloodied knife or iron bar was incontrovertible proof of guilt. Latents might survive for a long time at a murder scene: fingerprints had even been recovered from ancient Egyptian papyri in the Valley of the Kings.

Even if the murderer had taken the precaution of wearing gloves, he or she usually left other minute traces behind. A shoe, especially if worn for a long time, might leave a unique impression; textile fibres could be matched to a particular item of clothing; and a stray hair, if intact with its root, could work against a culprit, a unique genetic fingerprint.

The gathering of evidence was a tedious and painstaking business, and it wasn't every day you got a tour of a private torture chamber. I could dine out on this for months, if I ever had time to eat or to socialise, Fox thought. Police work demanded sixteen hour days and she hardly met anyone new these days, unless their pupils were fixed and dilated or they had previous for GBH.

The Home Office photographer was still taking flash photographs of the crime scene, while Fox and TJ stood there, their hands in the pockets of their white overalls, watching with the indifference of a sound crew on a pornographic film set.

Fox returned her attention to the girl lying spreadeagled on the table, handcuffed to the frame. She fought the urge to cover the girl up. Something obscene about dying like this. Cold candle grease, lurid and visceral green in colour, had leaked along the dead woman's torso. The nipple clamps did not look particularly severe; Fox decided she couldn't have filed her monthly bills with such flimsy implements. None of these minor torments had been enough to separate French Kitty from her mortality.

Fox would not need Professor Elizabeth Pakula's PM to explain the cause of death. There were contusions around her neck, pinpoint haemorrhages around the eyes called *petechiae*, and her tongue protruded from her mouth, blue and swollen. A probationer could tell you that she had been strangled.

Such a summary conclusion would not have impressed Pakula: she had a job to do, and went about it with professional diligence. Fearsome, grey haired and fifty, she was known as the Virgin Surgeon by TJ and the rest of the squad at Hendon Road.

Per usual protocol, the pathologist would not be called to the crime scene, but this was no ordinary crime scene and Fox had wanted Pakula to examine the body *in situ*.

Pakula began a thorough examination of the body, speaking softly into a voice-activated tape recorder, taking note of the room temperature, the positioning of the body and its bizarre presentation in a monotone drawl, as if she was reading the shipping forecast.

Fox moved to the end of the table, half crouched to see if she could catch a glimpse of the starchy residue of semen on the vulva or the insides of the girl's thighs. Pakula will tell us soon enough, she thought, feeling like a kid trying to see her test marks before the papers were handed back.

She caught a glimpse of herself, in her mind, as a stranger might have seen her, squatting down, peering at a dead woman's genitals. If Dad could see me now. Or Ma, or Ginny.

Fox thought she could just see what looked like wine-coloured bruises on the underside of the body. After death, when the heart stopped beating, gravity allowed the blood to pool in the lowest part. Lividity set in after about two hours and was fixed after eight, so that no matter how much you moved the body after that, the characteristic 'bruising' remained. It was a telltale sign if the body had been moved after death. In this case lividity was consistent with the supine position. The woman had died right here on this table, or very shortly before.

Rigor was fixed also. Jesus, she thought, wondering how the attendants would get the outstretched body on to the stretcher, even into the van.

The photographer had now discarded her Nikon and was taking a videotape record of the scene. No doubt this would be required viewing for the boys back at Hendon Road. Privacy was something you aspired to in life; when you were dead your body, even your fantasies, became public property.

Fox was happy to leave French Kitty's private dungeon to the forensics team and the pathologist. Corpses no longer fascinated her, if they ever had, and this particular cooling body left her feeling more than a little uneasy.

The dungeon was in the basement of a three storey semi-detached house in Highgate. It would have been grand once. Even now Fox could not decide if it was a street that was slowly becoming gentrified, or an area being reclaimed by the urban jungle. The garden was neat and well maintained, in contrast to the neighbouring front yard which was a tangle of grass and weeds, with empty bottles of Newcastle Brown strewn up the path.

From the outside it was unremarkable and in good repair. Not the kind of house that made you think, 'I bet some kinky stuff goes on in there.' The interior was similarly anonymous. There were vases with fresh flowers in the hallway and front parlour. On the coffee table was a novel — lying open face down, as if French Kitty had been disturbed during her reading. There were family photographs in silver frames, for God's sake.

Even bondage queens had lives, she supposed.

TJ was standing by the stereo in an airy sitting room that looked out over the street. He pressed the play button on the compact disc player with a gloved finger. Debussy. Fox frowned. Somehow she had expected heavy metal.

'Jesus, look at this,' TJ said.

Fox turned around. 'What is it?'

'She was reading Nicholas Sparks,' he said, nodding towards the coffee table. 'There you go. She lost the will to live. Case solved.'

One of the uniforms frowned. Fox felt embarrassed for him. Gallows humour was all very well but TJ went right over the line into mental illness.

Fox looked out of the window at the buzz going on outside. Neighbours and passers-by stood beyond the police cordon with the rapt attention of gawkers at a traffic accident. This was better than television, especially if you were unemployed and had nothing better to do with your Monday morning. A deadlocked Rasta in a woollen hat was watching, a Walkman on his head, singing along to the music; a Moslem woman, pushing a baby in a stroller, had stopped to stare; some white youths in leather jackets jeered at the police; a jogger in a London Marathon T-shirt, a gold rope around his neck, interrupted his exercise to indulge his curiosity.

'I'm going to check upstairs,' Fox said.

Two of Gold's team were at work. They were thorough, checking the water trap in the hand basin for blood, the lavatory for discarded cigarette stubs. Fox wandered into the bedroom and looked around, surprised. It was the bedroom of a little girl rather than a grown woman. The walls were candy pink, there was lace on the coverlet and – a poignant touch, Fox decided – a teddy bear on the pillow. Fox wondered what she had been expecting. A bed of nails and Gestapo memorabilia perhaps.

There was a mahogany dresser against one wall. Fox watched one of Gold's men rifle through the drawers. Chaotic. Woollen jumpers and lingerie had been thrown in together, nothing folded, just crammed in and the drawers jammed shut.

He took the bottom drawer right the way out and found a black lacquered box, which he showed to Fox. Inside were bondage cuffs that fastened with Velcro snaps, nipple clamps, a box of white candles, some spiked dog brushes, a purple vibrator, KY jelly. Their victim liked to mix business with pleasure.

There was still a part of her that felt uncomfortable about her role in the destruction of the dead girl's privacy. Everyone had secrets, things that no one knew: the blue movie kept on a shelf, the letters from a gay lover from many years ago, the lingerie meant only for the eyes of a lover, all of it safely hidden away. But people never considered death, especially sudden, unanticipated death, and what might happen to their secrets then. Sometimes Fox felt like a carrion crow, picking through guts like an animal carcass on a desert road.

As a murder squad detective she became both voyeur and intimate to the dead, got to know them through a jigsaw of observed and apparently inconsequential detail. She scanned the room, noting an *X Files* poster hanging on the wall beside a carefully framed Edwardian advertisement for Pear's soap; Covent Garden opera programmes stacked next to Arsenal FC match programmes on the bookshelf; a Victorian love seat positioned next to an Ikea lounge chair.

She wondered if French Kitty had ever dreamed that one day a perfect stranger would be dissecting and examining every private detail of her life this way. Death was a mugger. It not only took your life, it went through your pockets afterwards and took all your secrets too.

Gold put his head around the door. 'Think we've found something,' he said.

Chapter Two

Area Major Incident Pool, Hendon Road

As she walked into the Incident Room she was assaulted by the familiar stink of stale cigarette smoke. She glanced up at the whiteboard that ran the length of one wall. The operation already had a name: DARK LADY.

Fox sat down, sipped at the bad coffee, leaving a lipstick mark on the polystyrene cup. She consulted her notes, making sure the details of the crime scene were clear in her mind, that she was prepared for her DCI's questions. Greg Mills had taken over the squad from Marenko. Unlike Frank, who had become a legend in his own mind for intuitive inspiration and hands-on investigation, Mills was a career professional, who valued hard work and good dress sense, not necessarily in that order. He was on the square, next stop the flying squad.

Their victim's name was Kimberley Mason. So far they had kept a lid on it, feeding it to the media as a home assault, the assailant probably known to the victim. The tabloids would have a field day if they got hold of the details. If Kimberley Mason turned out to have a connection with the Royal Family or an Arsenal midfielder, the *Sun* and the *Mirror* would run with the story for months.

Mills walked in. She could hear WPC Stacey's sigh from across the room, like the whisper of the wind. Mills had a sexual aura about him, not crass and overt in the manner of a Terry James, he was too much the professional for that. She had never been able to define quite what it was, or declare herself completely immune.

Mills was one of those men to whom youth was a waystop *en route* to the peak. There was a photograph on his desk of him taken in the seventies as a beat cop, in a London Bobby's helmet, looking gawky and self-conscious. That creature had long ago ceased to exist, passed over with the uniform and the truncheon.

Now he was another creature entirely, well over six feet, lean and hard, only the tiny lines around his eyes and the dusting of grey at his temples betraying his age, which was reckoned to be early forties. He had been through four marriages, and was currently living with Sally, a blonde love goddess reincarnated as a fashion model, if Honeywell could be believed. Mills moved with the grace of an athlete, and his clothes could have been moulded on him by an Italian fashion designer. Love on legs, TJ called him behind his back, no doubt out of envy. Mills had a ready sense of humour, a keen sense of office politics and a ferocious constitution. He was, in short, superintendent material.

He was one of those men whose lives had assumed mythic proportion. One of his most famous exploits was getting drunk at a Freemasons' dinner and driving his car through a council roadworks sign and into a drainage ditch. Somehow he had survived even that episode, which would have been enough to finish most careers.

But the thing that had struck Fox immediately – apart

from his eyes, which had her stripped buff naked in ten seconds on their first meeting – was his portability. He was component-like, a module. He gave the impression that he had a toothbrush and a razor in his pocket, and if he was called – to Scotland Yard, to Interpol, to a policing conference at FBI headquarters at Qantico, or to the flat of an underwear model from the pages of *Cosmopolitan* – he could pick up a new suit from the dry-cleaners and be gone by morning, leaving not a trace behind. Not like Marenko at all: Frank had belonged here, he had left the impression of his shoulders in the walls, the outline of that massive behind in the DCI's chair, like a plaster mould. Mills was one of the new school, a good cop who had metamorphosed into management material. Hendon Road was just a way station to New Scotland Yard.

Mills sat down, took the Parker from his jacket pocket and crossed his legs. Not even a crease in his socks, she thought sourly. She saw TJ watching him, a hungry look in his eyes. He had at last found a role model.

'Okay people, let's get to work,' Mills said. 'What do you have, Madeleine?'

Fox opened her notebook. 'Her name was Kimberley Mason,' she said. 'Aged twenty eight. PM's not scheduled till three o'clock, but it appears that she was strangled. We also have this videotape from SO3.'

Fox put the tape in the VCR. She saw herself, in a pair of white overalls, standing with notebook in hand beside the torture table. There were close-ups of the nipple clamps and the dried candle wax on the dead woman's torso. The photographer then panned around the walls of the room, its sinister implements hanging on hooks on the bare brick. It seemed darker than she remembered from this morning, lending it an air of the macabre – or the erotic, depending on the way you viewed it, she supposed.

As the tape ended there was a shuffling silence in the room.

'Could this have been accidental, ma'am?' Rankin, one of the DCs, asked her.

She knew what he was driving at, and it was the crucial question that had to be answered before the investigation could really move forward. Had Kimberley Mason consented to some form of strangulation during the sex act, as a way of achieving a more intense orgasm? Had her partner miscalculated, then panicked and left her body? Fox had come across such bizarre deaths before, but only in solitary sexual rituals that had gone wrong.

Scarfing, the S&M crowd called it, starving the brain of oxygen to increase sexual pleasure. The trick was to stay alive to enjoy the afterglow. History recorded a number of men for whom this just wasn't possible: diarists as far back as the seventeenth century had noticed that the victims at public hangings became priapic and even ejaculated during their death throes.

Instead of coming, they went, as TJ would have it.

It wasn't a new thing: the Japanese had been playing this dangerous sexual game for centuries. Cerebral anoxia, together with the adrenalin rush of risk was a heady cocktail, particularly attractive to young males. According to the statistics, thirty per cent of adolescent suicides might be sexual experimentation gone wrong.

Everything they knew so far about Kimberley Mason suggested that such practices were well known to her. The question was: had she died playing games, or had her murderer been in deadly earnest?

'We still haven't formed a theory about her death at this stage,' she said to Rankin. 'The post mortem might tell us more.'

'Any clues on time of death?' someone else asked.

'Again, we'll have to wait on Pakula's PM, but rigor mortis was quite advanced. She thought that the victim had been dead for over twenty four hours.'

'Can you tell them what Forensics found in the kitchen, please,' Mills said.

She turned back to the room. 'One of Gold's team found a bloodstain on the refrigerator handle. There was also a broken cup in the rubbish bin. Tiny shards of crockery were still on the kitchen floor. It indicates that a scuffle took place there recently and someone cleaned up afterwards. Whether this was connected to the murder, we don't know as yet.'

'Fingerprints?'

'Again, we're waiting on the report. Forensics lifted a blood-stained latent from the fridge, but we don't know yet if it belonged to Kimberley or her attacker.'

'How did the assailant get in?' Rankin asked.

'There was no forced entry. So her assailant either knew her, and she let him in herself, or he had a key.'

'So it *could* have been accidental,' Honeywell insisted.

'It's possible, but until after the PM we can't start to form a theory,' Fox repeated.

'This girl was a tom?' Rankin asked. He looked up and caught Fox's hard stare. 'She was a prostitute, ma'am?'

'We're still looking into that, Dennis.' She referred to her notes. 'By day, she ran a small public relations firm with an office on Euston Road. It appears she was leading what amounts to a double life, though. While I was there, I got a phone call. A man asking to speak to French Kitty. He wanted an enema.'

'Was this on your mobile, ma'am?' Honeywell asked, and that was enough to bring the house down.

'Yes, and I've told you not to call me during working hours,' she shot back.

'Moving along,' Mills grunted with a sour look.

Fox returned to her notes. 'We checked the message bank. There were calls from her father and two from her secretary at work. Two other callers rang off without leaving a message.'

'That's it, ma'am?' Honeywell asked.

'That's it, Bill,' she said.

'Who found the body?' Nick Crawford, their new DS, asked her.

Mills cleared his throat and Fox let him take over. 'When Miss Mason didn't show up for work this morning, her secretary rang her at home. She got no answer. When she still hadn't appeared for her first two appointments, she decided to ring the police. Two uniformed officers from the Highgate nick broke into the house and found her body.'

'It wasn't them, was it?' Honeywell said. 'You know what some of these probationers are like. I wouldn't trust them to help my grandmother across the road.'

'I wouldn't trust *you* with your grandmother,' Mills said, and that drew more laughter, TJ giving it more than it probably warranted.

'Anyone see anything, guv?' Rankin asked.

'TJ has talked to the neighbours,' Mills answered, 'but they claim to have seen or heard nothing unusual.'

TJ nodded. 'The other half of the semi is owned by a couple of relics from the V & A Museum. He's deaf and she's got advanced Alzheimer's. I checked the other side but it's rented by half of Jamaica. They reckon she was a slag, though.'

'Why?' Crawford asked.

'She had blokes going in and out at all hours, apparently.'

'What about the family?' Rankin asked.

Mills nodded to DS Crawford, who was to be family liaison officer for the case, responsible for all contact between the SIO and the family. It meant taking statements from them in their home, helping them with funeral arrangements, keeping them informed about the investigation through weeks or even months, even staying with them throughout any criminal trial.

In Fox's opinion it was one of the hardest jobs to do well, considerably more stressful than looking at any number of mutilated corpses. As TJ had once put it: 'I can do hamburger. I can't do grief.'

Crawford had transferred to the Met from bandit country; he had been with the CID in Bristol, had worked on the Frederick West investigation. He had spent two years as DS at Catford before being transferred to the AMIP.

'Father's a retired oil executive,' he was saying, 'lives in the money belt, in Surrey. If his daughter was on the game, he says he knew nothing about it. Poor bastard. Wife's a mess, doctor had to sedate her.'

'When was the last time they saw her?' Rankin asked.

'About a week ago. She used to go down there for lunch most Sundays.'

'Boyfriends?'

'None that she told them about. It'll be a day or so before we can interview them properly.'

Fox shook her head. It seemed their victim had neatly dissected her life into two halves: Kimberely Mason, businesswoman and dutiful daughter, and French Kitty, trader in deviant sex.

'There was one thing,' Fox said. 'Why no little black book?' The penny dropped for most of them straight away but a couple of the new DCs on the squad appeared nonplussed. 'A girl like Kimberley would have kept a list of her clients somewhere,' Fox went on. 'We didn't find one. It might have been removed by whoever strangled her.' She looked at Rankin. 'Accidentally or otherwise.'

'You think that was the motive?' Honeywell asked.

Fox shrugged her shoulders. 'As I said, we don't know if it *was* murder.'

Mills had been making notes in a large red ledger book. He snapped it shut with a gesture of finality. 'I want to know everything there is to know about this girl: her friends, her lovers, her clients, her enemies, what kind of breakfast cereal she ate, whether she caught the bus or the Tube, everything. We also need to go house to house, talk to everyone in the area: someone might have seen something. The duty rota's on the board. Let's get to it.'

TJ got in the passenger seat of Fox's Sierra. There were plum-coloured bruises under his eyes and she detected the stale reek of sweat and booze under an overpowering blast of aftershave. A big night on the bevvy.

He started to wind down the window. 'Mind if I smoke?'

'Yup.'

He made a face and wound it up again. He muttered something under his breath. 'What's the difference between a Foster's and a woman?'

Here we go.

'A Foster's is cold but it's not bitter.'

She pulled into the traffic and headed south along Hendon Road. A spatter of rain on the windscreen. It wasn't that she minded TJ's jokes, his perverse humour at crime scenes. God alone knew, a little black humour now and then kept them all sane. But there was real misogyny behind TJ's attitudes. He came from a part of White City where you either became a cop or a crim, depending on chance. He was ex-Army, crop-haired, a lad. As far as she was concerned, a complete pain in the arse. But you didn't get to choose who you worked with. At least she was the boss. She guessed that was part of his problem.

'You really think this was accidental?' she asked him.

He fiddled with the air vent. Great stubby fingers like a bricklayer. He was going to break the bloody thing if he didn't leave it alone. 'Well, maybe she gets together with some geezer, they get their kit off, he straps her down, does the wax and all that business, then as the big finale, he climbs on top of her, and just at the vinegar stroke he starts to choke her, to send her needle off the register. But he gets carried away and holds on too long. Then after, when he realises what he's done, he decides to leg it. Maybe goes home to his wife and kids and hopes he can get away with it. It's possible.'

'Except for French Kitty.'

TJ thought about that. 'French Kitty. Fuck me.'

She could do without the language. She gave him a look.

'Fuck me, *ma'am*,' he added.

She tried not to smile.

'Doesn't make sense,' she went on. 'If he's a paying customer, why does he choke her? If he's a psychopath, yes. But not for any erotic stimulation for her. Come on. He just wants to get his own jollies away.'

He nodded, conceding the point.

'Have we done any research on this French Kitty, ma'am?'

'I've got Honeywell checking the personal columns in the local newspapers. If he has no luck I'll send him off to check all the telephone boxes between here and Tottenham Court Road for calling cards.'

'He's a married man. Shouldn't put temptation in his way.'

'I'd like to find out exactly what she was offering.'

'Whatever it was, she was making good money.'

'Looks like it. I wonder how much it costs to set up your own torture chamber?'

'Maybe she had a whip-round.' He gave a short, barking laugh and then fiddled with the radio, flipping up and down through the channels. Finally, he gave up.

Fox turned on the windscreen wipers. It had started to rain properly now, warm, sticky early-July rain. Must be Wimbledon time.

Chapter Three

Middlesex Hospital

Scrubbed tiles and the reek of disinfectant, tainted with the sickly-sweet stench of death. Fox could smell her own fear. She had grown accustomed to looking at dead bodies, but she had never overcome the suspicion that one day there would be a corpse that would be just too revolting, too hideously disfigured for her to look at and she would be unable to perform her professional duty, exposed as a chinless wonder. Irrational really, for she had sat through post mortems and seen bodies stripped back to the bone, even small children; seen faces degloved, organ trees weighed and examined as if they were prime steak in a butcher's shop.

She suspected that the effect of her work was cumulative. They said your back could take only a certain number of lifts in a lifetime; perhaps there was a limit to the trauma even the toughest spirit could take before it reached a breaking point. Her own dispassion in the face of so much violence and death surprised and sometimes even shocked her.

She put a little Vicks under her nose and handed the jar to TJ. He accepted it gratefully and did the same.

Just a bit of toast for breakfast this morning. She had once accompanied Marenko to the morgue after a big fry up and nearly brought it up for inclusion in the pathology report.

'Ready?' she said to TJ.

He was looking seedy. No doubt regretting the seven or eight pints of Guinness from the night before. 'Ready,' he said.

They followed the attendant through the doors of the waiting room and down the corridor to the dissection room, sometimes known as Graveney's Slice 'n' Dice after its previous incumbent. Now it was more generally known as the Junkyard.

Professor Aloysius Graveney had suffered a heart attack two months short of his sixty third birthday and had decided to retire to a cottage in Normandy before his own organ tree made its appearance in the stainless-steel trays. His replacement was Professor Elizabeth Pakula, sometimes Doc Peculiar or Dracula to the cops who visited her for the good word on the bodies that came through the door. But her abrasive manner and unmarried status soon earned her the sobriquet now favoured by TJ and the rest of the squad: the Virgin Surgeon.

She was an intimidating woman, over five ten, thick grey hair, huge spectacles like display windows, and a nose like a potato. She stood behind a stainless steel sluice table wearing a green gown and green rubber gloves that reached to her elbows, regarding them with a disapproving frown, reserved for all those lesser beings who had neither a degree nor a name tag attached to their toes.

Kimberley Mason lay naked in front of her. The SO3 photographer from the Highgate house that morning was taking more shots for the evidence file on a tripod-mounted camera. Final stage rigor had passed and Kimberley's arms now lay at her side, her hands bagged, her legs together; a lady at last, Fox thought, and experienced a moment's bitter self-reproach at her prejudice. Pakula had removed the clamps at the crime scene, but her torso was still striped with red candle wax. A label had been attached to the little toe on her left foot with her name and a number. No mention of French Kitty. In death she reverted to a single incarnation.

Pakula watched them, like an autocratic schoolteacher waiting for her pupils to give her their full attention. 'Murder,' she said, finally.

'Are you sure?' TJ said.

Pakula fixed him with a withering stare. Her spectacles flashed, reflecting the overhead strip lights. 'No, it was a wild guess,' she said, her voice thick with contempt.

Pathologists were an elite band of medical scientists and in Fox's experience they could be as pedantic as an Oxford linguistics professor. You could cut down a body swinging from the rafters on the end of a rope and they would still check for bulletholes and then tell you death by hanging was only a provisional diagnosis.

There was some justification, she supposed. Post mortems had been known to reveal bullets in bodies in which there were no visible entrance wounds, and on one celebrated occasion a man with gunshot wounds had lingered in a major London hospital for three weeks being treated for cardiac arrhythmia. One of Pakula's favourite pronouncements was that there were just two things that had no place in pathology – signs of life and assumptions.

But once she was convinced of her findings, years of professional experience and a firm belief in the perfection of science made Professor Elizabeth Pakula intolerant of doubters.

The professor referred to her notes. 'The body is that of a normally developed white female, five feet eight inches in height, weighing one hundred and twenty-six pounds. She has black hair and green eyes and appears to be in the mid third decade of life. There is lividity over the back, which is fixed.

'On initial examination this morning I registered a deep rectal temperature of sixty-two point four degrees Fahrenheit with final stage rigor present in the lower limbs. I would calculate time of death at between ten p.m. Saturday night and four a.m. Sunday morning.' Pakula addressed herself to the overhead microphone, speaking in a low monotone. Her findings would be transcribed later for the pathology report, which would find its way on to Mills' desk at Hendon Road.

Well, it gave them a start, but time-of-death estimates were notoriously unreliable. They were invariably contested in courts of law.

Pakula leaned over the corpse and pointed to the bruises on Kimberley Mason's neck. 'The *petechiae* and the swollen tongue identify asphyxia by strangulation as the probable cause of death. The bruises around her neck are consistent with manual strangulation. However, if you look closely you will notice that the contusions are more profuse in the anterior region, around the trachea, than they are here, on the sternomastoid.

'Simply put,' she said, 'if I placed my hands here, and tried to throttle her from in front, my thumbs would leave impressions here and here, on the soft tissue, while my fingers would cause larger areas of bruising at the back of the neck. In this case the pattern of bruising is reversed.' She stood at the head of the table and gripped Kimberley's neck from behind. 'If I reverse my position, you get a different pattern of bruising entirely. You see? Whoever did this, strangled her from behind.'

'They couldn't have done this while she was lying on the table?' TJ asked.

'Why would they? Certainly not for her sexual gratification anyway. And you could not easily exert the necessary pressure. The assailant would have to turn his wrists back towards his body.'

The point made, Pakula returned her attention to the external examination of the rest of the body. She noted an appendix scar and a fresh wound to the victim's right hand. Finally she peeled off the dried candle wax.

'There is bruising around her upper arms, indicating that someone, presumably her assailant, gripped her very tightly. There are no other contusions on the body. Which is significant.' Catching TJ's puzzled expression she took time to explain. 'Look at her wrists and ankles, Detective. There are no ligature marks from the restraints, which you would expect if she had struggled against the bonds. You may draw your own conclusions from that. *Livor mortis* is consistent with the position in which she was found. Of course, she could have been placed on the table soon after death. It would make no difference.'

Fox felt pieces of the puzzle clunking together. 'What about the wax and the clamps?'

'The pattern of the wax indicates it dried on the body while it was supine.'

'But you don't think she was strangled in that position?'

'No, Inspector, I don't.'

'So it is reasonable to infer that the bondage paraphernalia was intended to give the impression that her death had an erotic component, was therefore accidental, and took place after the supposed torture games.'

'Inference is your job,' Pakula said. 'I can only give you the facts as they pertain to my medical knowledge.'

Take that. Out of the corner of her eye she could see TJ grinning at her. He didn't mind in the least seeing someone beat up on his guv'nor.

Pakula carefully removed the plastic bags over Kimberley's hands. She clipped the dead woman's fingernails and placed the clippings into evidence bags and sealed them.

'The fingernails on the first, second and fourth fingers of her right hand are broken.'

'She fought her attacker,' Fox said.

'Well, it's possible,' Pakula said.

'Which she couldn't have done while she was tied to the table,' TJ said.

'Hiring university graduates now?' Pakula murmured, her voice thick with sarcasm.

Fox gave TJ a look: she's always like this on Mondays.

Pakula took oral, vaginal and anal swabs for semen. 'I think you're out of luck,' she said. Without body fluids they could not match a DNA profile to a suspect. It would make the job that bit harder. Perhaps Forensics would come up with something.

Fox shook her head. Just when she thought she'd seen it all. Had any murder detective ever seen it all? 'Murdered, then laid out naked in her own dungeon. Tortured post mortem. No sexual interference.'

'Christ.' TJ shook his head. 'What sort of people go in for this stuff anyway?'

Pure rhetoric, but Pakula took the question at face value. 'Mostly people who have a bit of spare cash, in my experience, Detective. The paraphernalia is not cheap. As a hobby, it's right up there with photography and mountain climbing as a money pit.'

Fox didn't say anything. She had come across similar bizarre deaths several times in her career. Each time they had started out looking for some crazed sadistic killer and signed off on a bizarre sex ritual gone wrong.

Bondage was the human being's quintessential mind game, one of those dark vices that people in the street found fascinating, even if they wouldn't admit to it. Occasionally its fashions and language surfaced in the mainstream, like the 'seventies *Rocky Horror Show*, or Billy Idol and Madonna making leather and chains a fashion accessory in the late 'eighties. It remained almost the last sexual frontier now that it was cool to be gay. She couldn't imagine scatology or necrophilia taking the same hold on the public imagination.

Pakula picked up a scalpel from the tray of shining steel instruments and made two neat and bloodless incisions along the collarbones to the base of the suprasternal notch and then down to the zyphoid process.

Fox saw no reason to stay for the formalities, which consisted of removing the brain and the organ tree for examination and weighing, and drawing specimens from the heart, stomach and bladder for laboratory analysis. She decided to wait outside.

Fox and TJ patrolled the sluice room in awkward silence. Fox thought about what Pakula had just told them. Murder. Kimberley Mason had been strangled from behind, was already dead when she was strapped to the table. Yet there was no sign of forced entry into the house. That left the scenario of her death open to debate.

'Would you say that woman's got an attitude problem?' TJ said, interrupting her thoughts. He nodded towards the dissection room, where Pakula was still at work.

'Spent too much time talking to corpses,' Fox muttered.

TJ nodded. 'I suppose we all have.'

Couldn't argue with that. The job could make you a little hard, a little cynical, after a while. You needed a reality check from time to time. Much of her own working life was taken up with talking to and bargaining with some of North London's most venal and unlikeable people, some of whom were solicitors; the rest of her time was spent studying various body detritus and fluids, such as semen, saliva, urine, vomit, tissue and hair. Not that different, she supposed, from being a prostitute.

Except that at least she only had to look.

'So what do we have?' Fox said, thinking aloud. 'A murder made to look like something else. A part-time prostitute offering bizarre sexual services, strangled from behind, but by someone she apparently knew. There must be a personal motive behind this.'

'At least we're not looking for a maniac,' TJ said.

Fox nodded, then thought: Okay, but who dribbles hot wax on a spreadeagled corpse if not some sort of headcase?

Wait till Ma hears what I'm working on now.

Chapter Four

———◆———

Belsize Park, NW3

James Carlton double parked his silver BMW outside the gates of the school, and thought about his life. He wondered if any of it was, really, his own fault. Such private debate came easily to him. Introspection had been a lifelong habit, so that often, when he should have been conducting conversations with other people, he instead found himself in silent dialogue with himself. As a result people thought him aloof, or arrogant, when in fact he was merely preoccupied.

The argument against his proposition of innocence, he told himself, was free will. But free will presupposed that men and women did not have turbulent inner lives, that life was an intellectual exercise where choices could be made based on judgment and critical thought. But life wasn't like that. The intellect, he thought, is something we use to justify our decisions after our longings and obsessions have already steered our course. It is the landscape veneer we apply to the lurid abstract scribblings of our lives. It makes us appear civilised and not just the play-things of the Devil.

It is why why marriages fail. It is why men and women die, too soon, and very badly. It is what drives others to suicide.

The sound of voices and laughter shook him from his reverie. Christchurch School for Girls was an imposing red-brick edifice, guarded by spiked railings and twelve-foot wrought iron gates. A statue of Edward VII stood in the forecourt. By all accounts the school still strove to impose the same values on its alumni as its Victorian forefathers had done a hundred years before, with diminishing success. The twentieth century continued to impinge on the school's traditions, as the electronic security gates and the burglar alarms mounted on the white portico attested.

At ten minutes before four o'clock a horde of schoolgirls burst across the asphalt courtyard, with the elegance and restraint of Chelsea supporters. They were dressed without exception in uniforms of claret blazer and grey skirt. The brown stockings and silver finger rings of the older girls were the only concessions the school had made to their blossoming gender.

Carlton watched them with a mixture of regret and satisfaction. I am no harm to anyone, he told himself. I have never corrupted innocence. I am no monster.

He watched his own daughter emerge, slouching, from the porticoed entrance, at the rearguard of this boisterous adolescent crowd. She was chewing gum, her schoolbag clutched in her right hand. Her tie hung loose around her collar, and there was a snag running the length of her grey tights. She grinned when she saw him and he experienced a sharp pang of grief. He already had too much, far more than he deserved. His wealth, some even said his luck, had been inherited. He had a trophy wife, a house in Hampstead, a foreign car, and this lovely daughter. Isn't this enough for you?

Apparently, the answer was no, it wasn't.

How can you keep living this way? he wondered. As you drive through London every night, on your way to your fine and handsome home, you pass countless people living lives of perpetual squalor, without food, without shelter, without hope, sleeping at nights in doorways or under bridges. Why not count yourself lucky and be satisfied with what you have?

Diana parted from her friends at the main gate. She threw her schoolbag into the back of the car and climbed into the passenger seat beside him. She rewarded him with a perfunctory kiss on the cheek and immediately went into her usual post-school rant about who had said what to whom, which teacher was a total prat, which of her friends had dumped which boy. Everything that was vital and important to a sixteen-year-old girl.

And he didn't mind. It was comfortable for him. He was not expected to respond, only to drive, and as she talked he allowed his mind to drift away. The gentle purr of German engineering reassured him; the Mahler symphony, softly distinct on the sound system, a distant anthem to his self-recrimination and sickening burden of guilt.

Chapter Five

Area Major Incident Pool, Hendon Road

TJ, Bill Honeywell and several other members of the team were staring at the scene-of-crime photographs that had been pinned to the noticeboard. The five-by-eight glossies had an erotic quality that was totally at variance with the tableau Fox had witnessed a few hours before.

'Look at that,' she overheard TJ saying, 'nipples like a lorry driver's thumbs.'

The Incident Room smelled of cigarette ash and stale sweat. Fox wrinkled her nose and sat down on a chair by the window. She took out her notes from her briefcase. OPERATION DARK LADY had been printed on the whiteboard in black marker, and underneath Mills had started a flow chart of Kimberley Mason's friends and associates in an effort to establish a pool of suspects.

Fox caught TJ trying to steal a look up her skirt as she crossed her legs. She ignored him. He spent too much time watching movies like *Basic Instinct*. If a glimpse of her cheap white cotton briefs from Woolworths made his day worth living, she wouldn't dream of denying him that small pleasure.

Mills made his appearance on the stroke of five o'clock, as scheduled. He sat down and brought the team up to date with developments. He read them the results of Dracula's post mortem, which supported the theory that Kimberley Mason had been strangled, possibly in her kitchen, before being carried or dragged down to the basement/dungeon below the house. Time of death was between ten p.m. Saturday night and four a.m. Sunday.

'I don't have the forensics report as yet,' he told them, 'but I've just spoken to Peter Gold. His team retrieved several woollen fibres from Miss Mason's body and from the kitchen. They're going to run some tests but the results will take a few weeks.'

'What about the blood on the refrigerator door?' Fox asked.

Mills shook his head. 'It was Kimberley's blood group. Again, we'll have to wait for DNA tests, but we shouldn't hold our breath for a result there.'

'What about the whips?' someone asked from the back of the room.

'You can't have them, we need them as evidence,' TJ shot back.

Mills ignored him, as did the rest of the room. The man's need for attention borders on the tragic, Fox thought.

'They have no connection to the crime,' Mills said, 'only to her clientèle.'

'So we're flogging a dead horse there,' TJ said to groans and catcalls.

'What about witnesses?' Mills said, ignoring TJ's inane banter.

Honeywell sat up straighter. 'We went door to door along the whole street, guv. No one saw anything suspicious, or saw anyone go in or out of the house that night.'

'Did you track down Kimberley Mason's girlfriend?'

Honeywell referred to his notes. 'Lila Mahmoud, aged thirty-one, lives in Islington, flat just off the Liverpool Road. Owns a porn shop off Brewer Street, in Soho. They've been friends for four or five years. The night Kimberley was murdered, they'd arranged to meet at a pub in Upper Street, near the Angel, about half past seven. They had a couple of drinks, then went to a nightclub off Leicester Square, shared a cab home around midnight, cabbie was going to drop Kimberley off in Highgate after. That was the last Lila saw of her.'

'She didn't meet anyone in the club? They went home alone?'

Honeywell nodded.

'Okay, well let's find the cab driver and talk to him,' Mills said. 'But that immediately narrows down time of death to between midnight and four a.m. It could be that Kimberley's assailant was already there waiting for her. Let's find out who else might have had a key to her house. Find them, we've found our prime suspect.'

Middlesex Hospital

George Mason looked as if he had been hollowed out with a sharp spoon. He was an exceptionally tall man, obviously not without means: a tailored wool suit, gold Piaget on his wrist, and when he sat his trousers rode up his long legs to reveal monogrammed socks. He was sixty three years old, but there was only a little grey in his hair and he spoke with an impeccable Home Counties accent, greeting her with the dignified reserve he might display at an afternoon tea. But there was nothing in his experience to guide his behaviour now, and he teetered on the edge of despair. He had neglected to shave, and the shadow of iron and salt stubble jarred with his demeanour, his face was sickly grey and there was a noticeable tremor in his hands. His dark eyes were shadowed with pain.

DS Nick Crawford had accompanied him from Surrey. They sat together in the mortuary waiting room. George Mason stood up when Fox walked in. Nick introduced her and he proffered his hand.

'I'm very sorry for your loss,' Fox murmured.

He seemed embarrassed by this admission. His Adam's apple bobbed in his throat, as large as a wine cork. He seemed about to say something, but then did not trust his own voice. He cleared his throat and sat down again.

The wait for the body seemed interminable. Fox paced the room, while Nick leaned towards George Mason, whispering words of encouragement and telling him the procedure they would follow for the identification.

George Mason did not seem to have heard any of it. Fox heard him say, almost to himself, 'You wonder how well any of us really knows someone else, even our family.'

Finally one of the mortuary assistants opened the door to tell them everything was ready. Mason stood up, took a moment to compose himself, but as he moved towards the door he stumbled, and Nick caught his arm to steady him.

Fox held the door open. They followed the assistant along a white-tiled corridor to the viewing room. They all trooped in, formed their little knot of misery around the body that had been laid out for them, covered with a green sheet.

Fox looked over at Nick, the signal to begin.

'Are you ready, sir?' he said to Mason.

She watched the muscles rippling in his jaw. He nodded. The mortuary assistant drew back the sheet as far as the dead girl's shoulders. 'Is this your daughter, Kimberley Julia Mason?'

Fox was immediately reminded of Walt Disney's Snow White. Kimberley Mason had black hair, cut in a bob, and in death her skin had that same translucent, marble pallor, like an ice sculpture.

George Mason barely looked at her. A quick glance, followed swiftly by an expression of unbearable pain. He looked away again. 'Yes,' he said, though the word was barely audible.

Nick nodded to the mortuary assistant who quickly covered her again. George Mason crumpled as if someone had punched him in the stomach. He gave a choking gasp, and his knees gave way beneath him. Nick caught him as he fell, and through sheer strength was able to hold him upright.

And then Mason did the most remarkable thing. He put his arms around the smaller man, as a small boy might do to his mother after he had fallen and grazed his knee. He buried his face in the detective's neck and made a sound as if he was choking. Fox took a step forward to help him, but Nick gave a slight shake of the head to assure her he was all right and nodded towards the door.

She guided the attendant towards the door and went out, shutting the door behind her. She looked back once through the glass panel, and saw Nick holding Mason in his arms, a young black cop supporting the sagging weight of the older, taller Englishman, shouldering the pain as if he had been doing it all his life. Fox felt herself warming to him. A good cop. A nice guy.

This was what it came down to. The job wasn't about forensics or painstaking police work or brilliant interrogation technique. In the end, no matter how good you were, no matter that you got the right result, you were still left with a crime that could never be compensated, lives irretrievably damaged.

As a cop, you could never right a wrong; you just tried to prevent it happening again, to some other poor sod.

Chapter Six

Off Euston Road, St Pancras

The windows afforded a view over the sweep of London to the south, the yellow afternoon sun filtered through the sepia veil of carbon monoxide rising from the glass and concrete canyons. Kimberley Mason's office still carried the faint signature of her perfume, but it was the only imprint she had left behind. Fox looked around the cream coloured walls, expecting to find Kimberley Mason, but unlike others she had known in the public relations business, Kimberley had not sunned herself in reflected glory. There were no framed photographs of her shaking hands with satisfied clients, sharing a Kodachrome moment with minor celebrities. There was a Hockney print, a large imitation walnut desk, a Habitat sofa against one wall, and a smoked glass coffee table. Her leather-bound appointment book revealed nothing of the private Kimberley Mason: her client base consisted of medium-sized corporations and charity foundations, her business life sterile and unimpeachable. Fox tried to put herself inside the mind of the dead woman who had separated her private and public selves as neatly as if she had divided the central cortex of her brain with a slide rule.

Kimberley's secretary gave her name as Rhiannon Strudwick. An unfortunate name, Fox thought, unless you happened to be a white witch. It took no prizes to guess the approximate date of her birth or her parents' musical tastes.

Rhiannon sat on the sofa, a box of tissues on the coffee table in front of her, weeping softly. She seemed as overwhelmed by the concentrated scrutiny of the police detectives, the activity of the murder squad detectives around her, as by private grief for her former employer.

'I can't believe anyone would do something like this,' she said.

People always said this, in Fox's experience, as if murder was something extraordinary. It was a reaction that continually amazed her. When people watched the news at night, saw the grainy photographs of crime victims and the gratuitous shots of bloodstains on the pavement, did they think the television programmers had invented this for the edification of their listeners, that it was scripted in the same way as a police drama? Or perhaps what they mean to say, Fox thought, is: *I can't believe this has finally happened to me.*

Rhiannon Strudwick was young and pretty with glossy blonde hair – natural, no black roots – and outrageously large breasts, which were accentuated by a tight black sweater. Fox was worried that TJ would ogle the girl, but to give him due credit, he was making a reasonable fist of ignoring her, or them. Fox wondered if Kimberley Mason had hired Rhiannon Strudwick for her tits. Women could be sexist too, at least when it came to business. They, as much as men, knew what the punters liked.

Fox sat beside her on the sofa, TJ on the other side of the coffee table, on a castor chair, a look of practised sympathy on his face. Occasionally he would solicitously pass Rhiannon the box of tissues.

'They said she was strangled,' Rhiannon said, not so upset that she couldn't fish for gossip.

'That's right,' Fox said carefully.

'Where did you find her?'

'In her basement,' Fox said, avoiding the more salacious details. Those, they would keep to themselves, to help them confirm a suspect later, should they be fortunate enough to obtain a confession. It would also spare the family from the wolves of Wapping.

'On Friday, she just seemed so . . . alive,' Rhiannon said.

Well, that's because she wasn't dead on Friday, Fox thought. 'I know this is hard for you,' she said, 'but we need to ask you a few questions.'

'I don't know what I can tell you.' She sniffed and blew again, screwing a sodden tissue into her fist. She shook her head. 'She just seemed so alive.'

Fox looked at TJ and she knew he was thinking the same thing. He wanted to throttle her, too.

Rhiannon Strudwick told them she had worked for Kimberley for eight months. Kimberley was, by her account, a good employer, but Rhiannon remained a little in awe of her. Apparently her former boss was a fashion statement in motion, a goddess adrift in a mist of expensive French perfume, who double parked her red cabriolet outside some of London's best clubs. Fox looked around. A goddess with a small public relations company and a staff of one. I wonder how she afforded it all? Perhaps French Kitty paid most of the bills.

'Did she talk to you much about her private life?' TJ asked her.

Rhiannon shook her head. 'No. Never. She kept that part of her life pretty much . . .'

Go on, Fox thought, say it.

'. . . well, private.'

'What about phone calls?'

'You mean, apart from work?'

Fox felt herself losing patience. 'Yes. Apart from business calls.'

'She had a mobile. I think she took all her personal calls on that.'

There was a flicker of hesitancy. Fox pressed on. 'You didn't take any personal calls for her in your eight months here? Didn't you ever get any through Reception?'

She reached for another tissue and blew hard. 'Mr Mason rang a few times. Her father. And there was this other man.'

'What other man?'

'I don't want to get anyone into trouble.'

'If he hasn't broken the law, he won't get into trouble.'

She blew her nose. 'His name was Gary.'

'Do you know his surname?' TJ asked her, his pen poised.

'I don't know. Just Gary. He rang a few times.'

'Did he ever come here, to the office?'

'Once. He seemed really nice. You don't think he did it?'

Well, what do you think? Fox thought, fighting down her irritation. That we'll fit up the first suspect you throw at us? 'We need to find out a lot more about Miss Mason's friends and associates, so that we can build up a picture of her life. Until we've done that, we can't possibly establish any suspects.'

Rhiannon seemed to accept that. She sniffed and wiped her nose again. 'He only came in here once. Miss Mason seemed a bit upset with him. I don't think she liked him coming here. They had a row. They went in her office but I could hear their voices through the door.'

'Do you know what they were fighting about?'

She shook her head, no.

'What did he look like?' TJ asked her.

'He had a lovely smile. And a cute bum.' She giggled like a schoolgirl. For Christ's sake. 'Know what I mean?'

'Perhaps we can get an artist's impression,' TJ said to Fox, deadpan.

'Can you give us a bit more, please?' Fox said. 'What colour hair did he have? How tall was he?'

'He was about your height,' she said to TJ. 'Only he had fair hair.'

'Is there anything else you can tell us? Did he have any distinguishing features? Apart from his butt.'

Rhiannon put her hand over her mouth to stifle another giggle. Fox felt her fingernails biting into the flesh of her palms. Really, she wanted to kill her. 'I don't think so. He was really well dressed. Double-breasted suit, silk tie, Oxfords. But then, I suppose he would, with his job.'

Fox stared at her. 'You know where he works?'

'While he was waiting for Miss Mason, we got talking. He told me he was a sales manager for a big stationery company down Camden Road. I didn't catch the name of it.'

Fox smiled. 'It doesn't matter. There can't be many. Thank you, Rhiannon. You've been very helpful.'

The interview over, TJ and Fox got up to leave. Rankin was supervising the boxing and removal of Kimberley Mason's records and private effects to Hendon Road. Perhaps there was a diamond in all that paper somewhere.

TJ nodded in the direction of Rhiannon Strudwick and raised his eyes heavenward. 'How do you make a blonde's eyes light up?' he whispered. 'Shine a torch in her ear.' He and Rankin both laughed.

'There is one other thing,' Rhiannon said.

Fox waited while the girl struggled with herself. It was

almost as if she felt she was betraying a confidence. As if that could matter to Kimberley Mason now.

'She was seeing this other bloke.'

'What other bloke?'

'Real high flyer. Well, I think he was.'

'High flyer.'

'It was just something she said. A couple of weeks ago.'

Fox waited. Rhiannon had a tissue between her fingers and was ripping it to shreds. 'Maybe it was nothing.'

This girl, Fox thought, would try the patience of a saint. 'Anything you can think of could be helpful,' she said, trying to keep her voice even.

'Well, it was an odd thing to say.'

'They're usually the things that are most useful,' TJ told her.

'She said, "How do you think I'd look on a polo pony?" I mean, the way she said it, it was like, I don't know, I got the impression she was going out with someone . . . you know, posh.'

'What did you say?'

'I said I thought she'd be great at polo. I mean, she paid my wages. What was I supposed to say?'

TJ grinned. 'But privately you thought . . . ?'

'She really wasn't the type. If she'd said she was going out with a rock star, I would have believed it, but I couldn't see her in the horsy set. I don't want to sound mean, but despite the car and everything, she was a bit . . .'

'Common,' TJ said, who seemed to understand how her mind worked.

'Well, yeah.' She grinned apologetically. 'Know what I mean?'

And, funnily enough, Fox did know what she meant. She wondered what Rhiannon Strudwick would say if she found out that Kimberley Mason's father had been an oil executive for a multinational in Kenya, that she had had servants pick up her toys and bring her lemonades on the verandah of her Nairobi home, that her father had numbered members of the 'horsy set' among his personal friends. In expressing the thought about polo ponies, Kimberley Mason had been perhaps expressing a desire to return to her roots, to go back to the life she had once rebelled against.

'Is there anything else?' Fox asked. 'Anything else she said that seemed odd?'

Rhiannon shook her head. 'Just that. I mean, maybe she was just daydreaming. We all want to marry rock stars or presidents, don't we?'

They sat in Fox's Sierra. Fox put the keys in the ignition and started the engine and then sat there, thinking.

'Do you want to marry a rock star or a president?' TJ asked her.

'No. Do you?'

'I've had my eye on that bloke out of Hot Chocolate for a long time,' he said.

Fox nodded. 'What about George Bush?'

'Boris Yeltsin is more me.'

Fox drummed her fingernails on the steering wheel. 'What did you make of all that?'

'Personally, I think we should go and find Gary.'

'What about the polo ponies?'

'I don't see how a polo pony could have done it. Pakula said she'd been strangled.'

Christ, she loved working with comedians. She put the car into gear. Moments later they turned into Euston Road. 'I'll be interested in seeing her telephone records,' she said.

Chapter Seven

Area Major Incident Pool, Hendon Road

During the first week of the murder investigation the team met twice a day in the Incident Room, so that Mills could review the case constantly and they could keep each other briefed on their progress. That afternoon when Fox walked in, most of the squad were already seated around the Incident Room, notebooks and folders open on their laps, some of them smoking and discarding butts in polystyrene coffee cups.

Honeywell was talking quietly into his mobile phone.

'Domestic crisis,' TJ mouthed silently at her. Honeywell was always having crises at home that he tried to sort out on the end of a telephone; he had four children and three dogs, and one of them was always sick.

As soon as Mills arrived, Fox debriefed the team about her interview with Rhiannon Strudwick.

'I asked her about boyfriends, but she was pretty vague. There's some bloke called Gary who evidently got a run in her first team on a regular basis.'

Mills looked at Honeywell. 'Gary. That was the name you came up with when you interviewed Lila Mahmoud, wasn't it?'

Honeywell nodded. 'Think so.' He rechecked his notes. 'That was it.'

'Did she know where we can find him?' Mills asked.

'She thought he worked at a stationery company on the Camden Road. Sales manager or something like that.'

'Think you can find him?'

'TJ and I did some checking. There's only one that fits the bill – Newell and Redpath. We made a couple of calls, the sales manager is one Gary Bradshaw.'

'Did you run him through the computer?'

Fox nodded. 'He's got previous. Assaulted his girlfriend three years ago.'

Mills nodded. It was starting to come together now. 'Okay, you two had better get round there now, see if you can interview him. Rankin, did you come up with anything from her office?'

'We're still working on it,' he said.

'I want that finished tonight. We need to know a lot more about this lady. Our victim had far more secrets than was good for her.'

Fox thought about George Mason, and what he had said to Nick at the morgue that morning. *You wonder how well any of us really knows someone else, even our family.* Fox wondered what secrets Kimberley Mason had lived with, what secrets she was still trying to conceal, beyond the grave.

Chapter Eight

Camden Road, NW1

Gary Bradshaw strode towards them from behind a large mahogany desk, a look of profound irritation on his face. She could not tell, therefore, if he really did have a nice smile, as Rhiannon Strudwick claimed. She also could not ascertain, from this position, his other pertinent feature.

What interested her more, was that he had previous, for occasioning actual bodily harm, on a former girlfriend, and had received a three month sentence at Middlesex Assizes in June, 1996.

He was, however, dressed well, as Rhiannon Strudwick had told them; power dressed, in fact, in a button-down two-tone business shirt, a double-breasted charcoal woollen suit and a dark blue silk tie. She could almost see her reflection in his polished black Oxfords. His long fair hair was perfect, and there was a diamond signet ring on the pinkie of his left hand.

She knew the type. He lived, she imagined, in a terraced house in Kilburn, and all his salary went on his car and his clothes. He was hungry and ambitious and would have seen someone like Kimberley Mason in her red cabriolet as a vital addition to his expanding CV.

He was certainly a class above the outfit he worked for, whose offices off Camden Road were functional but rather anonymous, housed in a dour two storey brick building with security gates and open plan strip lit office space.

'What's this about?' he snapped.

Fox showed him her ID. 'I'm Detective Inspector Madeleine Fox and this is Detective Sergeant Terry James.' She looked around the office. Heads were all turned in their direction. Can we talk privately?'

Bradshaw hesitated. 'I suppose so,' he said then turned on his heel and led them down a partitioned corridor to his office.

It had none of its incumbent's panache. There were two sombre metal filing cabinets, a company calendar on the wall, and the bookshelves were filled with bound triple ring invoice folders. He closed the door behind them and did not offer them coffee. He folded his arms and glared at them. 'I'm busy,' he said.

Fox sat down in one of the two vacant chairs, without waiting for his invitation. If the man was going to behave like a prat, it was up to him. TJ followed her lead, leaving Bradshaw standing there in his heroic posture shaping up to thin air.

'Do you know a Kimberley Mason?' she said.

He hesitated. 'I never touched her,' he said.

Interesting answer. 'Do you want legal representation?' Fox said. If there was going to be an immediate confession, she would rather have a brief there, so there could be no confusion later on about precisely what was said and why.

'I don't need a fuckin' brief,' Bradshaw snapped. 'I don't care what that bitch said. I never touched her. Jesus. It's because I've got form, isn't it? That's why you're here. You bastards never let anyone go, do you? That was a long time ago. I learned from that.'

'A long time ago. Are you referring to your conviction three years ago for assaulting . . .' Fox referred to her note-book . . . 'Karen Susan Jamieson.'

He realised he wasn't going to intimidate them, and slumped into the chair behind his desk. He tried to keep up a pretence of belligerence, however. 'She slept with some dosser she met down the pub while I was up north working.' He looked at TJ. 'She deserved a good slapping.' When he saw his audience wasn't to be persuaded about the righteousness of his past behaviour, he backed off. His voice took on a more plaintive tone. 'Like I said, I learned from my mistakes. Whatever that bitch has been telling you, I never touched her. I might have grabbed her and shook her up a bit, but I never hit her.'

Fox wondered if Bradshaw was just a very good actor or if he really did not know. Perhaps he had not seen the *Evening Standard* yet. 'When did this assault take place, Mr Bradshaw?'

'I told you, I didn't assault her.'

'When didn't you assault her exactly?'

Bradshaw looked at TJ, then back at Fox, and his eyes took on a hunted quality. 'Look, what's this about?'

TJ leaned forward. Oh, tell him, Fox thought. Make his day. 'Miss Mason was found dead in her basement at ten o'clock this morning.'

'You're joking.'

'If I was, it wouldn't be a very funny joke,' TJ said.

Bradshaw seemed to deflate in front of them. He rubbed his forehead with his fist. 'Oh, fuck.' He put his face in his hands. 'Oh, fuck me.' The penny dropped and he took his hands away. 'You think I did it?'

Another interesting reaction. If all Kimberley's friends and acquaintances were this transparent, Fox thought, this case is going to be a dunker. Events had taken on a surreal quality.

'Why would we think you did it?' she asked him.

'The neighbours. They heard the row we had, right?'

'Look, let's stop fencing, Mr Bradshaw. Why don't you just tell us what happened?'

Gary Bradshaw leaned forward, put his elbows on the desk, and his tone became contrite. 'Would you mind telling me what happened?' There was a chill silence. 'I mean, Christ, who found her? How did she die?'

'She was found in her basement this morning when she failed to show up for work.'

'I don't believe this.'

'Do you want to tell us about the argument you had with Miss Mason?' she coaxed him, gently.

'I didn't hurt her!'

'Just tell us what happened.'

Bradshaw got up, turned around and aimed a vicious kick at the metal filing cabinet. He slammed the flat of his hand down on the cabinet, twice. Fox wondered if this little drama was for their benefit. All it proved to Fox was that he was violent and potentially unstable. 'Please, Mr Bradshaw,' she said. 'I know this is a shock for you, but right now I'd like you to sit down and tell us what you know.'

Bradshaw slumped back into his chair, eyes darting everywhere like a trapped and frightened animal looking for a way out.

'You said you had an argument with Miss Mason.'

'It was just a shouting match,' he said. 'It didn't mean nothin'.'

'When did this row take place?'

'Friday night.'

'What time?'

'I don't know. Shit. Midnight, one o'clock. I was drunk.'

'What was the argument about?'

'You saw the little set-up she had in the basement?'

'We were going to ask you about that,' TJ said, mildly.

'Christ. I never understood that about her. Why she wanted to do that sort of stuff.'

'Was that what the argument was over?'

Bradshaw ran a hand through the perfect hair. 'I wanted her to stop.'

'Why?' TJ asked.

A hint of belligerence returned. 'Why do you think?'

'Jealous?' TJ said, deliberately goading him.

'Do me a favour.'

'You weren't one of her punters, then?'

'Do I look like a fuckin' perv?'

'I've known a few in this business,' TJ said, with disarming frankness. 'They come in all shapes and sizes.'

'Well, I'm not, all right? I don't go in for that shite. I'm a normal red-blooded bloke. I don't need leather studs and whipped cream to get me jollies, all right?'

TJ looked around the office. 'Paperclips and ring binders more your thing.'

He got the reaction he was looking for. 'You havin' a go at me?' He looked to Fox for support. 'I got a good job here. Good money.'

'I was going to ask you about that as well,' Fox said to him.

The light dawned. Bradshaw seemed shocked that they should think such things of him. *A normal red-blooded bloke.* I've been doing this too long, Fox thought. Am I the only one who can see these questions coming?

'Oh, right. I know what you're thinking,' he said. 'And you're way off. Way off.'

'What are we thinking, Mr Bradshaw?'

'That I was pimping for her. Let me tell you something: Kimmie didn't need a pimp. She could look after herself.'

The irony seemed lost on him. It was left to Fox to point out the obvious. 'Apparently not. Otherwise . . . Kimmie . . . would still be alive.' Fox let him think about that. 'How long have you known Miss Mason?'

He seemed confused by the question. 'I don't know. Couple of months.' He put his elbows on the table, hung his head. 'I can't believe she's dead. This is a nightmare.'

Let's stay on track, Gazza. 'Where did you meet her?' she asked him.

'What?' Trying to keep himself together. 'In a club. Near the Angel.'

'All right, was she?' TJ asked him.

'How do you mean?'

'I've seen the photographs. Tasty.'

'Yeah. She was. To die for.' Another unfortunate choice of words. The phrase fell into the room like a rusty anchor.

'Your usual type?' TJ said, after a beat.

On the back foot now. 'How do you mean, my usual type?'

'Well, you know, Gary. She looked a little high class for you. Out of your league, if you don't mind me saying.'

Bradshaw's cheeks flushed. TJ had succeeded in making him angry, which was what he intended all along.

Then, pressing the point: 'Bit of a trophy for a bloke like you, right?'

'A bloke like me?'

'She drives a sports car, has her own business, looks a bit like a fashion model. You must have been pinching yourself.'

'I get my fair share. I can pull birds.'

'Not like her, though, surely?'

'I do all right.'

TJ looked unconvinced.

'Let's go back,' Fox said, keeping him off balance. 'You

were telling us about the argument you had. Why did you want her to stop this little sideline of hers?'

'I told you, I was really wired, all right? I didn't know what I was doing.'

Fox raised an eyebrow and he realised, too late, what he had said.

'Look, I told you, I didn't hurt her! That's the truth!'

'This argument,' Fox said, trying to keep him focused.

'I was drunk.'

'And?'

'I wanted to talk to her. She tried to shut the door in my face. There was some yelling. I pushed my way in. That was when she told me she didn't want to see me any more. I grabbed her, on the arm. Maybe I shook her a bit, I don't remember. Maybe a few things got smashed. But I swear to God I didn't hit her. Then I left.'

'Is that how you got that cut on your hand?'

Bradshaw followed Fox's gaze. There was an abrasion on his right thumb, near the wrist joint. 'Yeah, that's right.'

'So what did you argue about?'

'This French Kitty shit. I wanted her and me to have a normal . . . relationship. I wanted . . . she was driving me nuts . . .'

Fox waited. 'What was it you wanted, Mr Bradshaw?'

She thought he was being furtive, realised that instead he was merely embarrassed. 'I wanted us to get married.'

'You told her that?'

'Yeah. I told her.'

'When?'

'When I grabbed her.'

There was a long silence as Fox and TJ conjured an image of the scene. It was TJ who broke the tension. 'Always been a romantic, have you, Gary?'

'You're a real fuckin' smartarse, aren't you?'

TJ smiled.

'Did Miss Mason ever give you a key to her house?' Fox asked.

He seemed confused by the question. 'No. Why?'

It can't be him, she thought. He's too transparent. If he killed her, he's had thirty-six hours to come up with a story. He would have done better. All he's done so far is incriminate himself. He must be smarter than this. Surely.

'Did you love her?' Fox asked him.

'No,' he said.

'But you asked her to marry you,' TJ said.

'I was obsessed.' He said the last word as if it was a mantra, slowly, precisely.

'Obsessed.'

Christ, he'd done it again. This was too easy.

Bradshaw kneaded his temples with his knuckles. 'I can't believe it,' he repeated. And then, 'I never had a woman like her.'

'Like what?' she asked, keeping at him.

'I don't know. I don't know what I'm saying. But you've made up your mind, haven't you? Should I get myself a brief?'

TJ leaned forward. He wasn't going to let him off the hook just like that. 'You just wanted what you couldn't have,' he said. 'Didn't you, Gary?'

Gary Bradshaw glared at them, daring them to ridicule him for his weakness. Fox didn't quite feel sorry for him, there was just weary acceptance of another human frailty exposed by tragedy. Despite his protestations about being a red-blooded bloke, Gary Bradshaw was just another mug punter, and Kimberley Mason had enjoyed humiliating him, free of charge.

'You say this argument took place on Friday night,' she said.

'That's right.'

'What were you doing in the early hours of Sunday morning between midnight and six?'

The question shook Bradshaw from his self-pity. A sense of self-preservation took over from his flashy displays of grief. 'The Saturday night me and some mates went down a pub in Finsbury Park. Stayed there till about ten o'clock. They went on to a club, I didn't feel much like it. I went home, watched Sky for a couple of hours, then I went to bed.'

'Alone?'

'No, my dog sleeps on the end of the bed. You can check with him.' He leaned back and folded his arms again. 'Look, maybe I had better get myself a solicitor. I can see the way this is going.'

'All right,' Fox said. 'Perhaps we can continue this down the station.'

'Christ, this could cost me my job,' Bradshaw said, and his face almost crumpled. He nodded towards the outer office. 'This is going to be all over the warehouse by tomorrow.'

TJ shut the door to Interview Room 4A in the basement of the Islington division station. Bradshaw had given them his statement, persisting with the story he had given them that afternoon.

TJ shook his head. 'Guilty as hell,' he said.

'You think so?' Fox said.

'He has motive, he has no alibi. He's got previous. Bastard.'

TJ was right: at this stage he had to be their prime suspect. He had agreed to a search of his flat in Tufnell Park, had given a blood sample that could be matched against the blood on the refrigerator. He had co-operated in every way, even over the advice of his brief. Or perhaps he was just being clever. He knew everything they had on him was circumstantial. The blood they had found in Kimberley's kitchen, the bruises on her upper arms, he had explained them away without actually incriminating himself in a murder. It wasn't nearly strong enough to take to the CPS.

'His brief's going to demand we release him,' Fox said.

TJ shrugged. 'What are you thinking, ma'am?'

'I'm thinking that if he did it, he'd have a better story than the one he's given us.'

TJ looked angry. 'He did it all right. He hated her guts, no question. I can see through him like a plate glass window. We've got to nail this tosser.'

Fox watched him walk off. An unwarranted display of anger, really. But then, it had occurred to her that there was a lot of DS James in their Gary Bradshaw. Both flash, both obsessed with women but didn't like them very much. Sometimes there was a fine line between the accuser and the accused.

Chapter Nine

Soho, W1

The shop was in a cobbled alley off Brewer Street under a candy pink neon sign that read, 'THE PINK PUSSY'. The alley was crowded with market traders selling bootleg CDs and tapes, Chinese cabbages and jackfruit and fat purple eggplants. The essentials of life arrayed in this wet Soho alley this July morning: vegetables, commerce, sex.

Fox and TJ slipped through the flystrips across the doorway and around a plyboard partition with the usual age requirement warnings tacked on to the bare wood with Sellotape. The shop had a familiar, if unimaginative, floor plan: tawdry porn stacked on two of the walls, a few lurid pink vibrators and sex toys arrayed under a glass display case.

There was an assortment of male customers: a couple of Asian tourists in cheap baseball caps emblazoned with the name of a Japanese tour company, a scruffy-looking man in a donkey jacket, two young men barely out of their teens. How anyone could contemplate so much bodily fluid before lunch amazed her.

The sales assistant's ponytail might have suited someone

half his age. He was slowly turning the pages of a *Daily Mirror*, and looked distinctly bored. Two lurid green latex pudenda lay on the glass counter beside his elbow, both boasting a bright bush of fake red-brown hair.

Fox hated these places. She always felt like a sheep on a guided tour of the abattoir. The man behind the counter looked up and his eyes grew immediately wary when he saw her badge. 'We're looking for a Lila Mahmoud,' Fox said.

TJ was examining an enormous green plastic dildo. 'Bit small, isn't it?' he said, and the man looked first at Fox and then at TJ, off balance.

'Lila Mahmoud,' Fox said, regaining his attention.

'She's not here.'

'Will she be back soon?'

'I guess. She just popped out to do some shopping. What's this about?'

'Who are you?'

'Ray. Ray Pratt. I work here.'

'Pratt by name, prat by nature,' TJ chirped and gave him a grin. He picked up a novelty keyring in the shape of a penis. 'Does this have a light in it?'

Ray Pratt stared at him, unnerved.

'We'll wait,' Fox said, and wandered away from the counter. TJ followed her.

At the end of the room was the specialists' section, a circular wire rack featuring leather corsets and chastity belts, a bright red rubber bikini, a French maid's outfit in washable black vinyl.

'You reckon this is where Kimberley did her shopping? Bought her stuff off the rack.'

'Very funny, TJ.'

'It's like a C&A for S&M,' he said, examining a plaited

leather whip. 'The Bizarre Bazaar. That'd be a good name for one of these places. I should copyright it.'

'Yes, do that.'

TJ's demeanour changed. Here at last was a place where he felt comfortable assuming the high moral ground. 'I don't know how people get off on this crap,' he said. 'There's some sick bastards around.'

Fox studied the cover page of one of the cellophane-wrapped magazines. Why did men enjoy this? The trouble with erotica, in her opinion, was that there was nothing erotic about it. It was like a gynaecology lesson conducted in a rundown motel under floodlights borrowed from Wembley Stadium.

A woman burst through the flystrips and made her way behind the counter. She was in her early thirties, no make-up, big-breasted, in a shapeless brown jumper and jeans a size too short, leaving much of her hips to bulge over the waistline. Like two legs of pork wrapped in denim, Fox thought. Some women just don't know how to dress. She plumped two plastic shopping bags on to the countertop. Vegetables spilled from one, there were two cartons of milk in the other.

TJ nudged her. 'That must be Lila,' he said.

Ray Pratt had disappeared into the little office at the back. Lila picked up the green latex pudenda on the counter and stared at them, puzzled.

'What are these cunts doing out here?' she shouted to Ray in the cubbyhole office.

'They want to talk to you,' he said. 'They wouldn't tell me what it was about.'

Lila Mahmoud frowned, her expression one of utter bewilderment. She picked up the latex organs and took them into the little office, out of view. Fox could hear her voice over the partition. 'What the fuck are you talking about?'

'What?'

'I asked you why these cunts are out here on the counter.'

'Oh, those cunts. This geezer brought them back. Said that one had a split in it.'

'Cunts are supposed to have a split in them.'

'Well, he reckoned he did himself a mischief. And he reckoned the other one was too small.'

'Too small? Christ, that means he's used the fucking thing. And you let him have a refund?'

'I never thought of that,' Ray grumbled.

'Christ, you're useless.'

Lila came back out of the office and slammed the two refunded pudenda on the counter top. TJ and Fox were waiting for her, TJ holding his ID.

'Miss Lila Mahmoud? I'm Detective Sergeant Terry James, this is Detective Inspector Madeleine Fox. We're investigating the murder of Kimberley Julia Mason. We need to talk to you, love.'

Lila gave a theatrical sigh. The light dawned; so *you're* the two cunts Ray was talking about. Her day was going from bad to worse. 'I wondered when you lot would come sniffing around again,' she said.

'We thought you might be able to help us some more with our enquiries.'

Lila looked irritated. 'All right,' she said. 'Not here, though. Look after the shop, Ray,' she shouted in the direction of the office, 'I've got to go out again.' She picked up her purse off the counter and stamped out.

They sat outside the coffee shop in the watery sunshine, listening to the thump of music from the leather shop across the street. It had rained last night, and the air was humid and rich with scent and stink: roasting garlic from the Italian restaurant next door, exhaust fumes from the delivery vans parked along Brewer Street, the stench of the drains and wet garbage from the black plastic bags piled at the end of the alley. Market day on Rupert Street had brought out a few early tourists, who were being halfheartedly propositioned by the girls in the doorways of the one-pound peepshows.

TJ bought three cups and brought them to the single plastic table pushed against the coffee shop window on the narrow pavement.

'It was only a matter of time,' Lila was saying.

'What makes you say that?' Fox asked.

'I don't know. You just get that feeling with some people, know what I mean? Couldn't ever see Kim some wrinkled old tart sitting in a pub trying to get some punter to buy 'er a vodka and tonic.' Lila spooned sugar into her coffee.

'How long had you known her?' Fox asked.

'Four years. Maybe five.'

'Where did you meet her?'

'What's all this got to do with anything?'

'We'd just like to know a bit more about her, Lila. It might help us catch the person who did this.'

Lila sipped her coffee, wiped the froth off her upper lip with the sleeve of her jumper. Hard to imagine small, dumpy Lila with long, slender Kimberley. By all accounts Kimberley was a class act. They must have looked an odd sight clubbing together. Perhaps it was deliberate. There were certain girls, Fox knew, who chose plain girls as best friends in order to make themselves look better.

'The Black Rose,' Lila was saying. 'We worked there for a while. I didn't have this weight problem then,' she added, seeing TJ raise his eyebrows. 'It was easy money. Christ, it was just like acting really. Better. You didn't have to fuck anyone to get a part.'

'Why did you leave?'

'Just sick of it. Working in one of those places is like working in a lunatic asylum. Gets to you after a while. Only so many nutters you can stand before you start to go a bit loopy loo yourself. Know what I mean? A bloke wanting to get some custard off his chest, well, that's just human nature. But some of the punters you used to get at the Black Rose, they were certifiable, if you ask me.'

'Did Kimberley get sick of it?'

'No, not our Kimmie. She loved it, the whole thing.'

'When did you quit?' TJ asked her.

'I stuck at it about a year.'

'But you and Kimberley stayed in touch.'

She shrugged. 'I suppose we had a lot in common. Intellectually.'

TJ snorted but Lila ignored him.

'Did you know she was still into the S and M scene?' Fox asked her.

'Yeah, I knew. I was always telling her to get out of that side of it.'

'Why?'

'Stands to reason. Too many risks, especially what she was doing.'

'What was she doing?'

'She was subbing, wasn't she?'

'Subbing?'

Lila gave her a look: don't you know anything? 'There's two kinds of girl, right? You can be a dom or a sub – a dominatrix or a submissive. If you're a dom,' Lila went on, 'you're pretty much in charge. Your clients want you to tie them up. But Kimberley liked the sub stuff. I mean she *really* enjoyed it. You let the johns tie you up, it can get dangerous.' Lila gave her a sly look. 'Is that how it happened?'

Fox let that one go. 'Did you know she had her own dungeon under her house in Highgate?'

Lila shrugged. 'I never saw it, if that's what you mean, but I guessed she had her place set up. Like, if you're going to have a business repairing videos, you need a workshop. If you're going to do S and M . . .'

'The dungeon must have been a big investment.'

'She didn't pay for it. She got one of her johns to put up the dosh. Some sugar daddy.'

TJ gave Fox a look. 'Buying your girl a dungeon,' he said. 'Makes flowers and chocolates look a retro.'

'Did she ever ask you to get stuff for her?' Fox asked Lila.

'Sometimes. I got it for her wholesale. It's not cheap, you have to have it made specially. It's not a big market.' The understatement hung in the air. A Chinese girl walked past their table, dressed completely in black. She even wore black lip gloss. Her eyes were hollowed out from drugs, and she teetered on outrageously high stilettos. Just the right background and cast of extras for a conversation like this, Fox decided.

'Did she ever tell you who she was seeing?' Fox asked Lila.

'Men?' Lila shook her head. 'She never mentioned names, if that's what you mean. Never gave anything away, our Kimmie. But I got the impression she had kept this rich bloke on a string. Could all have been crap, though. She liked to make you think she had more going than she really did.'

'Did she ever mention someone by the name of Gary Bradshaw?'

Lila gave them a look of utter derision. 'Gary's a dickhead. You don't think it was him did her in?'

'He's helping us with our enquiries,' TJ said, his voice thick with sarcasm.

'If Gary was a lolly he would have sucked himself to death

years ago. Look, there were a lot of blokes like him used to hang around her. They were all way out of their depth with our Kimmie.'

'How many times did you meet him?'

'Gary? Only a couple of times. Salesman or something, ain't he?'

'Was he ever violent with her?'

'If he was, I wouldn't blame him.'

'Meaning?'

'She used to like to torment blokes. For fun. I told you, she liked the mind games.'

'How did she torment Gary Bradshaw?'

'She'd fuck his brains out, then next day she'd ring him up and say she didn't want to see him any more. Then two weeks later she'd ring him up again and get him to take her out. Somewhere expensive. But then she wouldn't sleep with him. She'd keep him twisting in the wind for weeks, going hot and cold, putting him on a promise and then not showing up. She had cock teasing down to an art form. If you ask me, blokes like him love it.'

Fox looked at TJ. He seemed fascinated. Perhaps Lila had just told him the story of his life. It certainly put the relationship between Gary Bradshaw and Kimberley Mason in a different perspective. How would a bloke like Bradshaw have reacted to that sort of provocation? With violence, probably.

'So when was the last time you saw her?'

'I've been through all this before Saturday night. We went to a pub in Islington.'

'Did you meet anyone?'

Lila shook her head. 'We just went there for a few drinks. We weren't looking for blokes. When you've worked in the sex industry for a bit, men lose some of their mystique. Sorry, love,' she added with a cheap laugh and gave TJ a playful nudge with her elbow.

TJ sat back and crossed his arms.

'Did she seem worried about anything?' Fox went on.

'No, she was just the same. I reckon it was one of her punters did her in, you ask me. Look, I've told you everything I know. I've got to get back to the shop. Ray will be giving refunds on used condoms if I'm not careful.'

'Thanks for your time,' Fox said.

Lila picked up her cigarettes and made her way back down Brewer Street. In retreat she looked more like an underpaid typist than a former dominatrix and proprietor of a sex shop. It took all sorts. 'What do you think?' TJ said.

'What do I think? I think you could be right about Bradshaw.'

'Silly bastard. Got to feel sorry for him.'

'Sorry for him? Why?'

'Well, she was asking for it, wasn't she?' TJ said.

They didn't talk much to each other after that. Sometimes she wondered about TJ. The fact that he was on her side of the fence was more down to luck than anything else.

Chapter Ten

Kilburn, NW6

The Black Rose was set in a quiet mews of turn-of-the-century cottages in one of the better streets in Kilburn. Fox parked her Sierra between a black Saab and a late-model Ford and turned off the engine.

'I wonder what the neighbours think,' Fox said.

TJ stared at her. 'The neighbours.'

'You know. I wonder if they ever come over to complain about the noise. Could you keep the screaming down after eleven at night, my husband's got to get up early in the morning, that sort of thing.'

TJ didn't say anything.

'Are you all right?' she said.

'I don't like this sort of bollocks, ma'am. Women in stilettos standing on blokes' eyeballs, people having their toes sucked.'

'You sound as if you know all about it.'

'I think it's sick.'

'I didn't have you down as one of the Moral Majority, TJ.'

'Everybody has standards.'

'Not you, surely.'

He seemed irritated by the remark, which amused her. He got out, slamming the door, and stared at the house as if a plague sign was painted on the front door. 'Let's get this over with,' he grunted and followed Fox up the path.

Black railings separated the house from the street, and the heavy door was painted wine-red. A black coach lamp hung above the brass number plate, and below it another brass plate announced 'The Black Rose'. The uninitiated might perhaps think it was the name of the house, like 'Dunroamin' or 'Thistledome', or perhaps that the premises housed the editorial offices of a magazine or small advertising company. The curtains were discreetly drawn.

They were met at the door by Mistress Demonica. It was eleven in the morning and Mistress Demonica was now Catherine Rees-Fry, dressed down in jeans and a T-shirt. Fox tried to imagine what she looked like in costume. She was attractive, not much older than Fox herself, with a blaze of auburn hair. She was not plump, but heading that way, Fox decided. Her green eyes were an arresting feature, the corners of her mouth twisted upwards into a smile that hinted at some sort of secret knowledge, which in her case, Fox supposed, was probably warranted. She would have looked almost homely if not for the slogan emblazoned across her T-shirt: *Sticks and stones may break my bones but whips and chains excite me.*

Mistress Demonica led them into the reception area, where they took the weight off on one of two red plush sofas. She offered them a cup of tea and biscuits as if they were at the vicarage. 'I'll put the kettle on,' she said and disappeared down the hall.

Fox felt a perverse thrill at being in a place like this. One of the perks of the job, she thought, you got to see things few women, even most men, ever got to see and you had a legitimate reason for poking your nose in. There was a part of her that took a gratuitous interest in the sleazier aspects of the work. Part of her nature, she supposed: as a kid she'd been the little girl at the back of the class always leaning forward to watch the science teacher dissect a sheep's eyeball, the teenager who made sure she was there behind the bike sheds after school to watch the boys fight.

She looked around. Like any premises designed for the night, by day the Black Rose looked gaudy and cheap. There were velvet drapes on the windows, and the walls were painted matt black. There were several black and white framed photographs: a woman in black leather posing atop a Roman chariot, her muscles oiled, the chariot drawn by two leather-trussed men; another photograph showed a naked man with a dog chain around his neck being led along by a woman in a black latex jump suit.

Mistress Demonica reappeared with a red plastic tray with three mugs of lukewarm tea and a plate of Digestives which she set down on a smoked-glass coffee table. Fox noticed that it had ebony legs carved in the shape of naked black women.

'You're not from Vice, are you?' Mistress Demonica asked them.

Fox showed her her ID. 'Inspector Madeleine Fox, Hendon Road. This is DS Terry James. We're investigating a murder.'

The woman's air of weary resignation evaporated. Perhaps she had thought she was going to be closed down again, or hit for a cash payment.

'Look . . .' Fox wondered what she should call her. She decided it was safer not to call her anything. 'We're not interested in what happens on these premises. A former employee of yours has been murdered and we hoped you would be able to help us.'

Mistress Demonica frowned. 'Kim,' she said. 'I read the paper.'

'She used to work here. Is that correct?'

'That was years ago.'

Fox produced a photograph of Kimberley, taken by her father the previous Christmas. 'We're talking about the same girl?'

She nodded. 'That's her. The paper said she was strangled.'

'That's right.'

'Is that really what happened?'

Fox dodged the question. 'Did you know Miss Mason was still active in the business?'

'Yeah, I heard.' Mistress Demonica gave her a look of exquisite cunning. 'Is that what happened? One of her johns do her in?'

'We don't know.'

Mistress Demonica's expression said it all: stupid bitch got what she deserved. 'I told these girls a hundred times. It's not safe out there. But you couldn't tell Kim anything, she knew it all. See, my girls here are looked after. You have to be careful in this business. Most of the punters are pretty harmless, but some of them you have to watch.'

TJ had been quiet up to this point, but now he leaned forward, and by the expression on his face you'd have thought he'd just bitten down on a lemon. 'Perverts, you mean?'

'We like to say that our clients have special needs.'

Let's not get into philosophy, Fox thought. She shot a warning glance at TJ. 'How long ago did Kimberley Mason work for you?'

She shrugged. 'About three, four years ago.'

'She was a good worker?' she asked, as if Kimberley was a secretary or filing clerk, and she saw TJ raise his eyes in disgust.

'I suppose,' she said. 'I was sorry to lose her.'

'Why?'

She seemed surprised by the question. 'Well, it's hard to find girls who are good at this. It's very specialised work. Kim really enjoyed it. You need a sense of theatre. The client can always tell if a girl's just play-acting.'

'How long did she work here?'

'A year, I suppose.'

'Do you know why she left?'

'She said she was giving it up. But they don't, of course. Not the ones who are good at it, like she was.'

The doorbell rang. It was pitched to the tune: 'Do You Really Want to Hurt Me?' Someone had a sense of humour, at least. Mistress Demonica answered the door. Fox caught a glimpse of a man in a business suit conducting a whispered conversation with their hostess in the foyer. She heard her say, 'No, we get a lot of young men ask for that.' The caller cast an embarrassed glance in their direction. Not so young, Fox thought wryly. Mistress Demonica knew that charm came before abuse.

After a few minutes he left and Mistress Demonica returned.

'What was all that about?' TJ asked her.

'He wants a naked woman to walk over him in her stilettos,' she said.

TJ gave her a look. He wasn't sure. 'You're joking,' he said.

'If I were a psychiatrist, I wouldn't joke about you having schizophrenia or a phobia about spiders or having been abused by your father when you were a child. We're all different.'

'Bit early in the morning, though, isn't it?' Fox asked.

'To wear stilettos? I think so. I've made an appointment for him at one o'clock.' She picked up the Digestives. 'Biscuit?'

Fox put down her mug of tea. Undrinkable. 'Can we have a look around?'

TJ gave her a hard look. Oh, to hell with him. She needed to understand Kimberley Mason. And this was where they would do it.

Chapter Eleven

There must be good money in this business, Fox thought. Lawyers, prostitutes, undertakers. None of them would ever go out of business. The house had been extensively redecorated in the same lurid style as the reception area, hot Gothic: burgundy flock wallpaper with chrome wall sconces, heavy gilt mirrors, a narrow mahogany staircase with gargoyles on the balustrades.

'The thing you have to remember is we don't do sex,' Mistress Demonica was saying, as she led the way up the stairs, 'we're not tarts.'

'What are you, then?' TJ said.

'Therapists,' she said. 'We make it clear to everyone, no sex, no massage.'

'Then what do the punters get for their money?' TJ asked her.

Mistress Demonica stopped at the landing, put her hands on her hips. 'You can get sex anywhere. What you pay for here is fantasy. Fantasy custom made to your requirements.'

'Like a suit,' TJ said.

'What sort of fantasies?' Fox asked her.

Mistress Demonica opened a door and Fox peered inside.

What must once have been a bedroom had been transformed into a school classroom, with a blackboard, desks, even multiplication tables taped to the walls. 'If you can't get your sums right, the teacher has to take you down to the head-mistress' office for a good caning.' She opened one of the desks. There was a girlie magazine hidden under a history textbook. 'We have some very naughty boys in this class.'

'Jesus,' TJ sneered. 'Pathetic. What sort of sick bastards do you get in here?'

Mistress Demonica treated this outburst as if it were a serious question. 'Control freaks, mostly. The majority of our clientèle are the sort of men accustomed to wielding authority. Politicians, judges, teachers. And a few policemen,' she added, smiling at TJ. 'Powerful men find release in sexual submission.'

'I take it your services are not cheap?' Fox said.

'We go to a lot of trouble to provide a helpful environ-ment. Downstairs we have a fully equipped torture chamber with whips, chains and hoists. There's a large capital outlay involved. Fortunately many of our clients are powerful men with important jobs. They have expensive tastes and they can afford to indulge them.'

'Masochists,' TJ said.

Mistress Demonica made a face. 'I don't like that word,' she said. 'I prefer not to use it.'

Fox smiled. She was like a middle-aged matron lecturing debutantes about etiquette.

'You might think our clients are pathetic, but believe me that's not my experience. In fact, they're some of the most self-absorbed people I've ever come across. They have certain needs they want met and they go to enormous lengths to make sure everything is exactly right. You could say they don't think of anyone but themselves. If we don't do the job right, according to their specific fantasy, they just won't come back. You don't just lay into someone with a whip, like some people think. This is all about theatre.'

'And this is what Kimberley used to do?'

She nodded. 'Kimberley was special,' she said. 'She understood all the mind games that went with the job. She was a natural.'

'What's in here?' TJ said, pushing against a locked door.

Mistress Demonica took a key from a hook on the wall and unlocked it.

Fox thought she had seen everything in her thirteen years in the police force, but surprises were still there to be had. The room looked like a conventional lavatory, except the toilet was made of clear Perspex and was fitted with a matching Perspex lid and cover. There was a neck chain attached to the lid, presumably for securing the victim's head inside the bowl.

'Jesus Christ All Fucking Mighty,' TJ said.

Fox was surprised at her own reaction. It was the same physical sensation she had had on seeing her first corpse when she was a probationer, revulsion twinned with morbid fascination. As she often did in these situations, she imagined her father looking over her shoulder, shaking his head, and she heard him sigh: 'Oh, Madeleine, when are you ever going to learn to be a *lady*?'

'This is a popular item?' Fox asked, as if it was a brand of washing machine.

'It would have to be. The capital investment is enormous. Not many plumbers carry these.'

'Is that a fact?' TJ said and walked away.

Fox wondered again about Kimberley Mason. She had misjudged her; imagined her as just another sort of tom. The truth, it seemed, was more complex, and more perverse.

'These are mind games we're talking about here,' Mistress Demonica was saying. 'You need a rich fantasy life to understand what this is all about. Most people don't get it, not because they're what society calls normal, but because they just don't have the imagination for it. You have to remember, it's the client who makes up the script, not us.'

TJ rubbed his forehead. He looked like he was getting a headache.

'I have one valued client,' Mistress Demonica went on, in a conversational tone, 'who never comes here to use our facilities. He pays me like a salary to kidnap him. The crucial thing, see, is that he never knows when it's going to happen. I come up behind him in the street or an underground car park, or even in a bar, and I stick my fingers in his back and we both pretend it's a gun. Then I take him out to my car and I drive him somewhere quiet and make him change into women's clothes. Then I just drive off again.'

TJ stared at her. 'Then what?'

'I suppose he gets himself home somehow. I imagine that's the thrill. Walking through London in a dress, with no money, and worrying you might be recognised. There's no sex, no nudity, not even any physical abuse.' Then she added: 'He's a cop, too. I dare say you know him.'

'Honeywell, probably,' TJ muttered under his breath.

They went downstairs and Mistress Demonica led them along a narrow passage lit with fringed sconces that bathed the corridor in a lurid red glow. She opened another door and they followed her into what looked like an office: a desk, credit card franking machine, a telephone, a plain paper fascimile machine. There were framed photographs on the walls, stylish pieces of erotica in monochrome; a woman's slim and black stockinged leg wearing a stiletto heel; a close-up shot of a woman's pierced nipple.

There was a high-backed leather chair behind the desk and a window with a pulldown blind.

'What's this?' TJ said. 'Some kind of secretary fantasy?'

'No. This is my office.'

She went to the window and raised the blind. Fox found herself looking into a futuristic dungeon, with metal-studded walls – fake, but effective, Fox thought – the ceiling and floor painted black. There was a metal torture table in the middle of the room, padded with black leather. Shackles and chains hung from the pipes that snaked across the ceiling, whips and switches and other torture implements hung around the walls.

'The key word is fantasy,' Mistress Demonica was saying.

'Is this a one way mirror?' Fox asked.

Mistress Demonica gave her a look that let her know that she thought the answer to that was obvious. 'This is not a game for amateurs. People could get hurt.'

'Isn't that the point?'

'Of course not. We're not the IRA, we're not here to maim people. For instance,' she said, and turned round to look at TJ. 'I could whip your friend here without leaving a mark, or draw blood from his buttocks with a single blow from my hand. Depending on what he wanted.'

'I'm going outside for a ciggie,' TJ said and walked out. The door slammed shut behind him.

Mistress Demonica returned her attention to the one-way mirror. 'All the activities in this room are supervised. Especially if a client comes in here and wants a sub.'

'A submissive?'

She nodded. 'Our girls are mostly doms, but we also provide submissives, for a substantially higher fee. Of course, with one of our girls under restraint there's a chance a client may overstep the mark and do real damage. That's why we have the mirror.'

'You said Kimberley Mason was a sub?'

She smiled. 'A lot of the girls won't do it, even though it pays a lot more. Not Kim. Like I said, she enjoyed it.'

Fox stared at the grim, dark-lit room and tried to make sense of her feelings. Horror, mostly, but also a muted but disorienting sexual frisson. Christ.

Mistress Demonica pulled down the blind. 'I don't expect you to understand girls like Kim any more than you can understand any of us. People who are only interested in vanilla couldn't possibly know what it's like in our world.'

'Vanilla?'

'Straight sex, dearie. Vanilla. No added flavour.'

Fox was finding it hard to concentrate on the job at hand. Pull yourself together, Maddy. Just another day at the office. 'Did Kimberley take any of your clients with you when she left?'

Mistress Demonica saw where that was going straight away. 'I don't know our clients' real names, and if I did, I wouldn't tell you.'

'This could be important. Whoever killed Kimberley Mason—'

'Look, I'm sorry about what happened to Kim. But life belongs to the living, as they say. I have a business to run.'

The shutters had come down. Bad move, Fox thought. The interview was over.

'Thanks, anyway,' Fox said. 'It's been . . . instructive.'

'I don't know what you think I've helped you with, but you're not really any closer to understanding Kimberley, or any of us.'

Fox turned to leave but then stopped, her hand on the door. 'Do you enjoy your job?'

'I could ask you the same question. Staring at mutilated bodies, looking at blood and semen samples. You'd have to be sick in the head. Sorry, but that's just my opinion. No offence.'

Fox shrugged. 'None taken.'

Mistress Demonica led the way out of the office. There was a cupboard under the stairs. She stopped, unlatched the door, and switched on a light. A man was crouching inside dressed in a black tight-fitting corset and suspenders. He wore lipstick and mascara and was lashed to a waterpipe with a length of chain.

Mistress Demonica leaned in and kicked him. 'You piece of shit!' She latched the door shut again.

Fox stared.

'Twenty-five pounds an hour. All he wants is for us to abuse him about every half an hour and let him out at a pre-arranged time, so he can make his business appointments.' She looked at her watch. 'Been there since eight o'clock this morning. Has to be gone by quarter to one.'

Fox couldn't think of anything more to ask. She let herself out.

TJ was leaning against the Sierra, a cigarette in his hand, scowling at passers-by. 'I'd like to shop the lot of 'em.'

Fox unlocked the driver's door. Her cheeks felt hot and the muscles in her gut were tense and twisted.

'Waste of time,' TJ said.

'Was it?'

'Slags I can understand,' TJ said. 'Even the ones who do it standing up in doorways. But I can't understand why Vice sit on their hands and let people like her just do what they like.'

Fox got behind the wheel and started the engine. She turned on the radio loud so she wouldn't have to listen to TJ gob off all the way back to Hendon Road. Sometimes he really got on her nerves.

✻   ✻   ✻

Fox checked her message bank. There was a call for her from her sister, Ginny, and it was urgent. It's Ma, Fox thought and punched Ginny's number on the speed dial.

'Ginny?'

Ginny could hardly speak, she was so distraught. This is it, she thought. Ma's died and I haven't seen her for a month. I should have gone over last weekend. Now it's too late.

'Ginny, what is it?'

'Ian,' she sobbed into the phone.

Fox felt a wave of relief, followed by renewed panic. 'Is he all right?'

'He's left me.'

Fox stared at the windshield of the Sierra. It was starting to drizzle again. She stared at a grey, amorphous sky, a Lufthansa 747 disappearing into the overburden of cloud. The atmosphere in the car was like warm treacle. She felt a droplet of sweat trickle between her shoulder blades. She wound down the window. 'Oh, Ginny,' she said, because she couldn't think of a single other thing to say.

'What am I going to do?'

Fox felt a sense of *déjà-vu*; only instead of her friend Carrie on the end of the line, her life crumbling around her ears, it was Ginny: dependable, straightforward, big sister Ginny. She had spent the last eight years despising her, for her ordinariness and her happiness. She even had a private nickname for her house in Surrey: Ginnyworld, a theme park established to commemorate the twin towers of motherhood and marriage.

And now it had come tumbling down and Ginny needed her, like Carrie always had. Now she wanted her on-the-edge, ballsy little sister to be there to bail her out. Too late in life Fox realised she had been typecast, a female Mr Rick to every refugee in life. The tough loner with the key to the safe. Ms Fixit.

'I'll be straight over,' she heard herself say into the phone.

TJ was watching her, a concerned look on his face. 'Anything wrong?'

Fox shook her head. 'Family problems,' she said, and dismissed it with a wave of her hand.

'You want to take Bill, then,' he said. 'He's got a lot of experience of those.'

But she was already out of the door.

Chapter Twelve

Worcester Park, Surrey

Ginny and Ian lived on the better side of Worcester Park, in a three-bedroom semi with a paved front garden and lattice bay windows, coach lamps by the barred oak front door, and a red Montego Countryman estate and maroon Jaguar parked in the driveway.

Today the Jaguar was missing. Ian wasn't home.

Ginny answered the door, her eyes pink and swollen from crying. Fox saw the twins staring down at her from the top of the stairs, silent and moon eyed with consternation. Fox wondered how much their mother had told them. She followed Ginny into the sitting room. The curtains had been drawn against the setting sun, as if she was in mourning. Which in a way, Fox supposed, she was.

Ginny wore a long and shapeless dress, and for once she was without her subtle but carefully applied make-up. Her long, jet hair, which she normally kept tied in a ponytail, now hung loose around her shoulders, adding to the impression of dissolution.

'He's having an affair,' Ginny spat, without preamble.

'Oh, God,' Fox said. Predictable, she supposed. Someone had once said to her that men didn't know the meaning of fidelity. They thought it had something to do with sound systems.

'I told him to get out,' Ginny spat.

'How did you find out?'

'It was obvious,' Ginny said, as, of course, it inevitably was.

Ginny sat on the sofa, pigeon toed, a paper tissue clutched in her fist, but there were no tears to dry, only a deep and fathomless well of anger, bubbling to the surface, sulphurous and intoxicating. 'I hope he gets AIDS,' she said.

'Ginny,' Fox said, shocked at such a sentiment from her sister.

'I hope he gets a carcinoma in his dick and *dies*.'

Fox had never seen her like this. Behind the tears there was something else in her eyes, some part of her so deeply wounded that she had become vicious. Gentle Ginny had found a reservoir of poison. Really. She was shocked.

'She works in his office. *Tart*.'

'When did all this happen?' Fox asked her, but Ginny wasn't listening.

'And she's older than me!' Ginny wailed, pounding her fist on her knee in outrage at this final, terrible insult. 'If he had done it with some little bimbo just out of school, I could have understood it. But she's three years older than I am! *I hope he dies!*'

Fox tried to put an arm around her, but Ginny shrugged her away. So Fox went into the kitchen and made them a cup of tea, out of some unfathomable need to do something when there was nothing she could think of to do.

Later she made the twins their tea, and talked to them, and tried to explain the best way she could why Mummy was crying and why Daddy wasn't going to be there to tuck them in bed tonight. She used the same voice she used for the grieving relatives of murder victims, quiet, calm, solicitous.

Inwardly she was horrified.

When the twins were in bed she sat down and listened to Ginny spill out the harboured grievances of eight years of marriage, the real truth about Ginnyworld. Fox could not decide if she was relieved or dismayed by these revelations of trouble in paradise. For a long time Ginny's perfect marriage – at least, as relayed to her by her mother and the united front Ian and Ginny had always presented – had given her hope that perhaps one day there would be a Ginnyworld for her as well. Her own Maddyworld, perhaps.

All evidence to the contrary so far.

There had been David, a relationship that had consumed much of her twenties, and which had allowed both of them to defer important decisions about their futures. They became convenient for each other, a Clayton's relationship, the love affair you have when you're not really in love. When he traded her in for a younger model, rage was replaced by relief with startling rapidity.

And then there was Simon; almost a year since she had seen him and there were still times when her hand hesitated over the phone. Not longing, just loneliness. Not waving, drowning.

The revelation that her sister's happiness had been founded on sand was in many ways a *consolamentum*. In fact Ian's indiscretions gave her renewed faith in her own adequacy. After all, if the Wonderful Virginia could screw up, it exonerated her for her own thirty-four years of wretched relationships and failed commitments.

By the time she drove home at one o'clock that morning, the cases of Kimberley Mason and Virginia Johnstone *née* Fox had become scrambled in Fox's mind. Everyone, it seemed to her, had their dirty little secrets. People bluffed you out, poker faced, until you believed there really were no knaves in the deck.

But there was always a reckoning. For Kimberley Mason it came last Sunday morning, her body laid out with her secrets in her own private torture dungeon; now Fox's own brother-in-law, perfect father and loving husband to the immaculate Ginny, had been caught out in a sordid office affair.

At the end of the day, people were endlessly frail, relentlessly human. Who really knew anyone, deep down?

Hampstead, NW3

It was James Carlton's particular pleasure at the end of the day to stand by the windows in the drawing room with a balloon of Courvoisier, Mozart playing softly on the sound system, and stare at the quiet Hampstead night and the distant lights of the city. He would take this time to remind himself that he was lucky, and he would try to imagine life without such luck. He heard his father's voice: *You got to have class, son, that's what you need in this world. Got class, no one can touch you.* His father had class; just no money. They had lived in a perpetual state of crisis, and it was perhaps from him that James learned what it was to dissemble.

His father was wrong, of course, as he had been wrong about many things. Class was one thing, luck was something else. Napoleon had once said, 'It's good to be good, it's better to be lucky.' Or perhaps that was Kevin Keegan. Someone said it, anyway. And they were right.

Almost impossible now to imagine life without privilege, to remember what it was like to struggle, to live without this cushion of wealth, to have to bear the constant cold ache of dread. He reminded himself that this could not last, that he did not deserve to have all this anyway. He felt the same desperate urgency of a gambler who knows he must stand up and walk away with his winnings before his luck turns again. But he could not walk away. He had to see the dice roll again, if only for the thrill of finding out whether he would win or lose. The anticipation yet outweighed the fear.

'Should we have the Barringtons for lunch on Sunday?'

'What?'

Louise was watching him from the sofa, her glasses perched on the end of her patrician nose. 'Sunday. Should we have the Barringtons over?'

'Yes. Excellent. Fine.'

Louise removed her glasses and studied him, as a head-mistress would a recalcitrant pupil. 'You seem tense,' she said.

'Do I?'

'Is something wrong?'

'You know what it's like. Politics. Don't want to bore you with it.'

Louise regarded him, the cool violet eyes taking everything in. But she was accustomed to that kind of reply from the men in her life, her father had trained her to it. *Cosset them, chum them along, tell them nothing.* She closed her book, shutting it so dramatically that it sounded like a gunshot on this quiet Hampstead evening. 'I think I'll go up to bed. Are you coming?'

'Think I'll stay up for a while.'

'You're sure nothing's wrong, James?'

'No. Nothing. I'm fine. Absolutely.'

She folded her reading glasses into their case and gave him a peck on the cheek as she passed. She left behind her in the room the familiar perfume of *eau de bain*. The door closed, leaving him to his seclusion and apocalyptic thoughts.

Fucking hell. I'm fucked. Truly.

But before the sky falls in, I wouldn't mind doing it all again. Actually.

Chapter Thirteen

━━━━━◆━━━━━

Area Major Incident Pool, Hendon Road

Fox picked up the telephone in her office. So bloody small. She might as well shift her desk into the broom cupboard. A photostat of a news cutting stared back at her from the wall, her own face smiling and holding up a medal towards the camera. Hadn't she taken some stick for that.

'Fox,' she said into the phone.

'Maddy,' a voice said, breathless. It was Carrie.

Fox braced herself for good news. Lately she had found it hard to adjust to her friend's reversal of fortune. For so long their friendship had been established on the twin bedrocks of Carrie's misery and Fox's steadfastness. She had grown accustomed to the role of wise older sister coming to the emotional rescue of her profligate junior. Now Carrie had found a job she actually loved and a boyfriend who did not beat her, and her burgeoning happiness served only to illuminate Fox's own barren condition.

'I wanted you to be the first to know,' Carrie said, and Fox knew what was coming, and it felt as if she had swallowed a lump of cold grease. She immediately despised her own selfishness.

'I've got great news,' Carrie said.

Fox squinted at the black and white glossies arranged on her desk in front of her, trying to concentrate. Kimberley Mason, spreadeagled naked on a wooden table. In a torture chamber she had built herself. The lives we create for ourselves: monogamy, eternal love, erotic suffering, deadly violence. The endless permutations arranged by the mind.

'I'm pregnant.'

Fox rubbed a hand across her forehead. This biting headache. She'd had it ever since she woke up this morning. 'Pregnant.'

'Two months.'

Are you out of your mind? she wanted to say. Carrie, you have an eighteen-month-old daughter by a previous relationship that failed. Now you've got yourself knocked up again.

She rearranged the photographs of the corpse, as if it was a jigsaw and she was looking for a pattern among the separate pieces.

'Maddy?'

'Congratulations,' Fox said and tried to sound as if she really meant it.

'Can we do lunch?'

Christ, no, Fox thought. We're flat out here. First week of a murder investigation. Sixteen-hour days and no weekend leave. Who has time for lunch? Why doesn't anyone leave me alone to do my job? First my sister, now my best friend. I don't have a normal life like you. I don't have time for coffee and for lunches, for anything except *this*. Anyway, I couldn't bear it. I don't want to hear about how wonderful your life is right now. The only new and exciting thing in my life is Kimberley Mason.

'Sure,' she said. 'Have to celebrate.'

They arranged to meet in a pub in Camden. Fox dropped the receiver and turned away from her desk, watched the rain leaking down the windows, little beads of water refracting the strip lights on to a landscape of office towers and grimy terraced streets.

The newspaper clipping on the pinboard was becoming yellowed. Only a year old and already it was a part of history. She was smiling in the photograph, holding her award up to the camera, alongside her fellow recipients for that year, her months of rehabilitation in hospital behind her. She had fronted the Grosvenor House Hotel in Park Lane on that warm June evening, feeling like a fraud. The other nominees were all uniforms, plods who did the frontline grind, as she had once done, talking suicides back to the other side of the rails on Hungerford footbridge, taking handguns away from coked up Yardies in Birmingham, a Cornish copper who had taken a six-inch knife off a schizophrenic on a St Ives beach.

She knew beforehand that she was a lay-down to get an award: she had actually taken a bullet in disarming a man later discovered to be responsible for the abduction and murder of several children. She had made the front page of the *Evening Standard*. She also knew that she had been reckless rather than brave: she could – she should – have waited for back up. Her last governor had called her a glory hunter and she suspected that perhaps he was right.

Well, she had paid the price: despite the counselling the dream still haunted her nightscapes; that recurring image of a frozen moment of time, one split second when she had seen the black eye of death down the barrel of a revolver. A fragment of her personal history that now went on for ever.

The award was in a drawer at home, she hadn't even taken it out of the presentation box. Bravery was not supposed to be part of a murder detective's job. The hard stops were for SO19, not female DIs from the AMIP.

When she had returned to the squad, there had been a mixed reaction from the team: naked admiration from some of the men, not a little envy from others. They had all long suspected that she had balls; now she had proved it. Behind her back some of them – it had started with TJ, she suspected – called her Mad Maxine. Others made jokes about the Blair government passing laws to make shooting foxes illegal.

For her own part, her own recklessness had scared her. Before that she had never doubted the fact that she had bottle. Now she worried that it was all gone, bled away in the emergency room of St Thomas' Hospital A&E.

Chapter Fourteen

———————————◆———————————

M26 Near Cobham

Fox allowed herself a sideways glance at DS Nick Crawford in
the passenger seat beside her. He looked too soft to be a good
cop. He had skin like polished ebony, a lazy smile and spoke
like a Devonshire dairy farmer.

He sat there, perfectly composed, his hands resting on
his knees. Huge hands, like two salad bowls he was trying
to balance, with some difficulty, on his lap. You could tell
a lot about a man by his hands, her mother had always
said. Nick's fingernails were perfectly manicured, the cu-
ticles exquisite half moons. Not like Honeywell, who bit
his down to the quick, or TJ, who was always picking at a
hangnail.

Unlike TJ, he didn't wear a leather jacket; didn't smell
vaguely of rusks and small children, like Honeywell. His
perfection embarrassed her somehow. She was acutely conscious that her Sierra needed detailing; there were peppermint
wrappers strewn in the console, an empty Coke can rolling
around on the floor behind the passenger seat, the faint
but unmistakeable smell of fried chicken emanating from a

discarded container secreted somewhere underneath the driver's seat.

You're a slob, Madeleine. She could hear her father's voice echoing down the years. You're a lovely girl and I love you. But you're a slob. Why can't you be more like your sister?

She wasn't sure what it was about Nick that made her so nervous. She didn't fancy him, for God's sake. Did she? Besides, he had a reputation already. Ever since TJ had seen him in the King's Head with some skinny blonde, Crawford had been the subject of juvenile, if not racist, jokes in the canteen regarding the length and girth of his male organ. TJ had taken to referring to it, within Nick's hearing, as the Black Man's Burden. Or the Horn of Africa.

The rain had stopped but billowing cumulus loomed above London and there didn't seem to be enough air. Fox wound down her window, felt a bead of sweat make its long and inexorable way down her spine. She hoped her antiperspirant would go the distance.

'What do you think about this case?' she said.

Nick shrugged. 'Seems to me whoever did this knew just enough to make it look bizarre without really fooling us about anything. Botched job.' The West Country accent jarred with his appearance. Like Worzel Gummidge fronting a rap video.

'Have you got a theory?' she asked him.

'I reckon he strangled her in the kitchen where we found the blood. Then he took her downstairs to the dungeon, laid her out, went through this charade with the hot wax and the rest of it to try and throw us off the trail. We have to figure out what the motive was.'

'Someone who does this, we might not be able to understand the motive.'

'Well, you know, it crossed my mind, maybe there's some form of as yet unclassified deviancy at work. Torturing a corpse; perhaps there's a name for it. Sadistophilia, is that a word?'

The traffic on the M25 was gridlocked, as usual. The largest car park in Europe, some people called it. Another ten years and the motor car would become redundant she reckoned. There'd be a fast lane for pensioners with Zimmer frames.

It would be quicker to walk to Surrey.

Kimberley Mason's family lived in an old manor house out by Junction 10, near Cobham. Fox turned off at Wisley Common. There was a mist of rain on the windshield and the newsreader on Capital Radio said that the Wimbledon women's final might have to be played on the Sunday if the rain went on.

'How are the Masons holding up?' Fox said.

He shrugged. 'He's been pretty cool with me since that day in the mortuary. I suppose he's embarrassed. His wife's a basket case, truth be told. Been under sedation ever since we gave her the news. Haven't been able to interview her yet.'

'Not a pleasant job for you, either.'

'No, ma'am.'

'Tell me about them.'

'Well, ma'am, as you know, he used to work for Shell. Retired about ten years ago, but I get the feeling they're not as well off as they'd like people to think. Nice house, but it's inherited, her side of the family. Kimberley was born late in their lives, so this has hit them pretty hard. She was their only daughter. The way they talk about her, they didn't really live for much else. She was good enough to them, in her way.'

They drove for a while in silence, until Nick said, 'He keeps asking questions, wanting to knowing all the details.'

'What have you told him?'

'Only as much as I have to.' He fidgeted. 'I can't help but feel sorry for them. There was so much of her life they didn't know about, although I think they had suspicions about what she was doing. And now this. Suddenly there's us lot asking endless questions, sorting through every intimate detail of her life.' He shrugged his shoulders. 'I don't know, it can't hurt *her* any more, but they still have to get through it, have to deal with shame as well as grief. Don't seem right somehow.'

Nick was right. A perfect memory could be enshrined, but in a flawed life the legacy was stained with regret and unanswered questions: why didn't you tell us? Why did you do it? Questions that could never be answered, but would nevertheless intrude each time the Masons stared at an old photograph, grasped for a receding memory.

'I suppose we all have secrets,' Fox said. 'The best we can hope for is to keep them to the grave.'

'Do you have secrets, ma'am?'

That was quick. 'No. Do you?'

He shook his head.

'Well, that blows that theory out of the water, then.'

A few moments later they turned into a gravel drive, past a duck pond and a signpost that said, 'Millwater. Bed & Breakfast'. They came to a rambling house with Tudor beams and moss-covered gables. An old millhouse had been converted into a garage, a black Mercedes 500 series saloon parked outside. On closer inspection she saw the rust marks around the doors and wheel arches. Old money straining to keep up with inflation, Conservative England trying to keep pace with new Blair. As far from French Kitty as she imagined you could get.

'Bloody hell,' Fox said as she got out of the car, 'how did she get there from here?'

❋   ❋   ❋

The living room was cluttered, an eclectic mix of the cultured and the profane, Marcel Proust and Jean-Paul Sartre on bookshelves alongside Harold Robbins and Arthur Hailey; antique Chinese vases on display beside cheap African souvenirs, family wedding photographs on the walls next to nineteenth-century oils. There was a motheaten stag's head above the fireplace, which now housed a more efficient convection heater.

George Mason met them at the door, in the uniform of a country squire: a green woollen cardigan with leather patches at the elbows, dark cords, loafers. He had quite recovered his composure, as Nick had said. He appeared awkward now, as if by grieving for his lost daughter he had committed some gross breach of etiquette. Mother, which was how he categorised Mrs Mason, was upstairs, he said, the doctor still had her under sedation. He offered them tea. Nick, familiar with the house, said he would make it and went to the kitchen.

Mason slumped into a wing-backed armchair, and Fox sat on an ancient jade-green Chesterfield, the leather cold under her legs. Mason looked desperately ill, his cheeks bloodless, skin like old parchment.

'Mind plays funny tricks,' he said. 'Woke up this morning and for a moment it seemed like any other day. I was going to go out and mow the lawn. And then I remembered our Dumpling was gone.'

Dumpling. French Kitty, aka Dumpling. The woman and the child. What a long and winding road it must have been for twenty eight years.

'Have you found out who did this?' he asked.

Fox shook her head. 'Not yet, Mr Mason. It's still early days.'

He seemed neither surprised nor displeased by this news. Often in their grief and anger people thought that if you had not made an arrest inside the first twenty-four hours, you were dragging your feet.

Nick brought in a pot of tea, three cups on a tray, two small silver jugs, sugar and milk.

'We don't have to do this now,' Fox said, 'but there are some questions we need to ask you. About Kimberley. We think it could be important.'

He did not appear to be listening. 'She had her wild years,' he was saying. 'We thought all that was over.'

There was a framed photograph on the wall, a gap-toothed child in a school blazer. Fox thought it might be a grandchild and then remembered what Nick had told her, the Masons had no other children. She realised with shock that it was an old school photograph of French Kitty.

'There were drugs, when she was younger,' George Mason was saying. 'At university. We didn't know half of what she got up to, of course. You do your best, but it's never enough.'

He stopped and looked down at his hands. Fox sat there, let him talk.

'Mother had a nervous breakdown when Kimberley was eighteen. Worry, you see. We spent half our lives worrying about her. But we thought all that was over.'

'What sort of things worried you, Mr Mason?'

She could see it in his eyes, he was wondering how much they knew.

'Was there anything about her life, do you think, that she might not have wanted anyone to know about? That she might have tried to keep secret from you?'

'There were many things.'

'Such as?'

'You're fishing, Inspector. What is it that you know, that I don't?'

Fox took a sip from her cup. The English way to discuss a murder, over tea.

'The way your daughter was found, Mr Mason, led us to believe that she was engaged in certain . . . unusual . . . sexual practices.'

George Mason closed his eyes. 'God,' he said. He ran his hands across his face. 'What sort of . . . practices?'

'Sadomasochistic. We believe she may have been engaging in these acts . . .' She hesitated, then plunged on. '. . . Engaging in these acts on a professional basis. Did you know about that?'

He shook his head, like a man trying to clear his head of a persistent and annoying sound. He took a deep breath, cleared his throat a few times. 'Dear God,' he repeated.

She hated this. She could look at dead bodies all day, had seen her share of corpses during her years in the Met; there were drug overdoses and traffic accident victims while she was in uniform, then the legions of the stabbed and the strangled and the beaten-to-shit since her ascent to the murder squads. It's just meat, her old mentor, Marenko used to tell her. Just chain of evidence.

It was grief that was hard, the hardest thing to deal with. Confronted by emotional pain she took refuge in procedure, rehearsed phrases, simulations of sympathy, kept herself at a distance.

Few people had to face grief like George Mason's. This was not just death, as it came to everyone sooner or later: violent death in the manner of Kimberley Mason's was different. Even Fox and Nick Crawford, though it was part of their working lives every day, never came as close to it as the Masons had. For them, the manner of their daughter's death must seem as bizarre as if she had been eaten by a bear while waiting for the Tube. Utterly incomprehensible.

'You wonder sometimes if you wouldn't have been better off without them. Kids, I mean.' George Mason shook his head. 'This is going to kill Jean.'

He was not hysterical, Fox thought. This sort of loss really did kill people.

'You can't live their lives for them,' George Mason was saying. 'God knows we tried. She got a scholarship to Oxford, could have done anything she wanted. She was a bright girl.' He looked up and stared at Fox, hating her for knowing what she knew, seeing what she had seen. 'I know what you people must think, but she was a decent young woman.' There was a challenge in the dark eyes.

'Your daughter's private life is not on trial here,' Fox said. 'We just want to find who did this to her.'

'It's not on trial *now*. But if this gets in the papers. If it gets to court. You know what will happen.' He seemed to shrink from shame. 'What must you think of her?'

'We're not here to judge, Mr Mason,' Nick said, gently. Fox watched him, surprised by the compassion in the dark, handsome face.

Mason held up his hand. 'I don't want to know the details. I don't wish to know. I hope you will spare me that.' He glanced up at Nick. 'Yesterday morning, when this young man came here, I badgered him for details. He was good enough to spare me that, and now, upon reflection, I am grateful.'

Fox waited. Let him gather himself.

'I've been over and over it in my mind, but the fact is, she was always a stranger to us. You wonder if it was your fault. Do you understand?'

Fox did not answer him. She had never had children, perhaps never would. What could she say to him?

'You can't blame yourself,' Nick said. 'And you can't blame your daughter. She did not deserve to die.'

But he didn't seem to have heard. 'She was always a rebel,' he went on, his voice no more than a murmur, so that she had to strain to hear him. 'She was . . . what can I say? . . . perverse. I don't mean in a sexual way. She did things that . . . we found impossible to understand. When she was seventeen years old she had her hair cut . . .' He made a motion with his hands to indicate she'd had most of her hair shorn. 'She dyed it purple, had chains and pins put through her nose and her eyebrows. Punk, they called it. The look. Christ.' He rubbed his face with his fists, hard, grappling with the memory, the total lack of comprehension. 'She was intelligent, that was the hell of it. She could have done anything she wanted, but she dropped out of Oxford after a year, came back to live in London. God only knows what she got up to. That's when I thought something like this would happen. I was prepared for it then. We both were.'

He rubbed his palms together, as if he was trying to get rid of some difficult stain.

'But we got through all that, and over the last three or four years she seemed to have her life back on track. She got herself a decent job, public relations. It seemed to suit her. She had a flair for attracting attention.' A bitter smile. 'I helped her set up her own business about two years ago. I thought she had straightened herself out, I provided the capital, took out a mortgage against the house. We really thought . . .' For the first time he faltered, and the expression on his face showed utter bewilderment at the strength of his own emotions. 'We really thought she was going to be all right.'

'When was the last time you saw her?' Fox asked him.

'Just over a week ago. She came down every Sunday for lunch . . . except last weekend of course.'

'Weren't you worried when she didn't show up?'

'It wasn't the first time she hadn't shown up without

telling us. We rang, of course, just got the answerphone. We just assumed she'd had a better offer.'

'Did she ever mention boyfriends?'

He shook his head.

'Anything you can remember that may help us . .'

'You learned after a while just to shut up,' he said, and there was an edge to his voice now. 'Jean wanted grandchildren, but we both knew not to ask about her . . . private life. We were walking on eggshells the whole time we were with her. I suppose deep down we suspected that it was all just a sham.'

Fox nodded.

'Over Sunday roast we'd talk about this and that. She told us only what she wanted us to know, of course, the things we wanted to hear: how well her business was doing, films she'd seen, that sort of thing. Then she'd drive back to London and we would know nothing of her real life. It sounds quite sad now, doesn't it? But it was a sort of compromise we'd worked out between ourselves. A truce. And we were happy with that. In the circumstances, it was the best we could do.' He stared at her, daring her to say otherwise.

'I am sorry for your loss,' she said. 'We will do everything in our power to catch the person responsible for this.'

He sat there for a long time, listening to the clock on the mantel. 'I wish I could be of more help to you,' he said, at last.

Fox looked at her watch and nodded to Nick. 'We'd better get back to London,' she said. 'Thank you, Mr Mason, I realise how hard this must have been for you.'

'I'll come back tomorrow,' Nick said to him. 'I'll try and keep you informed of any progress. If you need a hand with the funeral arrangements . . .'

'You've both been very kind.' George Mason led them to the door, shuffling like an old man. As Fox stepped over the threshhold he stopped her, gently placing a hand on her arm. 'Will it get into the newspapers?'

'Not if we can help it.'

He stood there, his hands opening and closing into fists at his sides. 'She didn't suffer? You're sure?'

'The cause of death was strangulation. There were other, smaller, injuries. They were inflicted post mortem. After death.'

'Were you both there? Did you see her?'

Fox nodded. 'Sergeant Crawford wasn't there. There was another officer from the squad.' Fox decided not to mention the army of forensic officers.

For a moment she thought he would crumple, but then he composed himself again, his lips compressed in a bloodless line. George Mason would face down the world, no matter what they said about him or his daughter. Pride would get him through. There might not be much worth saving at the end of it, but he would survive.

Chapter Fifteen

Camden Town, NW1

There were some guys, she thought, who just should not be let out alone, who should have an escort just to get themselves dressed. He was standing at the end of the bar holding a drink with a cherry in it, wearing a leather cap – possibly stolen from Sly and the Family Stone at the end of the 'seventies – a thick black leather belt, ruffled shirt and a scarf. Unlike Kimberley Mason, he had no secrets, his sexual identity proclaimed in the crimson codpiece he wore over his black Lycra pants.

The barman ignored this apparition. Instead, his attention was fixed on the television above the bar, watching the one thirty from Ascot, occasionally muttering a comment to two of his regulars.

Carrie and Fox sat in a booth in the corner, Fox nursing a half of Greene King. She had switched from her usual gin and tonic; just lately they had been going down a little too fast.

Fox wished she could be enthusiastic about Carrie's plans. You only have to pretend, she thought, it can't be that hard. Instead she heard herself say, 'Are you sure you know what you're doing?'

Oh, that was subtle. If Carrie was hurt, she tried hard not to show it. 'Of course I'm sure.'

Fox tried to think of something positive to say. The silence dragged.

'We're going to get married,' Carrie said.

Married. Fox just stared at her.

'Don't look at me like that, Maddy. It's the right thing for me.'

'When?'

'Next month.'

'Next month?'

'I don't want to break my waters walking up the aisle. Everything's worked out. It's in the church where Steve was christened. His parents still live in the village. It's like a postcard, this place, you should see it. It's going to be so romantic . . .' She realised she was gushing and stopped herself. She saw the look on her friend's face.

'You're giving up everything?' Fox said. Thin ice, this, but she couldn't help herself.

'What is there to give up?' Carrie snapped.

'You've just got yourself back on your feet. Daisy's in nursery. You have your independence back.'

'Independence isn't *everything*. None of us is really independent, Maddy. I need Steve. I need you.'

'Carrie, I'm sorry. But, Christ. It's a big step.'

'A lot of people do it. It's not like sailing single-handed around the world or anything.'

It might as well be, Fox thought. For some of us.

This appalling silence, stretching far longer than was comfortable for either of them.

'You could congratulate me,' Carrie said.

'I *am* happy for you,' Fox managed.

'Now say it like you mean it.'

Fox drained her glass. 'I do mean it. If you're happy, I'm happy. I'm just scared for you as well. You've only known him two months.'

'You like him, don't you?'

'I've only met him a few times. I hardly know him.'

In fact Stephen did seem like a nice guy. He was the sales manager at the radio station where Carrie worked. Thirty-something, divorced, a flat in Fulham. He had a nice smile, seemed articulate and well read. Perhaps he would be good for her.

Carrie looked at her over the rim of her glass. Empty. Time for another round. Perhaps something harder this time.

'I was thinking of asking you to be my maid of honour.'

'Please. At my age.'

'Give me a break. You're to die for, Maddy, face it. You don't look thirty-four, you probably never will, you bitch. And you're my best friend. You've always been there for me when I've been down. I want you there for me now. When I'm up.'

Yes, Madeleine Fox, pull yourself together. Was it that hard to be happy for her? You pick holes in every guy you ever meet, half the world has no chance with you, right from the start. You could blame the Met, but the truth is, you'd be the same if you were a suit in the advertising business or, God forbid, a lawyer.

Give it a break. Give *her* a break.

She reached across the table and touched Carrie's hand with her fingertips. 'Don't mind me,' she murmured. 'I'm just jealous. I'd love to be your maid of honour. And I think it's great about you and Stephen. If anyone deserves to be happy, it's you.'

Carrie, bless her, took her half-hearted effort at felicity for what it was, and grinned. 'I've never met anyone like him,' she said. 'You'll see. It's going to work out.'

'I know it will,' Fox lied.

'I'll get the drinks.' Carrie got up and went to the bar.

Fox closed her eyes. Time. Moving too fast for her. She wanted everything to slow down, give her time to make some decisions. For instance: she loved her job, but was it going to be enough for the rest of her life? Would the succession of the dead and the damned take the place of a home, and children? A man could juggle both worlds but she had not known many women who had done it successfully. She had put off her decision as long as she could, but now life was speeding past her, as if she was staring at it from the window of an express train, going too fast for her to step off and seemingly powerless to change its direction.

Area Major Incident Pool, Hendon Road

Honeywell sat slumped on the other side of her desk, running his fingers through his thinning fair hair. He wore an habitual harassed expression, always looked as if he was on the edge of a nervous breakdown. Perhaps he was: his long-running domestic crises were the subject of much amusement among the rest of his team.

'You all right, Bill?'

'One of the dogs got run over this morning.'

'I'm sorry. Is it all right?'

He shook his head. 'I want to have it put down but the kids are hysterical. It's going to cost me a fortune. You know what vets are like. Shit, it's fourteen years old and it's got halitosis.' He chewed fiercely on his bottom lip. 'You wanted to see me, ma'am.'

'The house to house. The flat directly across from Kimberley Mason's, still no result.'

Honeywell pulled a notebook from his jacket pocket, flicked through, looking for a page. 'Sandra Devenish. Got the name from the landlord, lives downstairs. He thinks she's gone to visit her mother. Lives in Sheffield somewhere, no idea of the address.'

'How long's she been away?'

'Left first thing Sunday morning.'

'The morning after Kimberley Mason was murdered.' She looked at her watch. Gone six. 'Grasping at straws here, Bill. We still don't have enough to charge Gary Bradshaw.'

'Landlord said she never goes away for more than a few days. Do you want me to go back and check?'

She nodded. 'I'll come with you.'

Highgate, N6

A wet evening, humid as hell, the smell of leaf mould and decay from the cemetery hanging in the air. Fox got out of the car and spared a glance at the two-storey semi across the road where Kimberley Mason had lived her bizarre life and died her even more grotesque death. The blue police tape had been taken down, the house in darkness, locked up. Kimberley's red sports car was still parked there in the street. Life in the fast lane, Fox thought grimly.

Number thirty New Cross was an identical semi – chocolate-coloured brick with downstairs bay windows – but had been converted into flats by the owner, a retired Jewish businessman. Fox looked up at the second storey window, saw the muted yellow glow of a table lamp, and felt her spirits lift. Got lucky.

*   *   *

Sandra Devenish peered out at them from behind huge, owlish glasses and a shock of black frizzy hair. She was dressed in what Fox would have described as early Stevie Nicks, wearing what looked like a chenille bedspread over a tye-died dark green ankle-length dress. She was in her mid twenties, Fox guessed, but the post-Glastonbury look made her appear much older.

'Sandra Devenish?' Honeywell was saying. He showed her his ID. 'DS Honeywell, this is DI Fox. Can we have a word?'

The smell of incense was overpowering, like stepping into a Chinese temple. An oak table had a pentagram carved into the surface, and a large framed zodiac hung on one wall, another wall taken up with a large shelf of books rescued from secondhand bookshops, from dog-eared paperback horoscope primers to gnarled tomes with cracked spines on hermetic thought and Isis worship.

Fox peered into an ashtray on the mantelpiece. The remains of a joint. Oh, let it be. She wasn't here for that.

Sandra Devenish stared at them as if they were emissaries of the Dark Angel. 'Miss Devenish,' Fox began, 'we won't keep you long. We're investigating a murder that took place last Saturday night at the house across the road.'

'A murder?'

'The victim's name was Kimberley Mason. She lived at number twenty-nine. Did you know her?'

She put her hand to her mouth and shook her head.

'You didn't know?' Honeywell asked her. 'It was in the papers.'

'I never read the newspapers. They only print bad news.'

Fox bit her lip. The Devenishes of this world made the job worth doing. 'I understand you've been away.'

'I went to see my mother. I go every month. She's getting old.'

'The murder took place on Saturday night. Your landlord told us you didn't leave until Sunday morning.'

'You don't think I did it?'

Fox looked at Honeywell, then back at the woman. She couldn't help herself. 'Did you?'

Sandra Devenish again clapped her hand to her mouth. 'No!'

'We didn't think so. We already have a suspect. We just wondered if you saw or heard anything unusual last Saturday.'

She clasped her hands together in the attitude of prayer. 'Isis save me,' she murmured. She blinked at them, her eyes huge behind her spectacles. 'Do you want some chamomile tea?'

'We don't want to hold you up,' Honeywell said. He glanced at Fox, an almost imperceptible movement of the eyebrows. Loony.

'Please, sit down,' Fox said to her.

No furniture, just bean bags. Sandra Devenish flopped into one. Rather than stand over her, Fox did the same. Honeywell grunted and followed suit, really pissed off now.

'I did see something,' Sandra Devenish said, slowly.

'What, Sandra? What did you see?'

'There was a car, parked right there in the street.'

'What time was this?'

'About ten o'clock.'

'What made you notice it?'

'Something made me look out of the window. A sixth sense, as you would call it. I know things before other people, you see.'

Fox glanced at the ashtray on the mantelpiece, the crystals on the coffee table, the Egyptian carvings of black cats. You are now entering the twilight zone.

'What did you see?'

'There was someone sitting there in the car. I could see the glow of a cigarette. There was an aura of evil around the car.'

'What did you do then, Sandra?' Fox asked her, trying to keep her on track.

'I knew it was a man, I could sense it, and I thought he might be watching the house. I didn't know what to do. I watched a film on television until midnight and then I got up to go to bed. When I looked out of the window, the car was still there.'

'Did you ring the police?'

'I've rung them before, lots of times, and they never come. Anyway, when I went back to the window ten minutes later, he was gone. But I had a feeling that something bad was about to happen. I was right, wasn't I?' A look of triumph.

'Did you get the registration number of this car?' Honeywell asked her.

'I remember part of it.'

'What part do you remember?' Fox asked.

'The numbers. Triple six.'

Fox looked at Honeywell. Bradshaw's Ford was WHK 666M.

'Could you tell us what sort of car it was?'

'I just remember the three sixes. It's the devil's number.'

'Is that significant?' Honeywell asked her, losing his patience.

'It is for me. I'm a white witch.'

Honeywell dropped his pen on the parquet flooring. It sounded like a gunshot going off.

Chapter Sixteen

Tolpuddle Street Police Station, Islington

'Where were you on the night Miss Mason was murdered?'
Mills asked.

Bradshaw looked at his brief. His name was Marcus Lloyd
and he was expensive: a pinstripe suit, carefully knotted dark
blue silk tie, his initials monogrammed on his soft leather
briefcase in gold.

'My client has already answered that question,' Lloyd
said.

'He can answer it again, can't he?' Mills said.

Fox looked across the desk at Bradshaw. Was there a hint
of uncertainty? Bradshaw fidgeted, scratched at his nose.

Mills referred to his notes. 'We have a statement from a
neighbour, who believes she saw your client's car parked across
the road from Miss Mason's house between ten o'clock and
midnight on the night she was murdered. This is at variance
with your original statement, Mr Bradshaw. You told us you
were at home in bed. Could someone else have been driving
your car that night?'

Bradshaw glanced at his brief.

'You don't have to answer,' Lloyd said, 'but if there is some good explanation of the facts, it might be better if you did.'

Bradshaw looked at the two detectives and Fox could see him searching for his out, his thoughts as plainly written on his face as if they had been projected on to a theatre screen: he was wondering how accurate their witness statement was and whether he could bluff his way through this.

Abruptly, his face crumpled in defeat. 'If I'd told you the truth, I would have been dropping myself right in it, wouldn't I?' he said.

'Of course, this way is much better,' Mills agreed, deadpan.

Bradshaw folded his hands and stared at the table. 'Okay, I was there.'

'You wish to revise your earlier statement?'

'I went round there, all right. I wanted to talk to her. On the Friday night . . .'

'When you assaulted her?' Mills prompted.

'I didn't assault her. I just grabbed her arm!'

'Go on.'

Bradshaw continued, his voice strident now. 'On the Friday night, she said she didn't want to see me no more. I couldn't accept that.'

'So you went round to see her.'

He nodded.

'For the tape,' Mills said.

'Yes.'

'What time was this?'

'About nine o'clock, I suppose. I don't remember exactly. I'd been drinking.'

'And what did you do when you got to Miss Mason's house?'

'I told you, I just wanted to talk to her. She wasn't in. So I went back and sat in the car and waited.'

'And then what happened?'

'Nothing happened. I got pissed off and went home.'

'You went home. What time was this?'

'I told you, I don't remember. I was there about an hour, I suppose.'

'Our witness says you were still there at midnight.'

'Yeah, all right, maybe I was. I wanted to see Kim, she didn't show up, so I gave up and went home to bed. That's it.'

'What time did you come back?'

'I didn't come back,' Bradshaw said, enunciating each word with the care and deliberation of a language student.

'You didn't mean this to happen, did you, Gary?' Mills prompted him. 'What was it? Wouldn't she listen to you?'

'I didn't come back,' Bradshaw shouted, flustered by the line Mills was taking.

'Her being on the game. All these sick bastards she called her clients. The stuff she used to do. Made you angry, didn't it, Gary?'

'Yeah, it made me angry.'

'Enough to make any red-blooded man lose his head. I can understand that. I guess you didn't mean to hurt her.'

'I didn't strangle her!'

'She wouldn't listen to what you were trying to tell her, so . . .'

Bradshaw was on his feet. 'I didn't hurt her!'

Lloyd put a hand on his arm.

'Sit down, Gary,' Mills said, gently.

Bradshaw sat down, breathing hard. 'Do I have to take this?' he said to his brief.

'I believe my client has answered your question,' Lloyd said. 'If you are going to harass him in this manner, I shall end the interview now.'

Mills contrived to ignore him. 'I'm sorry if I upset you,

Gary. It's just that I understand how these things can get out of hand. We've all wanted to kill our wives or husbands at one time or another.' He smiled at Fox, inviting her to share in the charade.

'I never touched her,' Bradshaw said.

'Except for Friday night. You told us you had a big fight with her on Friday.'

'I never hurt her . . .'

'There was heavy bruising on her upper arms. It was in the pathology report. That must have hurt, surely?'

'I didn't mean to do it.'

'You just lost control.'

'Yeah, I . . .' Bradshaw looked like a cornered animal. Again, he glanced at his brief. 'Do I have to answer any more questions?'

Lloyd leaned towards Mills, his spectacles glinting in the strip lights. 'Do you intend to charge my client? Because if you don't, can I remind you you have only a little over two hours left in which to do so. It appears to me you have no evidence against him, and he has co-operated fully with your investigation.'

'Your client has lied to us once already,' Mills said to him. 'Is that what you would call full co-operation?'

'I explained to you about that!'

'Explain it to me again. And let's be sure we have our facts right this time. You waited outside her house. You wanted to talk to her again about her being an S and M slag, right?'

'She wasn't an S and M slag!'

'What would you call it?'

'She never had sex with any of those creeps.'

'When did you find out about French Kitty?'

Bradshaw took a deep breath, trying to calm himself down. 'There was a phone call one day, while I was there. I picked it up.'

'It must have come as quite a shock.'

'Yeah. It was.'

'You didn't suspect? How long had you been going out with her by then?'

'About a month.'

'Would you say you were naïve, Gary?'

'Look, she had all these like, compartments in her life. She kept that part of her life pretty well . . . hidden.'

'Right,' Mills said, letting him know what he thought of that as an excuse. 'So, you heard someone asking for French Kitty. What did you do?'

'I yelled at her.'

'Did you yell at her the way you yelled at her Friday night?'

'No.'

'Why not?'

'I just didn't.'

'And what did she say?'

'She told me to mind my own business.'

'And did you?'

Bradshaw fidgeted in his chair. 'I suppose I didn't.'

'I suppose you didn't. What about these other affairs she was having? She was seeing other blokes, right?'

'No.'

'No?'

'Look, it wasn't like she was a tart or anything. It was just one other bloke.'

'Who was he?'

'I don't know.'

'How did you find out about him?'

'She used to talk about him. About how sophisticated he was. How much money he had. How she was going to marry him. She used to torture me with it.'

Interesting choice of phrase, Fox thought.

'You must have wanted to kill her when she said things like that,' Mills said.

This time he saw it coming. 'I just wanted her to stop.'

'Did you try and *make* her stop?'

Bradshaw shook his head and stared at the desk.

'For the tape, Mr Bradshaw has refused to answer.'

'I asked her to stop, I begged her to stop. She told me she would but she didn't. All right?'

'You know, the thing is, none of us really blames you,' Fox said, more gently, working a familiar interview-room routine with Mills. 'I mean, I can see how much you loved her. It's obvious. And she was cheating on you. And these other things she did. For money. It makes your skin crawl. I don't blame you for being mad at her.'

'I never met anyone like her,' Bradshaw said in a pathetic voice.

'Any man might lose control when a woman does those sort of things.'

'I didn't kill her.'

Mills puffed out his cheeks. 'Come on. Tell us what really happened Saturday night. You'll feel better afterwards.'

Lloyd leaned forward. 'My client has already answered your question. He has told you what happened last Saturday night.'

'What time did you go back to the house that night?' Fox asked him, trying to keep him off balance.

'I told you, I didn't go back. I drove home. I told myself I was being an idiot and to forget all about her. The next I hear about her is you lot showing up at work to arrest me. I didn't do it, and that's the truth!'

His brief leaned forward. 'Let's face it, Chief Inspector, you have no evidence against my client in this matter. I demand that he be released immediately.'

Mills hesitated. 'Interview suspended, six fifteen.' He leaned across the desk and stopped the tape. He nodded to Fox and they left the interview room together.

'Shit,' Mills said.

'Can we hold him?' she said.

Mills shook his head.

'If he had a key to her house,' Fox said, 'he could have been in there waiting for her when she got home. He strangled her, carried her down to the basement, then drove home. It fits with Sandra Devenish's statement.'

'We don't have a single print of his from the basement. He said he's never been down there, and we can't prove otherwise. We can't prove he had a key to the front door, either. We're guessing. And then there's our only witness. Devenish never actually saw him get out of the car. Think about it. Plus, our chief witness is a fruitcake. White witch. For Christ's sake!'

'What about the blood on the fridge door?'

'It doesn't prove anything. We don't even know if the blood is his. Even if we get a match on DNA, he's already given us an explanation for how it got there. It's all circumstantial. The CPS will throw this one right back at us.'

'You're going to let him go?'

'We've been through his flat. It's clean. There's nothing in his wardrobe matches the fibres we found in that basement.'

He was right, of course. It was the thing she hated most about this job. Catching the violent and the insane was one thing, putting them in prison was an exercise in frustration.

Mills straightened, adjusted his tie. 'It's him, though,' he said. 'I can smell it on him.'

He went back into the interview room to tell Lloyd his client was free to go.

*   *   *

He was standing outside the station as they left in Fox's Sierra half an hour later. He practically threw himself in front of the car, forcing her to slam her foot on the brakes. Lloyd was with him and tried to pull him away, but Bradshaw was in a rage.

He ran around the side of the car. 'What are you trying to do to me, you bitch?' he shouted. 'I didn't do nothing!'

'Tosser,' Mills muttered in the seat beside her.

Bradshaw pounded on the window with his fist. 'I loved that girl!'

Fox put the Sierra back into gear and drove away. In the rear vision mirror she saw Bradshaw's brief drag him back on to the pavement by the arm. She looked over at Mills.

'He did it,' he said.

Chapter Seventeen

———————◆———————

Dartmouth Park, NW5

Karen Jamieson lived in a maisonette just south of Highgate Cemetery, on the ground floor of a grey shingle three-storey eyesore fronting Dartmouth Park Avenue. From the road you caught a glimpse of St Paul's and the distant towers of the Barbican; from the window of Karen's groundfloor flat, the only view was a concrete bus shelter, defaced with graffiti, and the occasional number 135 to Archway station.

Karen Jamieson was in her mid twenties, worked as a secretary in an insurance office in the City. She was attractive in a tarty and rather obvious way, her short black skirt riding halfway up her thigh, a black lace bra worn under her white blouse, which was open to the second button. Poor TJ didn't know where to look. She had a strident cockney accent, and false fingernails, painted black. Some cheap jewellery. Gary Bradshaw had raised the bar over the last three years. She certainly wasn't in Kimberley Mason's league.

Fox looked around. The flat was rented, and it was cramped. Plastic flowers in a vase by the window gathered dust behind the net curtains, a phoney bull fight poster hung on the wall, a cheap souvenir from Ibiza. There were some framed snapshots of her with a man, one taken in a restaurant, another on a beach somewhere. It looked as if she had a steady boyfriend these days. Fox hoped he was better for her than flash Gazza.

'We want to talk to you about Gary Bradshaw,' Fox said to her, sitting down on an ancient chintz sofa.

'That bastard.' She recrossed her legs, probably for TJ' benefit. 'What's he done now?'

'We're investigating the murder of a young woman in Highgate. Quite close to here. You've probably heard about it.'

'You don't fink he had anyfing to do wiv it?'

'We don't know. We know he was on intimate terms with her.'

'Poor bitch,' she said. 'He nearly bleedin' killed me 'n' all.'

'That's why we're here,' TJ said. 'That's what we want to talk to you about.'

She crossed her arms. 'Bastard,' she repeated.

'Three years ago he was convicted of assaulting you,' Fox said.

'Yeah. Bleedin' right he did.'

'What happened?'

'I'd been seeing this other bloke. You know, me and Gary weren't serious. Not like we was engaged or anyfing. Anyway, he found out.'

'And?'

'He came round to where I was livin' back then and started screamin' at me. Called me a slut and all like that. I told him to get out. Then he just went mental.'

'That's when he assaulted you?'

'Yeah.' Her eyes clouded over at the memory. 'I turned me back for a minute, I was going to call you lot. And that's when he did it.'

'Did what?' TJ prompted her.

'He came up behind me and put his hands round me throat.'

'He tried to strangle you?'

'Yeah. I suppose.'

Fox looked at TJ. So, they had not misjudged their man. He was a crime waiting for somewhere to happen. A nutter. 'And then?'

'He shook me. I fought he was going to bleedin' kill me, I'm not jokin'. Then he frew me against the wall and started hittin' me. See this?' She pointed to a small scar running along her eye. 'He did that. I couldn't see proper out of that eye for months. And you know what the judge give him? Three months. He was out in six weeks. He could have bleedin' killed me. I told the judge he was a headcase. He didn't pay any bloody attention, silly old tosser.'

'Did you ever see him again?'

'The judge?'

'Gary.'

'I know he still lives round here. I seen him a couple of times, in the street and that.' She paused, calculating. 'So now he's done for someone, I knew he would.' She leaned in. 'Are you going to put him away? 'Cos it's about bleedin' time.'

'We haven't got enough to charge him yet,' Fox said.

She made a face. 'I fought so. You lot are bloody useless.'

As Fox drove away, down Dartmouth Park Avenue, Karen's summation rang in her ears. We're not useless, she thought, we just don't have nearly enough to get that bastard banged up. And I wonder if anyone else will have to pay the piper before we do.

Chapter Eighteen

Kingston, Surrey

It was a narrow, leafy street, lined with parked cars. Many of the bungalows were of identical design, built in the post-war boom. Some showed signs of their age, others had been renovated or extended to add to their appeal. Fox spotted Ian's maroon Jaguar parked on the concrete forecourt of number twenty-four and turned her Sierra into the driveway behind it. She switched off the engine and took a deep breath to compose herself.

Why am I here? she asked herself. Am I the interfering in-law, am I conceited or arrogant enough to think my intervention can help achieve a reconciliation? But I can't just stand by and watch it happen. Not made that way.

She got out of the car and hesitated before making her way up the path. I wouldn't blame him if he tells me to get lost and mind my own business, she thought.

Ian had just got home from work. He answered the door in his shirtsleeves, his tie hanging loose around his neck. For a man who had just been kicked out by his wife of eight years, he didn't look too bad. 'Maddy,' he said.

'Hi, Ian.'

A sheepish grin. 'Did Ginny send you round?'

'The only people she wants to send round here are contract killers.'

'Uh-huh.' He stepped to one side. 'Come on in.'

'I can't stay.'

'Have a drink, at least. Cup of tea? Something stronger?'

'Just tea.'

The house smelled of cats and the noise from the television was deafening. Fox put her head around the living-room door and shouted a greeting to Mrs Johnstone, who peered back at her, both startled and befuddled. She started to get up, but Ian waved her back to her armchair where she was watching an afternoon game show.

Ian's mother was an old lady now, quite deaf, and riddled with arthritis and osteoporosis. She had had Ian late in life, the last of a brood of seven. Heaven only knew what she thought about having her youngest, married son back in the house again.

Ian led the way to the kitchenette and put the kettle on the range.

'So,' she said.

Ian crossed his arms and leaned against the bench. He gave a shrug of his shoulders. 'Been a bad boy,' he said, in a tone that betrayed no contrition whatsoever.

Now she was here, she wondered what she was going to say. 'Why, Ian?' was the best she could manage.

Another shrug of the shoulders.

'I thought you and Ginny were happily married.'

'I *was* happily married. I *am* happily married. It's Ginny who's unhappy.'

'It seems reasonable to be unhappy. In the circumstances.'

'Yeah. It's sad, isn't it?' he said. She thought he meant the

marriage, the children, until he added, 'Back living with my
mother at thirty-four.'

'What about . . . this other woman?'

'There is no *other woman*.'

'Well, she wouldn't be this mad if you were doing it with
yourself.'

'Did Ginny say it was an affair?'

'What else would you call it?'

He made a face. 'I just slept with her a couple of times.
Christ, we didn't even sleep. Once we did it standing up in the
coffee room.'

Fox winced. 'Too much information, thanks.'

The kettle boiled. He poured the hot water on the teabags,
got the milk out of the refrigerator. 'Let's sit outside,' he said.

'Sure.'

He put cups and saucers on a tray. There was a tiny patio
off the kitchen, with a wrought iron table and two chairs. The
house backed on to the local park. It was evening and sunlight
filtered golden through the horse chestnuts. She could hear
kids' voices, a group of ten-year-olds playing cricket with a
tennis ball. There was a slight chill in the air and Fox shivered
in her cotton shirt.

She sipped her tea. Awful. How did people drink tea made
with teabags?

'I didn't come here to harangue you,' she said.

'Then why did you come?'

She shrugged. 'Mediator?'

'We'll work it out ourselves.'

His confidence surprised her. 'I hope so.'

'I still love Ginny, you know. I . . . I just needed some
excitement in my life.'

'Is it worth breaking up your family for a little excitement?'

'Well, that's not quite how you phrase the question to

yourself at the time.' He smiled. 'We can't all be straight shooters like you.'

Straight shooter, she thought. Is that how he sees me? Is that what I am? I always thought I was the perverse one in the family, the black sheep: Maddy, the one with the odd life and the fund of grotesque cop stories. I don't think I want to be the straight shooter. 'How can you risk so much over someone you don't even love?' she asked him.

'I don't know,' he told her. 'I'm not saying what I did made sense.'

'No, it makes no sense at all. I thought you *loved* Ginny.'

He grimaced. 'This was just sex.' He made it sound almost reasonable.

They talked and allowed the tea to get cold, while a frail sun dipped below the rooftops and a golden suburban evening settled like dust over London. They tiptoed around the subject of Ian's infidelity: he spoke about it as if it were a minor infraction, no worse than forgetting an anniversary or a birthday. And as they spoke, she realised that after all this time she didn't know her brother-in-law at all.

It was as she was leaving that it happened; afterwards she even wondered if she had imagined the whole thing. He hugged her as she was getting into her car, as he had done a hundred times before, but this time the embrace lingered a little longer, his body was pressed too close and as she pulled away and looked up uncertainly into his face, she thought for one panicked moment that he was going to kiss her.

Fox woke to pitch darkness, her heart hammering painfully in her chest, body slick with sweat, eyes wide open and staring into the darkness. She threw back the sheets, concentrated on her ragged breathing, orienting herself once more to the wakeful world. She sat up, switched on the bedside lamp and got out of bed. She padded through her flat in a T-shirt, switched on every light in every room, then went into the kitchen and turned on the radio. She plugged in the kettle to make herself tea.

Her nightmares had taken on an epic reality of their own, had etched themselves into her mind like true memory, without the ephemeral fabric of dream. Even now, with her eyes wide open, she saw again the small, black eye of a revolver, hovering there a few feet from her face. She felt a cold grease break out over her body, her heart pounding to desperate cadence.

The same dream she had had ever since Lambeth. The silence of the night. The single black and remorseless eye of death.

Chapter Nineteen

Highgate

Carlton came home early from the Party meeting, showered, changed into a cardigan and cords. He passed his daughter's bedroom, saw a chink of yellow light through the door jamb. He knocked and put his head in. 'Diana,' he said.

She was at her desk in the corner of the room, still in her school uniform. She had a pen in her hand.

'Homework?' he said. 'Need a hand?'

She leaned forward and put her arm across what she was writing. No, not homework, he realised, a diary. 'It's nothing,' she said.

He felt suddenly awkward and embarrassed. 'Have a good day?'

'Okay,' she said.

A long and aching silence. He could not think of anything else to say, and he went out.

As he made his way downstairs James Carlton wondered what kind of secrets his daughter might be concealing in her diary. It worried him, of course, but he realised how hypocritical that was.

Louise was in the drawing room with a cup of tea, had just returned from a gallery opening in the village. Canapés and chardonnay and all things French, except the paintings, of course, which without exception were modern and damned awful, if past experience was anything to go by.

'Is Diana okay?' he asked, making his way to the sideboard and pouring himself a Bushmills.

'She's broken up with her boyfriend,' Louise said, thumbing through *Country Life*. Habit she had picked up from her father. None of them ever got muck on their boots, of course, but they owned half of Berkshire and so they considered themselves farmers.

Carlton took a moment to digest this information. 'I didn't know she had a boyfriend,' he said, trying not to sound concerned.

'A sixteen-year-old girl's not going to tell her father things like that,' Louise said. 'Anyway, she wasn't going *out* as we know it. It's just a school thing. Now he's dropped her and she's a bit blue.'

'I thought she seemed a little . . . quiet.'

'You know how it is at this age. Boys. Hormones. That sort of thing.'

He took a swallow of whisky and wondered how much he didn't know about his family. He knew precisely how much they didn't know about him.

'And she had a falling out with one of her friends last week,' Louise went on. 'Having a rough trot, poor thing.'

How could so much be going on that he didn't know about? he wondered. Poor Diana. Chip off the old block, as the saying went.

'Are you all right, James?'

'What was that?'

'I said, are you all right? You seem a little put out.'

'No. Fine. Headaches occasionally. You know. Lot to think about.'

She looked up at him over her half-moon reading glasses, as if she were looking for the telltale signs of a lie: the nervous rubbing of the nose, the averted gaze, the anxious lick of the lips. He knew she could see nothing beyond the opaque intensity of his smile, however, and she returned to her reading, satisfied.

He glimpsed himself for a moment in the long mirror in the hall: well dressed, at ease, Bushmills in hand, mellow and golden, a man of stature, at his prime, the devil who lurked there hidden, utterly. A fine performance. Virtuoso. If he had been able he would have stood and applauded his own mendacity.

Louise didn't know. Nobody knew. Almost nobody. If only he could make sure that it stayed that way.

Chapter Twenty

There were four murder investigations being run out of F team's Incident Room at Hendon Road; there was supposed to be only one. The names of the operations were scrawled on the whiteboards, along with names of the victims and the prime suspects, several identifit pictures had been taped on with Sellotape.

Fox looked up at DARK LADY; Gary Bradshaw was still their main suspect, there was an asterisk beside his name on the board.

Fox stared at the ancient green screen computer in front of her. All the details of the case, witness statements, contact reports, forensic minutiae, had been logged on via HOLMES – the Home Office Large/Major Enquiry System – so the welter of information that was the natural result of every large investigation could be easily retrieved. Names, addresses, telephone numbers, even individual words, could all be instantly cross-checked.

Their office manager, an experienced DS by the name of Haskons, ran the system with WPC Stacey and three civilian indexers to do the copy typing. It was nine o'clock now, though, and they had all gone home; only Fox was still there, a cold cup of coffee by her right hand, searching for the one elusive thread they may have missed.

It was expected, once you moved above the rank of sergeant. She and Mills would work sixteen-hour days the first week of a murder investigation. It would be three weeks into an investigation before they would cut back to eight-hour days. No overtime, of course. TJ and Honeywell would be earning more than her, perhaps even more than Mills.

There was a mild but insistent pain behind her eyes and a tremor in her fingers. Not enough sleep, too much caffeine. She tried to concentrate on the green jumble on the screen in front of her, searching for any clues to Kimberley Mason's other clients.

Something made her look up and she saw Mills standing by the door. He was holding his briefcase in one hand and carrying a dozen roses in the other. Must have been a bad boy last night, Fox thought.

'Still here?' he asked her.

Strange, but she always felt clumsy and self conscious around him. It infuriated her that a man like Mills could make her feel like a sixteen-year-old. He was, after all, everything she despised: a womaniser, a drinker, a smoker and a golden haired boy of the brass in Tintagel House; Madeleine Fox worked out three times a week in a martial arts gym, refused ever to grovel to her superiors and was, if gossip was to be believed, a ball-busting bitch.

'Flowers,' she said. 'Are they for your girlfriend?'

'No, the chief super. My review comes up next week.'

That was probably so near the truth it wasn't funny.

'Madeleine, can I give you some advice?'

'You're going to anyway, guv.'

'Well, you need to hear it.'

She glared at him.

'You're a good cop, Madeleine. No doubt about it. But in the end it doesn't matter one brass shite whether you're a good cop or not. If you want to get past a certain level, you don't have to get your hands dirty, you have to get your nose brown.'

'Thanks for that, guv.'

He held up the flowers. 'Actually, they're for Sally.'

'Is that the underwear model?'

He shook his head. 'I don't know where all this gossip starts.'

'Your private life is legend around the department, I'm afraid.'

'Is that right? Madeleine, if I really had a way with women, why did four of them divorce me?' He put down the flowers and the briefcase. 'Why are you always the last one out of the building? Haven't you got enough awards on the shelf?'

'You're only as good as your last gig.'

'Well, I'm glad you're still here. I need to talk to you.' He pulled up one of the office chairs, put the flowers on the desk and unlocked his briefcase.

'Phil's come up with something,' he said.

Phil Soskins was the fingerprinting specialist with their Forensic Science Support Unit. Kimberley Mason's basement, and in particular the shiny black metal struts of the rack, had yielded a bonanza of lifts. Although they could not be construed as direct evidence in the murder investigation, Mills had wanted them run through the computer anyway. If any of Kimberley's clients had previous for crimes of a sexual or violent nature, it would give their inquiry an extra focus.

Mills slipped a file across the table. Inside was a copy of the forensics report; an enlarged five-by-eight of the lift from the basement compared with a print on the national register.

The computer had found a match unusually quickly. She read through the accompanying file.

'Oh, shit,' she said.

'That's what I thought.'

The name the computer had thrown up was for a Clive Reece, fifty-four, with a last known address in Hampstead. Fox knew the rest of it without having to read the record. Reece had been a detective superintendent heading the Crime Division at Islington, had been charged in a major corruption investigation that had rocked the Met a few years before. It had been alleged that he had been using one of his informers not only to help him make spectacular arrests, but had also been demanding part of the reward money. As insurers generally paid around one tenth of the money recovered to the informant, the sums involved had not been inconsiderable. Although the charges were later dropped under controversial circumstances, it had been the end of Reece's career in the force.

'I knew the guy,' Mills said. 'He was my boss when I was at Holborn.'

'What's he like?'

'Tough bastard. Well connected, too. On the square, knows a lot of very influential people in North London.' Mills looked worried. Perhaps they still saw each other in chapter. Give them something to talk about at the temple, she thought, after they'd slaughtered the virgin and deflowered a goat.

'Always a bit of a nob jockey, but I didn't know he was into whips and chains.'

'So, what do we do about this?'

Mills bit his lip, his fingers beating a fast tattoo on the desk. She knew what he was thinking. It had never been clear why the charges against Reece had been dropped; she had heard Reece had friends in the highest echelons of Scotland Yard. Now Mills was wondering just who else had been through Kimberley Mason's basement. He must have decided he could still run an impeccable murder investigation from here and still see his career beached.

'I hope this is not going to get complicated,' he said.

He had to lean across her to retrieve the file and she was aware of the masculine smell of cologne – Mills always smelled good, TJ reckoned he'd had his sweat pores surgically enhanced by Fabergé – aware, too, of his physical presence. The leaning-across-her thing had not been necessary; he could have asked her to hand the file back. He never missed a chance to impose himself, but he always kept it within the rules.

'We'd better go and talk to him,' she said.

'Looks like it.' He snapped shut the locks on the briefcase and stood up. 'Good night, Madeleine.'

'Don't forget your flowers, guv.'

He grinned. 'No,' he said, his smile powder white. 'I'll be needing those.' And he walked out.

The pain behind her eyes had worsened, and a few minutes later she went home herself.

Chapter Twenty-One

Hampstead

Reece lived in a Georgian townhouse in Hampstead. Not bad for an ex cop. He might as well hang a sign out the front, she thought: 'Guilty As Charged'. He lived a few streets from where Oscar Wilde had once worked and lived. Now there's someone who would have appreciated Kimberley Mason and her way of life.

It was a quiet cul de sac, spiked black railings, white porticos, nowhere to park. Just one blue National Trust sign in the whole street to indicate the former home of a famous British landscape painter. Almost a slum by local standards.

Five years since Reece had left the Met. He had lived in Finchley in those days. Not bad.

Reece answered the door in a tracksuit and joggers. Grey chest hair sprouted like wild grass from the zippered top. His skin was tanned the colour of tobacco, and hung on him like a suit two sizes too large. Obviously a man who had shed quite a few stone at some stage of his life. Through the chest hair she saw the last few pale notches of a bypass scar. Compulsive overachiever and coronary case. That figured. Still, he looked fit enough now, for a man in his early fifties.

'Millsie,' he said with a disarming, gap-toothed grin. 'Fuck me. You've got a moustache now. Did you get a promotion?'

She saw her DCI wince. That was a bit familiar. They must go back a long way, she thought.

'Hello, guv,' he said, although it must have been a very long time since Reece was his governor. Habit, she supposed. 'This is Madeleine Fox. She's my DI.'

Reece turned towards her and shook her hand, gave her that predatory look that certain older men reserved for much younger women. 'Well, you fell on your feet,' he said to Mills. He stood aside from the door. 'Come in. You're early. I've just got back from my run.'

He led them through to the living room. Impressive. A gilt mirror hung above a Regency fireplace, white carpet, wall to wall, period furniture. Reece looked out of place in his tracksuit, like an ageing distance runner accidentally stumbling through a Jane Austen film set.

He poured himself a whisky from a decanter and stood there, legs akimbo, one hand in the pocket of his track pants. 'I won't offer you one,' he said to Mills. 'You're on duty.'

'Bit early for me anyway, guv.'

He didn't invite them to sit down and Fox noticed that the forced bonhomie with which he'd greeted them at the door had evaporated. She hadn't expected this. Reece must have guessed why they were there, and while she had not imagined he would be proud of his relationship with Kimberley Mason, she hadn't anticipated a display of belligerence.

Fox made a show of looking around. 'You've done all right,' she said.

'Got my own company now.'

'Doing what?'

'I'm a consultant,' Reece said but did not elaborate on what sort of advice he gave and to whom.

Fox felt her temper flare. When she was on division she had to deal with scrotes every day, but when they were one of your own it really turned your stomach.

'It's about Kimberley, isn't it?' he said.

'That's right,' Mills said.

'How did you know I was one of her clients?' Client. He made it sound like he was a shareholder of blue chip stock. 'Did you find her little black book?'

Mills shook his head. 'Fingerprints.'

Reece gave a croaking laugh. 'On her?'

Now that was obscene, in the circumstances. Fox decided to cut him off. 'What sort of services did she provide for you, Mr Reece?'

The smile fell away. 'Am I under suspicion? I know the score, you know. So don't play your silly games with me, girlie.'

Girlie. A sergeant at Brixton had called her that, when she was in uniform. A brilliantined smug prat, like this one. 'No, you're not under suspicion. Should you be?'

'You're the detective.'

Mills frowned. 'Go easy, guv. She's only doing her job. We have to ask.'

'Ask away, then.'

'Where were you between midnight and six a.m. last Saturday night?'

'I was in Marbella. With my wife and two friends of mine. Want to see my passport?'

'That won't be necessary.'

'Good.' He drained his glass.

'We're looking for some help on this,' Mills said, his tone conciliatory, trying a different tack.

'Sorry, Millsie. I don't think I can give you any.'

Bugger this, Fox thought. What was this? An old boys' club? 'How long had you known Kimberley Mason?' she asked him.

'None of your business.'

'We know you spent some time in her basement. That's where we found your fingerprints.'

His face set like stone.

'When was the last time you saw her?'

He looked at his watch. 'It was on a strictly professional basis, about two weeks ago. That's about all I can tell you, really.'

'How many times did you visit her?'

'I don't have to answer that.' He looked mildly irritated, as if his accountant had asked him how much he had spent the previous year on postage stamps. He turned to Mills. 'Don't you have a prime suspect yet?'

Mills nodded. 'Someone's helping us with our enquiries.'

'What are you wasting my time for, then?'

'How did you meet Kimberley Mason?' Fox asked.

He thought about that. For all his bluster, he wasn't sure how far they were prepared to push him. 'I got her number from a friend. She only took referrals. She was very careful. She had to be, in her line of work.'

'Who gave you her number?'

'I can't tell you that.' He checked his watch. 'Anything else you want to ask me? I've got an appointment at eleven.'

Arrogant bastard. She looked up at Mills, but she could see he didn't have the stomach for this.

'I'll show you out, then,' Reece said.

'Does your wife know you're into S and M?' Fox said. She heard a hiss from Mills beside her, a quick intake of breath.

Reece flushed but the smile stayed in place. 'I haven't got

time for this bullshit,' he said, and led the way to the door. The door slammed behind them.

Mills stood on the portico, his hands in his pockets, his face gloomy. Still raining. The second week of Wimbledon and they still hadn't started the fourth round.

'That went well,' Fox said.

Mills didn't even smile. 'Waste of bloody time.'

'I thought we might have got a little bit more help than that.'

'Why did you think that?' Mills fumbled gloomily in his pockets and found his smokes. He lit up, his face etched in hard lines. 'Last thing I want is that bastard to start naming names. Before you know it, we'll be running between the Old Bailey and Scotland Yard interviewing this girl's former clients. That's going to do my promotion a lot of good.'

'That's a very cynical viewpoint.'

The shower eased off to a drizzle. Mills' Ford was parked a hundred yards up the road, towards the high street. They set off at a brisk walk. 'To be honest, Madeleine, I don't want to go digging around this one too deep in case we find any more bones. I can see my career going down the toilet here. It's pretty obvious this Bradshaw bloke did it. Let's get him tidied away and put this one back in the files.'

PART TWO

There is nothing safe about sex, there never will be.

Norman Mailer

Chapter Twenty-Two

Strand, WC2

Carlton left the Savoy Grill later than he had intended, the roseate glow from a couple of nips of good whisky had calmed his nerves, the reassuring banter of politics had taken his mind off the maelstrom of his personal life for a few hours. Replete after a good dinner, he strolled out of the Savoy and set off to find his car, which he had parked behind the hotel.

A pleasant evening, a cool breeze off the Thames, the rain had finally cleared. Perhaps they were in for a little bit of summer. He turned down Savoy Row, his hands in his pockets, refused to think about her, even for a moment. Or him.

Something made him turn around.

The warm buzz of the alcohol evaporated, replaced instantly by cold panic. He recognised him straight away, the combat jacket, the jeans, the Doc Martens; but mostly just from the way he stood, hands pushed deep into the jacket pockets, utterly at ease with his own intimidating presence. Carlton realised he was alone in the narrow street, that it was dark.

He turned and started to walk, briskly, towards his car.

He was running too. He could not hear him, did not dare turn around and look. He fumbled in his pockets for his car keys, dropped them on the pavement, scrambled for them in the darkness, breaking a fingernail on the paving as he scooped them up again.

I could shout for help, he thought, seeing lights in the second storey windows around him, but he was throttled into silence by his own fear and shame.

The BMW's indicators flashed once as he unlocked the doors with the remote. He reached for the handle, heard the reassuring click of the lock, pulled open the driver's door, thought he was safe. Then something slammed hard into him from behind and he fell against the car, gasping at the pain in his ribs and the door slammed shut again. He was lying on the cold, hard road, the silhouette of his nightmares standing over him, and the bastard still had his hands in his pockets.

Chapter Twenty-Three

Hampstead

James Carlton heard the reassuring crunch of gravel under the tyres, the whine of the electrically operated gates swinging shut behind him. He pressed a button on the console to operate the driver's side window and breathed in the cool, summer night air. Louise had left a light on for him in the living room, and the glow of the green-shaded lamp behind the lattice windows was somehow reassuring.

He sat for a long time behind the wheel, waiting for the tremor in his limbs to subside. Only now he felt safe. God knows how he had got home without piling into another car or a lamp post. He put a handkerchief to his face. Blood. Christ.

What a mess.

With any luck Louise would be asleep. How was he going to explain this? He got out of the car, reached into the back for his briefcase. He staggered, almost fell. Christ, his head. He leaned on the boot, the world spinning around him; the gargoyles on the gateposts, the gabled roof, his wife's white Mercedes in the double garage. He wanted to weep with relief at the sight of these familiarities of his life. He could weep again when he realised how he had placed them all at risk.

He fumbled with his keys; it took several attempts to unlock the deadbolt and let himself inside. He stumbled into the drawing room off the hall, found the decanter of Bushmills and poured three fingers into a crystal tumbler. He closed his eyes, felt his muscles relax as the smooth liquid burned its way down his throat.

He heard footsteps on the stairs. Oh, Christ.

'James?'

'Louise,' he said, without turning around. 'I'm sorry. Did I wake you?' Just go back to bed, for God's sake. Leave me alone.

'James, are you all right?'

'Yes, perfectly. Just tired, that's all.'

No good, of course. Women sensed these things, they were like dogs and sharks, they could smell fear, were attracted by it. He heard her pad bare-footed across the carpet and suddenly she was at his elbow, in her nightgown, but wide awake. Hadn't been asleep, by the looks of it, must have been waiting for him.

'James? My God. What happened to your face?'

'It's nothing.'

'You're bleeding.'

'I was at the Grill Room with Geoffrey and Bill. Talking about these new beef quotas into Europe. Funnily enough, we all decided to have the fish.' It was a joke, a weak attempt to throw her off the scent. The look on her face. You'd think he'd just been shot. 'Somebody must have followed me back to the car.'

'Followed you? You mean a mugger? My God. Did you call the police?'

He shook his head.

'Why ever not?'

'It was all over in a moment. I didn't even get a good look at him. He knocked me down, I hit my head on the pavement. He tried to grab my wallet and I put up a fight. Then he just ran off. Probably just some kid. Drugs, I suppose.'

'You should have that eye looked at. Do you want me to call Dr Lill?'

He shook his head. 'It's nothing.'

Louise just stared at him. Did she believe him? The story had sounded convincing enough, even to him. 'I'll get some water. We'll have to bathe it. It's a nasty cut.'

'Honestly, I'm all right,' he said, but she had already taken herself off to the kitchen, the perfect wife, the perfect nurse.

He sighed and downed the rest of the Bushmills, poured himself another. Christ. Life could be so unbelievably complicated sometimes. What was that thing about chaos theory? You killed one butterfly and the whole world started to go out of kilter. The notion had once struck him as quaint and rather implausible. Now it just seemed unbelievably grotesque.

Chapter Twenty-Four

Area Major Incident Pool, Hendon Road

There was a funeral atmosphere in the Incident Room when she arrived the next morning. The office manager, Haskons, was already at work on one of the HOLMES computers, Stacey and two civilian typists putting yesterday's contact statements into the system. Honeywell and Rankin were already there, but no one was talking much or making jokes.

'What's wrong?' Fox asked.

'Bradshaw,' Honeywell said.

'What about him?'

'He tried to hang himself last night.'

'Oh, Christ. Is he all right?'

Honeywell nodded. 'He's in the Whittington.'

Fox wasn't sure how she felt about this news. If he had succeeded in topping himself, at least he couldn't hurt anyone else; but then they wouldn't be able to prove that he really was responsible for Kimberley Mason's death. Whether it was real or imagined, she sensed an atmosphere of collective guilt.

'It's not our fault,' she said to Honeywell.

Neither Rankin nor Honeywell said anything.

'Oh, for God's sake!' she snapped, and went into her office, slamming the door. Because someone tried to take their own life, did it mean they automatically received absolution? Besides, no one was ever really completely innocent, she thought savagely. Guilt was just a matter of degree.

Area 2 HQ, Colindale

Roger Kennett was an imposing man, six foot three inches tall, greying at the temples, dressed in a grey double-breasted Savile Row suit. His hair could have been parted with a slide rule. He reclined in a high backed leather chair, the sun shining through the tall window behind him and making it appear as if there was an aura, a halo even, around his head. Precisely what he intended, she supposed.

As DAC for Number Two Area, Metropolitan Police, he rarely stooped to discuss the details of criminal investigations with the minions out on division. Which was why Fox felt as if she had been summoned to Area HQ Colindale to meet God. Roger Kennett was not unlike how she had imagined Him to be: kind eyes, an indulgent smile, a fatherly attitude, and a well-earned reputation as a ruthless bastard.

When she walked into his office Mills was already there. They had been discussing the case, of course, and from the moment they saw her they acted like two schoolboys caught smoking in the toilets.

They stood up as she walked in, the perfect gentlemen. She found it patronising, as they were both her superiors in rank.

Something on the nose here. Conspiracy in the air.

Kennett waved her to one of the sumptuous leather chairs across the vast rosewood wasteland of his desk. Its highly polished surface was interrupted only by a leatherbound blotter, a Parker pen set, a gilt-framed family photograph, an imposing telephone, and a Wedgwood china cup and saucer. Not a trace of paperwork in sight.

Mills was balancing his teacup on his lap, like a vicar at a garden party. Christ Almighty. For some reason she was acutely conscious that she was the only one in the room who was not on the square.

'Coffee?' Kennett asked her.

'No, thank you, sir.'

'Mills here has been telling me what a good job you've been doing for the team. He says you show a great deal of promise.'

'Thank you, sir.' She glanced sideways at Mills, who gave her a fatherly nod. So, they had been filling in her report card before she got here. Bullshit, laid on with a trowel. All part of the softening up process. What was going on?

'I asked Mills to brief me on the Kimberley Mason investigation.'

He stopped talking and stared at her, not in an unkindly way, but obviously waiting for her to say something. It was a little interrogative trick she was familiar with. Sometimes, instead of asking a direct question you sat there and waited for the other person to speak. It could be quite effective, worked better with your own staff than with real criminals. People sometimes incriminated themselves in an internal investigation without you having to ask a single question.

Fox was ready for him and just sat there and smiled back.

'There are aspects of this case that concern me,' he said finally, and the smile vanished as rapidly as the sun disappearing behind a cloud, leaving only a chilly, granite countenance, the kind eyes now hard and uncompromising.

'Sir?'

'What I am about to tell you is not to leave this room. Do I make myself clear?'

Here we go. She wondered if this had anything to do with Clive Reece. 'Yes, sir.'

Kennett sighed, stretched his legs, and put his hands behind his head, completely at ease in this company. 'You've heard of James Carlton?'

'I think so, sir. He's the Shadow Minister for Trade and Energy.'

'Very good. I see you keep up with politics. He's also a friend of mine.'

Right. Now she understood.

'He rang me a couple of days ago, of his own volition, and asked to speak with me. We arranged to meet over a drink. He was quite agitated. Never seen him that way before. Of course, at that stage, I had no idea what it was all about.'

'He was one of Miss Mason's clients,' Fox said.

He looked shocked. 'You knew?'

'I'm anticipating what you're about to say, sir.'

He looked irritated. He apparently didn't like his staff doing that. 'It was much more than that, I'm afraid. He has admitted having an inappropriate relationship with Miss Mason over some years. When he learned that she had been murdered, he was left with what one might well describe as a moral dilemma. He wishes to give us all the help he can, but at the same time he is most concerned that any – disclosure – might affect both his marriage and his career.'

'Yes,' Fox said, deadpan. 'That is a dilemma, isn't it?'

'Jim asked me for an assurance of discretion, which I gave him.'

Fox thought about it. If she were Carlton, she would have known they would track him eventually, through the telephone records. Like any good politician he had gone into damage control.

'Their relationship goes back four or five years,' Kennett was saying. 'He was seeing her on a regular basis, perhaps once or twice a month, for the last three years. He said he found it . . . helpful.'

'Helpful,' Fox repeated.

'We're not here to judge anyone's morals. Our only concern is whether or not he has broken the law.'

'When was the last time he saw her alive?'

'He tells me it was on the Thursday before she was murdered,' Kennett answered.

Fox fought down a tide of anger. This bastard was trying to intimidate her. 'Do we know what blood group he is?'

There was a silence in the room.

'Well, we have to know,' Fox persisted. 'It might be his blood on the fridge.'

Kennett looked at Mills. 'I was discussing that with DCI Mills before you came in. Jim has already agreed to give us a blood sample for analysis.

'There is nothing to be gained,' he went on, 'from dragging James Carlton's good name into this sordid affair. This investigation has the potential to ruin the man's career. You can imagine what will happen if the newspapers find out about any of this. Besides holding high political office, he is a married man with a teenage daughter. I am sure you will both treat this matter with the utmost discretion.'

Mills knew a cue when he heard one. 'You can rely on us, sir.'

'That is why Kimberley Mason's telephone records are to be kept strictly confidential. You are to use a codename when referring to him in any transcriptions, and the rest of the AMIP are not to be told of our conversation.'

Fox shifted uncomfortably in her seat. The leather was sticking to the back of her thighs. She looked across at Mills, who was nodding, as if to reassure her that everything was absolutely kosher here.

Well, as long as their investigation was not compromised. She wasn't in the business of persecuting someone because they were a tall poppy or had morals and sexual preferences different to her own. She had nothing to gain by making enemies in Scotland Yard either. 'I understand,' she said.

Kennett stood up and guided her to the door. His expression was pleasant but his eyes glittered like steel. 'Thank you for your time, Madeleine. I have asked Chief Inspector Mills to keep me informed of progress in this particular case.'

'Yes, sir,' she said. The door closed behind her, Mills still in there, cosying up to the brass. Like a bloody club, this place. Impeccable manners, charm and grace, but when it was time for the port and the cigars, they shut the doors and left you the washing up.

Chapter Twenty-Five

Mills was in his office, whispering into the phone. It might have been a confidential call, he could have just been ordering his lunch. Mills always whispered into telephones; it was a lifetime's habit. The bureaucrat in him coming out. Secrets were power. Even if it was just whether you were having chicken and salad or avocado and ham.

He put the phone down and looked up. 'Madeleine.'

She sat down and stared at him. She didn't have to say anything.

'Look, Madeleine, you know how it is. There's no point in rubbing against the pricks, like they say. It doesn't do any of us any good.'

'Especially if you're up for review.'

It was a provocative comment to make, but Mills didn't seem to mind. In fact, he acknowledged it with a shrug.

Fox hated this, had only seen it happen a few times, police work crossing that grey borderline into Scotland Yard politics. She didn't think it would compromise their investigation, but how could Mills be so sure?

'So James Carlton was one of Kimberley Mason's customers.'

'Everyone's got a bit of a kink in their chain.'

'Everyone?'

'Carlton's a Conservative Party politician. Comes with the territory.'

'He's a married man.'

'Real world calling Madeleine Fox.'

'In my book, it's wrong.'

'Yeah, it's wrong, but it's not *very* wrong.'

'Womanising is one thing. You can get away with a bit on the side, even in politics. But this, this is different.'

'So you're going to plead the case for the anal retentives.'

'Just airing my opinion.'

'Everybody has fantasies.'

'Sure. There's been a few times when I've fantasised about throttling TJ. But I don't do it, because that would be wrong. Unlike some of our customers, I know where to draw the line between thought and action. I mean, if you could get arrested for what you'd like to do, we'd all be in Pentridge.'

'I think Jim Carlton was just stupid, that's all.'

'That's reassuring. He could end up in Cabinet after the next election.'

'Perhaps they'll make him Minister for Corrections.'

She sat there, didn't laugh.

'Heard the joke about God and Adam?' he asked her.

'Is it funnier than Minister for Corrections?'

'God taps Adam on the shoulder. Says, "I've got two great new gifts for you." Adam says, "Brilliant. I loved the woman thing. What else have you got?" God says, "Well, the first thing is called a brain. This is good gear. You can do anything with this: solve problems, make up languages, work out how to make any kind of tool or game you want, it's amazing." Adam says, "Fantastic. I'll take it. What's the second thing?" God says, "The second thing is called a penis. Unbelievable. It will give you indescribable pleasure, plus you can reproduce your own kind with it. But there's just one catch with these two gifts." Adam says, "What's that?" And God says, "You can't use them both at the same time."

Fox smiled.

'See, you do have a sense of humour.'

'When are we seeing Carlton?'

'Four o'clock this afternoon. And don't worry, he didn't kill her. I'd bet my house on it. Bradshaw's our boy. So tread softly, Madeleine. This is a live hand grenade, believe me.'

Chapter Twenty-Six

Hampstead

Immaculate was the word she would have used to describe Mills' car. It was an executive model Ford, the coachwork gleaming in the sun, the carpet recently vacuumed, coins of diminishing value neatly arranged in the coin rack in the console, lined up like the Von Trapp children. There were no sweet wrappers in the ashtray, no broken cassette boxes on the floor, no umbrellas, old newspapers or discarded rain jackets lying across the back seat. As there were in her Sierra. The only blemish was the taint of stale cigarette smoke that was overlaid but not overcome by the smell of pine from the air freshener.

As they drove down North End Road, she stared at the towers and spires of London jutting through the afternoon haze. Hampstead was a rich man's enclave, had been celebrity real estate for centuries: Peter Cook and Daphne du Maurier had lived in Church Row, Rex Harrison was buried in its cemetery, Judy Dench lived in a small cottage off Vernon Place, George Michael had a penthouse there.

They passed Boy George's Gothic home, a living shrine to stardom. Fans had written laudatory notes to him on the brick wall outside. 'I love you, Boy George.' 'Boy George, you are the greatest.' A less enthusiastic fan had scribbled, 'You Fat Poof.'

Do you really want to hurt me? she thought. Sticks and stones.

They turned off New End Road and down into the Vale of Health. Or the Vale of Wealth as they called it round here. The avenue was overhung with oaks. Carlton's home was imposing, a Victorian redbrick mansion with mossy gables and a Gothic-inspired turret. Two ancient and weather-worn gargoyles studied them with sinister interest from the gate-posts.

Mills stopped the car before the electronically operated wrought-iron gates and they announced themselves into an intercom mounted into the brickwork before being allowed entry to a short gravel drive, flanked by two Monterey pines.

'Let me do the talking,' Mills said, turning off the ignition.

'Guv?'

'I don't want you and your attitude fucking this up for me.'

'I don't understand what you mean.'

'Yes, you do.'

Fox got out and looked around. A BMW and a Mercedes were parked in the double garage. She glimpsed gilt-framed landscapes through the latticed windows. This sort of wealth was not just impressive, it was intimidating. Carlton hadn't got all this on an MP's salary, she decided. She had researched her subject and discovered that he had been born in rather less fashionable Romford. His father had owned a printing business. Carlton had used this modest financial base to do some spectacular, if dodgy, things in real estate and the stock market during the 'eighties. He had married old money, and won the house, the political contacts, the right friends, the right clubs, passed Go and collected a great deal more than two hundred pounds.

Carlton's father-in-law was a director at Lloyds, owned chunks of Berkshire, had all the right connections when Carlton ran for Parliament. If the Conservatives gained office again, he was well placed for the front bench. Always a good leveller, marriage. Your business might go pear-shaped, the stock market could turn bearish, or worse, you could be born middle-class, but while you were of a marriageable age, you could still turn things around.

Carlton was waiting for them on the portico in a cardigan and loafers, a glass of Scotch in his right hand. He was guarded on either side by stone lions, like some Ming emperor. Fox got the impression of a man unsure whether he should play the perfect host or the put-upon local squire. His attitude hovered between charm and peevishness.

He was tall, his grey hair reaching to his collar to add a touch of the bohemian to him, despite the patrician appearance. He was slim, with smooth, unlined cheeks, pink beneath the day's stubble. He was built like a county fast bowler, rangy with long skinny arms. Fox guessed him to be somewhere in his late forties.

'You found us all right, then?' he said, as if they had ventured into the wilds of Borneo rather than a small North London suburb.

Mills turned on the charm for him. 'Detective Chief Inspector Greg Mills. This is Detective Inspector Madeleine Fox. Good of you to see us.'

Well, you had no choice, Fox thought. But anyway.

'Come in,' Carlton said.

He led them through a carpeted hallway into a drawing room, with dark panelled walls and antiques. Semi-valuable nineteenth-century oils hung on the walls, and a Persian cat was curled in a ball on the rug. The furniture was mahogany and rosewood. Everything in the room hinted at age and old money. She felt as if she had walked into an Agatha Christie film set.

'Take a seat,' Carlton said, but she noticed he preferred to stand, his back to the fireplace, taking up a pose of relaxed if informal power. A number of family portraits in heavy silver frames had been carefully arranged on the mantelpiece. There was an apparently informal shot of Carlton taken at a West End restaurant, unprepossessing except that she recognised William Hague and Jeffrey Archer among Carlton's dinner companions. There was also a family portrait; Carlton, with an elegantly dressed woman whom Fox took to be his wife, and a Sloane princess, probably his daughter; beside this photograph was one of the same teenager in riding outfit posed on a dressage pony.

Mills plumped himself down on a burgundy Chesterfield. Fox decided on a Victorian wingback covered in faded rose brocade, less comfortable but a little more formal.

'Would you like some tea?' Carlton asked them.

Love a bourbon, Fox thought, lots of ice. But Mills politely declined for both of them. He seemed as nervous as Carlton.

'It's about this poor Kimberley Mason girl,' their host said, in a tone that suggested they were all members of the same club, and were about to discuss a junior associate whose membership fees were in arrears.

'Not exactly a girl,' Fox said. 'She was a high-class prostitute specialising in clients interested in sadomasochism.' She saw Mills' chagrin at her directness. Well, to hell with it. She wasn't going to be bossed around by some old boys' club.

'Terrible business,' Carlton said.

'It was for her.'

Carlton seemed disconcerted by her attitude. He glanced at Mills for reassurance.

'We have been informed that you had some dealings with this girl,' Mills said.

Carlton took a casual sip of whisky. His hands were steady. 'That is correct,' he said. With admirable coolness, he did not try to answer any questions that had not yet been asked. Instead, he shut up and waited for Mills to continue.

'Of course, we don't think you are implicated in any criminal dealings yourself,' Mills went on, in a tone that irritated Fox and made her want to slap him, 'but we have to pursue every lead at this stage.'

'Of course. I see,' Carlton repeated, and then said nothing. It was subtle intimidation, but it seemed to be working on her DCI.

'So would you like to tell us the substance of your relationship with Miss Mason?' Fox said.

Carlton didn't answer her question straight away. Instead he looked at Mills. 'You understand this investigation has the potential to ruin my political career . . . and my marriage?'

'If you have done nothing illegal, I think we can assure you of our discretion in this investigation.'

Carlton contrived to look embarrassed, for the first time. 'It's rather awkward.' He looked at Fox. 'I thought you would be bringing another man with you.'

Mills looked at Fox. 'DI Fox here has heard it all before, sir.'

'I meant, that it was embarrassing for me, not for her.'

Fox lost patience with him. 'This is a murder investigation, Mr Carlton. We don't really have the time or the inclination to get too prissy. We want to find Kimberley Mason's killer before he murders again.'

Carlton thought about this. 'Of course,' he said. He took a deep breath. 'My relationship with Miss Mason goes back around five years. I . . . frequented . . . an establishment where she worked.'

'This would be the Black Rose?'

'You've done your homework.'

'Go on, please,' Mills said.

'After she left we continued our relationship, on a private but still professional basis. That's really all there is to it.'

'How often did you see her, sir?' Mills asked.

'Perhaps once a month.'

'And what sort of services did she provide for you?' Fox asked.

Carlton looked like he wanted to hit her. Mills did, too. Perhaps that was a bit blunt.

'As you said, she was a prostitute offering certain specialised services. That was what I paid for. I believe a man's private life should remain just that. Private.'

'We're not here to make moral judgments, sir,' Mills said.

Fox shrugged. Weren't here to bow and scrape, either.

Carlton's attitude had undergone a sudden transformation. Forbearance had been replaced by barely concealed hostility. In her experience every overly humble man was just trying to conceal his natural arrogance.

'Why did you continue to see her when she left the Black Rose?' Mills asked.

'She was good at what she did,' he said.

'Five years is a long time,' Mills said. 'You must have been very upset when you heard what had happened to her.'

'Yes, I was.'

'Have you any idea who might have wanted her dead?'

'I have no knowledge of her private life.'

'When was the last time you saw her alive?'

'The previous Thursday. I had a lunchtime appointment with her.'

Christ, Fox thought. He makes her sound like his dentist.

A bit of root canal work, with fur-lined cuffs and no anaesthetic. 'How did she seem to you?'

'In what way?'

'Just in herself.'

'I don't know. She seemed a little . . .'

'Submissive?' Fox said.

'Distracted,' Carlton said.

Mills cleared his throat, trying to attract her attention. Clearly, he was upset that she had ignored his instructions and was going at Carlton herself. Well, to hell with him.

'You never, in five years, talked with her about anything except the business at hand?'

'No.'

'That seems a little remote.'

Carlton's bonhomie dropped away. 'That's something I don't care to discuss with you.'

There was a long silence. If this had been Gary Bradshaw, they would have hauled him down the local nick long ago.

Carlton shifted position, and as one side of his face fell out of shadow she could make out an unattractive yellow stain around his left eye, recognised the telltale signs of an old bruise. Quite a large one, too.

'What happened to your eye?' Fox asked.

His left hand went instinctively to his face. It took him several moments to recover his poise. 'I had a fall on the stairs. I hit my head, gave myself a black eye. Is that any of your business?'

'It must have been a bad fall.'

'It was.'

'Tricky things, stairs. Have to take them one step at a time. Like a murder investigation, really. Otherwise you never know when you're going to slip up.'

Another long silence.

'Did she ever threaten to blackmail you?' Fox asked.

That threw him again. His mind tried to catch up. 'Who? Kimberley? No, of course not.'

'Why not?'

'We were friends.'

He realised what he'd said immediately. Fox smiled, let him know how easily he'd been baited. 'How could you be friends if you only ever spoke about . . .' she made a show of referring to her notes . . . 'the business at hand?'

Carlton turned to Mills. 'Am I being charged with anything? Should I have my solicitor present?'

Mills shook his head. 'We're not accusing you of anything, sir.'

'Your co-operation would be appreciated,' Fox said. 'This is a very serious matter.'

'I know it is. My career and good reputation are at stake.'

'I thought we were discussing the taking of human life.'

Carlton raised an eyebrow.

He turned and addressed himself to Mills. 'As I said to you on the telephone, Chief Inspector, I will help you all I can, but I resent being interrogated in this fashion in my own home. I ask you again, should I call my solicitor?'

'I'm sure that won't be necessary,' Mills said.

Carlton checked his watch. Time was pressing. 'There really is nothing more I can help you with on this matter. My actions may have been inappropriate, perhaps even by some standards immoral, but they were not illegal and I resent the fact that you feel you can talk to me this way in my own home.'

Silence. The grandfather clock in the hallway struck four thirty. Carlton again looked at his watch, a theatrical gesture. 'Is there anything more you need? I have work to attend to, and I'm taking my wife and daughter out to dinner tonight.'

The man had ice in his veins.

'No, that will be all,' Mills said. He got to his feet. 'Thanks for your time.'

'I have co-operated with you in every way I can.'

'We appreciate that.'

Fox was seething. This whole business reeked. 'Just one thing,' she said. 'Where were you on Saturday night between midnight and six the next morning?'

'On Saturday night my wife and I went to dinner with the Deputy Leader of the Opposition. We arrived home at around half past twelve and went straight to bed.'

'Your wife can verify that?' she said.

A moment of stillness.

'I don't think that will be necessary,' Mills said.

Carlton escorted them to the door. 'I'm sorry I couldn't have been more help,' he said to Mills. 'I hope you catch the man who committed this appalling crime.'

'We will,' Fox said, and she caught the look in Carlton's eyes.

Real fear.

Mills did not speak until they were on North End Way. 'What the hell do you think you were doing?' he said.

'He wasn't telling us everything.'

'Kennett told us to go softly on this one. You talked to him as if you'd just dragged him in off some council estate for stealing videos.'

'He was lying to us.'

'Of course he was. He's been seeing a dead bondage queen and he's trying to keep a lid on it.'

'He knows something.'

Mills shrugged. 'No, he doesn't.'

'He's lying through his teeth.'

'Look, all I know is Kennett's handed us a live grenade. Keep doing things like that and you can forget promotion. That's exactly the sort of behaviour that stuffs careers. 'Your inability to handle matters with the necessary discretion will go on your record, Madeleine.'

Fox chewed on that for a moment. She had already risen higher through the ranks of the Met than she had ever expected. Prejudice had worked on her side up until now; she knew her stellar rise was not just because she was bright, diligent, hard-working and aggressive. It was because she was a bright, diligent, hard-working and aggressive woman, and her superiors had helped her up the ladder because such tokenism bolstered their own image. They could point to her and say: see, we're not prejudiced against women in here. But there was a point at which the natural animosity towards women was going to kick in. *Policing was man's work.* They thought it even if they didn't say it. *Your inability to handle matters with the necessary discretion will go on your record.*

Mills reached for a packet of Benson and Hedges, took one out and lit it, one handed. He breathed the smoke deeply in the manner of a man who has been dying for one for a while. 'Don't worry, if push comes to shove, you can always join the fire brigade. They need tough bastards like you.'

'Thanks, guv.'

'Pity, you know. You're not a bad copper.'

She took that as a compliment. A bit too little, though, and probably a bit too late.

Chapter Twenty-Seven

Carlton watched them drive away from the window of the drawing room, and his fist tightened around the crystal tumbler in his hand, the ice rattling softly in the glass.

You're on borrowed time, Jimmy boy. They're on to you, you know. That bitch from the police. She's got eyes on her like a polecat, they don't miss a thing. Sees in the dark, that one. She sees right through you.

He had known this would happen eventually. It's like having a body buried in the garden. If no one finds it after the first week, you think it can stay there for ever. That no one will ever go digging.

Got to come out sooner or later, Jimmy boy. All of it. Hell to pay, of course, and you're going to be the one doing the paying.

He saw himself clearly at that moment, naked and diminished, standing in the cold darkness, looking for a way home. The snap of a lever and a thousand floodlights bathed him in their phosphorescence, he heard the gasp of a hundred thousand throats. There you are, my boy, exposed. All over for you. Naked to the world, all those petty lusts and dirty little secrets out there. They found you out.

He watched the landing lights of a jetliner on its slow and

thrumming course over the city, so many lives wrapped in that slender metal cocoon, tentative and fragile as his own. He listened to the solemn ticking of the grandfather clock, was struck with panic. That's your time slipping away, Jimmy boy.

He toyed in his mind with his vision of Kimberley, her arms stretched taut above her head, groaning with the pain-pleasure of the candle wax, pleasuring him as he stood naked beside the upholstered table. A sacred and terrible relic from his hideous past. It had no place in his world, yet would not be exorcised.

'What did the police want?'

He looked around, tried not to appear startled. Louise. She glided about the house like a ghost, appearing suddenly in rooms as if she had just drifted through the wall.

'A girl, used to be on my staff. She was murdered last week.'

Louise studied him intently with those violet eyes that so unsettled him. 'What has that to do with you?'

'Just routine. They were asking me about her boyfriends and so forth. Not that I was able to help them much.'

'Couldn't they find a better time?'

'Getting desperate, I imagine. I spoke to them about this when it first happened, rang that old mate of mine, Roger Kennett. They've taken this long to get back to me. You know what they're like. Bloody inefficient.'

Louise bit her lip. He wondered if she suspected. A lie needs willing partners.

She left the room, floating in a fragrant and ethereal haze along the hallway to the kitchen.

He poured himself another Bushmills. Tough call these days getting the intake right, just enough to steady the nerves, not too much that you start to ramble, and say too much.

Hope this is settled one way or another very soon. Don't think I can stand much more.

Chapter Twenty-Eight

Hospitals always reminded her of when her father became sick, the smell of antiseptic and overcooked food from the hospital kitchens inseparably linked to memories of decay and grief. She never minded the A&Es or the morgues, they were part of work. It was only up here, on the wards, that she had to remember how her father had spent his last months on this earth.

Bradshaw's eyes followed her as she walked into the ICU. His neck was in a brace, and there were dark bruises under his eyes. He was hooked to a heart monitor and there was an I/V tube in a vein in the back of his hand.

'Hello, Mr Bradshaw,' she said.

'Bitch,' he croaked. She had to strain to hear him. He must have damaged his vocal cords.

Fox sighed and stepped nearer the bed. She wondered if guilt had driven him to this. Perhaps they were one step closer to a confession.

It was a desperate hope, because the investigation into Kimberley Mason's death had stalled. They had put up posters in the Highgate area, looking for witnesses, had posted enquiries on the internet, had even appealed for help on *Crimewatch*. Gary Bradshaw was still their prime suspect.

'Look what you did to me,' he rasped.

'I didn't do it, Mr Bradshaw. You did. Want to tell me why?'

'Fuck you. I've just lost . . . my fucking job.'

'I'm sorry to hear that.'

'No, you're not.' There was a froth of spittle at the corners of his mouth, and the taint of something foul on his breath. 'You don't . . . give a shit. I bet you're . . . well chuffed.' It hurt him to talk, couldn't manage more than a few words at a time.

'Why would I be pleased that you've lost your job?'

'It's all part . . . of it . . . isn't it? Can't fit me up for . . . what happened to Kim, so you get the . . . fucking TV and the papers . . . camped outside my . . . flat . . . make my life a fucking . . . misery.'

'That was not our doing, nor our intention. We have no control over the media, I wish we did.'

'You never had . . . anything on me . . . from the start . . . you stone-faced fucking . . . cow. I was the soft fucking . . . option.'

He was raving, poor sod.

'If you think I have behaved improperly, Mr Bradshaw, you should make a formal complaint to my Chief Superintendent.'

'I lost my job,' he said, ignoring her. 'They said it wasn't . . . 'cos of this . . . but it was. No one . . . was talking to me at . . . work anyway. They all . . . looked at me like . . . I was Jack . . . the Ripper.'

'Mr Bradshaw, you are not charged with any crime. If what you say is true, then you should decide whether your employer contravened the laws governing unfair dismissal.'

'Yeah, right,' Bradshaw said. His voice was no more than a cracked whisper now. His eyes flickered towards the water jug beside the bed. 'Give us some . . . of that . . . will you?'

Fox poured some water into a small plastic cup and held it to his lips. He took a mouthful and then, with great precision, spat it back in her face. Fox put the cup back on the bedside table and took a paper tissue from her bag. She carefully wiped her face. 'I'm sorry you feel that way,' she said. She looked down at her jacket. A stain on the collar, but it would be dry by the time she got back to the office. She turned to go.

'You never found . . . the other bloke . . . did you?'

Hard to be civil to a man who had just spat in your face, but she heard herself say, 'What other bloke?'

'The other ponce . . . she was seeing.'

She turned around.

'Who do you reckon paid . . . for the big house and the clothes . . . and the fancy car? She . . . was a naff fucking . . . PR agent. She was earning . . . fuck all. Or did you think . . . it all came from . . . French Kitty?'

'It might have done. There are no records that we can check.'

Bradshaw grinned, wolfishly, the point made. 'You bastards . . . make me sick. And that's the . . . truth.'

She went out, the smell of his breath in her nostrils and on her clothes. He would be with her all day. She supposed she should feel sorry for him.

But she didn't.

Chapter Twenty-Nine

Kingston, Surrey

Dappled light under the trees, birdsong on a warm summer afternoon. Fox and Nick Crawford followed the procession as it made its way along the path from the church. The knot of mourners huddled around the grave as the polished walnut coffin was lowered into the ground and a few final words were spoken.

An odd gathering, Fox thought: George Mason and his wife staring in baffled incomprehension at the likes of Lila Mahmoud and Ray Pratt. Rhiannon Strudwick was there too, still weeping into a ball of screwed-up Kleenex, her make-up perfect. All these people, she thought, had known or loved a different Kimberley Mason to the one consigned to the earth today.

'You saw Bradshaw,' Nick said.

'He still says he didn't kill her.'

'Pity he botched the suicide.'

'Maybe. It still doesn't make much sense.'

'It never makes much sense though, does it, ma'am? Unless we get a confession, we'll never really know what happened.'

'Does it matter, Nick?'

'I'd like to know what happened. For their sake.'

George Mason and his wife had turned away from the grave and were being helped back down the path towards the cars. For all his six feet and three inches, George Mason looked diminished, as small and frail as a child.

'Maybe then they can sleep again.'

'They'll never sleep again.' Fox said. 'Want a drink?'

He nodded. 'Meet you later at the King's Head?'

'About seven,' she said.

Nick moved away, wanted to be with George and Jean, help them through the wake. Not strictly part of the job description, but that was why being family liaison was so hard on the nerves. After a while you started to care a little too much.

Hendon Road

She got held up with paperwork in the office, and when she finally pushed through the doors at the King's Head he was already there, nursing a pint of Carling. She put a ten-pound note on the bar, got herself a gin and tonic and another pint for Nick.

She looked around the bar. WPC Stacey was sitting in the corner with a couple of other uniforms. This would be all over Hendon Road by the morning. She couldn't help that. A little salacious gossip wouldn't do her stocks any harm, as long as they both arrived from different directions for the eight o'clock briefing. The canteen gossip would have them shacked up and at it like rabbits, no matter what she did from here.

'How are you settling in?' she asked him.

'Honest answer?'

She shrugged. 'Why not?'

'I'm finding it a bit tough.'

'Millsie didn't do you any favours that's for sure.'

'I think he wanted me out of the way.'

'Perhaps he chose you as family liaison because you have great people skills.'

He grinned. 'No. He thinks I'm a hayseed. Or else he's a racist. It doesn't matter. I'll just have to get on with it, won't I?'

'For the record, Nick, I don't care what colour you are and I certainly don't think you're a country bumpkin.'

'You don't ma'am, but some of the other boys have been watching me, waiting for my jaw to drop.' He slipped into Farmer Giles. 'We don't do none of that bondage up on Daisy Hill Farm, mind.'

'I heard you worked on the Fred West murders.'

'That was just digging up bits of bodies and helping the boffins tie labels on bones.'

He ordered another round of drinks. There was a CD jukebox in the corner and someone had selected Boy George. 'Do you really want to hurt me?' Synchronicity. 'Strangest case I ever worked, I'd just been made a DC, got sent to Barnstaple, thank you very much. First week out, me and my new skipper were called out to a local farm to investigate a suspicious death. A hanging.'

'A suicide?'

'Well, we couldn't figure that out right off. I mean, usual thing, they do it from a tree, or off the rafters in a barn or some such. This bloke was found early one morning by one of his farmhands, swinging off the shovel of a John Deere backhoe. He was actually suspended in a kind of sitting position. Don't ask me how, there were ropes and shackles everywhere, it was unbelievably complicated. There was a kind of strap around his neck, padded with a towel, so it didn't look like he actually meant to kill himself.'

'How the hell did he get up there?'

'There was some plastic pipe fastened with duct tape to a lever in the tractor compartment. He'd attached a broom handle to the other end of the pipe and that was what he was sitting on. He could raise or lower the shovel just by pressure on the stick. The tricky bit was, the higher the shovel went, the tighter it made this strap around his neck.'

'Okay, you've got me. Why?'

'Well, the skipper thought there might be some sort of erotic element to it. You know, because of the asphyxiation angle.'

'Erotic.'

He nodded.

'What was he wearing?'

He smiled. 'No, it wasn't like that, the only rubber gear he had on was his wellies. In fact we were a bit at a loss, until we went inside the farmhouse and found his diary. It was full of love poems that he'd written. To his farm machinery. The backhoe specifically. Pure fantasy stuff. In the poems he said he wanted to soar with Hercules – that was the name he gave the tractor – soar with Hercules right up to the sky, where no one could hurt them again.'

'He got his wish.'

'Not really. The tractor got sold to some apple farmer in Taunton and he's in a cemetery in Barnstaple.'

'I was being poetic.'

'It sort of put me off poetry, to be honest.'

'So instead of finding a Dear John letter . . . it was a John Deere.'

He grinned. 'That was about it.'

'Well, that's one for the autobiography, when you retire.'

'Funny, I've been thinking about that case a lot this week, watching George trying to make sense of something that maybe the rest of us just can't hope to understand. He thinks this was about sex, that there was something wrong with his daughter, like she was crippled or something. But maybe that's not it. Greed, jealousy, you can understand that, but when it comes to what goes on inside people's heads, well, that's not something you can really hope to come to terms with. This isn't just about sex, like gambling's never just about the money.'

'Do you have an angle on this?'

He shook his head. 'I don't know, but Gary Bradshaw looks too easy to me. Killing out of jealous rage is for normal people. If there is such a thing.'

'Any theories?'

He shook his head and finished his pint. 'What about you, ma'am?'

'I think you're jumping at shadows. Look at the facts: we know she was laid out for us to put us off the trail, make it seem like some weird sex crime, when we now know it wasn't. So whoever did it either thinks we're all idiots, or really doesn't know too much about the world in which Kimberley Mason lived.'

'Gary Bradshaw.'

'He had motive and opportunity. And why did he try and top himself? Guilt, maybe.'

Nick frowned and said nothing.

'You're not convinced?'

'Just doesn't feel right, ma'am. Just intuition. Inadmissible in a court of law.'

A man with intuition, she thought. What's the world coming to?

'When I was a kid,' he said, 'I got caught stealing lollies from the local sweet shop. First time I'd ever tried it, and I got nicked with two Mars bars in each pocket. Two of my mates were with me, they'd been doing the same thing for months, but when I got sprung the miserable old bastard who ran the place blamed me for everything that had ever gone missing out of his shop.'

'You think Gary Bradshaw is just the kid with his hand in the cookie jar?'

'Just a feeling. But like you say, we don't have any evidence either way, really, do we?'

'I don't know about that, Nick. We have motive, opportunity, previous and no alibi. We're almost there.' She looked at her watch. 'I have to go. I have a cat to feed and two hours' paperwork to catch up on.'

'See you tomorrow, ma'am.'

She waited for him to hit on her, but he didn't. That was his cue, and he missed it. She wasn't sure if she was insulted. She hoisted her bag over her shoulder, and picked up her briefcase. 'Are you staying here all night?'

'If we leave together, we'll get talked about.' He nodded to the corner where Stacey was watching them, supposedly deep in conversation with one of the uniforms.

'See you, Nick.'

Outside the air was still warm, tainted with the smell of diesel. The sun had stained the sky salmon pink. Another night at home on my own. Nick Crawford might have been a pleasant interlude in an otherwise workaholic life, but he hadn't asked her to come home with him, so she would never know what she would have said. Probably just as well. All her life she had kept her working life and her private life separate. It was the only sensible thing to do in her position.

She wondered if she would regret it, one day.

Hampstead

Shadows on the ceiling, silhouettes in a demon play; the long fingers of the ash tree beyond the window reaching out for the slender body of the light, encircling and embracing.

And so, the night.

In the daylight hours it was easy to perform, to forget the lies, but with the setting of the sun the ghosts walked, and in the quiet of his bed he could hear the cry of the banshee and the wicked remembrances of the dead.

Louise rolled towards him, he felt the warmth of her body against him as her fingers entwined in the hairs on his chest. Her satin nightdress was electric against his skin. He kissed her on the forehead and turned away. 'Good night,' he murmured, hoping to evade affection.

But she would not let it go, her hand strayed down his belly and her fingers encircled him. She kissed him, her breath hot on the back of his neck.

'I'm tired,' he said, his body stiff. There was an ugly gnawing in his gut, spiders crawling inside.

He felt her stiffen at his rejection. She rolled away from him, the bedcovers stretched.

And he lay there, ashamed and relieved.

What is wrong with me? he wondered. Why is all that I have never enough? This compulsion working in his blood, like a drug. He was addicted, as sad and tragic a figure as any lank-haired and raving junkie sleeping in the subways and doorways of the city. Reason was daily pushed aside, his passion treating the rational man with loutish violence.

It was not sex he desired; if that was all that drove him, perhaps he might overcome this black dog that had him by the throat. Lust itself was not the drug. Like nicotine, like opium, he craved that rush of adrenalin that could only be found in his secret, fetish world.

And so he closed his eyes to the nausea that gripped him and thought of Kimberley Mason. Even now there was some comfort simply in the thought of her, though she could no longer touch him in the flesh.

Chapter Thirty

Guildford, Surrey

Carrie and Stephen had bought themselves a cottage in a small village just outside Guildford. The first time Fox saw it she thought of picture postcards. Roses and marigolds bloomed in the front garden, which was surrounded by a dry-stone wall, ivy grew over the front porch. There was an old Norman church directly across the road. The only jarring note to this rural concord was Stephen's black XJS, which was parked in the garage, a converted wooden shed.

Carrie met her at the door, as excited as a child at Christmas, and immediately gave her the grand tour: two small bedrooms, a tiny kitchen, a rusted claw-foot bath, nothing plumb, and the downstairs living room smelling of mould and cats. Still, it was a long way from the cramped flat in Chingford, the thump of reggae from the flat downstairs, and the drunken Irish boyfriend who beat Carrie up every payday.

The hallway and kitchen were stacked with packing boxes. Stephen had hired a van and had driven over to Fulham with two of his mates to clear out his flat; Daisy was in the other room, playing with Barbie dolls on a strip of carpet. Carrie was supposed to be unpacking. Instead she sat on an upturned packing crate among the screwed up newspaper and dust, playing house with her dreams and wondering, amid the excited laughter and tears, if she had done the right thing.

Fox made two mugs of PG Tips and carried them out of the kitchen on a tray with some chocolate Digestives. She set the tray down on the floor and sat on a wooden stepladder next to Carrie.

Carrie sipped at her tea. 'It's tiny, isn't it?' she said, echoing Fox's own thoughts. 'Like a dolls' house.'

Bloody expensive dolls' house, Fox thought. 'It's lovely,' she said.

A tremulous breath. 'Just two more weeks to the big day.'

Poor Carrie, Fox thought. Diminished to talking in clichés. Is this what happiness does to you?

'When are we going to fix *you* up with a bloke?'

How patronising was that? Fox thought. She's getting married and has a new house and now she is feeling sorry for *me*. She thinks she has everything life has to offer, and now she would like to distribute some largesse to her friends. There was a presumption among certain women that if she had a home, a husband, children, that she would be happy. A straight shooter, as Ian had said; as if life were ever as easy as that.

Would I give up my job to have what Carrie has? I don't think so. And yet being a cop, and a murder squad detective, isn't the top of the mountain any more either. At least, I hope to Christ it isn't.

'Fix me up?' she said, lightly. 'You make me sound like a cat.'

'I just want you to be happy.'

'What makes you think I'm not?' *Bitch.*

Carrie said nothing, sitting there in silent judgment of her life.

What was happiness, anyway? It was like smoke. It drifted past now and then, but if you tried to grab it, your hand always came back empty. Happiness was an accident, something that happened to you, like winning the pools. You either got lucky or you didn't. One night you got home and there was a letter lying on the mat: You have been chosen . . .

It had to happen that way because she figured most people were like her, didn't have a clue what happiness looked like. People were propelled through their lives like pinballs, bouncing off their desires and obsessions, giddy as lemmings half the time. At least, that's been my life so far. And Carrie's, too. She got lucky, yet here she is, looking to take all the credit.

'Carrie, how long will this last? How long before he has his first affair, how long before you get tired of changing nappies or looking through the window with a baby spitting milk curds down your shoulder, watching life go east and west while you slowly go stir crazy?'

But she didn't say that.

She said none of those things, because Carrie was her friend and she loved her, and because for this brief moment Carrie had captured a skein of that sweet smoke, and Fox, for one, did not not want to see it drift out of reach before she had at least had the chance to breathe in the elusive fragrance.

Chapter Thirty-One

Holmes Road Police Station, Kentish Town

He sat in Interview Room Number Two at the Holmes Road police station, dropping ash from his cigarette into an empty polystyrene cup. He was in his early thirties, good looking, well turned out; he wore a black leather jacket, pressed trousers, and a dark shirt. He worked in computers, owned a retailer's in the high street.

Fox studied him through the glass panel in the door; he looked worried, continually rubbing at his forehead with his knuckles, as if he had a migraine. Guilt written all over him. Which was odd, because they weren't about to charge him with anything. In fact, it looked as if he would become their star witness in the Kimberley Mason investigation.

Fox went in, TJ behind her. She introduced herself, then sat down, started the tape and went through the usual preliminaries.

'Can you give us your name please?' she asked him, finally.

'Stone. Peter Raymond Stone.'

'Where do you live, Mr Stone?'

'Seventeen B Burrows Court, Islington.'

'Thanks for coming in, Mr Stone. You believe you may have some information that may help us in our enquiries into the death of Kimberley Mason on Sunday twenty-seventh of June?'

Christ, he looked like they'd cornered him. Conscience, Fox thought. Whatever you've done, son, anything short of murder and I'm not interested.

'The thing is,' he said, 'I might have seen the bloke who did for that tart.'

'You are referring to Kimberley Julia Mason,' Fox said, for the tape.

'If that's her name.' His hands were shaking. He licked his lips.

'Well, we're all ears,' TJ said. The two men seemed to have taken an instant dislike to each other. Strange, because Stone and TJ could be brothers, to look at them. Christ, they even dress the same.

'I've been seeing this woman who lives up the road.'

'What's her name, Mr Stone?'

'Her name's Cheryl. Cheryl Davies.' He rubbed at his forehead again. 'Mrs. Mrs Cheryl Davies.'

'I see,' Fox said.

'Her husband's a sales rep. He was away in Manchester. That's why I didn't come in before, see. If I had, I'd have had to explain where I was and what I was doing.'

'And who you were doing,' TJ said.

Stone gave him a look. 'Whatever.'

'We're only interested in any evidence you have, Mr Stone, not your private life.'

'Well, it doesn't matter now. Her husband's found out, hasn't he?'

TJ, doodling on his notepad, made a tut-tutting noise with his tongue.

'It's been bothering me,' Stone said to Fox. 'I haven't been able to sleep.'

'That's commendable,' TJ said.

'Look, she was the one. Cheryl. She was the one who made me promise not to say anything.'

For God's sake, Fox thought. Never mind the murderers have excuses. Now I have to sit here and listen to the witnesses whine.

'Why don't you tell us what happened?'

'I was coming out of Cheryl's flat on the Sunday morning . . .'

'What time was this?'

'I don't know. About six, I suppose. It was just starting to get light. I normally don't stay over. She didn't want any of her neighbours seeing me. I must have slept in.'

'Hard night,' TJ said.

Stone ignored him. 'I always park my car in the next street. I knew about what's her name. She had a bit of a reputation. As I was walking past her house, I saw him coming out.'

'Actually coming out of the house?' Fox said, and for a moment her hopes rose.

Stone shook his head. 'Just coming back up the path. Well, he must have been inside, right?'

Fox didn't comment on that. A good defence silk would turn that right around. 'What did he look like?' she said.

'Tall, I suppose. Fair hair. Well dressed. *Bloody* well dressed for that time of the morning.'

Fox looked at TJ. Stone had just described Gary Bradshaw. They would organise an identity parade as soon as possible, get it confirmed.

'Did you see where he went?' TJ asked.

Stone shook his head. 'He got in his car. I heard him drive off.'

'What sort of car?'

'I don't remember.'

'Did you get a registration number?'

'Yeah. I got the odometer reading as well,' Stone said. 'No, of course I didn't. I didn't think anything more about it until I heard on the news, how she'd been done in.'

'Would you be able to recognise this man if you saw him again?' Fox asked.

'I suppose so. I don't know. I wasn't paying that much attention. I was just curious. You know, there were some real weirdoes going in and out of there, Cheryl reckoned.'

Interesting. They would have to double check Cheryl's statement on the HOLMES.

'He looked normal enough,' Stone was saying, 'but I knew he'd been up to something.'

'How did you know that?'

Stone laughed. 'That time of the morning, there's only milkmen and blokes like me up and around.'

Well, so much for feeling conscience-stricken, Fox thought. Scratch the surface of any penitent and you find someone who's actually pretty chuffed with themselves.

'And he had that look about him,' Stone said.

'What look?'

'Like he'd done something he shouldn't of.'

'You know that feeling well?' TJ said. Hypocrite. Suddenly TJ wanted to play the Moral Majority.

Stone said nothing.

'Why do you think this man you saw was Kimberley Mason's assailant?'

'Well, that's what it said in the papers. Cheryl reckons she was found on Monday morning, but you lot said she'd been dead for a day or two.' He shrugged. 'Only trying to help.'

'Yes. And you have been very helpful, Mr Stone.'

He looked happy enough with that.

'Interview terminated at four fifteen.' She switched off the tape. Stone started to get to his feet. 'You're not ordinary plod, are you? You're Scotland Yard.'

'No, we're with the Major Incident Pool at Hendon Road,' TJ said. 'Murder squad to you.'

'Right. Only Cheryl's husband's looking for me.' Stone said. 'If you find me down a dark alley, you'll know who did it.'

Tufnell Park, N7

Gary Bradshaw lived in a two bedroom terrace in Tufnell Park. There was the inevitable satellite dish on the outside wall, a tiny square of untended garden and a black Camden Borough rubbish bin by the front window. Bradshaw's black Ford Capri was parked in the street.

She barely recognised him. He had not shaved for several days and he was wearing a pair of white football shorts and an off-white T-shirt. He'd been drinking and his breath reeked.

He looked at her, then at TJ. 'What the fuck do you want?' he said.

'We'd like to talk to you.'

'Don't I get any peace?'

'Can we come in?'

'Have you got a warrant?'

'We just want to have a word, Mr Bradshaw. We can do it here or down the station.'

He hesitated, then moved aside. She and TJ stepped inside and followed Bradshaw into the living room. It was the first time she had seen how Gary Bradshaw lived; it all fitted. There was a black modular sofa, a German sound system, no doubt all of it on a credit card. Probably liked to impress his mates and his girlfriends, even if it was only Tufnell Park.

That was all finished now, however, and her nose wrinkled at the overpowering stench of tobacco and stale sweat. Lager cans, discarded clothes and cigarette packets were piled up on the floor and the ashtrays were overflowing. A pizza box lay open under the coffee table, the contents going to mould. The television was on, the volume up too loud. An Australian soap.

'Can we turn that down?' TJ asked him.

'I'm watching it.'

'Not any more,' TJ said, and he found the remote and switched it off.

'You never give up, do you? This is harassment.'

'Mr Bradshaw, why did you go back to Kimberley Mason's house on the Sunday morning?'

All bluff, our Gazza, she thought. Took nothing to make him crumble. His shoulders sagged and he sat down hard on the sofa.

TJ gave her a look. This bastard couldn't lie straight in bed. 'Look, Gary, we have just taken a statement from someone who says they saw you come out of Kimberley Mason's house that Sunday morning around six o'clock.'

Well, perhaps, Fox thought. It was yet to be seen if Stone could pick Bradshaw out of a line-up. But Bradshaw gave it up anyway. 'I didn't go in,' he mumbled. 'I just wanted to talk to her.'

The 'I just wanted to talk to her' line again. This was the second time they had caught him out in a lie. 'How many times did you go back, Mr Bradshaw?'

'I shouldn't have,' he said. 'I was still pissed.'

'Do you want to have another go at telling us what happened?'

'Nothing happened. I knocked on the door, she didn't answer, that was it. And that's the truth.'

'You wouldn't know the truth if it jumped out and bit you on the arse,' TJ said.

'I don't know. I don't know!'

'What don't you know?'

'Why I went back. I was just . . . crazy.'

'Did you go back to clean up?'

'There was nothing to clean up!'

You're lying, Fox thought. You waited for her until she got home, two, three in the morning, then you let yourself in with a key, and you murdered her. Then you laid her out in her own private dungeon and cleaned up. Then you went home and that's when Stone saw you. But you still can't accept what you did. You want to believe your own lies.

'I didn't hurt her,' he said.

TJ was looking at her, waiting.

'Gary Bradshaw,' she began, 'I am arresting you for the murder of Kimberley Julia Mason . . .'

As she went through the caution he sat there on the sofa with his head in his hands. He kept saying over and over, 'I don't fucking believe this.' Fox didn't quite believe it either, the way some people behaved. But she'd seen enough cold bodies to know that most people committed the most mindless acts of violence on the spur of the moment and still expected to get away with it. They made up all kinds of stupid lies and still managed to look surprised when they were caught out.

Poor old Gary, poor little Gaz. He hadn't meant to hurt her. And that's the truth.

Chapter Thirty-Two

Area Major Incident Pool, Hendon Road

'Have a good day?'

She looked up from her desk. It was Nick Crawford. 'Brilliant.'

'You arrested Gary Bradshaw.'

'We have a witness, saw him coming out of the house at six o'clock on the Sunday morning.'

'Has he admitted anything?'

She shook her head. 'Just changed his story again. No doubt he'll stick to it until we prove him a liar again.'

'So you were right, all along, ma'am.'

She remembered their conversation in the King's Head, Nick playing devil's advocate. 'Have to see what the courts make of it first,' she said.

He hesitated. 'It's eight o'clock,' he said.

Eight o'clock. Christ, she might as well sleep in this bloody place. She looked out of her window at a summer evening settling over London, weakening yellow sunlight filtered through the smog like mist. If she didn't finish the paperwork here, she would have to finish it at home.

Home: a change of clothes and a shower, masquerading as a one-bedroom flat.

'I'm going over the road for a pizza. Want to join me, ma'am?'

Oh, why not. If I go home it will be tea and toast and falling asleep in front of the late news. 'If you promise not to call me ma'am,' she said.

They found a pizza joint, just round the corner from the King's Head. They sat at one of two Formica tables, while a kid in an LA Lakers T-shirt played a basketball arcade game right behind them, the noise from the machine almost drowning out the sound of Capital Radio behind the counter.

Fox finished her Coke and started picking at the bits of cheese that had congealed on the cardboard box. They made small talk, music and gossip and food, but Nick seemed distracted. She waited, and finally he blurted it out: 'TJ reckons there's something going on.'

'Does he?' She found a stray piece of bacon in the corner of the pizza box and popped it in her mouth.

'There's been a lot of speculation about Grey Man.' Grey Man was the codename they had given Carlton in the transcripts of the interview.

'I thought there would be.'

'Now it's over, are you allowed to tell us who it was?'

'You know better than that, Nick.' So, here she was colluding in Carlton's protection. But as Mills had told her, sometimes that's just the way it was.

Nick frowned but didn't say anything. The kid in the Lakers T-shirt punched the arcade machine with his fist and walked away.

'It beats me how a man can put his whole life on the line over sex,' she said.

Nick smiled, crushed his empty Coke can in his fist and dropped it in the empty pizza box. 'Ever read Plato?'

'Not really,' she said. 'I'm more of a John Grisham type of girl.'

'Plato said a man's life was like riding a chariot, pulled by two horses. There's one tame horse, the spirit, and one wild, headstrong one, the libido. The charioteer is reason. Plato thought the course of a life was an ongoing battle between the reason and the wild horse for control.'

'Nick, I worry about you. Do you go home at night and read Salman Rushdie and Stephen Hawking?'

A shy smile. 'I read Classics at Oxford.'

'And then you joined the police force?'

'Natural career move for a well-educated black guy.'

'Seriously.'

'I thought about going into law, but I decided on the police force instead.'

'Very clever. How long did it take you to think that up?'

He shrugged his shoulders. 'I looked at my choices, banking, postgraduate studies, decided I'd go crazy with boredom.'

'What did your parents think?'

'My father was a Jamaican playing left back for Exeter. Anything I did was a step up.'

'Not a conventional life, Nick.'

'For a black guy?'

'For anyone.'

'You're not a cliché yourself, ma'am. Madeleine,' he added, remembering they were off duty.

'Personal question?'

'Depends how personal.'

'What lured you into the job?'

'I plan to save the world from evil.'

'After you've done that. What do you want from life?'

What do I want from life? What a conversation to be having in a pizza bar on a Tuesday night. 'Oh, you know, the usual. A red Ferrari. Ten kids. Peace on earth.'

He shook his head. 'I couldn't see you being happy with peace on earth.'

'Maybe at Christmas it would be nice.'

'I couldn't see you with ten kids either.'

'Well, you know, a girl thinks about it. The biological clock and everything.' She shrugged. 'I don't know, I want to be happy. I just don't know what it would take to get me there. What about you?'

He shrugged. 'I just want to get through each day without getting found out.'

'Found out?'

'Don't you ever feel like that?' He laughed and ran a hand across his tight black curls. 'Don't answer that. I don't want to know if I'm a freak show. I shouldn't have told you anyway. I just drank too much Coke and lost control, like. Don't put it on my record.'

But then she found herself saying, 'We all have doubts about ourselves, I suppose.'

'Can I ask you another personal question?'

Dangerous ground. Well, she could always lie. 'If you like,' she said.

'Have you got a bloke?'

She took a deep breath. 'No.'

'Why not? Girl like you.'

'I never found the right man.'

'You're not gay, are you?' Said with a laugh, but deadly serious.

She counted silently to ten, as her father had once taught her to do. *That temper of yours, Madeleine. It will get you into a lot of trouble one day.* 'Is that it? If I'm not the station bicycle, then I must be some sort of pinko dyke.'

'I'm sorry, I didn't mean to upset you. I apologise.'

She made a big play of looking at her watch but all she saw was Nick Crawford stretched out on the floor with a knife in his ribs. 'I'd better go.'

'Ma'am, I really didn't mean to offend you.'

'I'm not offended,' she said and walked out.

Hampstead

Carlton sat propped up in the bed, a hardback novel open in front of him, pretending to read. It had been shortlisted for the Booker last year and he felt obliged. Louise was sitting at the dressing table, carefully applying face cream. Their eyes met for a moment in the mirror. He attempted a weak smile, saw the hardness in her eyes, knew what was coming.

'What's going on, James?'

'Hell you mean?'

'Don't lie to me.'

He had to look away. 'It's nothing,' he said. It would not do, of course, but he was too tired to lie.

Louise stood up and walked over to his side of the bed. He wondered what she was going to do. Oh, Christ. She unbuttoned her nightgown. He didn't know where to look. It fell away on to the carpet.

She knelt over him and kissed him on the lips, growling deep in her throat, like a hungry kitten. He still had the book open on his lap. Bit late to fumble for his leather bookmark. Probably not the right thing to do.

Have to do *something*, he thought, so he cupped a breast in his palm and she squirmed against him in a most un-Louise way. You're snookered, Jim, he thought. Have to perform now. As if there isn't enough pressure.

His wife had never desired much physical contact between them, but lately, with his mind and his body elsewhere, she seemed to have discovered an appetite not evident before. Perhaps all this lovemaking was a sign of possession rather than passion, he thought, and this intuition dispirited him.

Christ. Never did fancy a woman who threw herself at you. Always preferred a lack of willing, really. That was his problem. Louise groping for him under the bedclothes. Won't find much there, but give me time to work on it. Always can produce when the pressure's on. Good old Jim.

Louise squirming against him, felt the wiry bush of her pubic hair pressed against his thigh. Not done it like this since before we were married. Christ, Lou, why now?

What a mess. You let the Devil in the back door just once, and before you know it, he's taken over completely and you're out on the street without a shirt on your back.

PART THREE

If you look long into the abyss, the abyss also looks into you.

Nietzsche

Chapter Thirty-Three

Camden Town

A grey and breathless summer morning, an amorphous sky clinging to the rooftops of Camden like a shroud. James Carlton parked in the street, spotted the yellow Corvette he was looking for on the other side of the street, with its customised number plate, HARD1. Carlton experienced the urge to get back in his car and drive home to Hampstead. But he couldn't: this wasn't going to go away on its own.

Carlton's black boots clipped on the concrete, as he made his way down the steps to the canal footpath. The water looked oily and dark under the lowering sky, the only splash of colour a lilac in exuberant bloom under the rail bridge, an old barge on the other side of the lock, the red and green paint on its cabin blistered by years of neglect. A train thundered across the girder bridge into the station.

Carlton looked up and down the footpath, hesitated. A few walkers around, tourists by the look of them, on their way back to the markets. He felt suddenly nauseous. How had things come to this?

Then he saw him, sprawled on a bench, about fifty yards

away, towards the rail bridge. He made his way briskly up the path, checked that no one was watching, then sat down on the end of the bench and crossed his legs.

The other man shook his head in disgust. 'Do you know how obvious that looked?'

'What are you talking about?' Carlton turned and looked at him. A face like a retired boxer, hair dyed with peroxide, by the look of it, and cut short in the style of a much younger man. He was wearing a brown bomber jacket and jeans, and he had a gold Rolex Oyster on his left wrist. Carlton had only met him once or twice before this, had taken little notice of him then. Did not remember him looking this loutish.

'Never mind.' The man shook his head and returned his attention to the *Daily Mirror* on his lap. 'You wanted to talk to me?'

'I have a problem,' Carlton said. 'I was told you might be able to help me with it.'

A curious smile. 'Only time people like you ever want to talk to me. Too busy the rest of the time.'

Typical of boot-lickers like this, Carlton thought. If you didn't have your boot on their neck, they had theirs on yours. Kept wanting to do you favours, then as soon as you took them up on it, the poison leaked out. 'Can you help me or not?'

He put the paper down with a sigh. 'Depends what it is you want me to do. You'd better start at the beginning.'

Carlton took a deep breath, the stench of the canal in his nostrils. Or perhaps that was just his imagination, his life turning sour, his last principles rotting away.

Chapter Thirty-Four

Little Rushmoor, Gloucestershire

A warm August day, the clouds soaring over the plains like mountains of creamy froth, the sort of sky enshrined in Constable oils. The limousine deposited them in a gravel car park at the foot of what looked to Fox like an old tumulus mound. A stile led to an overgrown footpath that wound its way up the hill to the church, the clocktower jutting over fields airbrushed with lupins and poppies, and a handful of cottages built from Cotswold stone. The bells of the old church had counted the cadence of the seasons for the villagers of Little Rushmoor for almost eight centuries.

Before she got out of the limousine, Fox quickly checked her appearance in the driving mirror. Her hair was tied in a French braid, she had on a little more make-up than she was accustomed to wearing, but she had to admit, the effect wasn't too bad. She was less comfortable with the dress Carrie had picked out for her as matron of honour, grey satin, yards of it. For God's sake. If TJ or Millsie saw her now, she'd never hear the end of it.

The chauffeur held open the door and she stepped out into

the sunshine. She took a quick look around the car park: BMWs, Jaguars, a couple of Mercs. She was in the wrong business.

But she had always known that.

A lot of excited chatter and laughter over by the stile, where the other wedding guests were crowded together, waiting for the bridal party to arrive. She looked them over, with practised, if cynical, eye: a lot of overdressed young men with designer ponytails and diamond studs in their ears, their women dripping jewellery and cutaway dresses. A curved spine here, a cleavage there. This was going to be a long day.

She helped the bride out of the car. Carrie and Stephen had opted for a medieval theme. Carrie was resplendent in a gown of ivory satin, a coronet of amethyst and silver on her head, her hair plaited into two pigtails.

Fox gave her her best and most reassuring smile. 'You look lovely,' she said.

You look like Maid Marian.

In accord with the unconventional wishes of the bride and groom, there would be no grand entrance along the aisle. Instead, the bridal party made their way up the path to the church followed by the hundred or so guests, in train. Torch bearers, dressed as monks, led the way, escorted by a Celtic bagpiper. It was a steep climb on such a hot day and Fox could feel herself starting to sweat. Stephen's father had to stop to catch his breath.

Should make for great wedding photographs, Fox thought, the bridegroom's father in cardiac arrest in front of a bent and mossy gravestone, the best man down on his knees trying to resuscitate him.

*　　*　　*

The sombre gloom of the Norman church was relieved by the dull glow of candles. Uillean pipes played a Gaelic folk song. She stopped at the altar, beside Stephen and Carrie, and watched the guests file in. Some of Stephen's friends were in morning suits. Impressive. She had almost expected the congregation to be wearing T-shirts with the radio station logo. The women looked like meringues, albeit meringues with highly prominent tits.

She looked along the aisle and was startled to find one of the men trying to catch her eye. She glimpsed a boyish face, a cowlick falling over one eye and hazel-green eyes that appeared almost luminous in the gloom of the church. He was immaculate in a charcoal woollen suit with a hand-painted tie in burgundy silk. His date was far too young for him, all teased curls and trainer breasts and quick, birdlike movements. She was wearing hot pink. Ridiculous.

He smiled. Nice teeth, jailbait girlfriend. Must be Welsh.

To Fox's surprise, from that point it was pretty much a formal service, apart from the readings from Browning and a medieval Spanish poet she had never heard of. Carrie had had the lunatic idea of making Daisy a bridesmaid, and she screamed right through the service, and had to be removed. Another of the junior bridesmaids, Stephen's three year old niece, wet her pants during the betrothal and Fox had to rescue her, so she missed the actual exchange of vows.

Despite her misgivings, she was touched by the ceremony, touched by its innocence and its hope, and she was happy for Carrie that she had finally found a man with decent intentions and a good job, someone who showed no inclination to beat her blue when he drank too much, or when Tottenham lost at home.

Chapter Thirty-Five

Stephen's father had money, lots of it, that much was apparent. Only the rich could still afford to live like Beatrix Potter. He and his wife lived in a thatched cottage, extensively renovated, with its own duck pond; the old stables now accommodated five hundred horses, all of them under the bonnet of a red Mercedes 500 SEL. A little piece of olde England hiding away from Blair and the motorways and urban sprawl.

The reception was held in the garden, on a long strip of lawn that would not have shamed the curator at Wembley stadium. A live band was playing in the marquee, the singer murdering John Lennon a second time.

As she had anticipated, she didn't recognise a lot of the faces. Carrie's parents were there, looking overwhelmed, her father deaf and still belligerent, grey stubble under the dewlap, wheeled out in a mothballed suit for the occasion. Carrie's brother was there too, the one who had once tried to feel her up in the family kitchen, thinking that she was irresistibly attracted to body odour and mossy teeth.

Fox took a deep breath and made for the champagne waiter, needing a little booze to bolster her flagging courage. She had prepared herself to be sociable to Carrie's old friends, but none of them now looked like making an appearance. One was still in rehab, another lived in an ashram in India. Carrie had pissed off many of the others during her drugs and living-with-crazies years.

Fox made her way over to the bride, who looked like she was planning a bender for old times' sake. She had the waiter in a death grip and was helping herself to the champagne flutes like a kid at a birthday party grabbing handfuls of Smarties before they were all gone.

'Take it easy,' Fox said. 'For a start, it's not good for the baby. Two, you still have the rest of the evening to get through.'

'Christ, that was nerve racking.'

'Looked okay to me. All you had to do was say yes. If you had trouble with that, you wouldn't be pregnant again.'

Carrie gave her a look, but she let that one go. 'Everyone's looking at me. I feel like I'm in a shop window.'

This from a girl wearing a medieval coronet to her wedding.

'What did you think of the service?'

'Great.'

'We planned it all ourselves. Stephen's really into the medieval thing.'

'Right.' Fox looked up and saw the man with the hazel-green eyes, from the church. He was standing with the girl in the hot pink, staring at her again. 'Who's that?' Fox asked.

'I don't know. Must be a friend of Stephen's. Do you fancy him?'

'He already has a date by the look of it.'

'He's coming over,' Carrie said. 'I'll leave you to it.'

And the bitch took off.

*　　*　　*

'Hi.'

'Hi, yourself.'

'I brought you a champagne,' he said, holding out a flute.

He looked nervous, and she found his diffidence somehow appealing. And so fresh faced. Surely he couldn't be as young as he looked.

She took the champagne. 'Thanks.'

'Rodney Ashcroft. Mate of Stephen's. Friends call me Ash.'

'Madeleine Fox. Schoolfriend of Carrie's.'

'Personally, I think you were a bad choice for matron of honour,' he said, and stood there, waiting for her to ask him why.

'Why?'

'You drew all the attention away from the bride. All my attention anyway.'

'Yes. I saw you staring.'

'Couldn't help myself.' There was an awkward pause. 'What did you think of the wedding?'

'It was very . . . medieval.'

'If the best man's speech is no good, we stretch him on the rack.' He leaned towards her. 'And as the bride and groom leave the reception we throw hot oil instead of confetti. You really are very beautiful.'

He said it all in one breath and she almost missed it. His technique was like a good interrogator's, mixing it up, keeping the victim a little off balance. It could appear clumsy or smooth, she supposed, depending on whether or not it worked. She might have been charmed, but she couldn't get her mind off Junior Spice. 'Is that your girlfriend over there?' she said, nodding towards the heady apparition in pink.

He smiled for the first time. 'That's my sister. Really. She's barely sixteen. Who do you think I am, Gary Glitter?'

'She does look a little young for you.'

'Yes, and also she's related.' He made a face.

She smiled back at him. Perhaps the wedding wasn't going to be as bad as she'd feared. At worst they were a long way from London, and provided he didn't do anything too repulsive between now and the departure of the bridal couple, like vomit on the wedding cake, she might put a notch on the bedpost tonight, let her hair down for once.

'So, Madeleine. What do you do?'

She hesitated. Always hated this question. 'I'm a security consultant,' she heard herself say.

'Sounds interesting,' he lied.

'Not really,' she said. 'Let's talk about you.'

They were seated at opposite ends of the marquee for the chicken and the speeches, and Fox was forced to make small talk to a dizzy twenty-two-year-old schoolgirl who sold advertising space at the radio station, and a sixty-year-old friend of Stephen's father who went into a long rant about the destruction of the green belt.

As soon as the formalities were over and the dancing started, he found her again and she allowed him to ply her with champagne through the rest of the evening.

So when Carrie and Stephen drove away in the limousine and she and Ash were left standing hand in hand among the drunk and cheering wedding crowd, she asked him if he would like to come back to her hotel for a nightcap. His Saab convertible was one of the boy toys she had seen in the church car park earlier that day. She realised as she got in the passenger seat that she had no idea what he did for a living. Nice car; she hoped he wasn't a drug dealer. She didn't want anything to spoil a great wedding.

Chapter Thirty-Six

Something about country pubs, the vague smell of rising damp, the lumpy beds, the heavy drapes on the windows, a view over the village square and a spreading horse chestnut tree. This one had all the essentials: a fake mahogany wardrobe, a plastic vase of flowers on the matching dresser, bedside lamps with fringes.

'Not the Savoy,' she said, 'but it's the best I could do.'

He shut the door and turned on one of the bedside lamps. She felt a tightness in her stomach and her chest. It was the first time she had done this since the Lambeth shooting. A long time between drinks, as they said. A very long time. She felt suddenly nervous, and so she just stood there, rubbing her arms as if she was cold, wondering what he would say when she took off her dress and he saw the scar from the bullet wound over her right breast. Would he hide his eyes and run from the room? Fetch a crucifix and henbane? Christ. She felt like Quasimodo, down from the tower.

Like wrestlers, she thought, circling, looking for the right hold. He looked as nervous as she was. The first time was never easy.

He kissed her, took his time over things, gentle. She kissed him back and they toppled on to the bed, felt it sag alarmingly.

'Does it creak?' he whispered.

'I've no idea.'

'You know what these hotels are like. The walls are like paper.'

She brushed away the cowlick, but it immediately fell back over his right eye. He kissed her again, cupping her face in his hands, a languorous kiss that seemed to go on for ever. She started to unbutton his shirt. A hairless chest, smooth and perfectly muscled, like a young athlete. So good to feel a man next to her again. Almost a year; she really wasn't the type of girl who went in for one-night stands.

He tried to unzip the dress, failed miserably, got the zipper caught in the bow at the back. 'Let me do it,' she whispered.

'Sorry,' he said. 'I was never any good at knots.'

She untied the bow, unzipped the dress, and slid it down from her shoulders and over her hips. It was like climbing out of a tent, for God's sake. She heard the heavy silk cascade on to the floor.

She started to pull at his shirt. He laughed; she was strangling him with his tie. He pulled it over his head, and as he did so, something made her put both her hands above her head on the pillow. He seemed to know what she was thinking. He looped the tie over her hands, pulled it tight and then knotted the other end around the brass headrail.

Her whole body seemed to flood with adrenalin, making her light-headed. Her heart started to race, it was hard to catch her breath, there was tingling in her hands and in her feet.

Lying back on the bed, helpless in her best lace underwear. No longer in control. She watched him, watching her; he ran a hand lightly along her body, wondered what he would do when he touched the scar. He seemed hardly to notice.

Was this what it was like for Kimberley Mason? she wondered. The act of surrender more powerful than touch itself, sex played in the mind. I have no power over what is about to happen, the apex of selfish love; I cannot give, I can only receive, my only choices between physical ecstasy and disappointment. The realisation of risk set off a rush through her body like the hit of some powerful drug.

She felt his fingers slide under the elastic of her pants, his hands cup her underneath, his lips at her breast. Helpless with a beautiful stranger. Sex doesn't get any better than this. Anonymous in some hotel room, her city reputation as ice queen intact.

She woke to a gentle rapping on the door, rushing back to the surface from a black and bottomless deep. She sat up, heart racing, wondering where she was. She remembered, suddenly, what had happened the night before, and she looked over at the pillow beside her and realised with dismay that he was gone.

There was a note propped against the lamp at the side of the bed.

Another knock on the door.

'Just a minute,' she called. She jumped out of bed. Big mistake. Her head was pounding and she felt suddenly nauseous and faint. Christ, hangover. She pulled a long T-shirt from her overnight case and slipped it on. It had belonged to Simon. It said LONDON MARATHON 1993 on the front and reached almost to her knees.

She drew the curtains. The light hurt her eyes. The sound of horses' hooves in the square, some Hooray Henries out hunting foxes or whatever they did in the country at this Godawful time on a Sunday morning.

She opened the door. It was room service. A young girl brought in a large tray and put it on the table in the middle of the room. Toast, orange juice, a pot of coffee, a plate covered with a silver lid.

'Cooked breakfast,' she said. 'Sausages, bacon, tomatoes, black pudding, two fried eggs.'

Fox felt her gorge start to rise. 'Thanks,' she said.

The girl slipped out again, shutting the door behind her.

She picked up the note by the bed. 'Dear Madeleine. Sorry I had to leave so early. I have to play Rugby this morning back in London. I never got your number. Please give me a call. Ash. P.S. Keep the tie till next time?'

There was an 0171 number and a drawing of a smily face. Last night started coming back to her. 'Are you out of your mind?' she said aloud. She looked over at the bed. His hand-painted silk tie was still wrapped around the brass rail at the head of the bed. My God. She had let him – encouraged him – to tie her hands. What was she thinking of? She hardly knew the man. He could have been a serial killer. He could have slashed her throat. He could have got her pregnant. What had got into her – apart, that is, from a couple of bottles of champagne?

She screwed up the note and tossed it in the bin, then she drank the coffee, got dressed and left, the fried breakfast congealing on the plate untouched. There were some things even a reckless single woman on the loose from London for the weekend just wouldn't touch, and black pudding was one of them.

Chapter Thirty-Seven

Worcester Park, Surrey

Ginny had remade herself in the past few weeks, had emerged from the dark world of her betrayal, angry, brittle and businesslike. Fox had never seen her sister like this before and did not quite know how to deal with her. Ginny went about the house plumping cushions, picking up the children's toys, tidying the kitchen, busy, busy, busy, in your face and burning up on her own fury.

'How was the wedding?'

Oh, you know, usual thing. Chanting monks, French champagne and a little rough trade to follow. 'Good.'

'Poor bitch,' Ginny said, throwing the toaster into a cupboard. 'She'll learn.'

'So. How are you?'

'Fine.'

'How are the kids . . . coping?'

'How are they coping?' Ginny echoed. 'Well, so far I haven't told them their father's a lying, cheating bastard. The books say it might damage them. So I'll let them find that out for themselves as they get older.'

'That wasn't what I meant.'

Ginny gathered the breakfast leftovers – a marmalade jar, some eggshells, toast crusts – in the wing of her right arm and swept them straight off the counter top into the rubbish bin. She put the bin in the cupboard under the sink and slammed it shut.

'The kids are fine. I'm fine. The weather's fine. Everything's fine. Maddy, you have to stop worrying about me.'

'Okay,' Fox said. 'Fine.'

And then Ginny burst into tears.

Ginny was angry with herself afterwards for breaking down in front of her little sister. She made some excuse about having to take the children to see their grandmother and ushered Fox out of the house.

'Don't write the marriage off yet,' Fox said to her as they stood by the car.

Ginny looked petulant, her eyes bright with tears.

'It's too much to throw away,' Fox persisted.

'Don't lecture me. Tell Ian your sob story. I didn't throw the marriage away. He did.'

'He still loves you, Ginny.'

'No, he doesn't,' she said, with deliberate clarity, as if she were explaining road rules to a small child. 'If he loved me, he wouldn't screw other women.'

'It was one mistake.'

'Two mistakes, if I have the facts right. Once in the coffee room when they were working late, once in the back of his car after a work dinner.'

'You two have so much going for you.'

'We did have. Past tense.' Ginny hugged her quickly, roughly. 'Thanks for coming round. Thanks for listening.'

And she marched back inside the house so the neighbours could not see her crying.

As Fox drove away she wondered why her sister's estrangement from her husband had affected her so deeply. She guessed it was because while there were Ian and Ginnies in the world, she still felt there might be a chance for her, that there was a road map to navigate by, a template for a normal life. Now they had split up, she was no longer sure.

Maddy Fox, she told herself, was always a little bit different, but there had always been a chance that she could be a little bit more the same. If Ian and Ginny couldn't make it though, what hope was there for her? She had idealised their marriage, told herself that if there really was a Happyville at the end of the Yellowbrick Road, then Ian and Ginny were living in it. While it survived it undermined her cynicism.

But there was no Happyville, it was a lie, and she was adrift in a desolate world, inhabited by Kimberley Masons and other lost souls without hope and without meaning, only their secret obsessions to guide them.

Chapter Thirty-Eight

Hampstead

They ate breakfast on the flagged patio. James Carlton had the *Observer* neatly folded into a rectangle beside his plate while he picked at his egg, his wife sipping her coffee as she flicked through the feature pages. Sparrows twittered and fussed in the marble birdbath set in the shade of the giant beech tree at the bottom of the garden. His wife's domain, the garden. Everything in ordered perfection, the rows of petunias like guardsmen in full fig below the stone retaining wall, the grass trimmed by the gardener she bossed around once a week, the square of lawn so perfect it could have been cut with scissors, nature ordered to the particular taste of an Englishwoman. A love seat, never used, sat under a sycamore, and there was even a little tree house for the squirrels, nuts placed inside every morning. Have to put in a spa for the rat-faced little bastards, Carlton thought. Can't have them getting jealous of the sparrows.

'How are the headaches?' she asked him suddenly.

'Headaches?'

They looked at each other, like strangers from different

countries. 'The headaches,' she repeated, as if speaking to a small child, and he remembered that the other day he might have said something about headaches to get her off the trail.

'Better,' he said, and looked away again.

Louise surprised him. He had always thought she would confront him if he gave her cause for suspicion, but instead she had colluded with him in his evasions. So far. As if she too felt that he had chosen the right course in lying to her. Like a child, she wanted to believe her own fictions as well as his. The truth in life was the same as in politics: a lie was not a lie if you were not caught in it. History was written by victors. It all depended on the way this turned out.

And so it was incumbent on him to make all this go away. If he could make it go away, she would forgive him.

'Have I been a good wife to you?'

'Good Lord. What a question.' He could feign outrage as well as any man. 'Of course. Hell made you ask that?'

A hollow laugh, as brittle as breaking glass. 'I've always thought I was a good wife. I'm so proud of you, you know. I have never wanted this public position for myself. I suppose I've been spoiled. All my life. But I have been a good wife to you, haven't I? The dinner parties. The charity balls. The constituency fundraising. I've been a help?'

'How can you possibly think otherwise?'

'It's just that, you know, Diana getting older, we are at that time of our lives, aren't we, when we could be most useful? Daddy always said you were a man who knew what he wanted, a man who was going places.'

Daddy thought so, did he? Daddy is not as smart as I thought he was. But then I've always been good at it, this game of bluff. Whole life founded on it. Only now I'm doing it to hide my carnal sins, not just the state of my finances.

'I know something is wrong, James. I don't know what it

is. I don't think I want to know. But I couldn't stand it if you were unfaithful to me.'

There it was, baldly said. It was as he had suspected.

He could think of no answer, so after a moment Louise returned her attention to the *Observer* colour supplement, while he watched a squirrel scampering across the neatly trimmed lawn. He had the mad desire to shoot the bloody thing, see fur and blood flying, just for the satisfaction of seeing some other poor bastard suffer like he was.

He was alone in this. To say he thought of nothing else would be a lie, because there was no rational thought any more. Just this constant nagging ache of guilt and fear that had developed a heartbeat of its own, a monster he had created for his own particular torment.

Area Major Incident Pool, Hendon Road

WPC Stacey was changing back into her civvies when Fox came out of the cubicle and went over to the washbasin to rinse her hands. Stacey was watching her in the mirror. She knew the look. Bit of rancour there, bit of resentment stirring.

'Have a good weekend?' Fox said.

'Yes, thanks, ma'am. How about you?'

'Went to a wedding in Gloucestershire.' And had some kinky sex with a total stranger. Wouldn't you love to hear about that? 'What about you?'

'Not much. Went to the pub with a few friends.'

Stacey finished buttoning her blouse while Fox put a brush through her shoulder-length hair.

'You heard about Chief Inspector Mills, ma'am?'

'What's he done now?'

'Broken up with his girlfriend. Heard he's been playing up again.'

'I didn't know that. How did you find out?'

'Everyone's a detective in this place, ma'am.'

'Everyone's a *gossip*.'

'I wouldn't mind people gossiping about me and DS Crawford.'

'I believe he already has a girlfriend.'

'So they reckon. Tell you what, he can slip his handcuffs in my bedside drawer any time. Not that there's much chance. I've heard he prefers blondes.' Oh, that was subtle. An innocent smile in the mirror and then she was gone.

Fox stared at her own reflection in the glass. Not bad, but you won't always look like this, Madeleine. You should go out and have a bit more fun, while you still can. If half the gossip they spread about you in the canteen were true, life would be a lot more interesting.

She thought about Ash. She wished she hadn't thrown away his number now. Impetuous. Perhaps she could ring Stephen and Carrie when they came back from their honeymoon. Or maybe not. Her team would be back on roster soon, sixteen hour days seven days a week. There just wasn't time for men.

Chapter Thirty-Nine

Camden Town

There were places in the Camden markets where Fox could imagine she was in a Middle Eastern souk or an oriental bazaar: the old tunnels where shire horses had dragged coal from the Regency Canal to the warehouses were now a labyrinth of incense, tandoori, and imported African and Asian furniture, a heady mix of races and accents. Every stall, every shop, blared its own brand of music: New Age, hard rock, reggae, Arab pop.

Camden had become the last refuge for London's punks. She watched two teenagers come out of the cyberstore, holding hands. They were dressed in black, their nose, ears and lips pierced with rings, hair teased into shades of purple and green, the girl's face transformed into a mask with white foundation. There were chains on the young man's jacket and the girl's torn jeans. Another bondage fantasy.

She wandered through the cobbled market by the canal entrance. It was packed with summer tourists looking for souvenirs and antiques and cheap jewellery. She bumped someone's shoulder, turned to apologise and found herself staring up into the face of her most recent lover.

'Ash,' she said.

He grinned. 'Maddy,' he said. 'Great to see you.'

'What are you doing here?' It came out a little harsh, as if she thought he'd been following her.

'I *live* in Camden. What about you?'

She shook her head. 'Bayswater. Came up on the Tube.'

They stared at each other. He was dressed down, old jeans and an open-necked shirt, hadn't shaved, still looked all right. 'You never returned my calls,' he said.

There had been three or four messages on her answerphone at home, asking her to call. She had been meaning to, but her team was about to go back on rotation.

'Love 'em and leave 'em,' he said. 'Is that it?'

He had a disarming smile, she couldn't help but smile back. 'I was worried I might have got you pregnant,' she said to him. 'How did you get my home number?'

'Stephen and Carrie,' he said. 'Stephen said I was wasting my time.'

'Really.'

'He thinks you're a bit of an ice queen.'

'It's nice of him to say so.' Bastard.

'Look, the wedding. I'm sorry I left so early. I ordered you breakfast before I went. Was that all right?'

'I would have been more charmed if you'd paid for it.'

'You're right. I owe you one. How about lunch?'

'When?'

'Now. I know a place.'

'Okay,' she said. 'Why not?'

It was a Thai restaurant, dark teak furniture, peacock chairs, wind chimes. Jim Thompson's house in Bangkok dismantled and transported to NW1. She almost expected to see opium addicts passed out in the corridor from the kitchen. The authenticity was spoiled by Julio Iglesias warbling on the sound system, and the waiters, who looked more Levantine than Asian.

'So how's the security business?' he said.

Christ. She couldn't remember what she'd told him now. This was the problem her customers faced every day: it wasn't keeping a straight face through a lie that was the hard part, it was keeping track of your untruths. Fabrications had the habit of multiplying out of control, like rabbits. 'Fine,' she said, trying to remain vague. 'There's a lot of business around here.'

'I guess there is. I should get you to check my place. There's been a lot of break-ins round our way lately.'

Shit. Tell him you're a cop and get it over with.

'What do you do?' she said, changing the subject instead.

He shrugged, looked suddenly evasive. 'What do you think I do?'

Strange answer. 'I've no idea.' She thought about the flash car, the smooth clothes. 'Some sort of drug dealer,' she said with a smile.

He stared at the tablecloth. Their lemongrass soup arrived. There was a long silence.

'Tell me you're not,' she said.

'Why, do you have some sort of problem with recreational cocaine?'

There was a moment there when she gave herself away, but he couldn't keep it up. He started to laugh.

'You bastard,' she said.

'Look, it's no big deal. I've been out with cops before on dates.' Another smile. 'The first female one, that's all.'

'This is not funny. How did you know?'

'Carrie told me. I was quizzing her about you.'

'Why?'

'I was interested. More interested than you, I suppose.'

Which was basically how it was. She had had her fun, without complications, then she had gone back to London, put on her other face, and gone back to her marriage, her faithful but demanding spouse called Hendon Road Number Two AMIP.

'By the way, I'm a futures trader.'

'At least it's legal.'

'Sort of.' He sipped his lemongrass soup. 'Is there a bloke you're hiding somewhere? Is that why you didn't return my calls?'

'No, there's no man. I work long hours. I have trouble making relationships work. I was doing you a favour.'

'Do me another one. Have dinner with me tonight.'

'We haven't finished lunch yet.' She leaned back in the wicker chair and wiped at her mouth with the heavy linen napkin. 'We go back on rotation tomorrow. If we get a murder I don't have time for anything but work or sleep for a couple of weeks.'

'So you arrange your love life around corpses?'

'I don't have a love life.'

'I got here just in time.' The boyish grin again.

'It's not quite that simple.'

'I knew you weren't a security consultant,' he said, 'the moment I saw you.'

'What did you think I was?'

'Honest?'

'Honest.' She waited for it.

'I thought you were a kindergarten teacher.'

'I do not look like a kindergarten teacher,' she snapped, but he was laughing again.

'Yes, you do. You look kind of simmering and vulnerable.'

Baiting her. She would not rise to it.

'I didn't mean it,' he said, seeing her expression. 'You looked mean and hard and exotically beautiful. Is that better?'

'Somehow, no.'

'So tell me about your job,' he said.

And so she told him, straight from the hip. Most of it, she said, was tedious, painstaking work; there were no car chases, no gun fights, no dénouements, few surprises. She spent most of her time in interview rooms or in people's homes, talking, prying. Her job, she said, was simply to gather evidence, as part of a much bigger team, in an orderly and lawful manner, so that the Crown Prosecution Service might get a conviction in nine to twelve months' time in a court of law. Never mind that she thought the sentencing procedures were feeble and sometimes scandalous. She did her job well.

'And you love it.'

'Yes, I do. It's my life.'

'I'd still like you to have dinner with me tonight,' he said. 'Unless the Yardies give you a better offer.'

She thought about it. Tomorrow was Monday. Tonight was perhaps her last night of freedom before the bodies started to drop again. She shrugged, heard herself say, 'Okay.'

Forty

Broadridge Estate, Tottenham

The man had been shot in the face.

He lay on his back in the hallway of his ground-floor flat, crumpled like a rag doll. Must have been dead before he hit the floor, Fox decided. There was a Glock automatic pistol fitted with a home-made silencer in his right hand and blood absolutely everywhere. It looked like someone had massacred a whole family in here.

'The occupant of the flat goes by the name of Robert Hatton,' TJ said, at her elbow.

'Is this him?'

'Hard to tell, but evidently Hatton only has two nostrils. This bloke's got three.'

Too early in the morning for TJ' suspect humour. She looked at her watch. Two a.m. when the duty officer had called her, almost three now. She put another peppermint in her mouth to disguise the taint of the red wine from the night before. She thought about Ash, still asleep in her warm bed.

She took a look around. Whoever lived in the flat was

probably not a regular churchgoer. *Soldier of Fortune* magazines were strewn about the living room, a punchbag was suspended from the ceiling of the bedroom, and there were Japanese ceremonial swords and fighting sticks displayed around the walls. The bookshelves were stacked with books on martial arts and studies of the Vietnam War and the Gulf conflict.

'North London ninja,' TJ said.

'Look at this.' Fox nodded towards the video cabinet. *The Deer Hunter*, as well as hardcore under-the-shelf porn, bondage and torture.

TJ bent down for a closer look. 'Not one Teletubbies video. A real hard case.'

One of the Forensics team called to her from the kitchen. He pointed to the window. 'There's your point of entry,' he said.

A professional job. A large piece of putty had been placed on the window and a square cut around it with a glass-cutter. The glass had then been removed and the assailant had been able to open the window from the inside.

The question remained, was the person responsible for the break-in now lying on the floor of the bedroom? Or was he the occupant?

Fox rolled the body. The dead man was wearing a black woollen jumper and jeans. There was no ID, but there was a set of car keys in his pocket. 'The intruder,' TJ said.

'Unless he'd just got home and his visitor was already here waiting for him,' she said.

TJ frowned, conceding the point.

There was at least little doubt about the time of death. The gunshot that killed him had been heard by everyone in the block.

Fox had seen enough. A local uniform stood at the door to the flat, logging everyone in and out. Two others were taking statements from the neighbours, who were now gathered in the corridor, watching the proceedings with unabashed interest. An elderly man in a dressing gown sipped tea from a bone china teacup, staring at everything that was going on as if it were late-night television. In the doorway of the flat opposite two younger men watched: a Jamaican with dreadlocks and oversized white shorts, and a tall, lean white youth wearing nothing but a pair of white underpants and a vacant expression.

'The weirdo finally get popped?' the skinny white boy said.

'Weirdo?' she said.

'Him think himself something special, man,' the Jamaican said, 'real hard. Me park me car in him space one time and him threaten to shoot me.'

'Only a matter of time before someone did for him,' his friend said. 'Dickhead.'

'It wasn't Mr Hatton who was shot,' the old man in the dressing gown said brightly.

Fox turned around. 'You are . . .?'

He held out a hand. 'Marwick's the name. Brian Marwick. Police officer once myself. Constable at Fulham and West End. Only stood it for three years, until I got married. Wife didn't like the hours.'

'You believe the dead man is not Mr Hatton?' she said, cutting him off before he could tell her his life story.

'No doubt about it. I saw him leave after all the shooting.'

'You're sure?'

'Quite sure. My wife and I both heard the gunshot, it woke us up, in fact. I came out to see what was going on. That's when I saw him, right there where that policeman's standing now. He took off pretty smartish. Don't blame him, I suppose. Not if he'd just murdered someone.'

Remarkable, Fox thought. There are still some people in

the world who just will not be intimidated. 'Perhaps we can go inside and you can tell me about it,' she said.

Unlike the boot camp next door, Marwick and his elderly wife lived in fussy, cluttered disarray. There were ornaments everywhere, a glass cabinet full of toby jugs and crystal animals, even, touchingly, Diana and Charles souvenir plates on the wall. Marwick's wife went into the kitchen and produced a pot of tea and a packet of Arrowroot biscuits arrayed on a plate. How to host a murder party.

'What time did you hear the shots?' Fox asked Brian Marwick.

'One forty-seven,' Marwick told her. 'I know because we have a digital clock beside the bed with a red display.'

'How many shots did you hear?'

'Two. Gave us quite a turn. It sounded like it was right in the bedroom. My wife's still shaking.' Marwick indicated his wife, who held out her hand to show Fox that she was, indeed, vibrating like a tuning fork.

'And what did you do after you heard the shots?'

Marwick smiled fondly at his wife. 'I said, "Someone's shot that Mr Hatton, Rita." Didn't I, dear?'

Mrs Marwick smiled and nodded, as if her husband waking up in the night to pass comment on a murder was just one more of the endearing traits she had grown accustomed to through their years of marriage.

'And then?'

'I put on my dressing gown and went outside to have a look.'

'What did you see?'

'Nothing at first. It was dark, of course. Then I heard someone moving around inside Mr Hatton's flat and I thought I'd better call the police. Which is what I did. Nine nine nine. First time I've ever had to do that.' He looked delighted with the happy circumstances that led to him fulfilling this humble ambition. 'Then when I came outside again, I saw him.'

'Mr Hatton?'

'He came out of the flat, carrying a canvas holdall. He looked like he was in a hurry.'

'You're quite sure it was Mr Hatton?'

'I've lived next to him for six months. There's no mistaking him.'

'Did he say anything to you?'

'I asked him if everything was all right.' He leaned forward and lowered his voice. 'He told me to get fucked, if you'll pardon my language. His exact words. But he was like that. I never took it personally.'

So, the dead man in the flat next door was not Robert Hatton. That made their job easier. They now had the name of their suspect, and his address. The next step was to identify the victim.

Not a whodunnit, Fox, as her old boss Marenko used to say, but a whowasit.

Chapter Forty-One

Area Major Incident Pool, Hendon Road

There were six squads in the AMIP, A to F, on a six-week rotation. Any murder in the Number Two Area during the rotation belonged to whichever team happened to be up. On average there was a murder every other day in London, shared between the five policing areas. The workload then was largely a matter of luck, though the increased use of firearms by the Yardies had put them all under more pressure. Fox had worked one rotation when they caught four murders in twenty-five minutes.

But this one looked like a dunker, and the atmosphere in the Incident Room was upbeat. The body in the morgue had been cold less than eight hours, and already they knew the name of their suspect, his address, and the time he had committed the murder. Cause of death was unequivocal. Unlike Kimberley Mason, there would not be hours of frustrating legwork. Once they had the owner of the Tottenham flat in custodial care, they could put this one to bed as soon as the paperwork was finished.

They had now identified the victim.

'His car was parked two streets away,' Rankin said at that morning's briefing, 'it had custom plates – HARD1.'

'We're going to get new plates for him,' TJ said. 'STIFF1.' That got a laugh around the Incident Room. They were all in a buoyant mood.

'We got inside using the car keys we found on the victim's body,' TJ went on. 'The registration papers were in the glove box. The car was licensed to a Dennis Thorpe, with an address in Islington. He's got previous.' TJ checked his notes. 'Two counts of GBH, one of aggravated assault. He's well known to the Islington CID as a hard man and a fixer. Usual MO, moving squatters out of empty rentals, bad debts, repossessing motors, that sort of thing. He was also prime suspect in the murder of a National Front member who pissed off one of the Reillys.'

'Have you searched his flat?' someone asked.

Mills answered for them. 'The Tottenham plod have got the place sealed off and Forensics are going through it now.'

Mills nodded to Fox who ran the videotape of the murder scene, HARD1 lying on the carpet in the hallway of the Broadridge Estate flat, staring up at the ceiling, his face resembling raw hamburger. Fox pointed out the SAS mementoes, the martial arts books and videotapes on the bookshelves, the weaponry displayed on the walls.

'We're still waiting on Forensics, but we have initial reports from Ballistics and Pathology,' she told them. 'There was a shell casing under the bed. It looks like our victim was shot with an automatic weapon, probably nine millimetre.' She referred to the stapled typewritten sheets on her lap. 'Professor Pakula found gunshot residue on the deceased's right hand, indicating that he had discharged his own weapon shortly before expiring. Cause of death was lead poisoning from a .38 calibre bullet ingested at the maxilla, on an upward trajectory, before lodging in the brain.' A few chuckles around the room. Dennis Thorpe's previous made it unlikely anyone here would die of a broken heart at his passing. 'The bullet was in reasonably good shape and Ballistics say that it was a full jacket manufactured by Winchester and probably fired from a Glock Model 19 automatic weapon.'

'What about the gun Thorpe was holding?' Honeywell asked.

'Smith and Wesson .38. There was a bullethole in the wall, it made a neat hole in the plaster, and Forensics string-lined the trajectory to the point where Thorpe was lying. Just where the other shooter was standing when he fired his own weapon is problematic. Pakula thinks the bullet entered his skull at an angle of about thirty degrees, indicating he may well have been crouching in the doorway to the bedroom. Neighbours reported hearing two gunshots, so we believe what happened was that Thorpe fired first, his bullet went wide of the mark, and this bloke nailed him with one shot, first time.' She paused to let that sink in.

'Do we know anything about this bloke?' Honeywell asked.

'Ex SAS,' Fox said. She nodded towards Mills. 'The guvnor's got the details on him.'

'Anything else?' Mills asked.

'Just point of entry,' Fox said. She ran the tape forward to the close ups of the neatly excised windowpane in the kitchen. 'Dennis Thorpe knew what he was about,' she said.

'If he knew what he was about,' TJ said, 'he wouldn't have tried to top an SAS marksman on his own turf.'

'What about all those knives and numchukkas on the walls?' someone said.

Fox nodded. 'It looks like he's something of a collector.'

'Or a complete nutter,' TJ said.

Fox nodded to Mills, who took over the briefing. He referred to the notes on his lap. 'The man we are looking for goes by the name of Robert Philip Hatton. He has previous: a juvenile conviction for breaking and entering dating back to 1979. Nothing since. We ran a check with the Army who confirm that he enlisted with them in 1980, served as a private in the Royal Guards. He earned a DCM in the Falklands War, transferred to the SAS at his second attempt in 1984. Left the SAS shortly after the Gulf War, we don't know what he's been doing since.' He held up a photofit. 'We've interviewed his neighbours, and this is what he looks like. Long hair, beard, tattoos on both forearms. Most of them described him as eccentric, aggressive in his manner whenever he was spoken to, but quiet in his living habits, didn't play loud music, have parties, that sort of thing. Not that they were comfortable having him around. For instance, it seems he wore military gear, fatigues or camouflage uniforms, just to go shopping.'

'Only camouflage you need over there is dreadlocks and a beanie,' TJ said.

'It's pretty clear what happened,' Mills went on. 'Dennis Thorpe broke into this Bob Hatton's flat armed with a revolver. Hatton heard him, and was waiting for him. Thorpe got off one shot, which missed the target, either just before, or at the instant of, death. He received a fatal wound to the head, which killed him instantly. Hatton then fled the scene rather than face the obvious and embarrassing questions that would follow. There is a warrant now pending for his arrest and we have issued an alert to Customs and Immigration to all air and seaports. Our job from here is to track down family, friends, anyone who might help him go to ground.' He pointed to TJ. 'I want you to drive up to SAS headquarters in Hereford, TJ, ask them to pull this nutter's file. Take Nick with you. Madeleine, you and me are going to check out this Dennis Thorpe.'

'Do we know what this was all about?' Nick asked.

'Not at this stage. Our fugitive is the only one who can tell us that for sure. So let's get to work, people. Get this one tidied away quickly and make your guv'nor look good.'

Hampstead

James Carlton adjusted the climate control in his BMW, tuned the radio to a classical station, a movement from Rachmaninov. The traffic on Haverstock Hill was heavy. He looked at his watch. He didn't want to be late for this morning's sitting. They were debating the new foxhunting legislation. The Whip had made it clear he wanted him there for the vote.

His mobile rang and he snatched it from the cradle. 'Carlton.'

'You bastard. You tried to do me in, didn't you?'

A red Ford Escort had stopped at the lights directly in front of him. Carlton was slow to react, and the brakes squealed as he fishtailed to a halt, narrowly avoiding ramming the Escort's boot. He was jerked forward in his seatbelt.

'Now it's personal,' the voice said. 'Your arse is mine.'

The line went dead. Carlton sat there, the receiver in his hand, staring ahead. The number 27 to Hampstead went through the lights, a banner for a new West End production emblazoned on the side. A man in a trenchcoat and a Homburg. J. B. Priestley. *An Inspector Calls*.

Christ.

The lights changed back to green but he did not move. The traffic banked behind him erupted into a cacophony of horns.

Chapter Forty-Two

Mills sat in the passenger seat, eyes closed, his head lolling against the headrest. He looked awful. That morning's shave had been less than perfect and there were dark shadows under his eyes. The smell of alcohol mingled with the expensive glow of his aftershave. His clothes, however, were perfect.

'You all right, guv?' Fox asked.

'Girlfriend kicked me out. Things have been a little rough lately. I suppose you heard?'

'What did you do?'

'It's a long story, Madeleine. It involves some friends of mine, a going-away party and a professional stripper.'

'That doesn't sound so bad.'

'That's what I said.'

He brooded, staring out of the window.

'So what happened?'

'Old mate of mine, he's an engineer, just got a contract in Saudi, five years. So we threw him a bit of a party. Got together with a few mates, paid for a stripper, hired a room in the Chiswick Arms, pretty bloody harmless if you ask me.'

She waited. 'And?'

'Well, we were all on the bevvy. One thing led to another. Sally got really pissed off when she found out about it.'

Fox slowed at a stop light. 'Because of the stripper?'

He shook his head. 'There was, you know . . . a bit of oral sex, thrown in. Sort of.'

Fox stared at him. Face of a film star, morals of a goat, was how Honeywell described him. But that was just jealousy. 'You had oral sex with the stripper?'

'It was only a bit of fun. We all slipped her a bit extra. A tip, I suppose. Sally did her block.'

'And that confuses you?'

He shrugged. 'Yeah. A bit.'

The lights changed to green. The taxicab behind them slammed on his horn and shouted something at her out of his window. Mills turned in his seat and gave him the finger. Fox slipped the car back into gear.

'It's not like it was an affair. She was a stripper, for Christ's sake. I'll probably never ever see the bloody woman again, unless I get transferred to Vice. Anyway, a blow job isn't sex, is it?' He waited for her to concur. 'Is it?' he repeated.

'What is it?'

'It's a bit of fun. Christ, I'll never understand women.'

'No, I guess you won't.' Fox drove for a while. 'So Sally kicked you out.'

'Yelling, clothes in the street, the full monty. Got dirt on my buttondowns, which really hurt. She knew that.'

'Where are you staying?'

'With my daughter, she's got a flat in Swiss Cottage. Dossed down there last night, on the sofa. Christ, it was like sleeping on a sack of potatoes.'

'How old is she?'

'Rachel? Twenty-five. She's my eldest. From the first marriage. In fact, she was the reason I got married. Great kid.'

'Twenty-five,' Fox said. 'How old was the stripper?'

'I know, I know. The point has been made many times, don't worry.'

'But do you get it? The point?' she added, when he still looked addled.

'I get it. I just don't care for the implication that because I'm in my forties I'm sexually neutered.'

'What does your daughter think, guv?'

'Rachel?' He shrugged. 'She knows what I'm like.'

'Do you get on?'

'We get on fine. As long as she doesn't marry a bloke like me, she can't go wrong.' He checked his appearance in the wing mirror. 'I don't suppose it was just the stripper.'

Fox raised an eyebrow. 'You didn't rape the DJ as well?'

He laughed, as if that might have been a possibility. 'I'm not an easy bloke to get along with, I suppose. I work long hours, I like a long chain. And Sally wants kids. Christ, I've got five. I don't need any more.' He shook his head. 'I never picked her for the broody type. I mean, why does a woman dress like that when she wants something different?'

'I don't know. How does she dress?'

'Well, not like someone who wants kids and a home life.'

'Can't help you there, guv,' Fox said. 'I've never wanted kids and a home life.' They looked at each other, and it occurred to her, as perhaps it occurred to him in that instant: we're a match made in heaven. He doesn't want kids or commitment and apparently neither do I. He's in love with the Job, just like me. She saw the future and the future was Greg Mills. It frightened her.

They drove for a while in silence. 'Do you know why men give their penises pet names?' she asked him.

'No. Why?'

'Because they don't want a total stranger making all their important decisions for them.'

He laughed at that. His one redeeming feature. At least he could laugh at himself.

Camden Town

Camden High Street sweltered under an August sun of tropical intensity. Fox kerb-crawled along a line of shops selling leather coats and Doc Martens, past the styrofoam effigy of Elvis, the green styrofoam bomber mounted on the wall above the Army and Navy store. The usual passing parade of winos from the Camden doss house, Jamaicans, crazies, punks and wide boys. And the occasional nationally recognised playwright.

The Camden Health Gym was in a side street two roads back from the markets. It followed a conventional design, an all-glass façade and full-length mirrors mounted around the internal walls so the clientèle could watch themselves as they worked out. Modern temples to narcissism, someone had called them.

The customers that morning were exclusively male. Just after ten but the place was buzzing, and seven or eight burly tattooed men worked on the high tech Swedish equipment. The acres of glass reflected infinitesimal tunnels of sweat, bulging veins and bad haircuts.

As they entered, Fox felt the evil eye.

'I love the smell of steroids in the morning,' Mills murmured.

'Don't these people have jobs?'

'Doormen, nightclub bouncers,' he said.

A tall fair-haired man came out from an office at the back

of the gym. He wore a muscle shirt and Nike shorts and joggers with treads the size of tractor tyres. He put a smile in place, crooked with both fear and suspicion.

'Can I help you?' he said.

Fox showed him her ID. 'DI Madeleine Fox. This is DCI Greg Mills.'

She waited, giving him an opportunity to speak, wondering if he would incriminate himself straight off, blurt something inappropriate or damning. This one looked genuinely confused.

'Is something wrong?'

'Your name?'

'Dave McCarthy. I'm the manager here. What is this about?'

'This gym is owned by a Dennis Thorpe, is that correct?'

'That's right.' He puffed out his cheeks. 'What's he done now?'

'He hasn't done anything, Mr McCarthy. He's dead.'

'Shit,' McCarthy said. 'Fuck. Shit.'

'That's pretty eloquent,' Mills said. 'Maybe you should read the eulogy at the funeral.'

McCarthy frowned. He looked irritated rather than distressed. 'Just when I had this place making a fuckin' profit.'

'I can see you're upset,' Fox said, deadpan, 'so shall we go into your office?'

Office; it was a cubicle really. A single laminated veneer shelf served as a desk, a one-way mirror allowed McCarthy to keep an eye on the gym as he worked. A planner was tacked to the wall next to a Nautilus calendar. It was like squeezing into a Tube carriage during the rush hour.

McCarthy sat down and Fox and Mills stood shoulder to shoulder, leaning against the wall. Through the glass Fox watched a bulging Neanderthal with pectorals the size of sofa cushions doing bench presses. The man was staring at his own reflection, brutality and abundant body hair all bound up in one tight little package. He couldn't take his eyes off himself. Pure lust, for Christ's sake.

'So how did it happen?' McCarthy asked.

'He was shot.'

McCarthy shrugged, and did not look particularly surprised, which was significant. 'Shot. Fuck. Jesus.' He scratched his head, caught their stares. 'Look, I knew about his reputation, all right? But he just employed me to run this place. I didn't get mixed up in any of that other stuff.'

'What other stuff?' Fox asked him.

'A lot of his iffy mates use this place. I know he uses it for recruiting people.'

'Recruiting people?'

'He's a standover merchant, ain't he? Everybody knows that. He has a security firm on the side as well. Doormen, nightclub bouncers. You're cops. You must know all about him.'

'We have a reasonable idea,' Mills said.

'Fuck it. This means I'm out of work, doesn't it?'

'Most likely,' Mills said, without sympathy.

'We'd like to have a look at your membership records,' Fox said.

'For suspects?' McCarthy said, with a tone of derision.

'Do you know of anyone who might have wanted him dead?' Fox said, turning the question around.

'Do me a favour,' McCarthy said. 'Half of bleedin' London, if you believe the stories. Look, like I said, I just worked for the geezer. I made it me business to know as little as possible about the rest of it. He scared the shit out of me, to be honest.'

'Did you ever hear him mention someone called Robert Hatton?' Fox asked him.

McCarthy shook his head. 'Is that the bloke who topped him?'

'Will you check your records please?'

McCarthy punched some keys on his computer, pulled up a list of names. Hatton's wasn't among them. 'Where did he get shot?' McCarthy asked.

'In the head,' Mills said.

McCarthy looked up at Mills who smiled back at him. 'I mean, where was he when he was shot?'

'He entered someone else's residence without invitation,' Fox said, and then, changing tack. 'Did you know he owned a firearm?'

'I would have been more surprised if he hadn't. But he never flashed it around here.'

'When was the last time you saw him?'

'Last Thursday. He came in once or twice a week to check the books, meet some people. Like I said, he got a lot of recruits from here.'

A goldmine, Fox thought. The Islington CID will appreciate the results of a search and seizure on the property, even if didn't further their own murder investigation. 'I'm afraid we'll have to impound the computer,' she said.

'You think the computer did it?' McCarthy said. Now it was his turn to take the piss.

'We have a search and seizure warrant,' Fox said, handing him the target copy. 'Be nice or we'll take your coffee cup as well.'

'Take what you like,' McCarthy said, getting to his feet. 'As soon as you're done, I'm off down the dole office, by the looks. Fuck. *Fuck.*'

Chapter Forty-Three

Hampstead Heath

Another sticky-hot day, a few drops of rain, fat and heavy, falling spasmodically from a grey sky, low over the Heath as if it were roofed in. A jetliner roared over Parliament Hill, the painted steel skin visible for just a moment before it disappeared into the overcast.

Rubbish spewed from the council bins; a jogger, overweight and over fifty, looking like a candidate for the cardiac ward, gasped past them along the footpath. Below them, two lovers were entwined on a bench. In the far distance, between the trees, a vista of cranes and glass towers, the Telecom Tower rising over the Tottenham Court Road, the grey dome of St Paul's among the jumble of high rise.

He and Diana sat down on one of the benches. '*In loving memory of Martin A. Tomlin.*'

Hard to know where to start, really. Never has been easy, explaining myself, especially to the people I love, who love me. Not been that many of them, when you think about it. Perhaps that's why.

'You know your mother and I are having some problems,' he said.

Diana bit her lip.

'I'm sure we'll work them out,' he added, quickly. Now what made him say that? Hadn't brought her here to reassure her.

'Whatever happens . . .'

Whatever happens, you know I love you, don't you?

' . . whatever happens, I'm sure everything will work out for the best in the end.'

Diana didn't say anything. He wondered if it would rain. Hadn't thought to bring an umbrella. A little dog yapped and chased a stick. People shouldn't be allowed to have dogs that weren't at least twice the size of your average cat, he thought. Up to me, I'd exterminate the bloody lot of them.

'Are you going to get a divorce?' Diana said, at last.

'I hope not,' he heard himself say.

This wasn't going the way he had planned at all. He had always been so clumsy talking to his daughter. He loved her in an oafish, helpless way, all fingers and thumbs with his feelings. Do anything for her. Absolutely. But always feel like I have this image to live up to. Can never get down there to her level. Be like Nelson getting down off his pedestal to shake hands with the tourists in Trafalgar Square.

How am I going to do this?

'I don't want you to worry,' he said, hoping she would say something, anything. Give him a cue.

'Okay,' she murmured, leaving him nowhere obvious to go.

This ache in his chest. Took himself off to his doctor a couple of weeks ago, thorough medical, thought it might be the old ticker. Clean bill of health. Just stress, the medicos told him. Oh, just stress, he had said. Christ, is that all.

He wondered what Louise and Diana would think if they knew about him, that he was just clay like everyone else.

Worse than clay. Much worse. Have to protect Diana from knowing about this.

And Louise? Well, have to protect *myself* there.

They sat there in silence for a while. 'How are things at school?' he said, suddenly.

'Fine.'

No good. We've never been able to talk, not since she grew out of white socks, anyway. Women still a mystery to me, all of them. I've provided for her. Always good at patting her on the head and telling her to run along and play. But now she's joined the other side, my only friend in the enemy camp, as it were. No idea what to say any more.

'I'm sure everything's going to be all right.'

Diana nodded, kept her eyes fixed on some point in the near distance, the running track down at Gospel Oak. I wonder what the hell she's thinking.

'It's *good* we had this chance to talk,' he said. 'Clear the air.'

He stood up and they started to walk slowly back across the Heath in the direction of Hampstead.

Bayswater, W2

Fox fumbled with the key in the lock. Too much wine with dinner again.

She switched on one of the table lamps, and went into the kitchen to make coffee. Ash stood in the living room, his hands in his pockets, making a casual inspection. She saw her flat through his eyes, cramped, untidy, perhaps even drab. I should put more effort into my living arrangements, she thought. Get Ginny over to give me some ideas. Ginny's good at that sort of thing.

She watched from the kitchen as he sat down on the lumpy

brown sofa. She had bought it in a secondhand shop when she left home twelve years before. She could afford better. Just never had much time for shopping. That day at Camden market had been the first time in months she had ventured out with her credit card. And look what I brought back, she thought, glancing at her new boyfriend.

Hard to know where this was going. She had gone looking for a one-night stand, a man who wanted casual sex and no commitment. Christ, a girl didn't have to look very hard for that. Yet Madeleine Fox had even somehow stuffed that up, found herself a man who seemed genuinely interested in her, even though she was a cop, even though she worked horrendous hours. Worse, he seemed like a nice guy, which would make this relationship all the harder to break, when it came to it.

When she had left Hendon Road that evening, after another sixteen-hour day, he was just leaving his office in the Barbican. Working the same ungodly hours, they had been happy to meet for a drink and a late night Chinese supper in a restaurant near her flat. Gone eleven now and she had to be up at six in the morning, she should be catching up on her sleep. Instead, here she was, canoodling, as her father used to call it.

'Are you allowed to tell me what you're working on?' he asked her.

She came out of the kitchen, leaned on the door jamb. 'A shooting.'

'The one in Tottenham? I read about in the papers. Christ, you have an exciting life.'

'It's not really exciting. Not once you've done it for a while.'

'Sure.'

'What about you? You don't have an exciting life?'

'I drop a million, I make a million, it's just numbers on a screen. It's not life or death. You do many shootings?'

'With the Yardies around, there's a few more these days.'

'Is that how you got the scar?'

She had wondered when he would ask her about that. She went back into the kitchen, started making the coffee. Give herself time to frame an answer. 'It's horrible, isn't it?'

He followed her into the kitchen. 'Yeah, I screamed and ran out of the bedroom, remember?'

'You were disappointed.'

'No, I was intrigued. You're a beautiful woman, Maddy. One small imperfection just makes you more interesting, not less. Besides, being disappointed has nothing to do with it. It's not like giving out presents at Christmas. You don't make love to a body, you make love to the woman inside it.'

She caught her breath. 'Please. Don't say things you don't mean.'

'I mean it.'

'No, you don't. Men like you don't exist.' It was said off the cuff, a throwaway line, but she looked up and found him staring at her, and there was an expression on his face she had never seen before.

'What happened, Maddy?'

To hell with the coffee. She leaned back against the kitchen bench, folded her arms. 'I made a mistake,' she said, her voice flat. 'Tried to do a hard stop, which is not my job, and I tried to do it without back up. I got shot. I arrested twice: once in the ambulance and once in the operating theatre at St Thomas'. When I survived, my bosses didn't know whether to throw me out of the force or give me an award. They gave me a bravery medal. I keep the medal in the drawer, but this . . . ' she touched the place above her right breast where the bullet had entered . . . 'this goes with me everywhere. I'm touched you find it so appealing. I look in the mirror and I see Quasimodo.'

'You're a fraud,' he said.

'What?'

'Take that look off your face. You're not sorry about what you did, or about the scar. You'd do exactly the same thing again. It's plain as day.'

She turned away, spooning coffee into a cup, so he couldn't see her smile. He was right. She was like that bloke, their witness in the Kimberley Mason killing, what was his name? Stone. Contrition was just a game. Yes, she'd done something she shouldn't. But she was still alive, and boy, had she shown those bastards what a real cop could do.

She handed him his coffee. He poured it down the sink. 'Coffee's bad for you,' he said and put his hands on her hips, pulled her towards him and kissed her.

Like being a teenager again, when sex was discovered for the first time, like she had found a secret no one else had ever known. She wondered how she had kept her body numb for so long. Ash had made her want him. He was complicating her plans, such as they were. Trampling into her neat and ordered life uninvited.

He lay naked on the bed. She stripped off her clothes and lay down next to him, but as he reached out to hold her, she pulled away. 'Wait a minute,' she whispered. 'I've got a surprise for you.'

She got up and padded naked across the bedroom. She came back with a set of handcuffs.

'You still haven't given me back my tie,' he said.

'That's for me,' she whispered. 'These are for you. It's your turn.'

She turned off the bedside lamp. The locks clicked softly into place.

Chapter Forty-Four

The team met in the Incident Room at nine o'clock the next morning to discuss progress on the case and share notes. TJ and Nick had just got back from SAS headquarters in Hereford. They had a captive audience as they regaled the others with their adventures. Anyone would have thought they had just come back from an undercover operation in Colombia, Fox decided.

'It's unbelievable,' TJ was saying. 'It'd be easier to break into Buck Palace. They check under your car with mirrors, the works. I thought they were going to strip search us.'

'You would have enjoyed that,' Rankin said and the others laughed.

Nick looked up and saw Fox. 'How did you go at the gym?' he asked her.

'Two circuits and bench pressed three hundred pounds. The usual.'

'All those oiled muscled bodies turn you on, ma'am?' TJ said, never one to miss a cue.

'Testosterone doesn't really do it for me,' she said. 'I prefer brain to brawn. Either way, you get zip out of two.'

Mills walked into the room. 'Okay, let's get to work,' he said, throwing a briefcase on to one of the desks in the middle of the room. 'TJ has no doubt told you about his little adventure yesterday in Hereford. It seems all the stories we hear about the SAS are true. They interviewed a Colonel Rice, trying to get information on Hatton, but they're dragging their feet a bit.'

'What he did tell us,' Nick said, 'is that Hatton's pretty much a rogue element. These SAS blokes get counselling when they leave the Regiment, as they call it. They help them find new jobs, that sort of thing. Hatton must have slipped through the net. I got the impression he went bad on them, jumped before he was pushed, then went missing soon as he got into civvies.'

'What about a photograph?' Fox asked.

'Rice said there were security problems with giving us photographs,' Nick said. 'Said they would have to be screened first, you know, the business where they black out all the other faces. But he said he'd see what he could do and fax something through tomorrow morning.'

Mills took several facsimile sheets from his briefcase. 'I've been in touch with Aldershot and they've given us a list of names, members of Hatton's old unit in the Guards. Most of them have left the Army now, we have their last known addresses here, but you may have to follow it up on the computer: electoral rolls, DSS, that sort of thing. There's a chance that he may have kept in touch with some of these blokes. They'll all have to be checked out.'

'So what do we know about this Bob Hatton?' someone asked from the back of the room.

Mills looked at TJ.

'When I was a kid,' TJ said, 'I had this Action Man toy. He could do just about bloody everything. Like Superman in fatigues. That's Bob Hatton. According to Rice, he has extensive training in sabotage and interrogation techniques. He's also an instructor in unarmed combat, jap slapping, they call it. Him and his squadron operated for two weeks behind enemy lines in the Gulf War without losing a single man.'

Honeywell puffed out his cheeks. 'Okay, so if we find him, who gets to slap the cuffs on and tell him to spread 'em?'

'Let Foxie do it,' someone else said. 'She's always up for another medal.'

There was nervous laughter. No one in the room intended scrapping with this bloke. Least of all Fox. If they found him, the hard stop would be down to a specialist firearms squad from SO19.

Mills nodded to Rankin, who referred to his notes on the clipboard in front of him. 'I've been running some checks on the computer. He doesn't own a vehicle, he's not on any electoral rolls, hasn't filed a tax return for eight years. No credit applications, nothing.'

'The Invisible Man,' someone said.

'Maybe he went freelance,' Fox said.

Mills nodded. 'That's favourite, at this stage. He's not trained for much else. It would make sense he's been working as a mercenary overseas. Nothing in his flat to verify that. We reckon he's taken everything he needs, passport, cash, in that holdall he was carrying.'

'That would also explain why there's nothing on the computer,' TJ said, nodding. 'He might have been travelling on another passport the last few years.'

'If he has a fake passport and ID,' Honeywell said, 'then he's probably out of the country by now.'

'I agree,' Mills said, 'but we don't leave any stone unturned.

We can't assume he's OS just yet.' He pinned the faxed list of names to the pinboard at the back of the room. 'I want these people found and interviewed. One of them might be able to point us in the right direction. As Bill just said, he might be long gone by now, but if he's still in London, we want him. There's something very bloody odd going on here and I'd at least like to know what it is.'

Chapter Forty-Five

Earls Court, SW5

It was an ancient six-storey block of flats that had been spared the Luftwaffe's bombs in the Blitz, and in the intervening years had somehow dodged the developer's jackhammer. The entrance was off a narrow street, almost permanently in shadow. An ancient Mini, covered with rust spots and bird droppings, was parked under a sign that read: 'Keep clear. Offending vehicles will be towed away by the police.' The smell of over-ripe rubbish emanated from the plastic bins in the forecourt. Rap music thumped from an open downstairs window.

Fox and Nick pushed through the heavy glass door.

Fox looked around. The badly lit entrance led to an ancient lift and a gloomy stairwell. She surveyed both alternatives in depressed silence. The address they had was on the top floor.

'I'm not walking up those stairs in these heels.'

'And I'm not getting in that lift. I've seen bigger telephone boxes.'

'Christ, what's that smell?'

'I reckon someone's had a Jimmy Riddle in that lift.'

'No, it's coming from down there. It smells like cabbage.'

'It's either ganja or some Chinese cooking their tea. All part of living in a cosmopolitan society, ma'am.'

Fox hesitated, making up her mind. 'I'm taking the lift,' she said.

'I'll see you up there, then,' he said, and made off resolutely in the direction of the stairs.

Fox pulled aside the lift's metal grille door. He was right, it wasn't much bigger than a telephone box. It was probably the same vintage as the building, the interior illuminated by a single low wattage bulb. It smelled of stale sweat and grease.

As she was closing the grille, a man in jeans and sweatshirt ran through the glass door at the entrance. 'Can you hold it?' he shouted.

He got in, no thank you, nothing. There was hardly room for both of them inside. First time I danced with a boy at a school disco we didn't get this close, Fox thought.

He fumbled with the grille and then, as he turned around, he managed to charm her further by leaning against all the buttons. 'Shit,' he said. 'Sorry about that. Hope you're not in a hurry.'

Now they would be stopping at each of the six floors. Fox considered getting out again and following Nick up the stairs. Too late. The lift gave a jerk and started to creak slowly up, unseen cables groaning and straining overhead. Fox thought about metal fatigue. Nick was right, it was a death trap. Should have got the exercise.

She was aware that her companion was watching her. She met his stare and he gave her a lazy smile. There were several dried scabs on his chain. A bad shave.

'What floor did you want?' he said.

She couldn't place the accent. London but with something else in there. South African perhaps. 'Six,' she said.

He nodded. 'Sorry about this. Bloody slow, isn't it?'

The lift clanked to a stop at the first floor. Fox reached over and jabbed the button for the sixth floor several times. A squealing noise like train wheels at an Underground station and then they began to ascend once more.

'You live here?' he asked her.

'No. Do you?'

'Fifth floor.'

Fox felt suddenly uncomfortable. His scrutiny was a little too brazen.

'Didn't you have a bloke with you when you came in?' he said.

'He gets claustrophobia.'

'Right,' he said. The lift stopped at the second floor, finishing the final part of the journey agonisingly, by inches. 'Sorry for all the questions. Only we've had a few break-ins here recently.'

'Do I look like I steal videos?'

'I don't have one.'

'I'll cross you off my list.'

Little bit too close in to be this abrasive, she thought. She didn't like being interrogated. She thought about all those police movies: *I'll ask the questions, if you don't mind.*

They stopped at the second floor and he turned around and punched the button for the fifth floor. It made no difference. The lift was running to an ancient timetable when the rhythms of life were much slower than they were now.

'Sorry about this,' he repeated. He smiled again, but his eyes were hard and bright and predatory. She wondered if he was trying to hit on her. 'Who are you looking for?'

Mind your own bloody business, Fox thought.

'Friend of Dave's?' he said.

'Dave?'

'Dave Youll. He lives on the sixth floor.'

'Know him?'

'Yeah, a bit. Relative, are you?'

You nosy bastard. 'Yes.'

The lift shuddered to a stop on the third floor. Christ, it would have been quicker to climb up the outside of the building with ropes and karabiners.

Fox hit the button for the fourth floor. He was still staring at her.

'There's a coffee shop on the corner,' he said.

She stared at him. Nutter's eyes, TJ would have called them. You saw them a lot in this part of London, at Chelsea games, at raves, around Hammersmith station. And here she was, close up and personal with the owner of just such a pair of eyes, in a lift designed, according to the maker's specifications, for a maximum of four people. Close enough to smell him.

'Is there?'

'You want to have a cup of coffee?' He gave her an ingratiating smile. He had a tooth missing, the left eye tooth, a nice counterpoint to the nutter's eyes.

'Can I bring my husband with me?' she said.

The lift rumbled on to the fourth floor. 'Husband?'

'The other man you saw me with.'

'Oh, right. Sorry.'

They rode the rest of the way in excruciating silence. The man got out on the fifth floor and Fox felt herself relax.

When she reached the top floor Nick was standing there, his hands in his pockets, looking smug. He looked pointedly at his watch. 'It's not that the lift is slow, but I think I missed a couple of meals while I was waiting.'

Fox slammed back the grille and got out. Her hands were shaking. She put them in her pockets.

'You all right?' Nick asked her.

'Of course I'm all right,' she snapped and walked past him and down the corridor.

A printed sign taped on the door said, 'Piss off, I'm having a bad day.'

Nick beat on the door with his fist. It opened.

David Youll did not look like a killing machine. He was a tall, rangy man with ginger hair falling over his collar either side of a polished egg-shaped skull. He had a scrappy beard and wore a shapeless grey T-shirt and loose-fitting tracksuit pants tied with a cord. He stared back at them from the doorway with dark and hostile eyes.

'David Youll?' Fox said and showed him her ID. 'Detective Inspector Fox, this is Detective Sergeant Crawford. Can we have a word with you, please?'

He folded his arms. 'What about?'

'May we come in?'

He thought about it. Eventually he shuffled aside.

Unlike Hatton's flat, which looked like a military museum, there was nothing to suggest that Youll had ever been in the Army. Fox took a quick inventory as she walked through: a bedroom, glimpsed through an open door, had one unmade bed and a week's washing piled on the linoleum; the living room was a pit, more clothes scattered on and around a stained and ancient sofa, which apparently doubled up as a laundry basket. Videos were scattered on the carpet around the television, action movies, no pornography.

Despite the mess, the living room appeared somehow sterile. There were no books, and no photographs or pictures on the walls. The only other piece of furniture apart from the television cabinet and the sofa, were a large, overstuffed armchair and a coffee table.

The air reeked of tobacco and the peculiar musk that some solitary men seemed to give off, something fetid and primordial, redolent of semen and sweat. Perhaps they spray it in the corners, she thought, like male dogs or cats marking out their territory.

'Sit down if you want,' Youll said.

He threw some clothes on to the floor to make a space on the sofa. Nick took the risk and sat there. Fox preferred to stand.

'So, what am I supposed to have done?' Youll grunted.

'We're looking for an old friend of yours,' Fox said. 'Do you remember a former colleague in the Army by the name of Robert Philip Hatton?'

'Yeah, I remember Dog.'

'Dog?'

'It was his nickname.'

'How long is it since you last saw him?'

Youll took a tin of tobacco and some papers from the windowsill and started to roll a cigarette. 'Fuckin' years.'

'Precisely when?' Nick asked.

'I dunno. Years, all right?'

'He hasn't been in contact recently? No phone calls or letters?'

'What would he want to fuckin' write to me for?' Youll tamped down the yellow, stringy tobacco and licked the paper. 'Why? What's he done?'

'We're investigating the murder of a man called Dennis Thorpe.'

'Did he off someone?' He gave a short laugh, like a bark. 'That'd be Dog.'

'Why do you say that?' Nick asked him. 'Did he like killing people?'

'That's what you do in the Army,' Youll said. 'Killing people is the fuckin' job.'

'Surgeons are paid to cut people open,' Fox said. 'It doesn't mean they can take it up as a hobby in their spare time.'

Youll found a box of matches on the floor, shook it first to check that it wasn't empty, then took out a match and lit his rollie. 'Either of you two ever been in the Army?'

Nick shook his head.

'I didn't think so.' He exhaled a stream of smoke.

Nice bloke. There were two dirty plates piled on the coffee table next to a pair of stained and crusted mugs. 'Live on your own, do you?'

'Mostly.'

Fox checked behind the sofa. There was a rolled-up sleeping bag on the carpet. Youll saw her stare and his expression went blank.

'Got a guest?' she said.

'Mate of mine called in last night, down from Birmingham. I let him sleep on the floor.'

'His name?' Nick said.

'What the fuck is this? It's not illegal to leave Birmingham, is it?'

'Not yet, but it should be,' Nick said, content to play with this bloke. Be careful, for Christ's sake, Fox thought. This one might be a jap-slapper, too.

'Where is your friend now?'

'I don't know. I think he went down the pub.'

'Is he coming back?'

Youll shrugged, like he didn't really care one way or another.

'You are familiar with the law, Mr Youll?' she said. 'Harbouring a suspected criminal, in these circumstances, carries with it a jail term.'

'Gee, that's scary.'

'I'll ask you again. Do you know where we can find Robert Hatton?'

'And I'll tell you again. No, I fuckin' don't.'

Nick looked at her. Well, they could always come back with a search warrant. In the meantime she would call in and have Mr Youll placed under surveillance. Perhaps the sleeping bag on the floor did belong to a friend from Birmingham. Or maybe not. 'Well, thanks for your help,' she said.

They let themselves out. Youll slammed the door behind them.

'Lift or the stairs?' Nick said.

'Stairs, I think,' Fox said.

She had an uneasy feeling. Something wasn't right here, not right at all.

Chapter Forty-Six

Area Major Incident Pool, Hendon Road

Mills was in his office, a courier envelope open on his desk. His door was open and Fox put her head in. 'Excuse me, guv.'

'Come in, Madeleine.'

'I think we have something.'

'Sit down.' Mills was shuffling through three ten by eight photographs. He put them aside as she entered. 'What have you got?'

'We've just interviewed one of Hatton's old mates from the Army. A David Youll. I'd like to put him under surveillance.'

'Why?'

'He was pretty hostile, straight off. I thought, okay, maybe he just doesn't like cops. Then he tells us he lives on his own, but there are two cups and two plates on the coffee table. There's also a rolled-up sleeping bag behind the sofa. He said he had a friend staying with him overnight. The friend could be Hatton. DS Crawford's still there, watching the place.'

Mills thought about it. 'All right,' he said. 'I'll get it organised.' He slid the photographs across the desk. 'By the way, you'll want to see these. Hereford came through with some mugshots.'

Fox shuffled through them. A dozen men in jungle fatigues, gathered around an APC, palm trees in the background. Every face in the photograph, except one, had been blacked out. It was not a good picture, smudged and grainy, but in the second glossy Hatton's face had been magnified to twice its size, and in the third by times ten.

He had been a much younger man when this was taken, even his neighbours on the Broadridge Estate might not have recognised him. His hair was tight cropped and he was clean shaven, without the beard and the wild unruly hair portrayed in the photofit picture that Brian Marwick had given them. In fact he was much the way he had looked earlier that afternoon, when he had run in off the street and she had held the lift for him.

Chapter Forty-Seven

'There was nothing you could have done about it,' Mills said to her.

'I feel like an idiot.'

'Look, it's better you didn't know who it was. There was no way you and Nick were going to take him on your own.'

'He must feel pretty bloody sure of himself to pull a stunt like that.'

'Who dares, wins,' Mills said, with a sour expression.

'Part of it was luck,' Fox said. 'He must have got back to the flats at the same time as we arrived.'

'How did he know we were cops?' Nick said.

'How many black guys did you see hanging around those flats in a suit and tie?' Mills said. 'Also, I imagine Madeleine here looked a little out of place in her blazer and grey skirt.'

'Well, excuse me. Next time I'll wear a micro mini and a leather jacket.'

Mills grinned. 'Suits me.'

Crawford shook his head. 'He's still got to be bloody cool, to follow us in and interrogate Madeleine on the way up to Youll's flat.'

There was a long silence. No matter what Mills said, Fox knew they were all thinking the same thing. Hatton had made a fool of her.

'When we arrest this bloke we'll be sending in an armed response squad,' Mills said. 'I still reckon you were lucky you didn't sus who he was.'

The sheer balls of it, Fox thought. Hatton had watched them go into the building and had then decided to follow them. To check. She remembered how close he had been, close enough to see the small mole on his chin, the tiny white scar under his right ear. And when he had satisfied himself that they were who he thought they were, he had covered his tracks by making it look like a casual pick-up. Who dares wins, indeed.

'What bothers me is why he is still in London,' Mills said. 'He can't hope to evade us for ever, no matter how good he is.'

'Has to be a reason,' Nick agreed.

Mills shrugged. 'We'll get a search and seizure warrant for Youll's flat and then I'll talk to your David Youll and see what he has to say for himself when we charge him with assisting an offender. And let's get this photograph released to the media. He can run, but he can't hide.'

Fox wondered about that. With the kind of training Hatton had received during his time with the SAS, he might well be able to do both for as long as he wanted.

Fulham Road Police Station

David Youll accepted the news of his arrest with equanimity. He took the formal caution seriously and refused to speak to any police officer unless he had a lawyer present.

He was not in the least intimidated by his surroundings. In

the Army he had received specialist training in interrogation techniques, which included experience of sleep deprivation and actual physical abuse; so sitting in a warm interview room with a brief beside him and a cup of coffee at his elbow, did not leave him shaking in his boots.

A search of his flat had yielded no further clues.

Youll seemed amused by their consternation. 'Yeah, Bob Hatton crashed at my place last night,' he said. 'So what?'

'You denied that earlier this morning,' Fox said. 'You said you had not seen him for several years.'

'Yeah, I lied. I needed time to think.'

Mills leaned forward, his elbows resting on the table. 'Did you know he was wanted in connection with the murder of Dennis Thorpe?'

'Not before you told me. He just turned up on the doorstep and said he was in some sort of trouble. We were mates. I said I'd help him out, I didn't ask any questions. I didn't want to know.'

'When was this?'

'Yesterday.'

'What time yesterday?'

'It was the afternoon. I don't know what time, I don't wear a watch.'

'Did he say how long he intended to stay with you?'

'I didn't ask.'

'You didn't ask.'

'Like I said, we were mates.'

'He stayed at your flat all night.'

Hatton nodded.

'What did you talk about?'

'Existentialism. Sixteenth-century French poetry. Third World economics.'

Mills knew he was being stuffed around, but he didn't rise

to the bait. 'Did he tell you why he had to leave his flat in Tottenham?'

'No.'

'You didn't ask?'

Youll ignored the irony. 'He said he was in trouble. Like I said to you a hundred times, I didn't want to know. If I knew, that would make me party to anything he'd done. Right?'

Mills silently conceded the point. 'What time did he leave your flat this morning?'

'I got up, he was gone.'

'He took his belongings with him?'

'Yeah. I told you you wouldn't find anything of his in my flat. I hope you bastards left it as you found it.'

'Now he wants us to go back there and empty all the drawers on to the floor,' Fox said.

Youll turned to his brief in mock outrage. 'Is she allowed to say that sort of thing to me?'

The lawyer, who had two surnames, Heath-Black or Hayden-Brown or some high-powered handle, had the good sense to just smile.

'He was last seen leaving his flat in Tottenham with a green canvas heavy-duty holdall. Did he have it with him when he got to your place?'

'I don't remember.'

'Were you expecting him to come back this morning?'

'No. Like I told you, he was gone before I got up.'

'Are you sure about that?'

Youll caught on fast. The corner of his mouth curled in a smile. 'Why? Did you see him? When you came to the flat?'

'Were you expecting him to come back?' Mills repeated.

Youll looked at Fox and grinned. 'He's really pissed all over you blokes, hasn't he?'

Mills pressed on. 'Did he bring his holdall to the flat?'

'You don't think a bloke like him would leave his gear with me? He was with the Regiment, for Christ's sake. He's stashed it somewhere. He's probably got safe houses all over London and drops everywhere else. He's an expert in E and E.'

'E and E?'

'Escape and Evasion. Don't you blokes know anything?'

'Where do we find him, Mr Youll?'

Youll grinned triumphantly. He knew they had nothing on him. He crossed his arms and leaned back in his seat. 'I've told you all I know. Go fuck yourself, copper. Is there any more coffee?'

Regent Street, W1

The pavements were packed with tourists, Hamleys and the Disney Store doing big business. Tourist buses were caught in the gridlock of double-decker buses and taxicabs spewing diesel into the air.

Carlton fretted behind the wheel of his BMW. The soft leather seats, the climate control, the Mozart playing softly on the Blaupunkt sound system were a womb-like sanctuary from the summer stench of the city, the carbon monoxide and grit.

His fingers tightened around the soft leather, locked away in the prison of his own personal torment, oblivious to the crowds and the traffic, focused solely on his own pain, like a marathon runner emerging into a wildly cheering stadium, aware only of the effort to keep his legs and arms moving. Everything in his life balanced on a knife edge now, ready to crash down at any moment. He had long ago lost control of it all, like one of those illusionists with the spinning plates, too many slowing down at once, and he knew he could not save his act now. Still he went on spinning more plates, acting from instinct, knowing he was doomed, waiting for the inevitable disaster and the public approbation that would follow.

He looked into the driving mirror, almost winced when he caught sight of himself. It was the face of a complete stranger, the shaved, elegant and perfectly turned-out wide boy made good who now dogged him everywhere he went. An Englishman and a fraud; he saw through the mask that others deferred to. This aloof but constant companion was no friend to him, more like a colleague with whom he had been forced to work with year after year. Though he had never liked him, he had, at least, understood his motives and his weaknesses. But now he had discovered new and uncharted depths to this ruthless stranger that left him feeling shocked and appalled. Now, as the day of reckoning approached, he wanted to distance himself from the criminal little shit who stared back at him from the mirror.

Too late, he thought about all he had placed at risk: his career, his wife, his family, his financial security, perhaps even his freedom. Danger stalked him from so many directions, he no longer knew which way to face, which fear should command his most urgent attention.

The lies he had told the police would only keep the dogs at bay for a few days at most. It had achieved nothing, except delay for its own sake, a few precious days of living what he had come to believe as normal life. A last-minute appeal on his personal death row.

Insane really, but in the darker recesses of his mind there still lurked the hope that some unexpected constellation of events he had yet been unable to fathom might save him even now.

He reached the lights at Regent's Park, knew he should turn right on to Baker Street, but instead he found himself heading west towards Kilburn. Insanity.

Nothing he could do, something in the visceral depths arguing for him to go back, to touch those memories again, feel warm flesh, the tableau arranged perfectly, limbs arranged as he so desired, the body stretched in front of him transformed to the blissful sanctuary of his fantasies.

Kilburn

He parked his car and walked two streets to a mews of renovated turn-of-the-century cottages, striding with a cold and liberated certainty. He was sweating in the humid evening, could feel the damp patches forming under his arms. He stopped outside the discreet door, gateway to the paradise of his private and ungodly yearnings, the charnel house of his life's dreams. He was almost panting as he rang the bell, his heart a jackhammer in his chest.

His mind a white haze. Thoughts moved like shadows behind a gauze veil, and he could not define their shape, desired only the anaesthetic of relief and abandonment. He ignored the pitiful protests of reason.

The security camera watched him with cold and dispassionate eye, and then the latch clicked back.

A woman in a black latex jumpsuit smiled at him as he walked through the reception. 'Hello again, Mr Smith,' she said, with a dazzling smile. 'We haven't seen you here for a long time. What can we do for you tonight?'

Bayswater

Madeleine Fox woke in the early hours of the morning, staring down the black eye of the automatic pistol, her body bathed in sweat. She turned on the bedside lamp, sat up, reached for her watch. Christ, look at the time.

She knew she would not be able to get back to sleep so she got up and ran a bath to try and relax. She lay there until the water became cold, then she put a towel around her and went into the kitchen to make herself a cup of tea. It was almost dawn by then, and every bird in the borough was parked in the tree outside her window squawking. No way she was going to get any sleep now.

They had put her through counselling after the shooting in Lambeth but the nightmares came back anyway. Not often, perhaps once or twice a month, usually around the full moon. Getting more frequent, rather than less. Perhaps she should talk to someone again.

She went to the window. Along Queensway a pile of newspapers and rags stirred in one of the shop doorways. The winos in the street got a better night's sleep than she did. She sipped her tea, watched a tom pay a cab driver and walk slowly into one of the apartment blocks across the street, knocking off for the night, if that was the right expression. Another dirty little dawn in Bayswater.

She wondered what unpleasantness this new day would drag along with it.

Hampstead

James Carlton undressed in the darkness and slipped into bed beside his wife, laying quite still under the bedclothes, listening for the sound of her breathing.

'You're late,' Louise said, and the words echoed in the silence like gunshots.

'This Euro thing,' he lied. 'Thought Willie would never stop talking.'

'What time is it?'

'Bit after midnight.' Two o'clock actually.

He lay there for a long time, guilt suffocating him like the weight of a dozen rugs and making him sweat. He thought she had fallen asleep, but then she said, 'What's going on, James?'

If ever there was a time.

For one dizzying, awful moment he actually contemplated telling her everything, drawing her into his dark conspiracy, unburdening himself utterly, kicking the tripwire of faith.

Confession. Christ. Where would one actually stop? You can't tell anyone everything. Cease to be interesting. Man has to have some secrets. Go to church every Sunday, that's one thing. But to believe it, that's another thing.

He tried for a moment to imagine what it would be like, down on the knees in sackcloth, his sins never forgotten even if ostensibly forgiven, beholden for life. Like having an affair on camera and giving the negatives to your wife. Insane.

Be like the time he was sent home from school when they found the dirty magazine in his desk. Called in to the head's office, parents rung, threatened with expulsion, uproar, his mother shaking him by the shoulders: *Why did you do it, son?*

On second thoughts, don't think so. Rather not, in fact. Maybe mention it in a suicide note, if one ever gets to that stage.

The moment passed and his heartbeat resumed its normal rhythm and there was no longer chance or fear of unburdening his soul to her and living a normal life. Besides, without the customary baggage, his whole existence would become unbalanced. It would be like learning to walk again. A new life, too frightening and too banal to contemplate.

'Nothing, Louise,' he whispered. 'Nothing is going on.' And he lay there the rest of the night, staring at the darkness, exhausted to his very bones, and wide, wide awake.

Chapter Forty-Eight

Battersea, SW11

A piss-poor block of flats, shit-brown brick, dried vomit in the concrete stairwells, graffiti on the walls, a nursery for drugs, crime and petty theft. Dickens would recognise this side of London, Fox thought, so would Hogarth. Except for the satellite dishes.

Some black kids were screaming, 'Old Bill!' from the balcony above, letting everyone know the law was around, they'd have to stop nicking video recorders and snatching handbags for half an hour.

An anonymous row of doors on the third floor, an open balcony overlooking a courtyard with one spindly tree growing in the middle of it, some kids kicking a football around the cement bollards. Nick rapped on the door, and it inched open. An old woman in a hairnet, smelling vaguely of cabbage and cats, peered out at them.

'Mrs Hatton?' Fox said, holding up her ID. 'I'm DI Fox, this is DS Nick. Metropolitan Police. We'd like to talk to you. Can we come in?'

Place absolutely stank of cats. It was dark, gloomy and

cramped, the television turned up so loud you could feel the vibrations through the walls. Fox perched on the edge of an ancient sofa thick with cat hair and unidentifiable stains. She explained to Mrs Hatton why they were there but was not sure she fully understood. When Nick showed her the photograph they had obtained from SAS headquarters in Hereford, she held it in trembling and arthritic fingers as if it were a childhood keepsake.

'Oh, that's lovely,' she said.

Nick looked at Fox and shrugged.

Fox listened to the slow ticking of an ancient chime clock on the mantelpiece. A moth-eaten tabby purred and fussed around the old woman's legs, which were encased in thick brown stockings. Nick received permission from the old woman to turn the television down; a glamorous woman with an American accent was explaining why a certain shampoo gave her hair more body and shine.

'Where did you get this?' Mrs Hatton said, staring at the photograph.

'From the Army, Mrs Hatton.'

'He does look lovely in his uniform, doesn't he?'

Fox looked around the room. The furniture was pitiful, ten quid the lot at an auctioneer's. The television sat on an old cupboard next to some framed photographs, a freckled schoolboy scowling at a camera, another of a young man in an Army uniform. They looked to have been taken a long time ago.

'Mrs Hatton, has your son been in contact with you lately?'

'I think he's overseas somewhere. He gets around a lot, you know. The Army sends him all over.'

'When was the last time you heard from him?' Nick asked.

'Oh, he writes when he can,' she said. She got up and

hobbled over to the mantelpiece, found a letter propped behind a toby jug. She handed it to Fox.

Fox looked at the postmark. Cape Town, 13 July, 1995.

'Is this the last you heard from him?' Fox asked.

'He's a good boy, my Bobby,' Mrs Hatton said and returned her gaze to the photograph in her fingers.

Fox looked up at Nick, who tapped his temple with his finger. It looked like Mrs Hatton was a longterm resident of la-la land and would be little use to them. Probably just as well, Fox thought. Living here, on your own. A reality like this was no good to anyone.

'Do you know where we can find your son, Mrs Hatton?' Fox asked, one last dogged attempt.

Mrs Hatton stroked the photograph lovingly with her finger. 'He does look handsome in his uniform. Doesn't he?'

When they got back to the street, the car was still there, something of a minor miracle. Nick sat behind the wheel, shaking his head. 'Hasn't heard from him since nineteen ninety-five,' he said. 'Christ.'

'He's had things on his mind,' she said.

'My old lady lives on her own in Bath,' he said. 'I make a point of driving down once a fortnight. Least you can do.'

He waited for her to concur. Perhaps it made him feel better, knowing he was a dutiful son. Fox thought about Ma. When was the last time she'd seen her? Well, more recently than 1995 anyway. But then she didn't have a mercenary war in Angola or a cooling body in her apartment hallway as an excuse.

Chapter Forty-Nine

They were heading north across Westminster Bridge when her mobile rang. The 'William Tell Overture'. Why couldn't the bloody thing just ring, like a normal phone? she wondered. All this progress was just gimmickry. Honeywell reckoned that in five years mobiles would be the size of lip gloss and you'd need a master's degree in classical music just to make the bloody things stop ringing.

Nick handed her the phone. 'Fox,' she said.

'Madeleine? Where are you?' It was Mills.

'We've just left Battersea, we're heading back to the office. Be there in about half an hour, depending on the traffic.'

'Good. I need to talk to you,' he said and hung up.

Area Major Incident Pool, Hendon Road

Mills was in his office when she got in. At a glance his usual sartorial elegance seemed unruffled but on closer inspection there were pouches under his eyes and she noted a pocket of bristles under his chin that the razor had missed. Must have slept through the alarm and then had to rush.

He was nursing a cup of coffee, industrial strength by the look of it, and had the back pages of the *Mirror* open on his desk. 'Christ, it's hard being a Tottenham supporter,' he murmured, without looking up. 'It's like a curse that follows you around all your life. For two months I glimpse contentment. Then the season starts again.'

'Did they lose?'

'Do bears shit in the woods?' He pushed the newspaper away. 'How are you this fine morning, Madeleine?'

'Fine. How about you, guv? You look a bit washed out.'

'I'm all right. Take a pew.'

She sat down, sipped her fourth coffee of the morning. Half a dozen before lunch at least, get the heart rate up a bit, need a little tachycardia just to get through the afternoon. Last night had confirmed one thing for her: you couldn't run murder investigations and love affairs at the same time. Too exhausting.

'Have a look at these,' Mills said.

He passed a file across the desk. It contained Kimberley Mason's telephone records. It had taken six weeks for the phone company to find them and print them out.

She wished they'd had these in the first week of the investigation. According to the file, Kimberley Mason had made thirty-eight calls in the last week of her life; eight of those calls had been to the same number, four of them on the day before she died. They had been ringed in red ink.

'Whose number is this, guv?'

Mills beat a tattoo on the edge of his desk with a Parker pen. 'Mobile phone. Registered to one James Carlton.'

'Right,' she said.

They looked at each other. A burst of laughter from the Incident Room. TJ making jokes at Honeywell's expense, no doubt.

'This isn't quite what he told us, is it, guv?'

'No,' Mills said. 'It isn't.'

'I think we should have another word with him.'

Mills nodded. He looked worried, could see his promotion being sidelined by this. 'I'll have to tell Kennett. He's not going to like this.' She knew what he was thinking. If Carlton walked away from this and Mills continued to rise through the ranks of the Met, one day Kennett would be either a well-placed friend of his or a firm political enemy, depending on the way this was handled.

'Thin ice,' Mills said.

'It was Carlton who wanted to go skate on it.'

'Don't rush to judge.'

'What the hell's going on with this?'

'I don't know. We'll have to find out. Softly, softly, all right, Madeleine? If we kick his head in for no reason, Kennett's going to get me transferred to traffic duty in Brixton. My arse is on the line here.'

'So is mine.'

'And a very nice one it is, too. So look after it, and look after mine. Let's find out what's going on here, and let's hope to Christ we haven't banged up the wrong bloke.'

She rang Carlton's office, but a secretary said he was in Brussels and would not be back until after the weekend. She left her number. When she hung up, she thought about the old saying: a week's a long time in politics. Eight calls.

Must have been a very long time in the life of a high class bondage queen, too.

Chapter Fifty

Camden Town

They were lying in bed in the second-floor bedroom of his house in Gloucester Crescent. Done all right, Fox thought. Perhaps crime doesn't pay, she thought, but Ash has done okay out of futures trading, which is almost the same thing. Only without the violence and the bad clothes.

She ran a hand across his chest, smooth and hairless like a boy's. How had he insinuated himself into her life so fast? She hadn't meant it to happen.

She listened to the night time sounds of the city, the traffic on Parkway, an ambulance siren, the distant rattle of a train, and obsessed about Kimberley Mason. Like everyone else in the squad, Fox had been convinced they had the right guy when they charged Gary Bradshaw. Now she was no longer as sure. And it kept her awake at nights.

Why would Kimberley Mason have rung James Carlton eight times in the week before she died? Hardly the professional relationship Carlton had hinted at. Toms, even specialist high-class girls like Kimberley, didn't harass their own johns. She had checked on the HOLMES. Both

Rhiannon and Bradshaw himself had mentioned another man whom Kimberley had referred to as a lover. The issue would have to be settled one way or another. Bradshaw's brief would have a field day with it in court whichever way it went. This was going to make the dailies, no question.

'What are you thinking?' Ash asked her.

She had thought he was asleep. 'Nothing,' she said.

Already he knew her better than that. 'Solving a case, Holmes?'

'Maybe.'

'The shooting in Tottenham?'

'No, we know who did that.'

He waited for her to tell him more, but she made it a point never to discuss her cases outside work, with anyone. 'Do you want to talk about it, or do I have to lie here listening to your brain clunking through the gears?'

Well, she thought, perhaps for once it would be good to talk to someone. 'It's one we've put to bed,' she heard herself say. 'It was a rather bizarre murder and we actually have someone on remand for it. But now we've found a couple of things that don't quite add up.'

'Is it breaking the Official Secrets Act if you tell me about it?'

'The victim was a prostitute, specialised in bondage . . . she was found strangled in her own dungeon.'

'Her own *what*?'

'It was in all the papers.'

'I was probably still in Hong Kong.' He rolled towards her, leaned on his elbow. 'Must have been a great headline.'

'We kept the details to ourselves. Besides, one of the royals did something that weekend, I don't know, got caught sucking someone's toes or fell off a polo pony, the usual stuff. It got pushed off the front page of the *Evening Standard* on to page three.'

'You have a strange life, Madeleine.'

'Tell me about it.'

'Is that why you brought the handcuffs home?'

'I suppose it made me curious,' she said. They'd only tried it that once. An interesting experiment, but a little too edgy to make a habit of.

'So, I was like, homework.'

She smiled in the darkness. 'You didn't seem to mind.'

'We all have our fantasies. You'd know about the psychology of that sort of stuff more than me. Being a cop.'

'Would I? I don't know. I deal with murder every day, but I'm no closer to understanding how someone can actually bring themselves to kill another person.'

He was quiet for a long while and she thought he'd gone back to sleep when suddenly he said, 'Friend of mine's into S and M.'

'Friend of yours.'

'Yeah. At the bank. A *real* friend. This is not a euphemism for me.'

She laughed. 'Okay.'

'His name's Michael. Gay as old Paris, and gets into some real kinky stuff. Went to a bondage club a couple of weeks ago.'

'He tells you all this?'

'Yeah. Doesn't seem to bother him. There's a bar we all go to after work on Fridays, we get together, he has us all pissing ourselves. Really camps it up. Total extrovert.'

'What sort of things does he tell you?'

'This club he went to the other week, for instance. I didn't know this, but evidently there's a strict dress code.'

'Like, you can't get in without a tie?'

'Without *being* tied. You have to have some sort of bondage costume anyway. So, Mike and one of his gay mates front up, Mike's wearing a dog collar, on all fours, his mate's holding the leash. He's already pissed on Babycham or whatever, and he reckons there's one of the staff, a girl, flagellating customers against the wall. So he thinks he'd like to try it. Gets himself chained up, and whipped. Then he looks round, sees the girl drinking at the other end of the bar, realises he's getting flogged by a total stranger that he can't even *see*. That's when he realises he's got in over his head.'

'Where was this place?'

'I don't know. Somewhere in Islington.'

Islington. Kimberley Mason's stamping ground.

'Why?' he said. 'Do you want to go?'

'No,' she said, 'it's not really me. I'm not that curious.'
Liar, liar.

She let him make love to her again, but it was hard to concentrate. Her mind was still on Kimberley Mason's curious life and death, on telephone logs, and on other people's fantasies.

Chapter Fifty-One

Islington, N1

The club was called The DomiNation. There were four levels, more hardcore the further down you went. The first floor was an open bar area, where a vampish girl dressed in black leather served Coca-Cola and orange juice. Fox's first surprise: there was a strict no-alcohol rule. A sign above the bar read, 'Don't get tanked, get spanked.' Humour, even, and she guessed the rule made sense. If you were going to trust someone to hit you with a leather-plaited whip, you wanted to be sure their judgment wasn't impaired.

She wandered through the musty Victorian arches, bare brick walls and open plumbing on the ceilings, a futuristic subterranean netherworld of glitter queens and vamps and freaks; a bare-chested man, his skin covered in tattoos, his hair teased into horns; a priest in black latex; a nun wearing a gas mask. Everywhere she looked there was leather, tattoos, pierced lips and nipples, wet-look rubber and black lipstick. Torture chic.

Fox had bought a hooded cloak from a speciality shop in Camden market, had cut slits along both hips, revealing glimpses of black stocking as she walked. Modest enough to preserve her anonymity, edgy enough to impress the doormen. She kept the hood pulled well over her face. She caught a glimpse of herself in the mirror behind the bar: scary.

She felt her heart hammering in her ribs. She wondered what she would do if she saw someone she knew. Oh, hello, Commissioner, I'm here undercover. You too? She started to descend the stairs, got a rude shock when she glimpsed a Metropolitan Police officer's uniform cap. Just part of another costume, she realised, taking in the girl's egg-yolk yellow rubber corset.

The next level had the same subterranean feel, bare walls, red lightbulbs on a bare black ceiling, Metallica thumping from the sound system. On one wall was a large showcase, with a selection of plaited whips and bondage equipment. In the corner a girl was draped over a spanking chair, her white pants had been pulled down by her lover, who was whispering in her ear between strokes, his hand leaving red marks on her white skin. There was a handful of spectators.

Fox was surprised. The atmosphere was upbeat, not intense at all. People were joking and laughing, like they were in their local.

The third level was not quite as upbeat, less people down here, the serious amateurs. There was a curious smell, like must and incense drifting in the air. A man in rubber pants and a waistcoat was chained in a set of stocks having his bare buttocks beaten with a crop by a black woman in a tight bodice. Fox realised with shock that the woman was actually a man. Daddy, she thought, your little girl's getting an education tonight. Even at thirty-four, you're never too old to learn.

The bottom level was for the hardcore players, with a medical room and a fully equipped dungeon. She passed a cubicle where a middle aged man dressed in black leather had been gagged and blindfolded and left hanging in chains. He grunted and twisted, apparently enjoying his Friday night.

At the back of the room was a small stage, illuminated by a red spotlight, a raised dungeon extracted by some giant hand from a medieval torture chamber. There was a wooden cross, leather straps hanging from the four arms, a whipping post, and what appeared to be a rack, suspended on an angle so that it could be viewed from the dance floor.

In front of the stage there was a blackboard with 'NAMES FOR WHIPPING' scrawled at the top and underlined. A number of men and women had chalked their names underneath, volunteering for this dubious privilege.

There was a couple on the stage right now. They had stripped naked, except for black G-strings. She had allowed him to tie her spread-eagled to a wooden rack, her wrists and ankles secured with leather straps.

Fox's eyes were drawn not to the stage, but to the man standing directly beneath it, in black leather and studs. His chest was bare, revealing very white skin and a great deal of black hair. It was the assistant from the porn shop in Brewer Street, she realised. Lila Mahmoud's help. She searched her memory for a name.

'Hello, Ray,' she said. She almost had to shout over the thumping bass of the music, another Metallica track. She threw back the hood. She supposed he might not recognise her. She had slicked back her hair, and was wearing black lipstick and eyeshadow.

'Do I know you?' he said.

'Brewer Street,' she said. 'I came to interview your boss, Lila.'

'Fucking hell,' he said. 'What are you doing here?'

She didn't answer. She looked up at the stage. 'Why do people do this?' she said.

He didn't answer her. He had looked weedy and a waste of time in the porn shop, but in here, in the leather and the studded belt, he struck her as sadder, but also a little more sinister.

'I thought you got the bloke you were looking for,' he said.

'I don't know, Ray. Did we?'

A large red candle was burning on a wooden table in the middle of the dais. The man picked it up and then held it upright over his partner's supine body for a long time, then slowly tilted it on its side. The woman mewed and squirmed as the hot liquid wax spilled on her torso, cooling rapidly to leave a red streak like blood along her flanks. Fox thought of Kimberley Mason's dead body. Her mouth was suddenly dry. It was hard to swallow.

Fox looked around at the faces in the crowd. The audience was transported by the scene in front of them, their faces immobile, their eyes bright and hungry. The atmosphere in the club had become intense. Her own hands were shaking. She finished her drink and put down her glass.

'Kimberley ever come here?' she said.

Ray shrugged. 'All the time.'

'You saw her here?'

'Look, what is it you want?'

'I don't know. What can you tell me?'

He looked her up and down, the cloak, the spiked heels, the black stockings. 'You should be careful,' he said.

'Of what?'

Ray Pratt chewed his lip.

'You look like a man with something on his mind,' she said.

'You don't think I was one of her johns?' he said.

'No, I don't. You're gay, right?'

He didn't seem too surprised that she'd worked it out.

'You were friends with her, weren't you?' she said. A stab in the dark, intuition, whatever.

'How much did Lila tell you?'

'She only told us about Gary.'

'Not about the other bloke?'

'What other bloke?'

'She said she was going to marry him.' He grinned, pleased that he knew things no one else did. 'She used to tell me stuff she'd never tell anyone else. Even Lila.'

'Why?'

'Because I was the only one she knew who didn't want anything from her.'

The man on the stage had withdrawn the candle again, and she realised, with sudden clarity, that he was not master of this tortuous choreography. His eyes did not follow the intense journey of the cooling wax, but were intent on the woman's face; and when the pain was too much he raised the candle a little and waited until the grease had cooled before he began again. It was the woman who controlled her torturer's hand.

The session finished. The man released the straps and the couple hurried backstage to change. They left the dais to applause, like a band in a club finishing a set.

A woman dressed in a black leather bikini called out the first of the names on the blackboard. A woman from the audience stepped up on to the stage, was unceremoniously stripped and tied to the whipping post.

'Who was this other man?' Fox asked. When Ray didn't answer, she said, 'Perhaps she made him up.'

'No, he was real. She even told me his name.'

Fox held her breath.

'Are you going to tell me?'

He laughed. 'I don't remember. I didn't take any notice. She said he was in the government, or something.'

'What about James Carlton?'

He shrugged. 'Like I said, I don't remember.' A lie. He leaned in closer. 'After what happened to her, do you think I really want to talk about it?'

She didn't stay for the whippings. Seen one and you seen 'em all, she thought, as she got in her car. Her hands were shaking on the wheel. That had been a little too hardcore for her tastes. She wondered how many of the people in there held down day jobs, even marriages and families, their lives compulsively ordered into separate compartments, each sterile from the other like Kimberley Mason.

Why do they do it? There are people who like to play with drugs, she thought, like there are people who jump out of aeroplanes or off bridges and call it recreation. And there were people who liked to bring that same appetite for pain and danger into their sex lives. Perhaps making Gary Bradshaw the killer had been too easy, too pat, just as Nick Crawford had said. Perhaps they had not yet dug deep enough into Kimberley Mason's underground past for the truth.

Chapter Fifty-Two

Down by Hungerford Bridge the homeless and the lost are dossed down for another night in the evil-smelling doorways and underpasses, huddled in filthy sleeping bags. Night-time coughing echoes from an ancient brick archway. A Thames police patrol boat motors past, a tug's horn booms mournfully across the water. There are footsteps on the bridge above as an office worker hurries to catch a train to a cosy home in Woking or Guildford or Basingstoke.

A commuter train rumbles overhead, bass counterpoint to the shrill piping of a flute some lost teenager is playing, busking to the late night commuters for their coins.

The Dickensian shadows are littered with empty aerosol cans, broken syringes and empty plastic Woodpecker bottles, there is a reek of methylated spirits and urine. A mongrel barks on the end of a piece of frayed rope, a wino slumped beside him shouts and gesticulates at an enemy only he can see.

Bob Hatton curls into a makeshift bed of newspaper and cardboard, but even here among the junkies and homeless rent boys he is an outcast. They watch him and pass the bottle among themselves, exchanging silent glances, for even they are afraid. A solitary street light lends satanic intensity to his sleeping face. Under his green Army jersey he fingers an automatic pistol, the same weapon he used to kill Dennis Thorpe.

His brain squirms like some pale subterranean creature exposed to the light. The enemy are around him everywhere, and in his paranoia he knows he is vulnerable even here, among the night people. He needs a safe house from which to launch the next phase of his suicide mission. Madness owns him. His reference to reality is now as fleeting as some foreigner, cast adrift in a vast and featureless desert.

He is both genius and fool, idiot and savant, has cast himself as hero in a Kafkaesque nightmare which he alone can dream. The descent to this point was slow but sure, and in that at least he and James Carlton have twinned their destinies, each coming to it along his own path, a long and spiritless journey into blackness.

Fox lay there in the darkness, wide awake. It was hot in her bedroom and she tossed off the bedclothes, but every time she drifted to sleep she woke with a start, the muscles in her legs and arms going into spasm, jerking her back to wakefulness. Finally she gave up on sleep and got out of bed to make a cup of coffee. She took some paperwork from her briefcase and worked until past four in the morning when she finally fell into a deep but restless sleep on the sofa.

Chapter Fifty-Three

Camden Town

They met for a late-night supper in an Italian place on Parkway. There was a bottle of Australian red on the table and Ash refilled their glasses. He looked nervous and he hadn't touched his cannelloni. The conversation had been stilted.

Here it comes, she thought. Well, to hell with it. They'd only been together for a few weeks, it wasn't like it meant anything.

'There's something I have to tell you,' he said.

'You're married.' It was a joke but he didn't laugh.

He watched her over the rim of his wineglass.

'Fuck,' she murmured.

'Hear me out. This is complicated.'

She pushed her plate away. Now she'd lost her appetite too.

'No, it's not complicated, it's simple. You should have told me.' She didn't feel angry, or cheated. Just disappointed. Which was crazy because she'd never intended this to go anywhere, anyway.

'We broke up just before I left Hong Kong. She stayed on.

I thought it was over.' He shrugged his shoulders. 'She told me it was over.'

'Now she's followed you over here.'

'If it was just me and her, I'd be happy to go our different ways. But we have two kids. A boy and a girl. *That's* where it gets complicated.'

Fox thought about Ginny and Ian. What a shitty thing life could be. 'How old are they?'

'Seven and four.' He shrugged helplessly.

'I see.'

'She was the one who wanted us to separate. Now she wants to get back together.'

'And you said yes.'

'It's the only way I can hang on to my kids. How am I going to get custody? I work twelve hours a day.'

Well, Madeleine you never wanted a longterm relationship. This is the easy out. It's better now, before you both started expecting too much from each other. It's been fun, let's leave it at that. 'Why didn't you tell me?'

'Why didn't you tell me you were a cop?'

'Because I thought it would spoil my chances,' she said. 'And because it was only meant to be for one night.'

'That's why I didn't tell you I was married.'

A long silence. A struggle ensues between the head and the heart.

'Look, you start off not telling someone something . . . and the longer you don't tell the truth . . . the harder it gets.'

'It's okay,' she said, but it wasn't okay because she couldn't make sense of her feelings at all. A lump in her throat the size of a golf ball. Shit.

'Maybe it's for the best,' he said. 'Nothing comes between you and the Job, right?'

'It's funny. I knew we'd have to break it off one day. I just don't want one day to be today.'

'Neither do I.' He leaned towards her, put his hand on hers. 'Perhaps we could still see each other.'

She took her hand away. 'No, thanks. That would be fine with me, but it wouldn't be fine for your wife or your kids.'

'I'm sorry,' he said.

'Don't be.' She put her bag across her shoulder, put some money on the table. One thing she'd insisted on. Always split the bill.

'You don't have to go.'

'I'm just not hungry any more,' she said and rushed out. She didn't trust herself. Long time since she'd cried over any man, or over anything really. Didn't want to start now.

Chapter Fifty-Four

Ma lived in a village about an hour's drive south. Before Fox left, she washed the car, even hoovered the carpets, threw out the Mars bar wrappers and takeaway boxes that littered the floor behind the passenger seat. Didn't know what made her do it. She didn't care what her mother thought any more.

Still.

On the drive down she thought about the two files on her desk back at Hendon Road. Tomorrow James Carlton would be back in London and perhaps they could tie up the loose ends on DARK LADY, and she could sleep at nights, not have to worry if Gary Bradshaw had been fitted up for a murder he really hadn't committed after all. The Bob Hatton case, operation Action Man, TJ's whimsical choice, was causing more concern. Hatton posed a deadly risk if he was still in London.

She just hoped more bodies weren't about to fall.

Near Farnborough, Surrey

Ma was in the garden, gloves protecting her delicate hands from anything as common as dirt, a Burmese playing in the hawthorn bushes close by. She was a handsome woman, had been beautiful when she was young, *a catch*, as her father would have said. Her skin was still remarkably clear for a woman of her advancing years, her English rose complexion protected from the afternoon sun by a broad-rimmed straw hat.

Ma looked astonished to see her, even though Fox had rung that morning to say she was coming.

'Madeleine!' she gasped. 'How lovely to see you!'

She gave her a bloodless kiss on the cheek and stood back to survey her daughter with the critical expression of an artist who is reasonably pleased with her creation but who still feels she hasn't quite got it right.

'Like some tea?'

'Yes,' Fox said. 'That would be great.'

Fox sat in the garden on a wicker chair, surveying the borders and rockeries with their profusion of hollyhocks and petunias. This passion for the garden had come to her mother late in life. She had spent her entire existence bossing people around in that quiet, orderly way of hers, and now there were no people left around, she had started on Nature.

Ma brought tea out on a tray, and took off her straw hat, brushing back the long strands of greying, golden hair. 'How have you been?'

'Fine,' Fox heard herself say, a bare-faced lie, but her mother couldn't know that. She wondered what her mother would do if she told her the truth, if she actually poured out her heart to her. It had only ever happened once in their relationship, when her father had died, after his illness. She could still remember it. Her mother had stared at her as if she had lost control of her bladder at the vicarage. '*Pull yourself together, Madeleine,*' she had snapped. '*Your father would not want to see you like this.*'

'Still ambulance chasing?' Ma asked, sweetly.

There was not really anything much she could say to that, so she changed the subject. 'Heard from Ginny?' she countered. Attack, they said, was the best form of defence.

Fox wondered how much Ginny had told their mother about her husband's philandering.

'We spoke on the telephone yesterday.'

'Have you been to see her?'

'She'll come here if she needs me.'

Fox had anticipated this answer, but it still hit her like a physical blow. Typical of Ma. She was like one of those sea creatures that dropped her spawn then swam away, as if birthing them had been her final responsibility.

'She probably would have liked you to go over and see her.'

'Dear, you know I don't drive. It's frightfully difficult for me.'

'I think she's pretty upset at the moment.'

'Not much I can do, I'm afraid. You're big girls now. There's some problems you have to sort out for yourselves.'

Fox watched the sparrows playing on the lawn. Witch, she thought. Don't know why I come. Don't know why Dad ever put up with you.

'What about you, darling? Any husband on the horizon?'

'A few,' she said, 'but they all belong to other women.'

A tart smile. And then: 'Good for you. You're the only one ever had any sense.'

It was an astonishing thing to say, the very last thing she'd ever imagined hearing from her mother. And then it hit her: we are so alike, you and I. We are both loners, both prickly, both do-it-our-own-way people, with no affinity at all for longterm relationships with men.

It was an epiphany of sorts, and it horrified her and threw a black cloud over the warm August afternoon. We become what we hate, someone had told her once. Oh, yes, she had thought, but that won't ever happen to me.

Yet in a way it had.

Ma must have seen the expression on her face. 'You all right, dear?' she asked her.

'Yes,' Fox said. 'I'm fine.'

Guildford

Carrie had not been employed at the radio station long enough to qualify for maternity leave, and besides, the station manager, Carrie said, had been utterly pissed off that his sales manager had knocked up one of the staff. The fact they were getting married was beside the point. Carrie had resigned, with a vague promise of consideration for another job in a couple of years' time when the baby was old enough for nursery school.

And so it fell to Carrie to start renovating their cottage in Compton. Her nesting instincts in full flow, she started by painting the nursery.

Fox found her up a ladder in one of Stephen's old shirts that reached almost to her knees. There were flecks of white paint in her hair and on her face, like tiny white freckles. While she worked Fox went into the kitchen and made tea. A few minutes later she came back out with two mugs of PG Tips and set them down on a trestle table in the corner of the room, among the brushes and paints and bottles of turps.

Looking at her friend, Fox experienced a stab of envy. She looked so happy. Only one thing to think about, the baby. Not even starting to show yet, no morning sickness, blissfully content. Lucky bitch.

Inevitably Carrie immediately started talking about the

pregnancy, the shopping expeditions to Mothercare, the visits to the doctor for check-ups.

'Do you know what sex it is?' Fox asked.

Carrie paused and dabbed her brush in the pot of paint that was balanced on the top step of the wooden ladder. 'I had an ultrasound last week. It's a boy. So we'll have one of each.'

'Does Stephen know?'

She nodded. 'He's over the moon.'

'That's great.'

Fox felt lost among so much domesticity. More at home with blood on the floor than spilled paint, more comfortable at crime scenes than in nurseries. Which was a facet of her character she took pride in. On the other hand, she knew she was losing Carrie as a friend, was being replaced as Carrie's confidant by Stephen, which was as it should be, she supposed. But where did that leave her?

'Stephen's so good with Daisy,' Carrie said, picking up on the undercurrent of their conversation. 'He's going to be a great father.'

Better than Daisy's anyway, Fox thought, though that won't be hard, provided he doesn't vomit through his nose and beat you up more than once a month. The mess us women get ourselves into. For a little love, for a shoulder to snuggle into at night, for sex.

'Do you like it?' Carrie asked her.

'What?'

'Do you like the colour? Blue seemed too predictable. That's why we went for this soft green. It's kind of restful. Makes you think of the sea.'

'It's great.' She felt strangely disconnected, as if she was looking into Carrie's world through plate glass. She could hear and see what was happening on the other side, but she could not experience it. Perhaps not even understand it. Instead she was lost in a world of her own choosing, veering between the daylight world of death and mayhem and by night some snatched happiness with unattainable men.

'I know what you're thinking,' Carrie said.

'No, you don't.'

'You look at me sometimes and you've got this expression on your face. You think I was mad, don't you? Marrying Stephen.'

'No, of course I don't think you were mad.' A lie.

'It's going to be all right, Maddy. Honest. This is right for me.'

'I know,' Fox said and handed her the mug of tea. Carrie balanced the brush on the paint tin and accepted it gratefully.

Fox sat down on an upended paint tin. There was a difficult silence. 'Why didn't you tell me, Carrie? About Ash.'

Carrie didn't say anything for a very long time, couldn't meet her eyes. Finally: 'Shit.'

'You knew.'

'You mean about his wife?'

'Right.'

She studied the wall, the concentration of a Michelangelo examining a masterwork in progress. 'Stephen said not to interfere.'

'Stephen.'

A flat silence. Carrie finally chanced a look at her over the rim of the mug. 'It's not working out?'

'Finito.'

'You dumped him?'

She shook her head. 'Wife came back.'

'I thought . . . Stephen said that was all over.'

'No, "all over" is divorce. Separation is time out.'

'Is that what he said?'

'No, he said he loves his children, and he wants to go back

to them. I just don't see myself as the bitch who stuffs it up for them.'

Carrie chewed voraciously on her bottom lip. 'You don't have much luck with blokes, do you?'

'You make your own luck, I suppose.'

Carrie shrugged, stared at the floor. Something lost here this afternoon. A lifetime's trust, perhaps. 'I hope it comes out all right when it's done,' Carrie said.

'Yes,' Fox said. 'So do I.'

PART FOUR

The unique and supreme pleasure of love lies in the certainty of doing evil.

Baudelaire

Chapter Fifty-Five

The vote was over early, at three thirty. Duty done, Carlton left the House. As he made his way through the log jam of rush hour traffic he grappled again with the prospect of discovery, imminent now. That appalling detective from the murder squad had called him again, wanting to talk to him. He had tried to stall her, but she had insisted. She was coming around at eight o'clock tonight. He had tried ringing Kennett, but he was at a policing conference in Paris or Geneva or somewhere.

Why had he allowed his life to spin out of control in this way? He had kept such a tight rein for so many years. How had this happened?

Perhaps I have sickened myself with my own ambition, he thought. How better to destroy yourself than with your own secrets? Or perhaps I have just become tired of the lies. Even the terror and despair he felt now was better than living without feelings, any feelings at all.

I have lived my life for all the wrong reasons; I have sought appearances over devotion, feigned love without passion, public service without humanity. Sex has filled those empty places where feelings should have been. And see where it has left me.

The post mortem could go on for ever. The truth of it is, I have surrendered control of my destiny now, I am a spectator in my own tragedy. Recrimination is pointless. It would only have purpose if there was some way out of this, and there is no way out. I can only watch and wonder what disasters may come.

Hampstead

When he got home there was a note lying on the hall table.

James.
I have decided to leave you. Please do not pretend to be shocked. Our marriage has been over for some time now. I am staying with Mummy and Daddy for the time being. Diana is with me. From here we should let our solicitors work out the details. That would be best all round, don't you think?
Louise.

Carlton knew he had to get out of the house, just walk, constant movement the only answer. He found the dog's lead, routed her from her kennel, ignored the look of reproach. She was too old now for long walks, but she was his dog, for God's sake, at least Louise had left him something. And if he wanted to go for a walk, well, the bloody thing could drag herself round the Heath one more time. There had to be some recompense for the smell and the vet's bills.

He tramped across the Heath, the scent of warm summer in his nostrils, looking south across London and the distant haze and murmur of traffic. *Knew this was going to happen, just a matter of time.* Now it had finally come to it, he felt numb, wanted to go back, change everything, have the time over again.

And you'd do exactly the bloody same, he muttered to himself. Just the way you are. Born that way. Pointless to think you could change.

What the hell have I done?

Ducks paddled gently across the black ponds, sunlight like mercury on the water, squirrels darted across the green, but the perfect peace touched him not at all.

The house was in darkness when he got home. It was always Louise who turned on the drawing-room lamps in the evening, gave the house its welcoming yellow glow. Tonight there were only shadows, a feeling of cathedral stillness. He found the bottle of Bushmills and a crystal tumbler and retired with it to his study, there to find succour in blessed oblivion.

Chapter Fifty-Six

Fox stared at the crouching figures of the gargoyles on the gateposts, the shadowed gables, the house in utter darkness. Half past nine and still no sign of Carlton, no sign of life at all inside the house. Where were his wife and his daughter? Someone should be home.

She thought about going home herself, but then she thought no, sod it, he's trying to avoid me and I won't let him. He can keep me waiting for an hour and a half but he can't get me off his back. I'll hound the truth out of this bastard.

It was cool for summer, and she shivered inside her jacket, wished she'd brought a jersey or a coat. The usual crap on the radio and she turned it off. It was running the battery down. Nothing to do but sit there. A man walked past with his dog, whistling tunelessly. Cars drifted past down the street, then she heard footsteps, a man hurried past holding a briefcase, arriving back late from a long day in the city.

Christ, she was tired. She thought about Kimberley Mason, and wondered what had led her from her ordinary, upper-middle-class family in Surrey to a sordid basement in Highgate. Was there some sort of conspiracy against women that had drawn her in, some intense and yellow flame that had hypnotised her? She thought of her favourite childhood stories: Snow White laid out in a glass coffin, Beauty held captive by the Beast, a whole flock of delicate heroines bruised, passive and wounded. Even as a child she remembered being excited by the fascinating prestige of martyred, deserted, resigned beauty.

She shivered inside her overcoat. Summer. The stars were very far away right now and it was bloody cold.

She woke with a start, checked her watch, couldn't believe it. Three o'clock in the morning. Christ. Months on end with never enough sleep, and now she had slept five and a half hours straight, for God's sake. In her car.

A debilitating pain in her neck. Her whole body was cold and aching and stiff. She was furious with herself. She must be out of her mind. Thirty four years old, single, sitting here in the early hours of the morning in a draughty and cramped Sierra. Wasn't even getting paid overtime for this.

Get a life, Madeleine.

Then she saw the gates open. She realised that it was not the cold that had woken her. Carlton's silver BMW was pulling out of the gates and on to the road. She felt a rush of adrenalin and groped for the keys in the ignition. It took her three attempts to find them, her mind still drowsy with sleep, her fingers numb and unco-ordinated.

The Sierra's engine coughed to life. She waited until she saw the glow of the BMW's brake lights a hundred yards away at the foot of the hill before she turned on her headlights, put the car into gear and followed.

At this time of night tailing another car was not as difficult as it might have been during the day. She followed Carlton's BMW across West Hampstead and Cricklewood. She kept her distance, was perhaps even a little over-cautious, was forced to run a red light on Finchley Road because she was hanging back too far.

Where could he be going this time of the morning? she wondered.

He turned off the North Circular and on to an industrial estate not far from Wembley Stadium. Fox pulled over. If she turned in behind him, he could not fail to spot her. She would have to wait.

She watched the BMW's red tail lights disappear down the lane among the jumble of factories and chain-link fences.

Something was going on. What was the shadow minister for Trade and Energy doing in an industrial estate at this hour of the morning?

She waited an impatient five minutes, then put the car back into gear and followed. A chain-link fence, some black plastic bin liners, overflowing with rubbish, were illuminated in the splash of her headlights. She wound down the window, listening, heard the barking of a guard dog close by, the rattle of a heavy chain as it threw itself against a gate.

I've lost him, she thought.

No voices, no sign of Carlton's car. Two alternatives: either he had seen her, and had driven into the estate to throw her off track, then driven out again, on another road; or he was parked in one of the complexes, out of sight, engaged in whatever business had brought him here. God knows what. Drugs perhaps. Was that what this was all about?

She passed a padlocked chain-link gate, topped with barbed wire, found herself at the end of a cul de sac. She stopped the car, kept her foot on the brake, weighing her options. Directly in front of her a brick warehouse was silhouetted against a half moon. A sign read, 'BEAUFORT ENGINEERING. Please ring bell for service.'

The yard was in utter darkness. She had lost him.

'Fuck,' Fox murmured under her breath. She reversed her car and drove home.

Bayswater

The black eye of the revolver was pointed at her head. She watched the finger tighten around the trigger, held her breath, waited. Would she hear the gunshot that ended her life, would there be a few seconds of comprehension before the world faded in her vision like the last scene in a film? Or would the darkness come quickly, abruptly, hammering shut on oblivion with the finality of a slamming door.

She held her breath, her muscles frozen, helpless in the silent gaze of death's small black eye.

Fox sat upright in bed, her T-shirt soaked with sweat, heart racing.

The dream again.

That dream.

Lambeth. Martin Lampard staring at her down the length of a revolver. Death returning for the appointment so narrowly missed before.

She looked at the digital clock beside the bed. Almost six, time to get up anyway. Christ, she couldn't function this way. Eyes felt as if they were full of grit, a pain behind her eyes like a migraine, felt as if her body was somewhere else. She stumbled out of bed into the shower, stood there for ten minutes, letting the needles of hot water slice over her scalp, trying to chase night's black dreams from her mind, bring herself back to the world, and life's nasty surprises.

Chapter Fifty-Seven

Area Major Incident Pool, Hendon Road

She stared through the glass partition in her office, at the rows of desks in the Incident Room, the silent computers, the windows looking back towards the city, dawn creeping like a malignant stain over the sky. She regarded her breakfast – dispenser coffee, black, a Mars bar she had found in her jacket pocket – and wondered why she was doing this.

TJ was out there, Bill Honeywell too. At least they were getting paid by the hour.

She saw Mills walking across the Incident Room towards his office, a burnished leather briefcase in his right hand, immaculate in a charcoal woollen suit. They said he had been a male model before he joined the police force, enjoyed the money and the work but couldn't tolerate people thinking he was gay.

He saw her and made a detour towards her office. Shit, she wasn't ready for this, not this morning.

He put his head round the door. 'You look bloody awful.'

'Thanks.'

'Call them as I see them. Hungover?'

'Late night.'

'Mind if I sit down?'

No, you can piss off, you slippery, ass-kissing bastard. 'Sure, guv.'

His presence was accompanied by the aroma of expensive cologne. He looked crisp and groomed and assured, which made her hate him more.

'You're in early,' she said.

'Rachel brought a boyfriend home last night. Wanted to get out of the house before either of them woke up, so I didn't embarrass her.'

'So you're not back with . . .'

'Sally? No. I've decided to give up women for a while. See if something better comes along.'

'Good call.'

'Did you talk to Carlton?'

She thought about telling him. Telling him what? That she'd fallen asleep in her car and then lost her trace? Admit to screwing up twice? 'He didn't show up.'

'I think you're right about him. The whole thing stinks.'

'Have you talked to Kennett?'

'He's in Geneva. Not back till tomorrow.' He scratched his moustache with a thumb. 'I know what you think of me, Madeleine, that I'm just shallow and ambitious and out for number one.'

'I never thought that.'

'Well, you should have. Most of the time you'd be right. But don't think I'm not going after Carlton if I think he's hiding something.' He stood up, was about to leave when TJ put his head around the door. 'Guv, just had a call from Hampstead. Big flap on over there. Someone's snatched their Member of Parliament.'

'Not James Carlton?' Fox said.

TJ looked at her, and then at Mills, and she could see him putting two and two together. Grey Man. 'Yeah, are we interested in him?'

Fox and Mills took off out of the office together. TJ had his answer.

Chapter Fifty-Eight

Hampstead

A DS Sanderson from the Hampstead CID led them out to the gravel courtyard, familiar to Fox from her visit a few weeks before. She could still see Carlton standing under the portico in his loafers and cardigan, the perfect English gentleman, his home his castle. Well, this time the barbarians had come and thrown down the gates.

'Whoever did this was a professional,' Sanderson was saying. 'Scaled the wall about here, we found scratchmarks on the brickwork, must have used crampons, or some sort of climbing gear. No blood on the broken glass at the top of the wall, so he found a way of getting over that as well. We've got some footprints in the flowerbeds, Forensics have taken casts. He deactivated the burglar alarm and the security lights, got into the house by cutting the glass out of the windowpane here.'

A perfectly cut square of glass lay in the garden bed, the putty used to extract it still attached.

A Yard forensics team, in white overalls and overshoes, were searching for fingerprints, blood stains, footprints. An SO3 photographer was recording the scene.

Fox said nothing. She thought about the silver BMW pulling out of the gates the night before. The wall the intruder had climbed over was down a shadowy lane fifty yards from where she had parked her car, impossible to see from her position. No fault of hers of course; she had been here for an interview, not surveillance.

Still, it wasn't going to look too good on her record. She wondered about the best way to handle this. 'No bloodstains inside the house?' she asked.

'No sign of a struggle at all.'

'What about his family?' Mills asked.

'It seems Mrs Carlton moved out two days ago. She and her daughter are staying with her parents in Berkshire.' Sanderson chewed on the ends of his moustache. 'Can I ask why you're so interested in this?'

'You can ask, but I'm afraid I can't tell you.'

She knew what Sanderson was thinking: elitist bastards, worse than the Flying Squad. Still, if they'd kept this from their own team, they certainly weren't about to spill it to a DS in a borough CID office. Kennett's instructions, after all.

They went inside the house. The house's Victorian charm had been violated by the grey aluminium powder smeared on all the flat surfaces, middle-aged men in white overalls crawling over the antique carpets searching for trace.

Sanderson led the way upstairs to Carlton's bedroom.

'Bed's unmade,' Sanderson said. 'Carlton must have been asleep when the intruder broke in. He doesn't seem to have put up a fight.'

'And they left in Carlton's BMW?'

Sanderson nodded. 'That's our information. His wife took the Merc when she left.' A grim smile. 'As one would.'

'You've got a trace on this phone call you received.'

'It came through the Thames Valley Police. It's a mobile

so we can only pinpoint it to a four mile radius of the nearest microwave aerial. That still leaves most of north-west London, Edgware to Ruislip. We have an All Points Warning on the BMW, but it's got to be in a warehouse or a garage, my guess.'

Mills nodded and turned for the door. 'Thanks.'

'We'll keep you informed,' Sanderson said.

'We'll do the same,' Fox said and she followed Mills out, leaving Sanderson wondering what the hell she meant.

The activity at the Carlton house had brought out the neighbours, crowds watching from behind the cordon, fascinated and appalled. Didn't get this kind of buzz in Hampstead every day. The actors and rock stars and financiers and the rest of their high-profile community guarded their privacy too dearly. Television crews and newspaper photographers were out there, too. Jim Carlton might have hoped to keep his private life before this. No chance of that now.

'Something I have to tell you, guv,' she said, her hand on the door of the Sierra.

'Is it about Carlton?'

'Could be.' They got in the car. Fox hesitated, her hands on the wheel. She wondered how this was going to turn out. 'Want to come for a drive?'

He stared at her. 'I've got bloody work to do, Madeleine. So have you.'

She started the engine. 'Bear with me. I'll tell you about it as we go along.'

Chapter Fifty-Nine

Wembley, NW10

The rattle of a train on the Wembley line. Ahead of them a lorry, loaded with pipes, turned into one of the warehouses. They passed a printer's, a welding works, a yard with a large sign that read, 'Caledonian Freight Services'. Rubbish, paper and plastic had blown across the road.

They reached the end of the cul-de-sac, stopped in front of some spiked aluminium palings. There was an abandoned Portakabin on the other side of the fence, the yard littered with oil drums and crates and a rusting garbage skip.

'This is it?' Mills asked her.

In the daylight it looked even more forlorn than it had the night before. Weeds pushed through the asphalt, waist high along the perimeter fence. The site must have been empty for months: the nightwatchman's caravan had been vandalised, all the windows smashed. The gate appeared to be locked, but when they got out Fox discovered that someone had cut through the chain with heavy duty boltcutters.

'Could he have come through here?' Mills asked her.

'Let's take a look,' Fox said.

She and Mills wedged the gates open and went back to the car. They drove across the yard to the former offices of Beaufort Engineering. Every window had been broken and the graffiti artists had been at work here as well, tags spray-painted over all the walls.

Mills got out of the car, looked around. 'So this bloke took Carlton from right under your nose,' he said.

Fox said nothing. She felt her cheeks burning.

'He could have driven out the north side of the estate,' she said, ignoring the bait.

'Could have done.'

'I guess we'd better look around.'

'I guess.'

Mills walked around the side of the office, kicked the door. Locked. She checked around the back; the smell of cat piss and diesel, the harsh buzz of a saw from a furniture factory.

'Kennett finds out about this, he's going to have your guts,' Mills said. He would, too, she thought, unless they found Carlton.

'He's not going to find out.'

'Let's hope not,' Mills said, his tone making it quite clear she was in this on her own.

She tried the warehouse doors. Padlocked and bolted. Waste of time. For a moment she had allowed herself to hope that whoever had taken Carlton had also cut those chains on the front gates, that Carlton's BMW, if not Carlton himself, was here, somewhere. It would have been a redemption, of sorts.

She went round the corner.

The warehouse backed on to a reservoir, there was a sports ground on the other side, a vista of goalposts and white rugby posts, acres of them. And there, partly in the shadow of the roof, was the silver BMW.

'Guv!'

On cue she heard a muffled banging from the boot of the car.

Mills ran around the corner, shook his head in disbelief. 'Bloody hell,' he murmured, 'you've found the bastard.'

Chapter Sixty

Rosslyn Hill Police Station, Hampstead

Carlton sat in an interview room at Hampstead police station, the hand that held the cigarette shaking so badly he spilled ash all over the floor. His skin was grey. Earlier that day he had been conveyed by an ambulance to the Middlesex Hospital, where the doctors had pronounced him in good health despite his ordeal. Shaken but not stirred, as Mills had put it.

Carlton told the story haltingly. A man had appeared in his bedroom in the early hours of the morning. No, he didn't know what time; no, he didn't see the man's face, he was wearing a balaclava.

He seemed to resent having to answer their questions, as if it was just all too tiresome to bother with, as if they were once again intruding on his privacy.

'I've told all this to the other detectives,' he said. Sanderson and his colleagues from Hampstead CID had had first crack at him.

'I'm sorry, sir, but we're not the other detectives,' Mills said. 'I'd like you to go through it again.'

'When I got home yesterday evening, I had a few drinks. I got drunk, in fact. I'd had rather a nasty shock.'

'Your wife . . .'

Carlton looked at Fox. 'Exactly. That was why I was unable to make my appointment with you, Inspector.'

'You were passed out.'

'As you say.'

'So what's the next thing you remember?'

'At some stage I must have taken myself off to bed. I don't know what woke me up. I opened my eyes and the light was on in the bedroom and there was a man standing over me with a balaclava pulled over his face and a pistol pointing at my head.'

'What did you do?'

'I have no clear recollection of what happened next. I was intoxicated, I was terrified, I was half asleep. I did whatever he asked me to do. The only thing I clearly remember is him bundling me into the boot of the car.'

'Is there anything about the man that you remember? Anything that you recall as distinctive?'

Carlton shook his head.

'What was he wearing?'

'A balaclava.'

'You've told us that,' Fox snapped, growing impatient. 'What else?'

'I don't remember. I told you . . .'

'Yes, I know, you were drunk and half asleep.'

Mills gave her a hard stare. Ease up. He turned back to Carlton. 'What about his voice?'

Another shake of the head.

'Did he have an accent?'

'No. I've gone through this with the other detectives, I told you.'

Carlton reached for the cup of coffee on the table in front

of him, but his hands were shaking so badly he spilled the lukewarm brown liquid over the table. A break while they mopped up.

Finally Carlton continued with his tale.

'I don't know how long we drove around. I thought he must be taking me somewhere to kill me. I was terrified. And I could barely breathe in there. I hate confined spaces. I went to pieces, I'm afraid.'

Mills nodded, sympathetically.

'Finally we stopped, and he opened the boot. He shone a torch in my eyes and told me if I wanted to see the light of day again I had to organise fifty thousand pounds to be left in a holdall by John Constable's grave in Hampstead church. He said if he got the money he would come back and let me go. Then he tossed something at me and shut the boot again.'

'Tossed something at you,' Fox said.

'A mobile phone. It had an illuminated green dial pad. I heard him doing something outside. He was making air holes in the metal with some sort of drill. Then he left.'

'Fifty thousand pounds is a lot of money,' Mills said.

'Yes, it is.'

'Do you have those sort of readies?'

Carlton gave him a look that could have shattered glass. 'No, I don't.'

'So what did you do?'

'I rang my wife.'

'Right. And what did she say?'

Carlton bristled with injured pride. 'It was less than twenty-four hours since we had separated. Her father answered the telephone, not in a pleasant mood at being awoken at that hour, and I suppose his opinion of me has been coloured by the recent acrimony with my wife. My telephone call must have sounded a little hysterical. He told me to stop bothering Louise and hung up.'

Fox bit her lip. Oh, you poor bastard.

'Hung up,' Mills said, deadpan.

'I tried calling back but he had left the phone off the hook. Deliberately, no doubt.'

'So then what did you do?' Mills said, his voice oozing sympathy. Fox didn't believe she could have managed it with quite the same amount of sincerity.

There was a deathly silence.

'Mr Carlton?'

'Well, what could I do?' Carlton said, his voice as shrill as a schoolgirl's.

'Who else did you call?'

Carlton closed his eyes. Fox had the impression that he was wishing them all away. 'Look, it's over. I appreciate all your efforts on my behalf. I don't want to answer any more questions.'

'Why didn't you ring us?'

Carlton drew on the cigarette, his hands trembling. He shook his head, rubbed his forehead with a thumb. 'What was the point? I didn't know where I was and I didn't think you'd be able to trace a mobile phone.'

'Let's see, this happened . . .' Mills looked at Fox . . . 'just after three a.m.'

'I've no idea what time it was.'

'You made the call to your wife just before four o'clock. You didn't call nine nine nine until just after five. What did you do in that hour?'

'I was lying in the boot of a car. My options were somewhat limited.'

'But you did ring your wife.'

'Yes.'

'But you've already told us you didn't think you could raise that much money.'

'Perhaps I thought Louise could put her hands on some of Daddy's millions,' he said with no small amount of bitterness.

'And you didn't try to call anyone else?'

Carlton looked like a cornered animal. 'Look, am I on trial here? Are you accusing me of something? I thought I was the victim in this!'

Fox leaned forward. 'Why did your wife move out?'

Carlton kept his eyes on the floor. When he spoke his voice was a monotone, without inflection or emotion. 'Personal reasons.'

'Had she found out about you and Kimberley Mason?'

Carlton stared at her. 'There were many reasons. I think in the papers they call it irreconcilable differences.'

'So she did find out about you and Kimberley?'

'I have no idea.'

'All right,' Fox said, 'let's talk about something else.' She opened the folder on the table in front of her and took out the telephone logs for Kimberley Mason's phone. She turned them around so Carlton could see them. 'This is a record of the telephone calls Kimberley Mason made in the week leading up to her murder. She made eight phone calls to your mobile number, another five to your home. Why?'

'I think I'd like to call my solicitor,' Carlton said.

Chapter Sixty-One

Datchet, Berkshire

Louise Carlton had one of those walks the rich perfect, Fox thought, like they have a carrot stuck up their arse. Fox knew her life story from the moment they met: a good girls' school, her own pony to ride at gymkhanas, debs' ball, a nanny to some upper-class friends, a suitable marriage, regular appearances in the social pages. Fox detested her on sight. She wore a dress that would have paid Fox's rent for a whole month and far too much jewellery for four o'clock in the afternoon.

Louise invited them to meet Mater and Pater — an aged gentleman with the remains of his afternoon tea down his shirt, the overbearing demeanour of an Army major, and dewlaps that hung over his collar like saddlebags; beside him a blue-rinsed doll with a look on her face as if she had just swallowed a lemon. She led Fox and TJ through to what she described as the conservatory, a glass room jungle-green with pot plants that looked over acres of well-trimmed lawns and topiary.

She brought them tea on a silver service and while they balanced the Spode china on their knee they were offered paper-thin sandwiches with little bits of cucumber in them. The gentility of it made Fox's teeth ache, but TJ seemed to be enjoying himself immensely.

Louise Carlton leaned back in one of the wicker chairs and gave them a chill smile. 'You wished to talk to me about my husband,' she said.

'We are looking into the circumstances surrounding his abduction this morning,' Fox said.

'Ghastly business.'

Ghastly. That was one way to describe it. My God, these people were like icebergs.

'Some of your people have already been here.'

Sanderson, Fox thought. They seemed to have been trailing him around all day.

'Do we really need to go through all this again?'

'Mrs Carlton, we're not actually investigating your husband's kidnapping. We're conducting a murder enquiry.'

'Murder? You think the man who kidnapped my husband may have murdered someone?'

She decided to sidestep that one. 'Before we get into that,' Fox went on, 'we'd like to ask you a couple of questions about last night.'

Louise Carlton crossed her legs and smiled, her face a mask.

'We believe your husband rang here to speak with you in the early hours of this morning.'

'That's correct.'

This is going to be like pulling teeth, Fox thought. 'He has told us your father answered the telephone.'

'Yes.'

'Can we speak with him later?' TJ asked.

'If you like, but you'll have to excuse him. He's a little volatile since his stroke. Gets agitated rather easily.'

Almost senile, then. That helps. 'When did you find out about this telephone call, Mrs Carlton?'

'The next morning. Pater was in quite a snit about it.'

'Did he tell you exactly what your husband had said to him?'

'Well, my dear, it was the middle of the night. Apparently, James said he wanted to speak to me and that he wanted money. Pater hung up. Then he rang back a second time and Pater took the telephone off the hook. He's always been rather protective of me. Especially where James is concerned.'

Fox decided to be direct. There really was no other way. 'You don't seem very upset,' she said.

Louise Carlton gave her a chill smile. As if she had broken wind and wanted to pretend it was the dog. 'We don't discuss our personal lives with the police.'

Jesus. This was like interviewing the Queen. 'I understand you have recently separated.'

A stare, the smile frozen exactly in place.

She tried again. 'You wouldn't have wanted your husband to have come to any harm, though.'

'Of course not. I was most relieved to learn that he is safe and well.'

'But?'

'I'm sorry?'

'I'm sorry, but you don't seem relieved. You seem angry.'

'As I said, I don't think it's appropriate to discuss one's private life with the police. It's not relevant.'

'It might be.'

Louise smiled and offered the plate. 'Sandwich?'

'No, thanks,' Fox said, but TJ leaned in and grabbed one. 'How's your daughter taken this?' Fox asked.

'You don't need to speak to her about any of this, do you?'

Fox wondered about that. 'I don't know. Has she anything to tell us?'

At last the mask came down and the real Louise Carlton stared back at her with genuine ferocity. 'I want to keep her out of this. She's only young. It's bad enough all of this being in the newspapers and on the television. She needs to be protected.'

For the first time Fox felt an emergence of sympathy for Louise Carlton. She stared at the Ladro figurines in their glass cabinet, the Chinese vases. All so expensive, but all so fragile and delicately balanced. One good shake and the whole lot comes crashing down.

'Where is she right now?'

'She goes riding in the afternoons. With a friend.'

Fox smiled and decided it was time to hit her with it. 'Mrs Carlton, did you ever hear your husband talk about a woman named Kimberley Mason?'

The blood drained out of Louise Carlton's face. 'She was in the newspapers a few weeks ago. The woman who was murdered in Highgate.'

'That's right.'

'What possible connection could there be between my husband and a woman like that?'

Fox said nothing. Louise Carlton knew what she was talking about, it was written all over her. The same old same old, she thought. James Carlton thought his wife didn't know, and she knew all along.

'I don't know anything about her, except what I read in the newspapers.'

The shutters came down. There really was nothing more to be learned here. She might hate her husband, he may have been unfaithful, he may have humiliated her, but for Louise Carlton this was family business. You didn't make things worse by involving the police. That, Fox supposed, would be just too *common*.

They saw Diana as they were leaving, a photograph on the oak mantelpiece, a pale, skinny girl with very white hair, shyly grinning at the camera, self-conscious of the braces on her teeth. Fox would remember the face in that photograph in the days to come, and it would haunt her, probably for the rest of her life.

Chapter Sixty-Two

Area Major Incident Pool, Hendon Road

She got to the office at seven the next morning. Mills was already there, ensconced in her office, his polished leather boots on the desk, flicking through a folder that lay open on his lap, nursing a mug of black coffee. As she walked in he saw the flicker of annoyance on her face and stood up. He tossed her the file. 'Thought you might like to see this.'

She took the file from him. It was Hatton's telephone records.

A printed sheet was attached to the last page. Most of the numbers had been traced, and the names and addresses of the registered owners had been typed in a neat column down the page. She skimmed through the list, supposed she should not have been surprised to find Carlton's name there. She took out a pen, circled the number on the records.

She stared at the numbers for a long time, her brain clunking through the gears, testing endless permutations.

'This isn't a coincidence,' she managed finally. Suddenly the Dennis Thorpe investigation, which a few minutes ago had looked so simple and clear cut, took on bewildering new dimensions. 'Does anyone else know about this?'

'Not yet.'

'What do we do?'

Mills looked at his watch. 'I phoned Kennett as soon as he got back from the airport last night. He's going to meet us in his office at eight o'clock. Grab yourself a coffee and we'll get going.'

Area 2 HQ, Colindale

Kennett stared at the file with the gloomy and bitter resignation of a man who had been checkmated by his twelve-year-old nephew. 'I don't understand this,' he said.

They were in the Chief Superintendent's office, Kennett resplendent in his dark blue suit, wearing his club tie. Across the desk Mills picked at an imaginary piece of lint on his sleeve.

When Kennett finally looked up at Fox, his expression intimated that he would like to deal with this news by shooting the messenger. 'What do we know about this Robert Hatton?'

'Former SAS,' Mills answered, 'left the Regiment in 1991, what he's been doing since that time is still unclear. James and Crawford went up to Hereford to interview his former commanding officer. They haven't exactly fallen over themselves to co-operate. You know how they like their secrets up there.'

'I can't imagine what an SAS renegade would have in common with a man like Jim.'

'Neither can I,' Mills said, carefully.

'We'll have to talk to him,' Fox said.

Kennett placed the file on his desk with the care of a man handling sweating gelignite. Anything that involved politicians or government officials always sent the fat cats in Tintagel House hurrying off for the antacids.

'First he appears on the telephone records of Kimberley Mason, now his name crops up again in the murder of a standover merchant in Tottenham,' Fox said. 'There's something not right here.'

'You think the cases are connected?' Kennett asked her.

'It doesn't seem likely, on the face of it, but it's clear our James Carlton has had more than one inappropriate relationship.'

Kennett nodded, conceding defeat on that point.

Fox took the forensics report from the Kimberley Mason investigation out of her briefcase. 'I think you should also look at this, sir,' she said.

Kennett snatched the report out of her hands, wordlessly, his lips compressed in a bloodless line. There was silence in the room as he read it.

'What in particular do you wish me to look at?' he said finally.

'The fibres found in the basement of Kimberley Mason's house. Forensics say that they are from a khaki Army-issue jumper commonly found in any Army and Navy surplus store. The kind of clothing Hatton was often seen to be wearing. In fact his neighbours say he dressed Army almost exclusively.'

'You're making a quantum leap of faith. They must sell thousands of those jumpers every year.'

'There's also this, sir,' Mills said. Another report, Hatton's censored file from SAS HQ in Hereford. 'His blood group was A rhesus negative, the same as the exemplar from the refrigerator door in Kimberley Mason's house, the same as

Bradshaw's and Kimberley's. Only the DNA tests now show that the blood did not match with either of the samples from the dead girl or the man charged with her murder. We've got a hair sample from Hatton's flat and I've authorised a premium service to pathology for DNA testing. In two days we'll know if it was actually Hatton's blood we found in the kitchen.'

'This is appalling,' Kennett said, shaking his head.

'So far Mr Carlton is hiding behind his brief,' Mills said. 'I'm hoping this latest information may persuade him to co-operate with us a little more fully.'

Kennett was silent for a long time, but finally nodded, conceding defeat. He turned to Mills. 'I want you to handle this, Mills,' Kennett said to him, ignoring Fox. 'Strictly softly, softly. If any of this gets out to the media and he's in the clear, it's your job.'

'Yes sir,' Mills said, and gave Fox a look of undisguised bitterness. Now look what you've done.

Chapter Sixty-Three

Carlton sat in the interview room at Hampstead station. His brief was beside him, a yellow handkerchief sprouting from the breast pocket of his suit, a gold Piaget on his wrist, Salvatore Ferragamo shoes, and a Savile Row suit that probably cost more than one of the patrol cars out in the compound. His initials were monogrammed on to his briefcase, which was of soft burgundy leather. The big guns were out now.

Mills started the tape and went through the formalities. Before he started the interview, however, the brief, whose name was Meyer — disappointing, Fox thought, I'd hoped for something grander — made a brief statement, to the effect that he wanted to record that his client had come here without duress in order to co-operate as fully as possible with the police in their enquiries.

Mills waited for him to finish, then opened the manila folder in front of him and slid Hatton's telephone logs across the table towards Carlton. Why one company should take six weeks and another twenty four hours to produce such records Fox wasn't able to fathom. You worked with what you got.

'Mr Carlton,' Mills said, 'we'd like to ask a few questions in regard to your abduction by person or persons unknown yesterday. In front of you are the records of phone calls made from the telephone your abductor left with you yesterday morning. We asked the telephone company involved to put an urgent trace on it. The telephone was registered to someone by the name of Robert Hatton, who is not unknown to us. This same Mr Hatton made five telephone calls to numbers listed to you, in the last two weeks. Are you still telling us you don't know who abducted you?'

A shudder seemed to pass through Carlton's body, like a ship foundering on a reef. Christ, he's going to come apart, she thought. He's right there on the edge. Here he was preparing himself for questions about Kimberley Mason, and now Mills has ambushed him from left field. Carlton managed to pull himself together. He leaned across to his brief and held a whispered consultation.

Finally: 'It was dark. He was wearing a balaclava.'

Fox looked at Mills. For God's sake.

'So you do know someone called Bob Hatton.'

A slight nod of the head.

'For the tape, please.'

'Yes.'

'Why didn't you tell us this yesterday, Mr Carlton? He gave you instructions on the ransom. If you knew him well enough to have five telephone conversations with him, you would have recognised his voice.'

Carlton thought about that. He could see the sense in it. She could see him wondering how to stall them.

Meyer looked at the ceiling. 'You don't have to answer these questions, James. You're not being charged with anything.'

'Perhaps you'd like to tell us the nature of your relationship with Bob Hatton?'

Carlton scratched his hand, perturbed for a moment. In Fox's experience, that was the trouble with telling porkies, it made it hard to remember what you'd said to whom. 'You're already looking for him?'

'You knew that.'

'The photograph you put in the newspapers. It wasn't a very good one. He looks a lot different now.'

'Would you like to tell us the substance of your dealings with Mr Hatton?' Fox repeated.

Carlton didn't answer her question straight away. Instead he looked at Mills. 'What will happen to Hatton when you catch up with him?'

'We have a warrant for his arrest.'

'He's still armed, I suppose. Do you think he'll surrender peacefully?'

'I have no idea.'

'I don't think he'll just give himself up,' Carlton said, almost as if he were trying to reassure himself about something.

'So can you tell us about your relationship with Bob Hatton?' Fox persisted.

'I employed him,' Carlton said, in a tone that he might use to a rude and over-inquisitive tabloid reporter.

'Employed him. To do what?'

'I believed I was being stalked.'

'I see,' Mills said.

Fox didn't see at all. He wasn't a government minister so he probably wasn't eligible for protection from MI5, but even so, his answer simply raised more questions than it answered. In fact, there were no circumstances she could imagine under which someone like Bob Hatton might find any kind of employment, albeit informal, with a wealthy Hampstead businessman and member of the Opposition front bench. 'Why did you believe you were being stalked?' she asked him.

'I was receiving nuisance telephone calls. Cars following mine through the traffic. Several times I thought I saw someone loitering in the street outside my house.'

'Were you threatened?'

'No, that was just it. I just suspected that something was going on.'

'Did you inform the local police?'

'I had nothing specific to complain about. I know you people are busy and I didn't want to waste your time. Besides, what would you have done?'

He had a point, if he was telling the truth. 'Go on,' Mills said.

'I decided to do something proactive.'

Well, I wonder what he means by that, Fox thought. Have the culprit shot in the head?

'How did you make contact with Bob Hatton?' Mills asked.

'Through Dennis Thorpe.'

'Ah,' Mills said. 'Mr Thorpe.'

'Hatton shot him, didn't he? I read about it. It's terrible.'

'Well, let's not get too maudlin,' Fox said. 'He was no great loss.'

'How did you know Dennis Thorpe?'

'He has a certain reputation and he likes to ingratiate himself. You know how these people work. He owns night-clubs, restaurants, makes sure you always get the best seat, sends over free champagne. That sort of thing.'

'You allowed yourself to be compromised.'

Carlton swallowed hard. 'He said if I ever needed help with anything . . .' He shrugged. 'I decided to take him up on his offer. It was stupid of me.'

No argument there. Even his brief looked disgusted.

'He said he'd see what he could do. A few days later I got a call from this Bob Hatton. We arranged to meet.'

'Where?'

'It was a coffee bar. Near Euston station.'

'A coffee bar,' Fox said.

'His suggestion.'

'What do you remember about Mr Hatton?'

'He drinks coffee black without sugar and he does not like to sit with his back towards the door.'

'Anything else?' Mills asked.

'He was wearing Army fatigues. It distressed me: I wanted to keep the meeting as anonymous as possible and I felt it attracted undue attention.'

Fox could imagine the scene. Hatton in his khakis, Carlton in his blazer and Gucci loafers. Not exactly the cappuccino set. 'Why did you want to remain anonymous?'

'Isn't it obvious? I have a certain position in the community.'

'Were you aware that what you were asking Mr Hatton to do might be in breach of the law?'

'No, I . . .' He looked over at his solicitor.

'You did realise that if Mr Hatton were to injure someone, you could be involved in a conspiracy charge?' Mills said.

'My client is trying to co-operate with you,' Meyer said. 'If you want to browbeat him, I will advise him to bring the interview to a close.'

For God's sake, Fox thought.

'What exactly did you ask Mr Hatton to do for you?' Mills insisted.

'It was a private security contract. I wanted him to keep me under surveillance, discover if there was actually someone watching me. I was told that he had certain skills in that area.'

'And he accepted this proposal?'

'Yes.'

'And that was all.'

'That was all.'

'How much did you pay him?'

Silence.

'Was it a retainer or set fee for his services?'

'We did not discuss money. I had already agreed a sum with Mr Thorpe.'

'I see,' Mills said. 'And what happened then?'

'He said he'd call me if he had any news.'

'And did he?'

'Yes. About a week later. He said he'd taken care of the problem.'

'When was this?'

'Two weeks ago.'

Long before Dennis Thorpe was murdered. They would have to check the MISPERS file on the computer, perhaps there was another body lying in a shallow grave somewhere or rotting at the bottom of the Thames. If Carlton's story was true.

'Did you ask him what he meant by taking care of the problem?' Mills asked.

Carlton shook his head. 'I was appalled, naturally.'

'Naturally,' Fox said, and Carlton glared at her.

'What did you think he meant?'

'I didn't know. I didn't want to know.'

'What did you do then?'

'I drove to Dennis Thorpe's flat in Camden and paid him the sum we had agreed on and that was that.'

Fox checked her notebook. 'The last call from Bob Hatton to your phone was made two days ago. Why was he still in contact with you if you'd paid him off?'

'He led me to believe he had not been paid for his services. I imagine that was why he murdered Dennis Thorpe. I suspect it was an argument over money.'

No, Fox thought. Too neat. He had wrapped it up and tied it with a bow and they were supposed to be grateful. If Thorpe was killed in an argument over money, as Carlton said, what was he doing in Hatton's flat? It didn't make sense. And it still didn't explain the connection to Kimberley Mason. It was too early to tackle him on that until they had the DNA results from pathology.

Carlton seemed to relax, like the actor at the end of a long and demanding performance, ready to take the curtain calls. Thinking it was all over.

She looked at Mills. 'Interview suspended three fifteen,' he said and turned off the tape.

Chapter Sixty-Four

———◆———

Windsor, Berkshire

Late afternoon, the light dappled through the oaks and the horse chestnuts beside the road, the royal castle at Windsor visible through the haze. A bright green poster nailed to one of the trees advertises a country fair, HRH Prince Charles the prime attraction, appearing as a guest player in a polo match.

Two riders appear from a copse of beech, cantering along a bridlepath that leads from a nearby stables and riding school. The riders are teenaged girls, dressed in jodhpurs and helmets. They slow their horses to a walk as they reach the road, the blinkered bay gelding skittish with the traffic.

The two riders are blinded by the sun. An opentop 4WD goes past too fast, carrying four teenagers not much older than themselves, and the bay rears up.

Struggling with her mount, Diana pays little attention to the blue Combi van that comes around the bend ahead, out of the sun. But her friend sees it and watches with disbelief as it keeps on coming, across the white lines in the middle of the road and towards her friend fifty yards in front of her. Her stomach turns. Why doesn't he swerve? Can't he see them?

The Combi does swerve, at the very last moment, but not soon enough to prevent the impact, the side of the van hits the horse a blow on its right shoulder, snapping its foreleg. The bay rears up again, his metal shoes hit the roof of the Combi, sending up sparks, its body leaving an imprint in the right side of the vehicle.

The horse's eyes are wide as dinner plates, from pain and fear and panic. He stumbles and falls, screaming in pain. Diana tries to hold the reins, bounces once in the saddle and is thrown, lies stunned on her back on the road verge. All the breath has gone out of her, there is a terrible pain in her right ankle, and she stares up at a woolly, wondering sky, unable to rise.

Fifty yards away the other girl watches, this moment suspended in time, settling her own horse. She sees Diana on the ground, her horse scrambling blindly with its hooves, trying to get up. The blue Combi stops and a man jumps out of the driver's seat.

The girl waits for the man to take control, to rescue them from this disaster. She can only gape at the long, silenced barrel of the handgun that he draws from the pocket of his donkey jacket, has only a moment to admire the sunlight that reflects on the metal, as he aims it at her head.

And that is the last thing she remembers.

Chapter Sixty-Five

———————— ◆ ————————

Rosslyn Hill Police Station, Hampstead

You could almost feel sorry for him as he sat there, his head in his hands, the knuckles kneading his scalp, a man destroyed by desires he understood no better than voodoo or black magic. He had invited the devil into his house and now he was utterly lost.

No expensive brief in sight. No more playing games.

Mills sat down. 'Would you like to have your solicitor present, Mr Carlton?' he asked him.

Carlton shook his head.

Christ, he's aged, Fox thought. Even since this afternoon.

They went through the formalities and then Mills leaned forward, his elbows on the desk. 'You'd better tell us the truth now,' he said softly.

'They're going to crucify me,' Carlton whispered.

He was right, of course. No way to keep a lid on this now. The kidnappings were headlining every newspaper, leading every television and radio bulletin in the country. A young girl had been brutally slain in broad daylight, another abducted, and less than forty eight hours since her father, a shadow front bencher had been kidnapped from his home. The tabloids were in a feeding frenzy. So far Kimberley Mason's name had not surfaced, but that was just a matter of time.

'Why haven't you found her?' Carlton said.

Fox said nothing. She expected him to blame them. What else could he do?

Hatton had stayed a step ahead of them. Almost from the moment they found the BMW at the Wembley warehouse, he must have been planning his next move, preparing to twist another knife into Carlton's tormented soul. The snatching of Diana Carlton was his contingency plan, ready even before he abducted Carlton from his home. This was personal, that much was clear now.

'Just tell us what happened,' Fox said, softly.

'I never meant for any of this. It just got out of control.'

'Just the facts, Mr Carlton.'

He ran a trembling hand across his face. 'You know about my relationship with Miss Mason,' he said.

Fox nodded. 'Let's do this again. For the tape. How long had you known her?'

'Four years. From an . . . establishment called the Black Rose. When she left, our relationship continued. Of course, I never expected my political career to take off the way it did, but I don't suppose I would have been able to stop anyway.' He could not look at Mills or Fox, kept his eyes on the table. 'You can't change how you're made, I suppose. When I met Kim it was like a dam broke. Before her, it was just for money . . . ' His voice trailed off, lost in bitter remembrance.

'What happened?' Fox prompted, trying to keep him on track, away from introspection.

But Carlton had been waiting to unburden himself, was determined to state his case. He was going to have his say. 'You'd be surprised how many powerful men patronise places like the Black Rose. Even there, I was different. I wasn't interested in humiliation as recreation. I wanted a fantasy woman I could dominate, utterly. That's where Kim was such a treasure. She actually enjoyed it, almost as much as I did. It wasn't just for the money.'

Mills fidgeted in the chair beside her.

'I was like a drowning man being thrown a line,' Carlton was saying. 'I couldn't let go. I'd finally found someone who really understood me. She made me feel that I was . . . okay.'

'But you paid her for her services?' Mills asked.

Carlton shook his head. 'Not after she left the Black Rose. She was like a mistress, I suppose. A very unusual mistress, I admit, but a kept woman, as they used to say.' He shrugged his shoulders. 'I helped her, financially. She lived far beyond her means. I didn't mind.'

'When did it go wrong?' Fox asked him.

'She got this notion that I should leave my wife and marry her.' He smiled. 'I suppose that was her fantasy. Not as base as mine, but less attainable. I imagine she dreamed of being the wife of a public figure. She had the right pedigree, that was the irony of it, but cabinet ministers don't have wives with a past. Besides, Louise has all the money.'

He stopped, and perhaps for the first time the utter implausibility of his position really hit him. A man could not be both public and private, ultimately the shadow of one would fall on the other.

'I'd always told myself that I would finish with Kimmie one day, finish with that world. Every time I went there, I said it was the last time. I always came away feeling so utterly disgusted with myself that I wanted to throw myself under the next bus. But then I always went back, it was an obsession with me, I was powerless.' Carlton swallowed hard, fighting his own emotions. 'Finally she told me that if I didn't leave Louise, she would ruin me. That she would sell her diary to the tabloids. Sheer spite. She started to telephone me, at home. Well, you can imagine. I didn't want even my wife and my daughter to find out, and here she was, threatening to tell the whole world.'

'What did you do?' Fox said.

'I met this chap about a year ago. He was in the arms business. He wanted a favour, and at the time I helped him out.'

'What sort of favour?'

'Let's say I oiled some wheels.' A fevered smile. 'No money changed hands. It was done on the understanding that if I ever needed his help, his door would be open to me. I decided to call in my marker.'

'Go on.'

'I went to see him, asked him if he knew someone who could take care of a little problem for me. I just wanted to frighten her, I swear. I didn't mean for him to kill her.'

'You are talking about Bob Hatton.'

'I didn't know his name, I didn't want to know. A certain amount of money changed hands. I thought it was all over. Then, I heard that Kim had . . . then I got this telephone call.'

'From Hatton.'

'He didn't give his name. Said he had a diary and an address book I might be interested in buying.'

'Exactly what Kimberley had threatened to do.'

'Yes.' A chill and bitter smile. 'Ironic, isn't it? Anyway he asked for an unreasonable amount of money. I panicked. I tried to get hold of my . . . friend . . . but he was overseas and I couldn't contact him. In the end I gave Hatton the money, but he got angry, said it wasn't enough.'

'Is that when he beat you up?' Fox said, remembering the

first time they had interviewed Carlton, and the faded purple bruise over his eye.

He nodded. 'I knew I'd never get rid of him, not now he had his claws in me. That's when I approached Dennis Thorpe. He had a reputation in North London, of course. One of those hard men who like to associate with politicians, actors and pop stars. You know the type.'

'Why didn't you go to him in the first place?' Mills asked.

'I thought my way was better.' A brittle laugh, like glass breaking.

'You asked Thorpe to kill Hatton?' Fox asked him.

Carlton looked startled. 'Christ, no. I just wanted the diaries.' He looked at Mills. 'You know what it's like. I didn't want this in the papers, I wanted to keep the police out of it, I thought I could handle it myself.'

Mills' face was like stone.

'Why didn't you tell us all this yesterday?' Fox asked him.

'I suppose I still thought I could get away with it. Keep it quiet. The connection with Kim.'

A long silence. *He still thought he could get away with it.* How long had he been wriggling on the hook? The dilemma of a man who thought he could have it all.

'You really have dug yourself a hole, haven't you?' Mills said, finally.

'I don't care what you do to me now. Just get Diana back. That's all I care about, she's all I've got left.' He put his head in his hands. 'This is all my fault.'

Mills leaned forward. 'We'll do our best. First, you have to give us the name of the man who put you in contact with Bob Hatton.'

Chapter Sixty-Six

The room is used as a store room; there is an old bed, some beer crates stacked in the corner, an ancient dartboard leaning against the wall, a disused jukebox, a green canvas holdall on the floor. There are bare boards on the floor and the plaster is flaking off the ceiling.

Bob Hatton sits on one of the beer crates, smoking a cigarette.

He runs a hand across his freshly shaved head. The moustache is false, bought in a fancy dress shop, his anorak and brown cord trousers purchased separately at charity shops in the high street.

He is toying with a knife, a long-bladed dagger, a souvenir from his years with the SAS. He runs a finger lightly along the edge of the blade, instantly producing blood. He licks at it, not to staunch it, but lovingly, as if it is juice. The essence of him. The essence of life.

The girl is tied to the bed, blindfolded, and there is a gag in her mouth. She has stopped struggling, lies pliant and exhausted. Her ankle has swollen to twice its normal size, a ragged edge of white bone can be seen just below the now purple skin. She has fainted twice from the pain. Whenever he gets bored, he prods the fracture with the stub end of the knife.

Now he watches her silently, debating what to do with her. He can't keep her here. Nails wouldn't like it.

In fact he'd be really pissed off if he found out what he'd done. Perhaps it was time to collect his debt and slip away. Nothing much to keep him any more.

Paddington W2

The offices were above a travel agent's off Praed Street near the Station. A plaque downstairs read, 'International Specialist Employment Services', a name that told the casual passer-by absolutely nothing. Mills and Fox went up some narrow, wooden stairs. International Specialist Employment was a one-room office, with a desk, a telephone/fax machine, a computer and a filing cabinet. The sort of equipment that could be moved overnight with the minimum of fuss.

They heard a man's voice speaking into a telephone. He looked up as they reached the landing and covered the mouthpiece. 'Can I help you?' he said.

Everything looked out of whack here. He looked too smooth, too prosperous, for the sort of operation he was running here; a double-breasted wool suit, a silk tie with a button-down collar. He had iron-grey hair, cut short, and his face was too tanned for an office worker. There was a hardness about him that belied the surroundings.

'We're looking for a Peter Robinson,' Mills said.

The man's eyes were wary and calculating. 'Can I ask who wants him?'

'I'm DCI Mills and this is DI Fox, Metropolitan Police.

You're Robinson, right?' Mills getting down to business right off, letting him know he wasn't in the mood to be yanked on.

They had already done a little checking on Peter Robinson. He had been a major in the Army, educated at Sandhurst, all the right connections. He had retired after the Gulf War, was under investigation for his role in an illegal arms shipment to a Kurdish separatist group in 1997. He travelled frequently to Africa, and was believed to have supplied former Army personnel, under private contract, to provide specialist training to the armed forces of Nigeria and Chad.

'I'll call you back,' he said into the telephone and hung up.

There was only one chair. Mills and Fox looked at each other. Mills nodded for Fox to sit down. The helpless female, she thought, and decided to stand.

Robinson got to his feet. Over six two, powerfully built, an aura of compact strength about him. GI Joe in a suit.

'Can I see your IDs?' Robinson said.

'Of course,' Mills said.

Robinson examined them closely – a simple little power play, Fox thought, buying himself time to gather his thoughts – then parked his behind on the radiator under the window.

'Can I ask what this is about?'

'I think you know,' Mills said.

Fox gave him her best smile. 'You read the newspapers, you watch television. You know about your friend Mr Carlton.'

Robinson shrugged his shoulders. 'Silly bastard.'

'He speaks well of you too.'

'I told him to be careful.'

'He tells us you hired Bob Hatton to rough up his girlfriend?'

Robinson sighed and crossed his arms. 'Is that what he told you?'

'Is it true?'

He went back to the desk and picked up the telephone. 'Excuse me. I think I'd like my solicitor to sit in on this conversation.'

Chapter Sixty-Seven

Newcastle Place W2

They sat in Interview Room Two at Paddington police station. Robinson had his solicitor beside him; another fashion statement, like Robinson himself. He doodled on a yellow legal pad with a Parker fountain pen, looking vaguely bored.

Fox set the tape running and Mills walked Robinson through the formalities. Robinson admitted his relationship with Carlton and after consulting his diary he also admitted to speaking to him in his office on 23 June.

'Can you tell us about the conversation?' Mills asked him.

'I don't remember the details. I believe he asked me if I would do him a favour.'

'And you agreed?'

'I felt honour bound. He had done a few things for me in the past.'

'Such as?'

Robinson looked around at his brief, who glanced up at them over his gold-rimmed spectacles. 'I don't think that has any relevance here.'

Mills shrugged. 'Go on,' he said to Robinson.

'Carlton said he had a problem. He told me he was being threatened, and asked if I could give him the name of someone who could advise him on questions of personal security.'

'And what did you say?'

'I gave him Bob Hatton's telephone number.'

'How do you know Mr Hatton?' Fox asked.

'He served in my unit for three years from 1988 to 1991. I've also placed him in various positions overseas.'

'What sort of positions?'

'Military adviser, places such as Rwanda and Uganda.'

'A mercenary,' Mills said.

'A military adviser,' Robinson repeated.

'Why did you give Carlton his name?'

'I knew Bob needed the money. And he was available.'

'But you didn't speak to Hatton yourself?'

'Certainly not. I wasn't exactly sure what Carlton wanted. It might have been illegal.' A chill smile.

'Are you aware that Mr Hatton is wanted in connection with the murder of a young woman in Windsor two days ago? He is also thought to have shot dead another man in Tottenham six days ago. We also want to talk to him regarding the death of a woman in Highgate on the twenty-ninth of June.'

'I see.' His face gave nothing away.

'Do you think Mr Hatton is capable of murder?'

'Capable? What do you think they train people to do in the Army?' Fox saw Robinson's brief wince at that.

'But you still put Mr Carlton in touch with him?'

'He said he wanted advice on personal security. Mr Hatton is an expert on such matters. Whether he paid him to kill someone was a matter between them. It was certainly not mentioned to me.'

Mills leaned forward. 'Mr Robinson, as you will appreciate, we want to find Hatton pretty urgently. He's committed
two murders, we think he might have committed a third. We
also believe he is responsible for having kidnapped Mr
Carlton's daughter.'

A hint of a smile. 'Yes, I read about that.'

'You think it's funny?'

'No, but a tad ironic, don't you think? In the circumstances.'

'We're not about giving you grief, Mr Robinson. We just
want to catch this bloke before he does any more damage.'

Robinson sighed. 'There's a bloke in Earls Court. David
Youll.'

'We've spoken to Mr Youll. Hatton stayed in his flat for
one night and then moved on.'

'Well, there is one other bloke. He was in the same unit
with Youll and Hatton. I've set him up with a few things over
the years. You could always talk to him.'

'What's his name?'

'He runs a pub in Lisson Grove. The Lancaster, or
something like that. His name's Andy Naylor, everyone calls
him Nails. If Youll doesn't know where he is, Naylor might.'

Fox and Mills ended the interview.

'Is my client being charged?' his brief asked them.

'He's free to go,' Mills said.

But Robinson just sat there, his fingers drumming on the
desk. There was something else on his mind. 'This is strictly
off the record,' he said.

Mills and Fox looked at each other. Why do I get the
feeling I don't want to hear this? Fox thought.

Robinson rubbed at his temples with his fingers.

Mills sat down again. 'Off the record, then,' he said.

'Look, I didn't know this had anything to do with a

woman. I mean, when Carlton rang, he didn't say *anything* about a woman.'

'Why is that important?'

'Well, if he'd told me that, I wouldn't have put him in touch with Bob Hatton, would I?'

'Why not?' Christ. Come on, spit it out.

Robinson stared at the ceiling. 'Bob used to be one of my clients, right. Last year, I got him some work in Uganda. Thing was, I had to get him out of the country in a hurry three months into his contract. Some business involving two women in a village near the training camp. Pretty sick stuff, in fact.' He tapped his forehead with his finger. 'Turned into a bit of a nutter, our Bob. Unreliable. I've steered clear of him ever since, for contract work. Obviously.'

'Obviously,' Fox said.

'I just thought you should know.'

Fox and Mills exchanged glances. Great.

Just bloody marvellous.

Chapter Sixty-Eight

———————◆———————

Lisson Grove, NW8

The Lancaster in Lisson Grove had seen better days. It was an old fashioned boozer that hadn't had a penny spent on it since the blitz. The yard beside the pub had corrugated-iron gates with 'NO PARKING' written on them, the white paint streaked down the metal.

The black and red paint on the fascia was cracked and peeling, and there were two plastic tables and chairs thrown out on the footpath as a token effort for summer. There was a dark saloon bar with filthy frosted-glass windows, and a faded sign with a picture of a World War Two bomber hung above the entrance to the public bar.

Nick parked on the other side of the road, on a yellow line. Fox checked the wing mirror, saw Mills behind the wheel of a Ford from the car pool, TJ and Honeywell with him. A unit of SO19 waited around the corner, eight well-armed specialists in body armour and helmets, in two armour-plated Range Rovers.

She heard Mills' voice on her radio, telling everyone to hold their positions.

'No sign of the blue Combi,' Nick said.

'Might be around the back,' she said. 'Or in the yard there.'

She and Nick were to go in first, to try and establish if Hatton was on the premises. She got out of the car and started across the road.

Just as she reached the pavement Fox heard what she thought was an explosion, and she and Nick threw themselves on to the ground. She looked up and saw the gates to the yard hanging on their hinges. A blue Combi van had driven straight through, and was already turning on to the cross street, fifty yards away, its tyres smoking. Fox heard a squeal of tyres as a black taxicab slammed on its brakes to avoid a collision. A Rasta in a beanie stopped to gawp, customers spilled out of an antique shop on the corner, pointing.

Fox shouted into her radio, 'All units. Target escaping in a blue Ford Transit van along Broad Street. Go, go, go!'

Seconds later a panda car, sirens wailing, emerged from one of the side streets, followed by one of the blue SO19 carriers. They roared away down Broadley Street. Fox got to her feet and started to dust herself off. Nick swore and ran back towards the cross section.

A sucker punch.

Fox didn't know what made her look back, some instinct perhaps. As she turned, she saw a man with a shaved head walk out of the public bar of the Lancaster carrying a canvas holdall. There was something about him that was familiar, something she remembered from a lift in a block of flats in Earls Court.

Do you live in this building?

He started to walk faster, when he saw her staring after him he broke into a run.

'All units, this is Fox. He's still here, I've seen him! He's on foot and heading south on Daventry!'

Nick was too far away, she couldn't wait for him. She started to run.

Chapter Sixty-Nine

The hard stop on a man like Hatton should have been an SO19 responsibility. At the least, she should have waited for Nick to catch up. But she didn't want to lose the bastard a second time.

Hatton turned down a lane and she followed. The dirty brown brick of a block of council flats on one side, a disused factory on the other, the walls obliterated by graffiti. Directly ahead a wire mesh fence separated the alley from a primary school playground. Two discarded Tesco trolleys were propped against the wire.

Hatton stopped, turned around. He had run into a cul de sac.

Well, Madeleine, what are you going to do now? That wasn't very smart. This bloke is an unarmed combat instructor, has killed people with his bare hands. He'll go through you if he has to.

You should have waited for back-up.

Hatton's face split into a grin. He had something better than his hands. He reached into the canvas holdall and his hand emerged holding a long-barrelled pistol. He cocked it and aimed, one handed.

She froze.

And there it was, the nightmare returned to haunt her. She looked again into the deadly black eye of death. Nowhere to run to, no cover.

This is it, Maddy, the sum total of your life. It ends right here. No time for valediction, or even to prepare.

You're over, you're done.

Fox watched him line up the centre of her forehead, his finger closing around the trigger. She stopped breathing, heard a whimper escape her throat.

She closed her eyes. Couldn't bear to see the look on his face as he pulled the trigger.

She heard the traffic on Marylebone Road, the distant wailing of police sirens, the SO19 squad she had sent off in the wrong direction. She found herself thinking about Ash. He would know he had been right when he heard the news. Typical Maddy. Had to be the hero. Funny, but despite the way things had turned out, she had always thought she would see him, at least one more time.

This is all wrong, I can't die now. Still so much unfinished business.

Something made her open her eyes. She saw Hatton lower the gun, turn around and shin over the wire.

The bastard. He had let her live, without obvious reason. Crazy. Killed the girl, turned his back on her. Death, in its arbitrary way, had stepped over her and moved on.

'Ma'am. Ma'am, you okay?'

It was Nick. Out of breath, sweat glistening on the handsome brown face.

She fumbled in her coat, found the radio. Her hands were shaking so hard she couldn't depress the talk button. She tossed it to him. 'He's gone through the schoolyard,' she said.

She couldn't lose him, not now.

She started running, jumped at the fence, started to haul herself over, her fingers hooking in the mesh, ripping fingernails. She snagged her coat on the wire, slipped, landed heavily on the asphalt, tearing the skin on her wrists, wrenching her right knee.

She heard Nick on the other side of the fence, shouting their location into the handheld radio. 'Target escaping on foot heading south towards Marylebone Road. Still in pursuit.' He started to climb the fence. 'Ma'am. Be careful! I've called back-up! Wait!'

She started to run across the basketball courts. She could see Hatton shinning an eight-foot wire fence, making it look so easy, just a bit of training. She heard laughing and jeering from one of the second-storey classrooms, was vaguely aware of kids' faces at the windows, the astonished face of their schoolteacher.

Keep him in view, she told herself. Don't get too close. Pray that back-up isn't too far away.

Chapter Seventy

He was fit, outran her easily. She saw him head up Marylebone, towards the pedestrian underpass on Edgware Road. He sent a woman tumbling on to her knees as he shoved past her and disappeared down the steps.

Losing him.

There was a stitch in her side, she was breathing hard when she reached the underpass, her footsteps echoing in the concrete tunnel. A startled wino looked up as she ran past, shouted at her, his filth and anger reverberating in her head. She reached the subway, hesitated. There were two metal kiosks, an engraving booth and a newsagent. Hatton had spilled a postcard rack as he ran through. The Pakistani newsagent was crouched over his trampled stand, cursing at the world and white bastards with no respect.

She kept going. To the left or to the right? She went to the right.

He was waiting for her.

She was halfway up the steps when she saw him, crouched

there, grinning the gap-toothed smile she remembered from the lift in the Earls Court flats.

The wino had staggered after her, agitated by the activity, she could hear him shouting his craziness from the other end of the underpass.

'Looking for me, blondie?' the hunched figure said.

He was holding something in his lap, cradling it like a mother would a sick child.

She couldn't make out what it was. He tossed it to her, and instinctively she caught it.

Hatton leaped to his feet and ran off, up the steps to the street.

She felt something warm and liquid oozing down her fingers. She took a step back, nearly tripped on the stair.

The lips were drawn back from the teeth in a silent scream, the skin waxy and grey, eyes half-lidded, as if the owner was merely dozing. Glassy in death, they rebuked her for being too slow, too far away, too late to protect the innocent.

Blood was seeping from the severed neck veins and down her dress. She heard screaming as two shoppers entered the underpass behind her, to be confronted by a panting, blood-stained woman holding a severed human head. Common sense told her to drop her terrible burden, but some irrational maternal instinct shrank from damaging Diana further.

And so she cradled her in her arms, too shocked to move, dazed by horror and guilt. And that was how Nick found her, still surrounded by the screaming women and the crazy dosser.

'Ma'am,' he said.

The blood had formed a pool at her feet. One of the shoppers fainted, hitting her head on the concrete steps as she went down.

'Ma'am?'

Fox looked around at Nick. 'It's all right,' she said to him. 'It's all right. We found her.'

They heard the squeal of brakes from the street above, the dull thud that followed it. Fox seemed unable to react, or even to move. It was Nick who made her put down her terrible prize, sat with her until the back-up arrived.

They heard a commotion at the top of the stairs, shouts, screams, car horns. It didn't seem to matter any more.

Above them, a few yards from the entrance to the underpass, a small crowd had gathered around the shaven-haired man lying face down in the road. A passer-by had stopped to give first aid, but on seeing the body was now vomiting noisily into the gutter. The driver of the number 98 bus to Willesden was repeating over and over, to anyone who would listen, 'He just ran out in front of me, I didn't stand a chance.'

Onlookers were bemused by the arrival, just moments later, of CID detectives and armed police in kevlar vests and riot helmets, holding assault rifles.

Mills stood in the middle of the chaos, shaking his head. Nick finally appeared and whispered something in his ear, pointing down the steps of the underpass. Mills took the news calmly, spoke softly into the hand-held radio in his right fist, then went back to his car and kicked the door, causing serious damage to property belonging to the Metropolitan Police Force, that would later on have to be written up and justified on a form.

Chapter Seventy-One

Fox stared out the window of the Incident Room, watched the kaleidoscope of headlights on the Hendon Road, looked again into death's single black eye, heard death's cold whisper: *Looking for me, blondie?*

Someone walked into the room and she turned around. It was Mills.

'Madeleine.'

'Guv.'

'You all right?'

She looked down at her clothes. Her jacket and stockings were torn, her blouse and skirt stained with blood. She must look a sight. She should go home, shower, change her clothes, but she didn't want to go home, not yet.

'I'll be okay,' she said.

Mills didn't seem to know what to say. 'Bad day,' he managed, finally.

'Had better.' The truth was, she really didn't feel anything right now, not emotionally anyway. Just a bit dazed. She had a bruise on her knee and two sutures in a cut on her right hand, but the physical pain was out of proportion to the minor nature of her injuries. She welcomed the discomfort, it was something she could focus on, better than thinking about Diana.

Mills put his arm around her. She felt herself stiffen at his touch. 'Do you want to talk about it?' he said, his face much too close.

'Honestly, guv, I'm all right.'

At that moment Nick walked in and Mills casually detached himself. Nick gave her a look. Mills walked back into his office.

'Ma'am?'

'Hello, Nick.'

'A few of us are heading over the King's Head. Want to come?'

'Celebrate?'

That was a bit tough. He frowned, embarrassed. 'Thought it might be a good idea to wind down a bit.'

She shook her head. She wanted to be alone.

Nick hesitated in the doorway. 'You're bloody fearless, you are,' he said.

'If I'd waited for back up, he would have got away.'

'You could have got yourself killed.'

Too right. Most beat cops, even most firearms officers, wouldn't face a loaded gun more than once in their entire careers. Now it had happened to her twice in the space of a year. The first time there had been no time to think about it, she had not even been aware of the gun until it was all over. She had acted instinctively.

This time, she could have held back. She couldn't believe what she had done. It was like she was cuffed to some suicidal stranger, dragging her along, against all sense and better judgment. As if she had a death wish.

'That bloke was a psycho.'

'Why didn't he kill me?' she said.

He shrugged. Who knew what the bastard had been thinking? The frightening thing about men like Hatton was the arbitrary nature of their violence. Killed Diana, killed her riding companion, let Fox live. No logic, no pattern.

'That poor girl,' Fox said.

'You can't always have a happy ending,' he said.

'No,' she murmured. 'Life doesn't always have happy endings.'

There was certainly no happy ending for James Carlton, he had paid a heavy price for his secrets. And still she suspected he had not told them everything. Had he wanted Kimberley Mason dead? It was clear to her now that it was he, not Gary Bradshaw, who had the key to Kimberley's flat and had given it to Hatton that night. But knowing it was one thing, proving it was another.

Only Bob Hatton knew the truth, and he was dead.

The worst that might come out of this would be a conspiracy charge. It had been left to Life itself to exact true penance. It had robbed him of his marriage, his reputation, and his political career; a pitiless judge of men, it had taken his daughter also.

But James Carlton did not suffer alone: five others had died for his secrets. She thought of a line from her childhood Bible, something about the Lord making it rain on the just and the unjust. Two innocent teenagers had lost their lives, as well as two natural-born killers. And then there was Kimberley Mason – did she belong among the sinners or the saints?

She changed her mind and joined the rest of the squad for a drink over at the King's Head, after all. It was a muted celebration, everyone finding excuses to leave early and go home. Finally there was just Nick and herself left at the bar.

He put his arm around her as he was leaving. 'You be okay, ma'am?'

She didn't mean to do it. Too many G&Ts on an empty stomach, probably. She turned her face up to his and kissed him. Just like that. But the kiss did not provoke the response that she had hoped for.

'Sorry,' he said, as if it was his fault.

'I don't want to be alone tonight,' she murmured.

He shook his head. 'I can't.'

'Nick, you don't—'

'There's something you should know,' he said.

She waited, knowing she was about to be burdened with another secret.

'I'm gay,' he said.

She smiled, more a grimace really, and sat down hard on the nearest bar stool. 'Oh,' she said, feeling like a complete fool, 'I didn't know.'

'I don't advertise it,' he mumbled.

'What about all the girlfriends?'

'My cover.'

'Christ.'

'This is just between us, ma'am. Please? It's hard enough being black, but being gay *and* black. In the Met? This gets out, TJ just won't leave it alone.'

She touched his cheek lightly with her fingertips. 'Sure,' she said.

Then she watched him leave.

She toyed with the coaster, then after a decent interval she got up and followed him out of the door. London in summer, still stewing in its own juice, the moon blood-red behind the veil of diesel fumes and heat. Her knee had started hurting like hell.

She took her mobile from her shoulder bag, there was a call on the message bank from Ash. She wondered what he wanted. In no frame of mind to ring him right now. She had her night planned: a few more G&Ts at home, in front of the television, fall asleep on the sofa. Happy just to be alive on this warm summer evening, to have choices and to have breath, and the promise of another shot at redemption tomorrow.

Chapter Seventy-Two

Hampstead Heath

Carlton parked his car on a lonely road overlooking the Heath. He sat there for a long time before getting out and opening the boot. Everything he needed was in there and he set to work. He clamped a hose on to the exhaust, fed it through the back window. He sealed the gaps at the top of the glass with masking tape, then got back into the driver's seat.

A good night for it, as the saying went. A full moon darted between high, dark clouds, the sky phosphorous and ink. Funny, he had never noticed the moon before, a night in London meant only lights on Westminster Bridge and the neon of Piccadilly. Nature and all its rhythms had passed him by utterly in recent years.

He remembered that as a child he had often watched the moon from his bedroom window. When we become adults, we lose touch with the stars and the magic of the sky, he thought. Hard now to remember himself as a child. The small boy he had once been could not have imagined that the man would come to this.

How did I get myself into this mess? What could I have been thinking? But of course, we don't think, that is the nature of irrational acts, by their very definition. We all have a fatal flaw, it is what makes us human; some of us succumb, some of us prevail. Once I thought myself so far removed from the wretches I saw every day in the City, filthy and begging. But they are not so different from me, after all. Their addictions led them to their despair, as my obsessions led me to mine.

I believed that if I indulged my darker side just once it would be enough, that I would be sated, but that was self-delusion. Later, I even tried to persuade myself that I was in control, that I would go back just once more and it would be over. But it never was. I was a junkie for my own particular perversion. I could not let it go. You know, of course *you know* that you are going to be damaged by it. But it is always enough that you are not damaged by it *today*.

And I had the right training. For years I had pretended to be rich, assured, confident; pretending to be happily married did not seem such a difficult balancing act.

Kimberley. My Kim. My real sin was that I loved you and did not want the world to know it. That would have shouted to the whole world who I really was. Every other evil was spawned from that betrayal.

And so.

He put a white sealed envelope on the dashboard, and started the engine. The quiet purring of precision German machinery, the soft piano of a Chopin movement on Radio Three. They said this was a painless death, that one just drifted away. At least this way he would be spared the indignity of scrutiny. The tabloids could not hound him beyond the gates of the cemetery. At least he would be safe behind the portals of Hell.

Though he might meet up with those newspaper bastards

at some later time, he thought grimly, when we are all shrieking down there together.

Diana: I adored you with a dumb and helpless passion. I could never articulate it, or demonstrate it to you. Love was distilled into its white and purest essence with you, the only time I was ever capable of it. You died never knowing how much I wanted for you, or how terribly I had let you down.

Tomorrow morning, people I have never known will judge me and the choices I have made. I wonder if what I have written in the letter on the dashboard will not only excuse the innocent, but also find pardon for myself in the hearts of those I have loved.

But I don't suppose I will ever know.

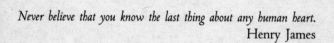

Never believe that you know the last thing about any human heart.
Henry James

Acknowledgments

My thanks to Detective Chief Inspector David Brown for his generous hospitality and invaluable guidance on investigative procedure in the Metropolitan police. And a great bloke as well. I couldn't have written this book without his help. Thanks also to DI Phil Wheeler, and Phil Soskins and Phiros Christadolou from the Forensic Science Support Unit for their time.

Once again thanks to Tim Curnow in Sydney and Anthea Morton-Saner, my London agent, for helping with leads for research when I got stuck. To Barbara and Stanley Slinger for friendship, hospitality and black pudding. A belated thanks to Dr Mostyn Hamdorf for certain medical anecdotes and to Sydney author Gabrielle Lord for being kind enough to let me unashamedly steal her story about the porn shop.

Photo credits: Carol Wooders

COLIN FALCONER

ROUGH JUSTICE

A YARDIE IS SHOT IN THE FRONT SEAT OF HIS CAR IN CAMDEN TOWN.

A TWELVE-YEAR-OLD CHILD IS RAPED AND MURDERED IN A NEARBY ALLEY.

Two unrelated murders.
The same squad called in to investigate.

Madeleine Fox, the only female detective in the team, has a prime suspect for the murder of the child: the owner of a sweet shop. But there's no evidence to convict him.

Then her disgruntled boss DCI Marenko gets a break in the Yardie case. But the witness is murdered and their suspect walks away.

But if law and order can't be found in the courts, it can be found in the streets, where justice is on the side of the angels.

HODDER AND STOUGHTON PAPERBACKS